UNSUPPRESSED DESIRE

In the buggy, he had a basket of flowers which he'd bought from a peddler who was on the wharf. He'd chosen bright red blossoms because she was so vibrant and full of spirit. He leaped out of the buggy with his wines and the basket of flowers and in long striding steps marched up the pathway to the cottage.

He couldn't have been more pleased when the beautiful Elena opened the door and stood before him. Her black eyes flashed excitedly and her thick lashes fluttered nervously.

"Mateo," she cried in surprise. "It is you!"

In her simple skirt and drawstring tunic she was a more exciting young lady than any he'd seen dressed up in fancy gowns. He swore he'd never seen more beautiful hair than Elena's.

He could no longer suppress the desire to take her in his arms and kiss her firmly on those luscious lips. Such honey he'd never tasted before and her tiny body swayed against him as his strong arms held her. Such flaming fire consumed him that he had to call on his strong will to release her.

But as he let go of her he murmured in her ear, "God, Elena, don't be mad at me. Damned if I could help myself."

WANDA OWEN

GOLDEN DESIRE

ZEBRA BOOKS
KENSINGTON PUBLISHING CORP.

*This book is dedicated to
the memory of my dear friend
Lola McGrann.
You are missed so much, Lola!*

ZEBRA BOOKS are published by

Kensington Publishing Corp.
475 Park Avenue South
New York, NY 10016

Zebra and the Z logo Reg. U.S. Pat. & TM Off. The Lovegram
logo is a trademark of Kensington Publishing Corp.

First Printing: May, 1994

Printed in the United States of America

Part One
Half Moon Bay

One

A warm summer gleamed down over the wharf where Mark Mateo sat with his old pal, Alonso. Their fishing poles and lines stretched out over the waters of Half Moon Bay. Since he was just a young lad, Mark had come here to this wharf to sit and fish. He loved the old man as sincerely as he did his own two grandpas, Carlos Mateo and Paul Aragon.

Alonso was no longer able to put in the long full days he used to around the estate, but Mark's father Mano was generous. He provided the old man with comfortable living quarters, for he never forgot how he had helped him on his land and in the winery, Golden Splendor, when he and his beautiful young bride, Aimée had come seeking their future as newlyweds.

Alonso was a part of their family, for he'd seen Mano and his lovely wife work hard to make this estate grow and flourish.

He'd also been there as their family had come along. Mano's firstborn had been his son Carlos, but Alonso had never been able to warm to him as he had the second son, Mark. Young Mark trailed around the place with him since he could walk. Alonso had called him his "little *amigo*."

The last of Mano's children was a daughter; they'd named her Markita. Alonso had been so happy that the sweet Señora Aimée had finally had the pretty little daughter she'd always wanted. Young Mark reminded Alonso of Mano, while the older boy, Carlos, was more like his Grandfather Mateo. He was nothing like the funloving, carefree Mark. There was no hint of mischief about the serious young fellow.

Mano was a typical Latin father—very protective of his only daughter, who looked exactly like him. There was no denying that she was pampered and spoiled.

Alonso had watched all of them grow up. Carlos no longer lived at Golden Splendor. He had moved to Sacramento to join a law firm there. Young Mark was at a restless stage, not knowing what direction he wanted his life to go. He'd just returned from Mexico where he'd visited relatives who raised fine bulls as his grandfather did over at La Casa Grande, his vast ranch.

The pretty little Markita was beginning to rebel against her father's restrictions, so it was always Mark she rushed to for sympathy.

Markita had found that her oldest brother, Carlos, would not be understanding about her feelings. Mark had a more generous, kinder heart.

Old Grandfather Mateo was pleased to hear about his younger grandson's interest in the prized Mateo bulls. Once he'd traveled to this region around San Jose as a young man, he'd never sought to return to Mexico where his family lived. He'd worked long and hard to acquire his vast holdings here. At his ranchero, La Casa Grande, he'd raised and bred his own prized Mateo bulls.

It had not pleased him that his son Mano had not chosen to follow in his footsteps. He had considered Mano a renegade when he was young. Once he'd met Aimée Aragon, the beautiful daughter of a French vintner in the valley, Mano was determined to woo and win her. It had mattered not to him that there was a feud going on between the Aragons and the Mateos. A bull had broken out of the corral and trampled the vineyards of Paul Aragon. Paul Aragon and old Carlos

Mateo were arrogant, unrelenting men who refused to bend to one another.

So Mano had been forced to play a game of deception when he'd courted Mark's mother, Aimée. Mark had found their courtship very romantic when he'd first heard the tale, for he knew how deeply devoted and in love his parents were. He was the only one who'd inherited her deep violet eyes, though all of them had his father's jet black hair.

That afternoon, as Mark and Alonso sat on the wharf fishing, the old man asked him about his plans. "Are you staying here awhile?"

"I'm not sure, Alonso. I got excited about the bullfights when I was down in Mexico visiting Uncle Mario. They made my blood churn!"

Alonso shook his thick grey mane and told Mark, "Oh, your little momma would not draw an easy breath if you went into fighting the bulls, Mark."

Mark shrugged his concerns. "Ah, just a thought, Alonso," he told him. "Now you don't mention a word about this to Mother, for we wouldn't want to worry her, would we?"

"You know how I feel about the señora, Mark. I'd never tell her anything that I thought might worry that pretty head of hers. Your mother is an angel here on earth if there ever was one. Only last week she came over to my quarters with a new blanket for my bed, a pouch of tobacco for my pipe, and a new woolen sweater. She knows I get chilled in the evening hours."

Mark smiled. "That's my mother. She has a heart of pure gold. But then she loves you, Alonso." He confessed to Alonso that until he found a girl like his mother, he would not marry.

Old Alonso chuckled. "Then you prepare yourself, Mark, for you are going to remain a bachelor for a long time yet."

The sun was beginning to set in the western sky over Half

Moon Bay and Alonso and Mark were just preparing to get up when Mark's eyes caught sight of a most beautiful little creature strolling the plank wharf. She was a sight to behold. Her dainty feet wore no shoes, but what impressed Mark was the sensuous swaying of her hips in a full-gathered bright floral skirt cinched in around her tiny waist. His violet eyes could not have overlooked the way the soft batiste blouse clung to the full-blown breasts underneath it. Soft, glossy black hair flowed over and around her shoulders in a loose, free way. Her skin looked like golden satin, as though it would be so soft to touch.

Since old Alonso knew everyone around Half Moon Bay, Mark asked him, "Who is she, Alonso? She's absolutely beautiful!"

"Ah, that's little Elena—Elena Fernandes," he grunted as he struggled to get up with Mark's strong hand supporting him.

She sat down on the pier and leaned back to take a deep intake of the breeze. All the time he was trying to help Alonso and gather their gear, his eyes kept darting back to this beauty sitting some twenty feet away from them.

Suddenly a huge mountain of a man marched down the long wharf. He was fierce looking with a bushy head of black hair and a beard. Mark could not remember seeing a man with a broader chest.

But he didn't think about this when he saw the man reach down and yank the tiny little señorita up from the landing as if she were a rag doll. But she was a little spitfire even though she could hardly win a fight with him. She was most exciting to Mark, who watched her eyes spark with fury and her arms try to break loose from his hold.

"That bastard!" he muttered.

Old Alonso realized that Mark was ready to go to her rescue, so he quickly warned him, "Don't interfere. That's her brother Vasco. Don't worry about little Elena. She can take care of herself. She's been doing it since she was six years old. Come on. It's time we get back to Golden Splendor."

Mark never questioned old Alonso's wisdom and he did as the old man advised him, but he could not resist turning back to watch the huge man lead his protesting sister down the wharf. He had to wonder what had riled the brother so much.

While he and Alonso were traveling home in the buggy, Mark questioned him about the divine little creature, Elena Fernandes.

"She's the daughter of Sebastian Fernandes, a Portuguese fisherman, and she's rarely out of Vasco or her father's sight. I'd guess she slipped away from the two of them just to catch a moment of freedom this afternoon and that was why Vasco was so mad. I feel sorry for her."

"Why are they so overly protective of her? God, I thought father was unusually strict on Markita, but he's not that bad."

"Well, need I point out to you, Mark, how beautiful Elena is? It was not that way when she was a child. Back then, she roamed the wharves at will; but when she got older, Sebastian and Vasco began to watch her carefully. Perhaps it is because of what happened to her mother, Miranda. She was a gorgeous woman and she used to make quite a stunning sight aboard Sebastian's fishing boat. Many a man would have liked to have bedded her, and many a man probably tried. Anyway, she was found murdered in their cottage on the bay one night. They never discovered who did it. Some say Sebastian killed her in a jealous rage."

Alonso's tale of the Portuguese family intrigued Mark, but not half as much as the dark and sultry Elena herself. Never had a young lady fascinated him as she had, innocently seated on the wharf.

Alonso confessed to him that he had speculated about the murder of Miranda Fernandes and whether it had been Sebastian who'd killed her. Everyone knew that he was a very jealous man and Miranda was a very beautiful woman. "But no charges were ever brought against Sebastian, and that happened many years ago," he told Mark.

When the two of them arrived back at Golden Splendor, they went their separate ways. Alonso was tired and ready to seek the comfort of his quarters. He was not as well as he tried to appear. Mark guided the buggy on toward the stables.

The beautiful face and figure of Elena Fernandes haunted him into the evening as he sat with his family in the elegant, spacious dining room. That night he paid little attention to the fine food he ate or the wines his mother had chosen to go with the meal. Aimée Aragon Mateo had brought the French traditions of the Chateau L'Aragon to the Mateo ranchero. To her, it was important that the right wine be served with their meals. Her father's winery was well known throughout California for its fine vintage.

Mark loved that his mother and father had managed to blend so perfectly their two grand heritages. Mano's Latin background, immediately obvious at the country estate of Golden Splendor, mingled pleasantly with his mother's French customs.

Mark admired both his parents. He hoped to equal his father, but he was honest enough to admit that he wasn't sure in what direction life was going to take him.

There were times when it bothered him that he was twenty-three and still had no idea what he wanted to pursue for his future. But then he would remember that his own father had been twenty-five and aimless when he'd met the beautiful Aimée Aragon. Mano Mateo had not been willing to settle for raising bulls although Grandpa Carlos had expected him to. "I was reckless and restless," Mano confessed to his son.

Mark prayed that sometime within the next year it would be made known to him what he should do with his life and how to plot his future. He didn't like this limbo state he was in.

Alonso told him that he'd know when the right thing came along. "Your instincts will guide you if you'll listen to them," he promised.

There was a devious streak in the happy-go-lucky youth, and he loved to tease old Alonso. Alonso suspected this was why he found it more fun to be around young Mark than his older brother.

"What about a beautiful little señorita, Alonso? Should I let my instincts guide me too?" His violet eyes twinkled with mischief as he watched a sly smile come to the old man's wrinkled face.

"We both know that you know the answer to that, Mark." Alonso grinned.

Mark liked the simple way old Alonso always put things in proper order. The old man made a lot of sense to him. They always had lighthearted, good times together and yet, Mark knew he often dropped sage hints in the course of their afternoons.

That afternoon as they'd entered the gateway of the five-foot greystone fence, Alonso had remarked, "This is one lovely place."

"It sure is, Alonso. Mother and Father have made it so." Mark smiled at him.

"It was a two-story greystone house, bleak and dismal looking, when they took this place over. But Señor Mano had that grillwork installed, and your mama put me busy getting the grounds in order. I did most of those flowerbeds, Mark, but then I was a husky hombre back then. That mama of yours sat on the ground, digging holes in the beds I dug up, and planted her garden. She didn't have no servants. Not then."

Alonso told him that only a few of the rooms had had furniture and the three of them had worked from sunup to sunset seven days a week. "But there was never any shortage of love, Mark. I've always said this place was built on tender love and caring. It was amazing what those two young people accomplished during that first year here."

"They have a right to feel a great pride about their Golden Splendor, don't they, Alonso?" Mark remarked.

"They sure do, Mark. It makes me happy to see your pretty mama able to be a grand lady and wear her pretty gowns. She deserves the fine life she's having now. She didn't have to do what she did for your father for she'd come from a wealthy family, but she wanted it that way."

"I know. I—I just hope I'll find a woman like her one day, Alonso," Mark confessed.

"You'll find her, Mark. I've no doubt about that."

Later that night as he lay on his bed and stared out his window at the starlit skies shining over the California valley, he found himself thinking about the feisty little bare-footed girl he'd seen on the wharf.

He couldn't deny that she'd sparked a fever in his blood.

Two

Vasco Fernandes might have seemed fierce to Mark Mateo and Alonso that afternoon, but they were not privy to the conversation as the sister and brother walked down the wharf away from them. The little Elena gave her older brother a harsh tonguelashing. "Damn you, Vasco," she shrieked. "Those big hands of yours hurt me when you yanked me up like that. I want you to quit doing that."

As docile as a dutiful puppy, he told her, "I'm sorry, Elena. You know I wouldn't hurt you for anything in the world. Don't tell Pa I hurt you. He'll knock me up beside the head. But he was the one who sent me out looking for you. You know how he gets when you get out of his sight for a minute, Elena."

"Well, Pa is going to have to accept that I'm no child anymore and I'm not going to settle for just being around you and him all the time, Vasco. I want a chance to breathe and be free of the sight of you two once in a while," she declared to her husky brother.

"Pa don't feel like you need to run away by yourself. You're too young, he says," Vasco told her.

"Well, he's not right, Vasco. I can take care of myself."

"*You* can tell him that, for I'm not going to," Vasco told her. He might tower over the short pudgy Sebastian, but his father was still an intimidating figure to Vasco. For a man his age, he was as strong as a raging bull.

But Sebastian Fernandes did not have this same effect on his seventeen-year-old daughter. She dared to defy him and argue with him. There were times when her volatile temper gave way to tossing something angrily when she got riled.

The fire in Elena reminded him of his beloved Miranda, whom he had loved so much even though they had had violent fights and fusses. Ah, but what sweet making up they had always enjoyed later!

He knew that rumors circulated around Half Moon Bay that he was the one who'd murdered her, but only Sebastian knew the truth. Never would he have harmed a hair on her beautiful head. Never had he ever laid a hand on her except to caress her.

He knew the man who'd probably done the foul deed and he knew the reason. Miranda had resisted his advances when he'd come to their cottage while Sebastian was working late at the docks on one of his fishing boats. Miranda had fought him off, and he'd killed her in a fit of rage.

It was one of his own men—José Martinez. The next morning, Martinez did not show up for work. When he did not come in the next day, Sebastian knew who'd killed his wife. He'd told the authorities, but they had never pursued the obvious clues. Sebastian could not track down the killer himself, for he had a dead wife to bury and a young daughter and son to care for. He shrugged aside the speculation and rumors spreading around the village; his true friends knew how much he had adored Miranda.

The wives of the other Portuguese fishermen offered a helping hand, watching out for Elena and Vasco when he had to be gone on his fishing boat all day. They admired Sebastian, for they knew that he devoted his evenings to his children and didn't go to the taverns to carouse.

By the time Elena was nine, she went with her father during the day on the boat or Vasco stayed with her at the cottage. No one observing Sebastian walking down the docks holding his little daughter's hand as they strolled homeward could have doubted his great love for her.

By the time Elena was thirteen, Sebastian allowed her to become the little mistress of their household. She enjoyed puttering around the cottage and keeping it clean, and she would prepare dinner for her father and Vasco. It gave her a great sense of pride to be in charge of the cottage, and she worked diligently to keep it nice.

Conscious of her own needs and desires, she sought the advice of a neighbor lady to learn how to sew so she could make herself some colorful gathered skirts and tunics. She had never had a frock bought in the mercantile store in the village.

When Elena turned sixteen, Sebastian realized that Miranda would never be dead as long as her daughter lived, for the girl was the image of her mother. A year before she had been like a lovely rosebud, but now she had blossomed into a rose. Sebastian saw how her full breast jutted against the thin batiste of her tunics and he was aware of her firm, rounded hips in the old pants she wore when she went out on his boat with him. She had that certain sway of her young body that was exactly like Miranda's sensuous lilt when she walked. It was enough to tempt any man. So he became more watchful and protective of her.

He'd not had a woman since Miranda had been murdered, but he could still remember the fever a woman could stir in a man!

For this reason he didn't encourage his daughter to go out on the fishing boat. He saw how his men ogled her. Elena had also noticed how the young sailors looked at her from the top of her head down to her toes, and she had to admit that it excited her. But she had yet to see the handsome man she'd envisioned in her girlish daydreams and she knew that she would know him immediately when her black eyes gazed at him.

As it happened, this particular afternoon a very handsome young man appraised her beauty, but she had never turned around to see him standing on the wharf. If she had, she would have been stirred with excitement, for most ladies found Mark Mateo's face and firm-muscled body appealing.

His deep blue-violet eyes had turned a deeper shade as he stared at her until she disappeared down the wharf. Old Alonso stood beside him, an amused smile on his wrinkled face. That pretty little Elena Fernandes, he noted, was tempting Señor Mark something fierce.

Mark detested those days when rains moved in over the California coast and he was forced to remain inside the sprawling old mansion and couldn't take his daily ride on his fine stallion. He became restless, for he was not a man who could content himself with sitting and reading a book as his father could.

Aimée was aware of his impatience as he paced the house. Markita was just as fretful as her older brother, and Aimée knew why. She'd planned to go over to her friend Roberta's home, but the rains were coming down too heavily. However, Aimée figured that it was Roberta's older brother that Markita had really anticipated seeing this afternoon.

None of the young men who came to Golden Splendor to call on Markita had any effect on her, for she'd set her sights on Roberto Estrada. Aimée feared that Markita was due to get her heart broken for Roberto showed no interest in her. In truth, Aimée didn't care for the arrogant young man and she knew that he merely looked upon Markita as his sister's friend. But Markita was so attracted to him that she didn't give any other suitors a chance. Aimée wanted to shake her firmly to clear that pretty head of hers.

Often Markita and Roberta spent the weekends at each other's homes. Ironically, Roberta Estrada acted like a love-sick calf when she was around Mark. While he was always polite to his sister's friend, Mark was certainly not attracted to her, and the girls' attempts to get him to join them when they went riding never worked out. Mark always had an excuse; he knew what Markita was up to.

Her hot temper had exploded the last time he'd refused to accompany them. "You were downright rude, Mark," she'd accused him. "It wouldn't kill you to ride with us."

Mark had smiled. His sister was as cute as she could be when she was angry; her dark eyes flashed so brightly. "Roberta is not my guest," he'd reminded her. "She's yours, so you entertain her. I've no time." He'd strolled casually out of the room.

He was thinking as he went out to the barn that Markita was rolling those big black eyes of hers for nothing where Roberto Estrada was concerned. He was interested in another young lady, and Mark had seen the two of them together several times over the last few months.

He didn't know who she was and Mark didn't find her particularly striking, but it was obvious that Roberto was very intrigued.

It had been almost two weeks since Mark and Alonso were up on the fishing wharf. Alonso tried to go to Half Moon Bay every two or three weeks to see his widowed sister, Lola; she was the only family he had left. She lived in a three-room house and hired out as a laundry woman to keep food on her table and a roof over her head.

Lola, aware of her older brother's failing health over the

last six months, had told him that he should come to her house to live so she could look after him. But Alonso figured that it was better that he remain in his comfortable quarters at Golden Splendor, rather than be a burden on Lola. He had a nice place to live and, thanks to Señor and Señora Mateo, he never lacked for plenty of food for his belly.

However, a few days after their fishing jaunt, Alonso became ill and had to take to his bed. Mano sent for the doctor, and the doctor's diagnosis was not encouraging. "The old man's heart is just worn out," he said. "I wish I could have given you better news."

All the Mateo family were very concerned about Alonso. Mark checked in on him two or three times a day and so did his mother. During one of Mark's visits, Alonso asked him, *"Amigo,* would you do me a favor? Would you go to Half Moon Bay and bring my sister here. I've a need to see her."

"I'll go tomorrow," Mark assured him.

That evening when he told his parents about Alonso's request, his mother did not hesitate. "Get Lola to come here to stay with her brother," she said. "Permanently. He needs her; and, should something happen to Alonso, we could provide her a much better home than she has now. Golden Splendor could find a place for her services. Alonso has told me how hard she works to keep a roof over her head and food in her cupboards. She could have a much easier life here and also be with her dear brother."

Mano marveled at his wife, who had to have the kindest heart of anyone he'd ever known. It wasn't any wonder that the people who worked his vineyards and the servants in the sprawling house called her the golden *reina*. She deserved the title, for she certainly was a queen. But then she'd always been his queen.

The next morning as the sun was rising in the eastern sky, Mark guided his buggy through the double iron gates which enclosed the property. An hour and a half later, he pulled into the road leading up to Lola's small three-room shack, hoping he'd arrived before she'd left for her laundry jobs.

Luck was with him. He leaped out of his buggy as Lola emerged from her front door. She recognized him immediately, and seeing him without Alonso panicked her. Hesitating, she asked, "Señor, what brings you here?"

"I've come to you because of Alonso," he told her.

"Alonso's dead, ain't he, Señor Mark?" she stammered.

"No, no, Lola—he's just real sick and wants to see you," he quickly assured her. His hand went out to take her arm for she looked faint. "Let's go inside and talk," he said gently.

He explained the situation quickly and outlined his mother's proposal. "Alonso has nice roomy quarters that could accommodate both of you," he concluded. "And, God forbid that something should happen to Alonso, my mother told me to assure you that Golden Splendor would still be your home. You see, my family loves Alonso quite devotedly."

"Lord Almighty, you've got this lady's head swimming! You mean to tell me your mama is offering me a home there, too?" Lola asked, feeling that she had surely heard wrong. Señora Mateo didn't even know her, but she was offering her a home. Lola hadn't believed such good-hearted people really existed, and yet, she should have from all that Alonso had told her about the Mateo family.

"I'm here to help you in any way I can to get you moved—if you agree to come with me." Mark grinned.

A smile etched Lola's face. "Well, I'd have to be some kind of fool to turn down such a generous offer as that. Your mama must truly be a saint, Señor Mark. We've never met, but I've heard Alonso sing her praises for years."

"If you come with me, you can see for yourself," Mark said.

"Well, I don't have anything to keep me here and my rent is paid up for another month. This old furniture will be a welcome gift to a struggling young couple down the road, so I've not much to take. I can get my personal belongings packed and be ready to leave by tomorrow morning, if that's all right with you."

"I'll help you," Mark offered.

"Oh, no, señor, I'll be able to do that. But I do have one favor to ask of you," she said, hesitating to ask him to take her to the homes where she'd worked regularly for years to let them know she was leaving Half Moon Bay. Lola felt she owed them that consideration.

Mark readily agreed, and a short time later he was surprised to find how long it took to make the rounds of all the households Lola had worked for weekly.

When he returned her to her house, he told her that he would return the next morning. He sensed that Lola wished to spend this last night alone in the little shack where she'd lived so many years.

Mark could understand how she must be feeling for she was finding her own comfortable world interrupted. It was surely not easy on a lady of her age to make such a big change so suddenly. Mark felt much compassion for her as he headed for the inn.

With a wave of sadness, she watched her young neighbors take away her worn and battered furniture. They left her the bed for the night. In the morning they would come for that, too.

Sitting in her empty house that evening, Lola could not have known that fate was being very generous to her. Going to Golden Splendor was to be the best thing that had ever happened to her—and the most rewarding.

Old Alonso's illness was to spur changes in several people's lives, including Mark Mateo's.

Three

It was mid-afternoon when Mark deposited his canvas bag at the inn. He had no desire to linger in his lodgings. Nothing was more boring to him than killing time in the room of an inn or hotel. So he decided that he'd take a jaunt around the village before the evening meal.

When Mark left in his buggy, he might not have admitted to himself why he was heading toward the wharves, but the truth was he hoped to see the divine little creature who'd caught his attention the last time he and Alonso were in Half Moon Bay. He couldn't erase her from his mind. Her beguiling image had haunted him constantly for the last weeks.

He stopped the buggy and went down on the wharf to the spot where he and old Alonso had sat that unforgettable afternoon.

The wharves were busy, but he saw no one who looked like the petite and sensuous Elena. However, other pretty young ladies sashayed along the levee. Some openly flirted with the handsome Mark Mateo. He gave them a smile but did not invite them to join him, which they would have done had he crooked his finger.

His violet eyes kept searching the parade of people for some sight of Elena to no avail. He took one last puff on the cheroot he'd been smoking and tossed it into the bay, rising to go back to his buggy. It had been foolish for him to dare to hope that he would see the lovely Portuguese girl again.

He was ambling back to his carriage when he heard an angry shriek. He turned to see the little Elena fighting like a wildcat with a young man, who was obviously trying to embrace her.

In long striding steps, Mark rushed toward the two of them. The tall trim youth was no match for the strong hands that grabbed his shoulders and flung him aside. "Leave her alone, *bastardo!*" Mark growled fiercely at him.

The young man, who was probably about eighteen or nineteen, was taken by such utter surprise that he broke and ran like a scared gazelle.

Elena, too, was taken by surprise. This stranger's presence startled her, just as Emilio had with his sudden amorous embrace. She found herself gazing up into the face of the most handsome man she'd ever seen. He towered over her by many inches and there was a forceful manner about him that made her ask why he had interfered in her life.

Her volatile temper exploded indignantly. "And who appointed you my protector, eh?" she snapped harshly, raising her hand to slam his face. Mark quickly restrained the dainty palm and fingers.

He grinned down at her. "Now why would you want to do that, *chiquita?*" he inquired. "I was only trying to help you."

Cockily, she tilted her head to one side and looked up at him with flashing black eyes. Haughtily, she declared, "I did not need you. I can take care of myself."

A deep voice broke through the air to contradict her. "I have to disagree with you, little one. You did need this gentleman's help."

They both turned to see a stout, husky man approach them. He was a fierce-looking fellow with an unruly mane of thick grey hair and a heavy beard. Mark Mateo had never seen such piercing jet-black eyes.

"May I introduce myself, señor? I am Sebastian Fernandes, the father of this ill-tempered hellcat who should be graciously thanking you."

Mark held out his hand, a slow grin coming to his face. "My name is Mark Mateo," he told the old Portuguese man.

"Mark Mateo, eh? The name—I have heard that name before. You live around here in Half Moon Bay?"

"No, sir, I live east of the bay at my father's estate, Golden Splendor. He has a winery."

A broad smile came to Sebastian's face. "Ah, a winery, eh? Please come to our house, and we shall share the best wine you have ever tasted. It is a fine Portuguese stock. What better way could I express my gratitude to you for what you did for my little Elena?"

"It would be my pleasure, sir. I've heard about your Portuguese wines," Mark told him.

"Then shall we go?" Sebastian asked. Mark ushered father and daughter into his buggy.

"You guide me to your house, sir," Mark suggested as they both reached for the reins.

Elena had become very quiet since her father had made his appearance on the scene. But her curious dark eyes had been active. She scrutinized everything about the handsome stranger who'd suddenly appeared out of nowhere to yank that silly Emilio away from her. This afternoon the annoying boy had given way to the yearnings she'd suspected he'd harbored for months. He claimed that she was the most beautiful girl in the fishing village and that he had only to watch her stroll down the wharf and he was afire!

A lot of young men sought her affections, and Sebastian reacted protectively. He realized that this was a time in her life when she desperately needed the mama she didn't have. Dear God, if only his Miranda were there with him to help him raise Elena! He had to ask as he had time and time again why fate had been so cruel to him and their young daughter. Since Vasco had been older when the tragedy occurred, Sebastian didn't have as deep a concern for his son's well-being.

He knew he made this fiery woman-child angry all the time, especially in this last year. Those black eyes constantly glared at him, demanding to know, "Why are you so strict on me, Papa? I am not a baby."

He always gave her the same response. "Because I love you. That is why." Sebastian spoke the truth, for he worshipped her. It was a special love he felt for Elena, who'd come to him and Miranda some years after they'd had Vasco. They had feared that they would never have any more children until the day that his excited wife told him he was to become a father again.

Sebastian could not have been a happier or prouder man. There had always been a fierce pride in him. Some might look on him as a simple fisherman who lived in a small little house so he really had nothing to crow about, but Sebastian saw things in a different way. He was a man who earned an honest living by the sweat of his brow and he owed no man any money. His little plot of ground was not large nor was his five-room house fancy, but it was bought and paid for. As were his two fishing boats. His family always had clothes on their backs and plenty of food in the pantry.

So that was enough to make Sebastian a very proud man.

Something about the manner of Mark Mateo told Sebastian that he was prideful, too. He had taken an instant liking to this young man who had gallantly rescued Elena when she was being pestered by Emilio, that randy little rooster. Sebastian decided to speak with Emilio himself the next day and put the fear of God in him so that he'd never bother Elena again.

They traveled down the dirt road for about a half-mile

before Sebastian directed him to turn in the next drive. "To the right, Mateo. That's my place."

Mark immediately recognized the husky young man at the side of the house chopping wood. He was the older brother he'd seen with Elena that first time on the wharf. Vasco, Alonso had called him.

Vasco quit his work, a quizzical look on his face as his father, Elena, and the stranger dismounted from the buggy. He approached them slowly, his dark eyes scrutinizing Mark.

Sebastian introduced them before he guided Mark toward the front door. "Welcome to my home, Mark Mateo," he said with a warm friendly smile on his rugged face. Elena and Vasco trailed into the house behind them.

Elena knew that her brother was as curious as a cat about this stranger that their father had brought to the cottage.

Mark found Elena a most intriguing minx. Every time his eyes glanced down at her, he found her watching him; but the minute their eyes met, she quickly turned her head away. He wondered if she were just shy and bashful or if she'd not wanted him to think she was staring at him.

"Please, have a seat, Mark Mateo," Sebastian urged. "I have no wife. It is just me, Vasco, and Elena living here now."

"So, Elena, you must be the one in charge of the house." Mark directed his conversation to her.

"Yes, I clean Papa's house," she told him.

Everything was clean and neat. The furnishings were worn and old, but there were simple additions that gave a pleasant air to the room, like the clay pots of blooming flowers on the window sills. Floral curtains matched the ruffled pillows that lined the old sofa, brightening the room.

"Elena, you and Vasco entertain our guest while I get the wine I promised him, eh?" Sebastian headed for the kitchen, leaving the three of them in the front room.

Vasco had taken a seat in one of the large overstuffed chairs. Elena sat on the sofa, playing with one of the pillows as she attempted to carry out her papa's orders. "You said you were not from here," she recollected. "Where do you live?"

"I live at a place called Golden Splendor," he replied. "My father is a vintner."

"A vintner? What is that?" she asked, her brow arching.

"He grows grapes," Mark told Elena. "My father's vineyards grow the finest grapes in California; and when they harvest them, they make wines. His winery sells to merchants all over the state."

That got Vasco's attention and he asked, "Your papa makes his own wines?"

"Yes, he does, Vasco, and a finer wine you'll never taste," Mark boasted proudly. "The next time I come to Half Moon Bay, I'll bring you some bottles to sample for yourself and you will see that I speak the truth."

The usually quiet, reserved Vasco brightened with a broad grin and a nod of his head. At that moment, Sebastian entered the front room carrying a tray laden with glasses of his cherished Portuguese wine.

He stood, waiting for Mark to take a sip of the wine. When Mark took a second sip, Sebastian asked, "You like, eh?"

"Very good, sir. It is a very fine wine indeed." Mark declared.

A pleased smile covered Sebastian's face. With a nod of his head, he sat down with his own glass of wine. Sebastian took a long, slender cigarette from the tin on the table by his favorite chair, so Mark felt free to take out one of his cheroots from his case and light it. He also offered the cigars to Vasco and Sebastian.

Since Elena was not served a glass of wine by her father, she saw no reason to stay in the room. Besides, she felt ill-at-ease every time Mark's deep violet eyes darted in her direction. She didn't care that she would appear to be rude for leaving the room, for after all it had been Sebastian who'd invited this Mark Mateo to their cottage. She was very angry with her father for not serving her as he usually did. She knew why he had overlooked her. He was trying to impress on this Mateo that she was too young, which was just not true. Had only he and Vasco been present, Sebastian would have also poured her a glass of the wine.

Father and brother had been so engrossed in Mark's description of his father's winery and vineyards that neither noticed her exit, but Mark's deep violet eyes followed her as she left. She was in a pout, reminding him of his own sister when she was riled and fuming.

He lingered longer and accepted a second glass of Sebastian's good Portuguese wine, since he had nothing to return to but dinner at the inn and a long evening in his room.

Savoring the warm, red wine, he told Sebastian of his mission in Half Moon Bay, striking a bond of friendship.

Sebastian stood up and declared, "I think I like you, Mateo! You've got to eat somewhere tonight, so eat with us. I'll fix you my fine *paella*—best *paella* you will ever eat! Then you can go back to the inn, have a good night's sleep, and leave in the morning for your Golden Splendor."

A half-hour later, Mark was indulging himself with Sebastian's tasty, spicy *paella,* and it was most delectable. Now that he had been at the cottage for over three hours, the beautiful little Elena had become talkative and not as shy around him. They sat at the table, eating the *paella* and huge slices of fresh baked bread, enjoying more wine. They all laughed and talked lightheartedly.

Elena could tell that her father was not the only one who responded positively to their guest. Her brother was outgoing and seemed to like Mateo. For Vasco, this was very unusual.

Mark couldn't have been more pleased when those flashing black eyes looked at him, transformed into warm, friendly eyes sparkling as brilliantly as diamonds.

An hour after dinner was over, Mark was taking his leave from Sebastian's cottage. Before Sebastian escorted him to the front door he bade Vasco and Elena good night.

Mark knew that one way or the other he was going to see Elena Fernandes again. For one brief second, their eyes met and something about the way she looked at him betrayed that she would like to see him again, too.

At the door, he told Sebastian, "I'll bring you some of my father's wines the next time I get into Half Moon Bay."

"Our door is always open to you, Mateo," Sebastian replied, giving him a friendly pat on the shoulder.

"Thank you, sir. Thank you again for that grand dinner," Mark graciously declared before he went down the steps to his buggy.

It had been a far more exciting evening than Mark had anticipated. He had found Sebastian Fernandes an entertaining, interesting gent. He was certainly justified to boast about his *paella* as he had. Mark had found it magnificent; he'd never eaten any dish quite like it before.

But there was no question about the attraction in the cottage. It was the sensuous little Elena he'd watched. Her eyes were like black fire, and he was intrigued by the way she spoke his name, igniting the wildest desires within him.

No woman had ever affected him as Elena Fernandes had tonight.

Four

Mark went to bed early that night but he didn't go to sleep too quickly, for a lovely face kept haunting him. When he finally slept, a most fantastic dream about Elena woke him in a cold sweat.

At sunrise, he got out of bed and dressed. He went down to the dining room for breakfast, then checked out to go to Lola's house.

Around seven-thirty he pulled into her narrow drive. As she'd told him she would be, she was ready to leave. All her belongings were packed and her house was bare except for the bed she'd slept on last night.

"I'm ready anytime you are, señor," she greeted him.

"So let's get going. I'll get all your things in the buggy and we'll head for Golden Splendor."

A half-hour later the two of them were in the buggy and going down the dirt-rutted road toward Golden Splendor. The trip was long enough to allow them to have long conversations.

"I must tell you, Señor Mark, that my head is spinning this morning. It's not easy for an old woman to pick up and leave her place as quickly as this," Lola confessed to him.

Mark completely understood her feelings. "I should have helped you, Lola. I was there ready to do just that as you know. I know it must be a little scary for you to uproot your life so quickly."

"Oh, I want to be with Alonso. I truly do. As for the emptying out of my house, that was no problem, señor. That little couple was glad to come down last night and take everything in my little shack. This afternoon when Jeanine's husband gets off work he'll come down to get the bed. As you can see from the baskets here in your buggy, I don't have much in personal possessions."

What she said was apparently true for she had very little to show for a lady her age as far as clothing and personal belongings. On her meager wages she'd had to live very frugally and could not afford anything but necessities.

Mark smiled at her, "You're going to find yourself loving Golden Splendor, Lola, once you get settled in." What he didn't say to her was that life was going to be far easier on her than it had been back at Half Moon Bay. She was going to be living in much finer surroundings than the shack she had lived in.

"Oh, I'm sure I will, señor. I still can't believe your mother's offer to me that I could remain there if something happened to Alonso. My, what a generous, good lady she is! Now I know why Alonso was always singing her praises."

A twinkle came into his deep violet eyes. "That's probably why I'm still a bachelor, Lola. I can't find myself a girl to measure up to my mother. I can't settle for anything less."

The middle-aged woman smiled at him as she told him, "Now, Señor Mark, that is asking a lot of a young girl. Your dear mother had many things to learn and to experience over the years in order to become the woman she is today. You just ask her and I'll bet she'll tell you that."

He laughed, "Oh, I guess you're right, Lola. The truth is I'm not ready to settle down yet."

She gave a chuckle. "Now that's more the truth. But mark my words, one day a pretty girl will come along that will turn that head of yours and you'll forget everything you said to me today."

Mark laughed, "You're just like Alonso, Lola. You're just too darn smart."

The sun was setting when they entered the grounds of the estate and Mark guided his buggy toward Alonso's quarters. He heard Lola give a gasp and exclaim, *"Madre de Dios—what a lovely place this is, Señor Mark!"*

A few minutes later she and her brother were having a most happy reunion. Mark didn't linger after he'd carried Lola's possessions to her quarters.

But he did tell Lola before he left that dinner would be sent over to them this evening.

It was almost dark by the time Mark arrived at the back entrance of the house. He paused long enough in the kitchen to tell Celia to send two fine dinners up to Alonso this evening, for his sister Lola had arrived. Then he swiftly mounted the back stairs to the second landing, and to his room.

For Alonso and Lola it was a glorious evening. They feasted on the fine food sent over by Celia and chatted for hours. Lola quickly saw that her ailing brother lived in a much nicer place than the one where she had lived all these years. There were several pieces of fine furniture in Alonso's rooms.

When she'd raved about the fine meal they'd had, Alonso told her how the señora always saw that he had good meals daily. Lola shook her head in amazement as she told him, "Alonso, what a lucky man you are to have such good people to look after you."

"You'll not regret coming here, Lola. I promise you that," he said.

They did have one disagreement before the evening was over but Alonso won out in the end: he insisted that she have the bedroom. "I sleep on my old daybed most of the time anyway, Lola. Now, you go in there and get yourself cozy and settled in. I'm ready to get on my daybed and go to sleep."

Lola didn't wish to upset him and she, too, was beginning to feel ready to lie down. Already, she was enchanted by the splendor of this place.

Mark dominated the conversation that night as he joined his family for dinner. They were delighted to hear that Lola had returned with him.

"I told Celia to take two dinners over there this evening, Mother," he told Aimée. "You'll like Lola. She's a very dear lady. She'll be a great tonic for Alonso."

"I've no doubt about that, Mark," Aimée told her son. "I'll meet her in the morning."

Mark also told them of the fascinating old Portuguese fisherman he'd met and how he'd dined with him one evening in Half Moon Bay. He told his father about the fine Portuguese wine Sebastian had served. "I've got to tell you, Father, that was a very fine wine, especially with the pot of *paella* he cooked for our dinner. I never saw so many things thrown into one big pot."

"This Sebastian sounds like a very interesting character," Mano told his son.

What his son *didn't* mention was Sebastian's beautiful daughter. He wasn't ready to speak of Elena Fernandes just yet.

He didn't linger in the parlor with his family, but they understood why he needed some well-deserved rest after his trip to Half Moon Bay to bring Alonso's sister back to Golden Splendor.

Mano excused himself from Aimée and Markita shortly after dinner to go to his study to get some paper work done.

Aimée was looking forward to meeting Alonso's sister in the morning.

Lola had no trouble adjusting to life at Golden Splendor. She had never expected to live in a place as grand as Alonso's quarters. There were surely no nicer people than the Mateo family. The first two days she was there she did little cooking, except for brewing pots of the black coffee she and Alonso liked. Dinner trays were brought over from the house with such generous servings that there was usually enough for her to fix the two of them a light lunch the next day.

But Aimée realized that Lola might enjoy preparing some of her own favorite foods, so she told Lola to come over to their big pantry and pick out whatever she'd like. "I doubt that you found much in Alonso's pantry for he'd not been up to cooking for the last few weeks before you arrived. You just put what you want in the baskets and I'll have young José bring the baskets over to you."

"Why thank you, señora. I'll come over this afternoon after I fix Alonso's lunch and while he's taking a nap," Lola told her. She was ready to start puttering around in the kitchen for she wasn't used to sitting around most of a day.

"You've been a good tonic for him, Lola. I'd swear that he's looking better today," Aimée told her.

"Being here has been a good tonic for me too, señora. My goodness, I've had free time to sit in your beautiful gardens to listen to the birds sing or watch them come to the fountain to get themselves a drink of water. Why this place is like living in paradise."

"I'm glad you like it here, Lola. Mano and I love it so much and we wish all our people to find it pleasant."

Lola had a simple explanation for her. "Love lives here, señora. One feels it immediately. I know I did."

Aimée gave her an affectionate pat on her shoulder and

nodded. "Yes, love is here and always has been since the first day we moved here."

She turned to leave for she had things to attend to since they were having dinner guests tonight. Two hours later, Lola left the quarters to go over to the big house to gather up some groceries as the señora had suggested.

Never had she stepped into such a vast pantry! None of the wealthy families she'd worked for had anything to compare with it. There was a long row of cured hams, sausages and slabs of bacon hanging from a wooden rack. Shelves of jars containing vegetables and fruits extended down the full length of the room. There were jars of all kinds of spices and dried herbs. She helped herself to some of the potatoes and onions in the bins, along with flour and corn meal. She also gathered eggs, for Alonso loved bacon and eggs in the morning. She lifted one of the smaller hams to put in her basket. She also took a jar of the blackberry jam.

She felt a wave of guilt wash over her when she suddenly realized she'd filled three baskets. But she could not resist gathering up a sack of dried beans. She could just taste them cooked along with chunks of that fine cured ham.

The Mateo's cook, Chita, observed how carefully Lola kept checking out her baskets. She knew she was hesitating about taking too much, so Chita sought to ease her concern. "Now, Lola, take as much as you want, for there's enough to feed two armies," Chita told her. She and Lola were about the same age and she knew that she had not had an easy life, for old Alonso was always talking about Lola when he was around her.

Like Lola, she was a widow. She had worked in the Mateo kitchen for over fifteen years. Before her husband died, he'd been Mano's foreman in the vineyards and they'd lived in one of the little cottages on the estate. But when her husband died and she was left alone, Mano had moved her into the main house. A room a short distance down the hall had been converted into a bedroom for her. She was more than delighted to be there in the spacious house after Jorge was no longer with her. It gave her a very secure feeling.

When she was through in her kitchen in the evenings she had only a few steps to take before she was inside her cozy bedroom. She ate the same fine food that the family ate, so this Mexican lady in her fifties felt like she had a very good life.

She had all the comforts she needed and more than she expected. Señora Aimée had taught her to read and she was free to select a book from their library anytime she wished. That had provided her many hours of pleasure.

When Lola was ready to leave the pantry, she told Chita, "I'll be fixing our supper tonight so you won't have to send Anita over with a dinner tray."

"All right, Lola, but I'll send Cola over a little later with some milk and fresh-churned butter. I do have something to give you cause I know how that Alonso likes his fried chicken."

Lola laughed. "Oh, you sure know him well."

That evening when Alonso ate Lola's dinner he told her, "That's the best meal I've had in a long time, Lola honey."

It had done her heart good to see him eat with such relish for she'd fixed the fryer Chita had given to her and made the nice thick, creamy gravy which he liked to spoon over his biscuits.

She teased him. "You keep eating like this Alonso, and you'll get fat."

He chuckled. "Now wouldn't that be something!"

It was a most pleasant meal and they lingered at the table for a while to have one last cup of coffee.

Perhaps Señora Mateo was right; Alonso seemed very alert and lively tonight. Lola had to admit the extra hours of leisure here had done wonders for her. It was quite a different routine from the days she put in back at Half Moon Bay when she'd walk home so weary she could hardly make it through her door. Some nights she'd just snack, for she was too tired to cook dinner for herself.

"You're liking it here, aren't you, Lola? You sure don't look as worn out after three days and nights here as you looked in Half Moon Bay those last few months."

Lola laughed, "I'd be some kind of fool if I didn't like this place, Alonso! I can tell you that I'm not as tired cause I'm not working that hard."

"I have a confession to make to you, Lola honey. It wasn't that I thought I was on my deathbed that I sent Mark to have you come here to me. Now, I might have been and just didn't have enough sense to know it. Oh, I'm not saying to you that I don't know this old heart of mine is acting up. The doctor told me that, but I am feeling better each day, Lola, and it's thanks to you."

"So you sent for me because you wanted me to stay with you for awhile, Alonso?"

"Oh, sure I wanted that but I also wanted you to see what this place was like. Then I was hoping that you and Señora Aimée would meet and she might offer you a job right here. I never figured it would work out as it did. But that little lady did me one better. That little lady doesn't waste time when she makes a decision. She puts the wheels in motion. From what Mark tells me, she instructed him to gather you up to bring you back here to live. Should something happen to me after you got here, then you could remain here. I've never met a lady like that one in all my life, Lola."

"Nor have I, Alonso. Well, that is just what Señor Mark did, so here I am," she smiled.

"And I'm so glad you're here, Lola. Life's going to be a lot easier for you now and that's enough to make me happy.

Should something happen to me, you are not to fret that they'd turn you out, Lola. They'd never do that. You'd have a home here as long as you'd want it."

"I know that, Alonso." Lola smiled over at him as he sat in the overstuffed chair.

The two of them fell into a quiet contentment after that. Lola began to knit as she usually did in the evenings and Alonso read the newspaper Mark had brought over this afternoon. Being able to read a newspaper was something he had to thank Señor Mano for; he hadn't known how to read until Mano taught him, years ago, as Aimée had taught her cook, Celia.

Alonso was a very grateful man this evening. The luckiest day of his life was the day he came upon this place desperate to work to earn some wages and he was hired by Mano Mateo.

That seemed like a lifetime ago to Alonso!

Five

Mano had asked his son to accompany his new foreman, Leon, to Half Moon Bay the next morning with a load of his wines being shipped to southern California. "I'd feel better if you went with him, Mark. Leon is a good man but he hasn't been with us all that long."

"Sure, I'll go with Leon in the morning," Mark quickly responded. Going to Half Moon Bay would give him a chance to pay a call on the Fernandes again. Just maybe, if he were lucky, there would be an opportunity for him to spend some time alone with Elena. That was what he really yearned to do.

Knowing how overly protected she was by her father and that husky brother of hers, it was going to be a miracle for that to happen.

As the three of them were preparing to leave the dining room, Mano reminded Mark that he should go to their cellar tonight to choose some bottles of fine wine to take to his Portuguese friend.

"Oh, I plan to," he told his father as he parted company with him and his mother that evening. As they went toward their parlor, Mark went to the far end of the hall and entered the last door, which led down a flight of stone stairs into a cellar.

He took a lantern to light his way down the darkened rows of racks of stacked wines. He picked four bottles of his father's finest vintages of red and white wines to take to Sebastian, then took them to his room to put them in the canvas bag to take with him to Half Moon Bay.

Often in the last few years, Mark had accompanied the wagon taking shipments to the bay. Just lately, now that he had been carrying more of the load around the winery and vineyard, he'd learned to appreciate the responsibility that rested on his father's back while he and Carlos were growing up. He had it all to do with the help from old Alonso. It was no wonder he was so willing to take good care of him since he was old and ailing. Alonso had been a godsend to him back some ten years ago.

One evening when his father was in a reflective mood, speaking to him about the early years around Golden Splendor, he'd told him that Aimée's life was not always as leisurely as it was now. She bore his children and tended to all of them for they'd had no servants then.

While he worked all day in the vineyards and winery, Aimée had taken full charge of the bookwork in his office along with raising and overseeing her three very active children.

"She worked from sunup to sunset every day along with me and then some, Mark. A remarkable lady, your mother."

But the day came when Mano could relieve Aimée and start keeping the books, which could be very time-consuming. Aimée had been free to run her spacious home and spend time with her growing children. She still rode with Mano when he inspected the grapes on his vines for he valued her opinion. The daughter of a respected vintner, Paul Aragon, Aimée had learned much from him as she grew up at Chateau L'Aragon.

All the old hatred between the Mateo family and Aragons had long been forgotten after Aimée married Mano. Paul had seen what a happy woman his daughter was after she'd married Mano. He respected Mano for the vintner he'd become over the last twenty years. Perhaps, he also felt a little smug that old Carlos' son chose to be a vintner instead of raising the prized Mateo bulls.

Paul's two sons had taken over the running of his winery and he and old Carlos had both mellowed over the years. Now they could sit and laugh about the time the Mateo bull got out and ravaged Paul's vineyard.

The two cantankerous gentlemen were getting too old to argue and fight one another anymore!

At sunrise, Mark's buggy, followed by Leon and Diego in the flat-bedded wagon, pulled through the double iron gate at the entrance of Golden Splendor. It had been a beautiful, clear morning, but the closer they got to the bay they ran into fog. The closer they got to Half Moon Bay, the thicker the fog got. It wasn't easy to see Mark's buggy ahead of them, and it was so dense that Mark and Leon both slowed their pace. When they arrived at the wharf, they learned that the fishing boats were delaying taking out of the bay. The wharf was crowded with disgruntled fishermen impatiently pacing.

But Mark didn't see Sebastian or Vasco. There was very good reason why: Sebastian had not allowed the dense fog to hold up his day. He and Vasco were already out on the waters.

Everything was moving slowly on the docks that early morning, and it was almost noon before the shipment of Mano's wines was taken aboard the boat to southern California.

Once the loading was accomplished, Leon and Diego started back to Golden Splendor in the wagon. Mark, however, guided his buggy in the direction old Sebastian ha shown him on his last visit to Half Moon Bay. He had no trouble at all finding the little cottage. Some of the fog had begun to burn off by the time he pulled his buggy into the drive.

In the buggy, he had a basket of flowers which he'd bought from a peddler who was always on the wharf. The flowers were for Elena for he wanted something to present to her. He had noted that Sebastian didn't allow her to drink wine as his father allowed his sister Markita. He'd chosen bright red blossoms because she was so vibrant and full of spirit. He leaped out of the buggy with his wines and the basket of flowers and in long striding steps marched up the pathway to the cottage.

He couldn't have been more pleased when the beautiful Elena opened the door and stood before him. Her black eyes flashed excitedly and her thick lashes fluttered nervously. "Mateo," she cried in surprise. "It is you!"

"Yes, Elena. It is me." He grinned down at her. "Did you think I would not return?"

"How could I know? But please—please, come in," she invited him.

Mark entered the front door and held out the basket of flowers to her. "For you, Elena," he told her.

"You brought these for me?" she asked, slowly reaching out to take the handle of the basket.

"Of course. A beautiful lady should have beautiful flowers," he told her as he watched her admiring the lovely bouquet. He was convinced that she was not used to receiving flowers from a young man. But then he had only to remember how very protective Vasco and Sebastian were of her.

"Oh, Mateo, I've never had a basket of flowers before, so I thank you very much," she confessed.

"Well, now you have, Elena. I brought wines for your father and Vasco from my father's winery, but I remembered that you weren't served wine that night I was here," he remarked as the two of them moved on into the front room.

A devious twinkle lit up in her eyes as she grinned, "Ah, but I drink Papa's wines. What he doesn't know doesn't hurt him. Papa is very strict. So I have my little secrets, you understand?"

Mark's deep violet eyes danced over her adorable face and she reminded him of a pixie, full of mischief. "I understand, Elena. My father is also strict with my sister Markita. Fathers just seem to be that way about their daughters," he told her.

"You have a sister?"

"A younger sister and an older brother, Carlos," he told her as they went over to sit down on the old sofa. This time she seemed perfectly at ease with him and he found her talkative and most inquisitive. She asked him many questions about himself and his family. In turn, he asked her about her life.

She smiled a most lovely smile as she declared, "I've never been anywhere, Mateo, but right here at Half Moon Bay. As you already know, Papa and Vasco are fishermen. Most of the Portuguese men here are fishermen. It is a very simple life we live and certainly nothing like what you have at Golden Splendor. But I plan to see more of the world than Half Moon Bay."

"Perhaps, one day you'd let me take you to Golden Splendor," Mark suggested.

"Me, Mateo? You would wish to take me to your home?" she asked him as if she were slightly amazed.

"Of course, I would. I've been to your home and met your family, and I'd like for you to meet mine. I—I like you, Elena. I like you very much," Mark declared to her.

In her frank, honest manner she admitted to him, "I've never met anyone like you, Mateo. I have only met the

Emilios of the world living all my life here at Half Moon Bay. I find them very stupid."

Mark found her absolutely fascinating. She was animated, and she spoke with dramatic gestures of her lovely dainty hands. Everything about this tiny miss seemed delicate, but he knew she was full of spice and ginger. He'd witnessed her hot temper exploding when she was riled, and he remembered she would have slapped him soundly had he not caught her hand.

In her simple skirt and drawstring tunic she was a more exciting young lady than any he'd seen dressed up in fancy gowns. He swore he'd never seen more beautiful hair than Elena's. It fell around her shoulders and down her back in soft waves and curls.

He sought to tease her, "Pray tell me that you don't find me stupid, Elena."

She gave a shrug of her shoulders and turned her dark eyes on him. "Come now, Mateo, you know better than that." She got up from the sofa and led him into her kitchen. "We shall have coffee—yes? Do you like bean soup, Mateo? It is time for lunch. I also have some cold chicken to serve you if you like."

"I like chicken hot or cold, Elena," he told her. He followed her, completely spellbound by this guileless, childlike creature.

He watched her ladle up two crocks of the bean soup and bring out a baked chicken, slicing off two huge servings. She looked at him and smiled. "I baked two hens yesterday. As you may have guessed, Papa and Vasco are hearty eaters."

With the coffee poured, she was ready to sit down at the kitchen table to join him. She was delightfully pleased to see how quickly he consumed the soup and asked for a second bowl. She filled another crock to the brim.

When he had finished, he looked over at her to declare, "I've got to get your recipe to give to our cook. It was delicious."

She giggled. "A lot of beans, a ham hock, and a little bit of this and that."

"That little bit of this and that sure made it taste good," he told her.

What amazed Mark was how long he lingered at that table after they'd shared lunch just to talk. The chiming of the kitchen clock made him aware of how many hours he'd been at the cottage.

Reluctantly, he rose, announcing that he had to get started back to Golden Splendor. "Give your father and Vasco my best regards and tell them I hope they enjoy the wine."

"You will come again, Mateo?" she asked him.

"I will come again, Elena," he told her. He could no longer suppress the desire to take her in his arms and kiss her firmly on those luscious lips. Such honey he'd never tasted before and her tiny body swayed against him as his strong arms held her. Such a flaming fire consumed him that he had to call on his strong will to release her.

But as he let go of her he murmured in her ear, "God, Elena, don't be mad at me. Damned if I could help myself. I've ached to kiss you since the minute I saw you. You're the most beautiful thing I've ever seen."

His kiss had shaken her to the core of her being, but that didn't stop her from boldly replying, "I'm not mad at you, Mateo. I—I wanted you to kiss me." She even dared to confess to him what he already knew; she'd never been kissed before by a man.

"I know, my little Elena, and I'm glad I was the man to first kiss those rosebud lips of yours." He bent down to kiss her one more time before he left. Reluctantly, he took his leave, but he paused to tell her, "You've now been kissed twice, Elena. I'm selfish, and I want no other man to taste that sweet nectar but me."

She stood watching him leap into his buggy and travel down the narrow drive. He turned back to wave to her before he guided the carriage onto the main dirt road and she waved back to him. Her heart was pounding erratically as she went back into the cottage, and for the next few minutes she roamed the rooms like someone in a daze.

It was apparent to Sebastian and Vasco that she was in a very happy mood that late afternoon. They both smelled the bean soup simmering on the back of the stove and the ham baking in the oven. The aroma of the cloves permeated the cottage, and their appetites were whetted to a high peak.

When Sebastian went into the kitchen to lift the lids of the pots as he always did to inspect what his daughter was cooking, he spied four bottles of wine on the cupboard shelf. "What is this, Elena?" he asked her as he ambled over to look at them.

"Mateo came today and brought you some of his father's wines," she told him.

"Mateo was here?" he quizzed, yanking off his cap.

"Yes, Papa, but he couldn't wait for you and Vasco to get home because he had to start back to Golden Splendor," she told him.

The first thought coursing through Sebastian's mind was that the dashing, handsome Mateo had been here, at his cottage, with Elena—alone. He wondered if this explained Elena's high-spirited mood.

Sebastian remembered how it was to be a hot-blooded young man like Mateo. He also recalled how it had been with Miranda, whose passions and desires had run as torrid and intense as his. His little daughter, Elena, was very much like her mama. He'd seen her eyes glancing over constantly at Mateo that evening he'd dined with them. Those all-knowing eyes of Sebastian Fernandes had not missed how the good-looking Mateo's eyes had danced over his beautiful daughter.

Being the very protective father that he was, Sebastian was most curious about what had happened in the afternoon while he was away and Elena and Mateo were alone.

Several miles away from Half Moon Bay, back in the valley of Golden Splendor, another father saw his offspring in high, elated spirits. Mano knew that Mark had arrived back home many hours later than Leon and Diego, and he had concluded that this time had been spent with the Portuguese family Mark had spoken about. But Mano also knew that Portuguese fishermen were out on the bay all day until late afternoon. So to whom had Mark delivered the wine? An amused smile came to Mano's face, for he had figured that the Fernandes family had to have a daughter and he'd wager that she was a beauty.

While they dined, Mano asked him, "Did you get your wines delivered to your friend Sebastian Fernandes?"

"Yes, I did."

"I guess you had to give it to his wife then, since the fishermen stay out so late on the bay," Mano commented casually.

"No, sir. Sebastian has no wife. She's dead. I gave it to his daughter Elena," Mark replied as he continued to eat.

"Oh, I see." Mano knew that he was right. His son was attracted to the daughter of the Fernandes family. He questioned Mark no more while they dined. It was later, when they strolled around the gardens to enjoy their cheroots, that Mano pressed him. "Tell me about Elena Fernandes," he urged. "Is she a beautiful young lady? Portuguese girls can be most exquisite."

Once again, Mark realized what a shrewd, clever man his father was. But he didn't hesitate to tell him, "She's the most extraordinary girl I've ever seen."

Six

By the time the two men reentered the front door, Mano had a vivid picture of Elena Fernandes. His son had told him more than he realized, and Mano recalled how he might have made the same detailed description of Aimée Aragon had he and his father shared the closeness that he and Mark did.

Mark was not aware of his father's thoughts when they parted company that evening. It would have come as a surprise to him just how much he had given away about himself and his feelings for Elena. He had no inkling how obvious he'd been to his astute father.

Later, when Mano and Aimée were sitting in the parlor, he told her about his conversation with their son in the courtyard. "I don't think Sebastian Fernandes whets Mark's interest as much as the pretty young daughter he spoke to me about tonight. Now I know why he was delayed for about five hours getting home from Half Moon Bay." He grinned.

Aimée sat up in her chair with a quizzical look on her face. "You think Mark is infatuated with this fisherman's daughter?"

"Oh, *querida,* I would swear to it! I'm not so old that I can't remember how every delicate feature of your face was etched in my memory after I met you. The same is true with our son when he describes Elena Fernandes."

"Oh, Mano, do you suppose Mark has found himself a

young lady who can tame that restless heart of his?" Aimée smiled.

"As we both know, *querida,* time will tell. But I am inclined to believe so."

Mano knew his son well. Always he had been able to relate to Mark more easily than he could to Carlos. Although he loved both sons just as much, Mark's ways were more like his ways when he was a young man in his twenties.

Lying in his bed tonight, Mark was thinking about Elena Fernandes. He wasn't sure that he could restrain himself the next time he was around her as he had this afternoon. Now that he'd tasted those honeyed lips of hers and she'd responded so eagerly to his caress, he could never again be as gallant as he'd been today.

The desire to possess her completely would be far too overwhelming. Mark knew that just kisses would not be enough to satisfy him, and he sensed that Elena Fernandes felt the same way.

Mark knew one thing about Elena, and that had been obvious to him when he kissed her: she was a woman of fire and passion. She'd honestly admitted to him that no man had ever kissed her as he'd kissed her. He was determined to be the man who'd make love to her the first and last time.

After her talk with Mano, Aimée found herself very curious about this little Portuguese girl up at Half Moon Bay. Was it possible that her elusive bachelor-son had finally fallen in love? She had never doubted for a minute that Mark would be the first to take a bride.

As far as her son Carlos getting married, Aimée figured he might be well into his thirties if he should marry at all. He was so absorbed in his profession that it left him little time to get distracted by a pretty face.

Aimée had the impression that Carlos had no desire for any lady to interrupt the regimented, routine lifestyle he was now living in Sacramento.

He'd bought himself a nice two-story house and had a housekeeper and cook who saw to his immediate needs. He spent long hours at his law office and came home to enjoy a quiet evening. From what he'd told her, he went upstairs shortly after dinner to go over papers and briefs before he retired.

He did have one constant companion—the big fluffy cat he called Amigo.

All that mattered to Aimée was that Carlos seemed happy and content with his new life in Sacramento. That was all she wanted for her sons and daughter.

As she puttered around her house that day, her thoughts kept going back to the Portuguese girl, Elena, that Mano had told her about. She found herself very curious to meet this little charmer. Suddenly, she was struck by an idea how she might meet her. She'd have Mark invite the Fernandes family to their Festival of the Grapes, which would be held very soon.

It was a special occasion—not only for the Mateo family, but for all the workers and their families who labored throughout the year in the winery and vineyards. And, of course, the Mateos always invited their family and friends.

They'd held the first such celebration after Mano had gotten his vineyards started and taken in his initial harvest. Every year thereafter, they had continued the festival.

Mano was excited about this year's yield. It had been a dry, cool summer with some sunny days, and Mano had learned that the grapes had to be picked at just the right time. Hot, moist days caused the picked grapes to deteriorate quickly. He'd declared to his wife that he felt this was going to be their grandest year.

Aimée found herself caught up in his enthusiasm and began to make plans for the annual affair. Her courtyard gardens would be teeming with guests, so mountains of foods had to be prepared. A platform had to be constructed for the dancing in the evening. She always engaged three or four gentlemen to stroll through the gardens, playing guitars.

That night before they went down to dinner she spoke to Mano about inviting the Fernandes family to the festival.

Mano bent down to kiss her. "A curious little vixen, aren't you, *mi vida?*"

She laughed. "And I'm never going to change, *mon chéri.*"

"I don't wish you to ever do that, and I think that's a fine idea you have," Mano told her.

"Then I shall say something to Mark tonight at dinner." She smiled.

An hour later, having just finished the dessert, she suggested that he invite the Fernandes family to their festival and took Mark by surprise.

"You wish me to invite them, Mother?" he asked her as though he were questioning if he'd heard right.

"I think it would be very nice to have them come, dear. I'm anxious to meet these Portuguese friends of yours." She smiled across the table at him.

Privately, he couldn't have been more pleased. Now he had an excuse to see the lovely Elena again as he was yearning to do.

So the next morning, he worked his usual routine around the winery before returning to the house to change his clothes, have a light lunch, and go to the barn to prepare his buggy for the trip to Half Moon Bay.

But this afternoon when he arrived at Sebastian's cottage, no one answered the door when he knocked. Elena was not home, and he'd not expected Sebastian and Vasco to be there, for it was too early.

So he got back into his buggy and headed for the wharves in hopes of finding Elena there. Perhaps she had gone out on the fishing boat with her father.

Some of the trawlers were returning to the wharf, but he knew that Sebastian put in a much longer day, staying out until five or five-thirty.

He knew he might have a long wait, but he didn't mind if he could get to see Elena.

So he sat down on the wharf and leaned up against a post after he'd lit up one of his cheroots. Across the water he could see a couple of fishing boats, but they were too far away to identify.

Mark enjoyed observing the various people going up and down the levec. He was in a quiet, thoughtful mood as he indulged himself in this most relaxed surrounding, and the rhythmical currents of the bay had a hypnotic effect on him.

Suddenly, he felt two dainty hands reaching around to cover his two eyes and a soft feminine voice giggling, "Guess who, Mateo?"

No one called him Mateo quite like Elena did. Her soft, accented voice spoke his name in a special way.

He sought to tease her. "Darned if I know," he said.

"Don't you lie to me, Mateo. You know who it is," she retorted as she jerked her hands away and whirled around from behind him to sit down beside him.

With a husky laugh, he reached out to take her hands in his. "Of course, I knew it was you, Elena."

A slow smile came to her face. "I—I stood back a moment to be sure it was you."

His dancing violet eyes excited her. It was a feeling she'd never experienced with any other young man. Only with Mateo did it happen.

"I went by your house and found that you weren't home

so I came here in hopes of seeing you. I knew Vasco and your father wouldn't be in yet," he told her.

"I was visiting my friend Marietta, but I always try to get home before Papa and Vasco or they get in such a stew. I don't know when the two of them are going to realize that I'm not a baby anymore," she declared.

"No, you are certainly not," he agreed. That was probably exactly why Sebastian and Vasco got in "such a stew."

"Well, Mateo, this is a nice surprise to see you this afternoon," she remarked.

"I came here to invite you and your family to come to Golden Splendor to our Festival of the Grapes. It's an annual affair my family has every year when the grapes are harvested. My mother wished to have you come," he told her.

Wide-eyed and slightly stunned, she stammered, "Your mother wishes us to come, Mateo? But she doesn't even know us."

"I told her about your family, Elena, and the hospitality your father showed me that evening I ate his *paella,*" Mark told her.

"You must have a very nice mama, Mateo. This festival your parents have—tell me about it," she demanded curiously.

Mark told her that it was a celebration that began in the afternoon and lasted late into the night. It was a time when the workers of his father's vineyards and winery came to their home to be treated to a feast and the fine wines that they'd help produce. He told her that later there was music and dancing. "Ah, Elena, you must come, for it is a most wonderful day and night. I want you to come to share it with me," he said.

"I would love to come, but Papa will decide that, Mateo. Your mama must have to cook for days for such an affair," she said. She had no inkling of the servants a spacious home like Mateo's home required. One woman could never have managed it. Celia the cook had two young Mexican girls who helped her.

"My mother could not possibly do that, Elena. She has to have servants to help run the house. But she makes all the plans for the festival."

Perplexed and apprehensive, she stammered, "I—I guess I had not realized just how wealthy your family is, Mateo. How could we possibly fit in to such a grand affair? My father is a simple man—a fisherman."

"Of course you could fit in. Remember, Elena, I told you it was a festival where all my father's workers and their families come to our house to celebrate. Yes, my parents are wealthy, but they are not snobs. They both worked hard to make Golden Splendor the grand place it is today."

She smiled. "I am eager to come, Mateo. Now you must convince Papa that we should come."

"I'll convince him," he assured her.

To Elena's delight, Mark easily persuaded Sebastian to attend the Festival of the Grapes. In fact, Sebastian felt very honored to be invited to the grand affair and he didn't hesitate a moment in accepting the invitation. Something Elena had not thought about that Sebastian considered was that Mateo's father's workers had no fancy buggies to drive to the fine country estate. They'd arrive in their flatbedded wagons as would he.

But Sebastian was certain that his daughter would be the most beautiful young lady there, and he was going to see that she had herself a fancy new gown for the occasion. He'd be the proudest fellow when he introduced his daughter to Mateo's parents.

"You tell your mama that the Fernandes family is very honored to accept her kind invitation to the festival, Mateo," Sebastian told Mark.

"I certainly will, sir. I will be looking forward to seeing you there," Mark replied. Actually, he couldn't have been happier. His beautiful Elena would be at his home for the gala!

It didn't come as a surprise to Sebastian when Vasco told him that he would not be going. But that didn't dampen Sebastian's enthusiasm. It would not keep him from going and taking Elena.

The celebration was a golden opportunity for his seventeen-year-old daughter and he'd not deny her that. Something like this might never come her way again, and he wanted her to experience this grand affair. He didn't care that it might cost him a whole week's earnings to buy her a fancy gown. It would be worth it.

He had not been able to give Elena many luxuries, and at times, it had pained him. But he could take her to Golden Splendor and it would be a memory that would last her the rest of her life.

She could talk of nothing but the festival the entire evening, and Sebastian realized how much she was anticipating the harvest fete. So that night, before she retired to her room, he handed her a pouch of money he'd had in the drawer of a chest in his bedroom and told her to buy herself a pretty gown to wear to Golden Splendor.

Later in her bedroom, when she emptied the purse and counted the coins, she wondered if her papa had taken leave of his senses. She couldn't believe how much money he had given her.

She would buy herself a pretty gown as well as slippers, but she'd not spend every penny. She knew how hard her papa worked to earn his money and how long it had taken him to fill the pouch that full.

After all, how many times would she wear a fancy gown?

The opportunity to attend a harvest gala might never come again for the Fernandes family.

So, Elena decided, she would enjoy herself at Golden Splendor. She would wear an exquisite costume with new slippers to the festival. She wanted to look beautiful because she knew that many pretty girls would be there for Mateo's eyes to appraise.

But she wanted him to think *she* was the most beautiful girl there.

Seven

Elena felt ill-at-ease and awkward going into the mercantile store to purchase this special dress for herself. She had
made her full-flowing skirts and drawstring tunics since she
was about twelve. Luckily, she was approached by a very
nice middle-aged clerk who sensed her apprehensions.

"My, you're so pretty that you could wear just about any
color of gown. What is your favorite color, dear?" Sarah
Colter asked her.

"I love the pale yellows," Elena told her.

"All right, let's you and I see what we might find for you.
Is there any other color you like should I not have a pretty
yellow dress that pleases you?"

"Well, I don't know what you would call it, but I call it
robin's-egg blue. I love that color," Elena told her.

"All right, dear. Come with me, and I bet we can find you
a pretty frock," Sarah told her.

Sarah found a beautiful frock with a low scooped neckline
edged with a wide ruffle and trimmed in dainty white lace.
It was sleeveless with the ruffling flowing over her upper
arms. The bodice molded to Elena's small body and a full
gathered skirt ended with a flounce.

Sarah unearthed a pair of pale-yellow leather slippers
which matched the dress perfectly. Sarah told her that she
needed only one other thing to complement her ensemble:

hair ornament. She chose for Elena a beautiful cluster of yellow flowers attached to a comb to tuck in her hair.

She smiled at the young girl and told her, "My, I'd love to see you when you're all dressed up in this. You're sure going to be a pretty little thing."

"Thank you. It is very important to me to look just right, Mrs. Colter. You've helped me so much," Elena told her.

"It was a pleasure, my dear. You come to see me again when you need another new dress. It was nice to have served you," Sarah Colter told her.

Elena jauntily left the store to go back home. What she did not know was that Sarah was reminded of her own daughter, who would have been about Elena's age but had died the year before. She had been Sarah's pride and joy, and so her heart had gone out to Elena that afternoon.

Elena was a most happy young lady when she left the store and walked toward her home with her armload of packages. Never had she had a frock this beautiful with dainty slippers to match. In fact, she had only two pair of shoes in her closet. There was a pair of shoes that laced up, which she always wore on her father's fishing boat, and there was a pair of leather sandals.

Emilio spied her walking down the street and dashed to catch up with her. It seemed to him that he had forever been enamored with her, but he had never been as brash as he'd been several days ago when he'd tried to force his attentions on her. He was in awe of the fierce Vasco. Later, when the strange young man had come to her aid, he had left in fear of what Vasco might do to him. But nothing had happened, so he'd begun to breathe easier the last few days.

His intentions were to apologize to her so he could get back in her good graces now that he had finally caught sight of her. When he neared her, he called out. Elena stopped for a brief moment, turned, and saw him, but she began to walk even faster.

"Elena, I'm sorry I acted like an oaf. Wait up," he cried, running after her. Finally he was able to catch up with her. "I said I'm sorry. I apologize. All right?" Emilio pleaded, but she only gave him a haughty glare.

With a saucy air, she told him, "All right, I accept your apology. Now, I've got to be on my way. I've got to get home, Emilio, so I've no time to talk with you."

Elena Fernandes could be the most exasperating female he knew, and it was probably why she attracted him so much. She was not like the other Portuguese girls in the fishing village.

He threw his hands up in the air. He shook his black curly head and sighed. "Damn, Elena, how can you have the face of an angel and have such a cold heart?"

Elena laughed. "Oh, come on, Emilio Santiago. I've got no cold heart, but I've a house to clean when I get home since I've been shopping for the last two hours. So I've no time to waste talking."

"Could I just come home with you and we could sit on your porch to talk awhile?"

"No, Emilio. You'd be sitting in the swing by yourself. I'm going to be in the house cleaning it up," she told him.

"So what were you shopping for that took two hours, eh?" he asked her.

"Well, not that it's any of your business, but I bought a gown to wear to the Festival of the Grapes," she declared smugly as she continued to walk on down the street.

"Festival of the Grapes?" He sniggered. "I never heard of any festival around here called that, Elena."

"Did I say it was in Half Moon Bay, Emilio? The Festival of the Grapes is held at Golden Splendor. Golden Splendor is a fine old estate with a winery and vineyards," she informed him.

"Elena," he rebuked her. "This is Emilio you're talking with. How would you get an invitation to such an affair?"

She whirled, fire sparking from her black eyes, and lashed out at him. "That is none of your business. What makes you think you've got the right to question me about anything? Go on your way, Emilio, before I scratch your eyes out."

Right then, she looked like a wildcat ready to pounce, so Emilio turned away. As angry as she was, she still excited him. No other girl in the village could compare to the fiery Elena Fernandes.

Elena was not the only one eagerly anticipating the festival. Lola McGrann was also keyed up.

"Señor Mano has had a good vintage year and I could not be happier for him. He will have every reason to celebrate his harvest," Alonso had told his sister. "Ah, Lola, it will be a memorable occasion. I'm so glad you're here to share it with me."

"I have to say you've got me curious, Alonso. I'll have to take your word about the grapes and harvesting them. The only thing I ever harvested was my vegetables from my garden." She'd laughed, but a few days later she'd begun looking through her clothes to see what she could wear to the festival.

Lola had only two dresses to choose from. She had a berry-colored gown with a dainty, white-lace collar and cuffs. The other good dress was bottle-green with a shawl neckline. She always wore a pretty broach on it that Alonso had given her. The only other jewelry she owned was her wedding band and the gold hoop earrings her husband had given to her on her wedding day. Those she wore constantly.

Deciding on the bottle-green dress, she pressed it along with Alonso's best pants and shirt.

She was pleased about her brother's improved condition over the last few weeks. Señor Mano, ever-thoughtful, had taken him in his buggy to see the final picking of the luscious grapes the week before the festival. It had done Alonso a world of good to be with Señor Mano that afternoon, and he'd returned to the quarters in the highest spirits.

Lola could not have been happier and more content with the life she was now living. It was far easier than her lot had been in Half Moon Bay, and she missed nothing.

She now knew why Alonso sang the praises of the Mateo family, although she had yet to meet the older son, Carlos, and she'd had little contact with the señora's daughter, Markita.

Alonso had already prepared her for Carlos. "There is a proud dignity and reserve about Carlos," Alonso told her. "I've known him for years, and I still don't feel that I know Carlos, so don't expect him to be the warm fellow Mark is."

But something happened a few days before the festival that changed things for Lola and Mark's sister. Lola had baked some pies for dinner and she had a pot of chicken simmering slowly on the stove. At the last minute she would add her noodles, so while she waited, she went out to enjoy the serenity of twilight in the courtyard.

She loved to watch the gentle flow of the fountain in the gardens and the birds that flocked to the feeders for the last time that day before they went to the nests and branches of the many trees. She always sat on one of the little benches in a secluded area surrounded by tall shrubs.

She saw a girlish figure dash through the wrought-iron gate with her skirts held high as she rushed across the grounds to seek a secret place. Lola sat only a short distance away.

Lola knew why she'd rushed there, for she could hear her deep sobs. As she listened, she hurt for the pretty girl whose heart was breaking. Something had hurt her very deeply.

After awhile, Lola could not resist the urge to comfort her. She walked around the flowering shrub and joined Markita. In a soothing voice she told the girl, "Come here, sweet child, and cry on old Lola's broad shoulder."

Markita saw her kind, compassionate face and fell into her outstretched arms to sob for an endless time. Lola, saying nothing, held her close.

When her crying finally ceased and Markita broke away from Lola's embrace to look up at her, her lovely face was tear-stained. "Oh, Lola, please keep this our little secret," Markita pleaded.

"You don't worry that pretty head of yours about my saying a word, child. Are you harmed in any way, little Markita?" Lola asked her with a concerned look on her face.

"Not the way you're speaking about, Lola. Just my foolish heart's wounded, I guess. I've been so silly—so foolish. I should have realized a long time ago that Roberto was not interested in me, but I kept throwing myself at him," Markita confessed.

"Oh, Markita. You're just guilty of doing what all we women do until we finally learn better. You'll be smarter next time, and that's all that matters." Lola took a wisp of the hair that fell over the tear-stained face and brushed it back. "Believe me, child, next time it will be different."

"Did—did you ever do something so silly, Lola?" Markita asked her.

"Lord yes, Markita. I did it three times before I finally got wise." Lola chuckled. "I figure that you will be smarter than I was."

Markita had chanced to witness with her own eyes what Mark had seen often over the last six months. She'd seen

Roberto in his buggy with a young lady snuggled close to him. She'd seen the most intimate way Roberto had looked at her. Markita was devastated as she watched the two of them. Her heart was crushed.

She found Lola easy to tell this to. "Oh, Lola, why didn't he discourage me? I was around him all the time since his sister and I are best friends. I'm always going over to her house, and she's always spending the weekends here with me. I thought he was being reserved because I was Roberta's best friend. Now I know different."

"Oh, child, a man's ways and thinking are not like a young lady's. His ego was heightened to think a pretty young thing like you was attracted to him. He must have enjoyed that feeling, for he could have easily discouraged you. This Roberto is a selfish man, Markita. Forget him and turn your attentions to another young man eager for your regard. I'd bet you know some young swain right now who'd welcome your interest."

"I know such a young man, Lola," Markita smiled, reminded that Francisco Renaldo had always wanted to court her.

"Then give that suitor a chance. You might be surprised what you'll discover about him," Lola declared.

"You might be right, Lola. I've never considered Francisco because I was always too dazzled by Roberto. Now that I think about it, Francisco is far more handsome and he's a very nice, considerate person."

"Now, see this, child, you give this Francisco a chance and forget this Roberto, who is not worth your tears. You may be in for a pleasant surprise." Lola patted her shoulder.

Markita perked up. "I will, Lola. I'll do just that. I'll invite Francisco to be my escort to the festival, and I'll ignore Roberto completely." Her hands went up to her cheek to wipe away a few remaining tears from her eyes.

"You see, everything will be fine, little Markita. You're going to have yourself a fine time at the festival," Lola predicted.

Markita was as animated and affectionate as her mother, and she reached out to warmly embrace Lola, telling her, "I'm glad you were here for me to talk to. I couldn't have brought myself to talk to Mother about this just yet."

"Well, I'm glad I was here too, child. But I've got to get up to my chicken before it goes dry in my pot, or Alonso and I won't have any supper tonight." Lola chuckled.

Two strangers had met in the back gardens that late afternoon, but they parted as close friends because of the intimate moments they'd shared one with the other.

A bond of friendship was formed that would last a lifetime.

Eight

Markita Mateo could be a cunning, crafty young lady when she wanted to be. The next day she decided to pay a call on Francisco at his father's country estate, which was only a mile-and-a-half away from Golden Splendor.

The unsuspecting Francisco, eager to be her escort, never realized that she was seeking her sweet revenge, still seething about Roberto. His father and Mano Mateo had settled in this region, which they called the Valley of the Moon, with their young brides the same year. Both of them had built their estates by working long hours and their wives had worked right along with them and had their children.

Mano had planted his vineyards and Francisco's father had planted his orchards, but both of them had prospered through the years.

His mother, Maria, was Aimée's dearest friend. Long before Mano had married Aimée, Pablo Renaldo had been his best friend. It was Pablo that Mano had talked to when he faced the dilemma of trying to court Aimée Aragon when their fathers were feuding so fiercely. Many a night Pablo had listened to Mano vent his frustrations about how he was ever going to court the young lady who'd stolen his restless heart. But Pablo never doubted that he'd find a way, as determined as he was to win Aimée Aragon's love.

No one could have been happier than Pablo when he heard about the wedding of Mano and Aimée. He had just taken himself a bride a month earlier. So the two couples and their growing families shared many good times together.

Like Mark, Francisco was a middle son. He had an older brother and two younger sisters. The Renaldo family always looked forward to the Festival of the Grapes because it was such a gay occasion, but Francisco was especially excited about it this year since Markita had requested that he be her escort.

Markita rode her thoroughbred back home feeling happy and smug. She'd show Roberto that she didn't plan to mope over him and that she was interested in another young man. She just hoped that he didn't have the audacity to bring that red-haired girl to the fete.

As soon as she arrived home, she started checking through her armoire for her prettiest gown. Her friend, Roberta was going to be stunned to find out that Francisco was to be her escort for she had so wanted Markita and Roberto to get together. But, Markita finally realized, it was never going to happen.

Roberta would quiz her unmercifully but Markita had already determined what she would tell her best friend. After all, she had her own fierce pride, so she could not tell Roberta that she'd seen Roberto with another girl and that there was no question in her mind that it wasn't the first time they'd been together.

She was going to tell Roberta that she'd decided that her older brother was really too old for her and far too serious.

That evening as she dined with her family she announced that Francisco Renaldo was going to be her escort. Mano could not have been more pleased, for he considered Francisco a fine young man. Aimée was just as delighted, although she wondered at the change of heart. Mark was glad that she was finally over that lovestruck infatuation that had lasted over two years. Mark didn't like Roberto. He felt that the self-centered, conceited rascal was far too experienced and sophisticated for his naive little sister. Francisco was an outgoing, honest young man closer to Markita's age.

Throughout the next few days, the large, roomy kitchen was a beehive of activity. The pantry shelves were lined with an array of pastries, loaves of fresh-baked bread, and huge jars of fruit punches. The Mateos' guests would consume tremendous amounts of food during the afternoon and evening of the harvest celebration. But that was what the festival was all about, for Aimée and Mano wanted everyone to feast, drink the fine wines, and dance to the music. It was their way of showing their gratitude to their workers for the hard labor they put in at the winery and in the vineyards.

Mano and Aimée didn't just sit back to watch the others dancing after they'd stuffed themselves with food and good wines. They joined into the dancing with the workers and their wives to have just as gay a time.

Like Markita, Aimée had carefully chosen the gown she would wear for the occasion. It would be one of Mano's favorites in a deep lavender color.

Today he had presented her with a gift as he always did at festival time. This year he'd bought her a pair of exquisite amethyst earrings, so there was no question about it: she must wear her lavender gown.

Markita had chosen her pale-pink gown and the pearls her parents had given her on her last birthday. In her dark hair she was going to wear the large mother-of-pearl comb that had belonged to her Grandmother Mateo.

Grandmother Mateo had had a vast jewelry collection and over the years old Carlos had given his daughter-in-law Aimée many exquisite pieces. He had not presented any to Markita until he had decided that she was finally old enough to appreciate them. He'd given her a lovely ruby ring which she wore all the time. Other pieces of the collection were being held for the brides of Carlos and Mark.

Markita was very much like her mother in that she possessed a most curious nature. She often pondered what young ladies her older brothers would choose for their wives.

She envisioned that Mark's wife would be completely different from Carlos's. He would want a more sophisticated woman who would fit into his world and his career in Sacramento.

He was so engrossed in his law practice that he would hardly find time to marry any young lady for a few more years. She just hoped that he would take time off to come to the festival, for her parents would be most disappointed if he didn't get home for the occasion.

She also hoped that Mark would choose to remain at Golden Splendor to run the vineyards and winery with her father. Although Mano openly dreamed of handing his business down to one of his sons, Markita knew it would certainly never be Carlos. That left Mark.

Maybe that was what he had in mind. He had been working long hours in the winery lately and had not mentioned the bullfighting which he'd been so enthused about when he'd first returned from Mexico some weeks ago.

Would he be bringing some pretty lady to the festival, she wondered? She knew about the Portuguese fisherman Mark had met in Half Moon Bay and that he had been invited to the festival. She'd told her mother that she thought it was very nice of her to invite the Fernandes family.

"Well, Sebastian Fernandes sounds like a gracious man and Mark seems to like him very much," Aimée told her. "If they accept the invitation, I've told Mark that they must stay overnight as our guests for it is a long trip for them."

"What about Carlos, Mother? Do you suppose he will be bringing a guest?" Markita asked.

The expression on her mother's face told her that she was a little out of patience with her oldest son. "I don't know Carlos's plans, Markita. We've not heard whether he is coming or not. It's been almost three weeks since we had a letter."

"Oh, he will come, Mother," Markita tried to assure her. "He knows how special the festival is."

"Well, we shall see, dear," Aimée said with a casual shrug of her shoulders as though she could not concern herself if he did or didn't come. As she turned to go out of the room to speak with her cook about another detail involving the festival, she told Markita, "Carlos is his own man now, living in his own home. He has his own life, but then we also have our own life here at Golden Splendor."

Markita understood.

Excitement mounted in those last few days before the festival. Mano could see it in the faces of his workers around the winery and so could Mark.

But the same was true at the house and within the Mateo family. Mark was eagerly anticipating seeing Elena Fernandes again since Sebastian had assured him that they would be coming.

The evening before the festival, Carlos arrived in his buggy. He'd brought no guests with him, but that didn't surprise Mark. When all the family gathered around the dining table, it was apparent that his parents were most pleased about Carlos's returning home.

Had Carlos hurt his parents by not coming home, Mark had already made up his mind that he would have a few choice words to say to him. He might be the younger brother but he'd never felt intimidated by Carlos.

On the other hand Carlos had always envied Mark. His

manner and ways were like Mano Mateo, and Carlos admired no man more than his father.

By the time he'd reached the age of twenty, Carlos recognized that he'd inherited grandfather's personality and airs. Grandfather Mateo was a stately, dignified gentleman who didn't give way to lighthearted laughter and easygoing ways. Yet Carlos had also gathered from listening to his mother and father jest with one another that Mano had been a restless, reckless rake in his younger days.

Carlos Mateo just wasn't a man who sought daring adventure.

Quite unlike his grandfather, he could never have been interested in raising and breeding bulls; but neither was he interested in the art of making fine wines or developing the vineyards with their lush clusters of grapes.

He had no great appreciation for fine horses or riding wildly over the countryside as Mark and his sister did. He'd never sat as fine in the saddle as they had, even when they were young children.

He could remember before Mark had even celebrated his eighteenth birthday how the young ladies were fawning over him. There was a certain animal magnetism about Mark that drew the girls to him like bees are drawn to the sweet nectar in the blossoms of flowers. They'd dash right by Carlos, rushing over to Mark.

Actually, he'd never had a serious love affair with any young woman to this day. Oh, he'd played escort for various maidens. But most of the time it would be a one-occasion affair and he'd rarely called on the lady a second time. None of them had ever intrigued him enough to seek to pursue a relationship.

Lately, he had come to the conclusion that he was meant to remain a bachelor. He liked living his life the way he chose to live it without the yoke of a wife or children hanging around his neck. It was nice and quiet when he went home in the evenings from his law office with only Amigo, his cat, to keep him company.

He couldn't imagine this peaceful atmosphere being disturbed by a crying baby in the house or a wife chattering away at him. When he'd gone to the homes of some of his acquaintances, he found their toddlers obnoxious brats. Their parents might consider them little darlings, but to Carlos they were pests.

One day he would be faced with nephews and nieces when Markita and Mark had their children, but he had grave doubts that he'd be much of a doting uncle. Bouncing a small babe on his knee didn't appeal to him whatsoever. He much preferred Amigo on his lap, lying quietly curled up, making no noise.

No, he was very content with his routine in Sacramento, going to his law office daily and coming home to the nicely furnished, comfortable house he'd recently bought. He had a capable housekeeper who prepared him a fine meal each evening.

He furnished the funds for her to purchase whatever she needed to make the house run smoothly. It was a well-organized life, and he enjoyed it. He'd never regretted his decision to leave Golden Splendor.

It was nice to see his family again for he loved all of them dearly, but the festival really didn't excite him in the least. He tolerated it for his parents' sake, but he had little to discuss or talk about with the people who gathered there.

Two days there and he'd be eager to get back to his cozy, quiet home and law office in Sacramento.

Nine

Elena Fernandes was titillated by the time she boarded her father's flatbedded wagon. Sebastian Fernandes had never been dressed in such fine attire as he was today. He wore new black pants and a new white shirt. Around his neck he wore a deep-scarlet silk kerchief. Atop his thick grey mane of hair he wore a new flat-crowned hat.

Elena knew why he had made such an effort for the occasion: he wanted her to be proud of him. That endeared him to her so much.

It was a beautiful golden autumn day with mild temperatures and a calm breeze, so Elena didn't have to fret that her beautiful hair was being blown. She had placed the cluster of flowers to the left side of her head as the clerk had suggested.

Both Vasco and Sebastian had told her how lovely she looked. Her mirror had also told her that. She didn't know what this afternoon and evening would be like, but she was anticipating a grand time.

It did not take as long as they'd anticipated to reach Golden Splendor. When Elena saw that they were rolling under the impressive archway, she exclaimed to her father, "Papa, maybe we'll be arriving too early. That would be rude."

Sebastian soothed her. "Honey, how were we to know how long it would take to get here since we'd not made this trip before, eh? You don't fret that pretty head of yours. Mateo will understand."

It was Mark Mateo who was fretting and pacing out on the south patio as he kept looking toward the entrance in hopes of spying Sebastian's old flatbedded wagon. As soon as he'd dressed in his fine-tailored black pants and white silk shirt, he'd left his room to go downstairs where he could have a perfect view of the entranceway. Like Sebastian, he had tied a bright-scarlet silk scarf around his neck.

He'd lit a cheroot and puffed nervously on it and he was unaware that his sister had breezed through the doors leading onto the patio with two glasses of wine in her hands.

"Here, Mark, I thought you might like this. You're as nervous as a cat."

He gave her a sheepish grin. "Have you been spying on me, little sister? Well, I guess I am, but let me say you look as beautiful as a pink rosebud."

"Madre de Dios, you can be sweet at times, big brother! May I say you look very dashing? No doubt all the girls will be flocking around you as they usually are every year," she said impishly.

He took a sip of the chilled white wine and gave a shrug of his broad shoulders. "Oh, come on, Markita," he protested. "Not all the girls flock around me. Sure, some of them come over to talk to me, but that's it."

"Mark, this is your sister you're talking to—remember? Why don't you just come over here and sit down to enjoy your wine?"

"I'm watching for the Fernandes to arrive, Markita. They're going to feel strange. They'll know no one here but me, so I wanted to personally greet them," he explained.

Markita giggled. "Sit down, Mark. You're pacing like a caged animal. Maria is stationed by the door, and she ca let them in. I've no doubt that you've already told her to let you know the minute they arrive."

He grinned for she was exactly right about that, so he did as she suggested and sat at the table with her. For a brief time they had a nice brother-sister talk as they often did. Mark confessed to her that he was glad Francisco was to be her escort this evening.

"You've never liked Roberto, have you, Mark? Since you're both about the same age, I've wondered why the two of you weren't friends," Markita remarked, taking a sip of the wine.

"I don't dislike Roberto, Markita. I just never found that I had anything in common with him. Let's put it this way: his personality and mine didn't click even though our parents were close friends. In other words, he and I could have never enjoyed the friendship that you and his sister have shared."

"I—I think I understand, Mark. It's for sure that Roberta is nothing like her brother."

Suddenly her dark eyes flashed as she chanced to see a flatbedded wagon rolling through the opened gates and she exclaimed that they must have their first guests arriving. "It must be one of father's workers, for they are coming in a wagon. None of them own a buggy. My goodness, they're arriving almost an hour early!"

Mark leaped up from his chair and declared excitedly, "No, that's the Fernandes, and they've arrived early because Sebastian was just not sure how long it would take him to travel here in his wagon."

Like a gazelle, Mark dashed from the patio, striding across the grounds. Markita, watching his towering figure move across the grounds, had a perfect view of the wagon and its occupants as they pulled up at the front entrance. She saw a hefty, robust fellow and a very tiny young lady.

As far away as she was, Markita could see the long flowing

black hair that fell slightly below Elena's shoulders. She noted the attractive yellow gown that displayed a tiny waistline. The Fernandes girl was a ravishing beauty with a very curvy figure. Markita now knew why Mark had so anxiously awaited his guests. It was Sebastian Fernandes' daughter that had her brother so excited.

When Mark reached the wagon and his hands reached up to lift Elena to the ground, the sight of her took his breath away.

"Welcome to Golden Splendor, sir, and you, too, Elena. Come with me. My parents have not come downstairs yet, but I'd like you to meet my sister Markita," he invited.

"I apologize for the early arrival, Mateo, but we just weren't sure how fast that old mare and wagon would travel," Sebastian told him.

"I'm glad you got here so we'll have a chance to visit before the other guests arrive," Mark told him as they headed to the patio where Markita still sat at the table. The closer they got Markita could see that the petite girl walking beside her brother was even more beautiful than she'd first thought. She had no inkling of what Mark was saying to her, but Elena gazed up at him with a lovely smile on her face. She had a saucy air, and she walked with a feisty pace. With both her father and Mark towering over her, she almost looked childlike.

Mark was rewarded by Elena's smile because he'd commented on how beautiful she looked and she, in turn, had told him, "You look very handsome yourself, Mateo."

When the three of them arrived at the patio, Mark introduced his friends from Half Moon Bay. Markita realized that Sebastian Fernandes was a mountain of a man once he stood within a couple feet of her. With that thick mane of grey hair and his dark coloring he struck an imposing figure. He gave a graceful bow when he was introduced to her. There was a certain charm about the man, Markita thought.

Elena's features were just as striking. Her light olive complexion looked like smooth satin, and her black eyes flashed with life and spirit. Markita liked her immediately, and Elena gave her a warm, friendly smile. "It is so nice to meet you, Markita," she said.

"Please, have a seat while Mark gets you a glass of wine," Markita insisted, and he left them in her care.

It took only a few minutes of conversation with Elena for Markita to see why Mark would find her so refreshing. She was unpretentious and down-to-earth. No silly little-girlish games would she seek to play. But her black fiery eyes also told Markita that she could probably be a real hellcat if her temper exploded.

Seated at the table with Mateo's sister, Elena thought how beautiful the girl looked in her pink gown. Impulsively, she exclaimed, "You are as beautiful as the pink rosebuds on our rosebushes, Markita."

"Why, thank you, Elena." Markita was used to young ladies flattering her to win her good graces because they were interested in Mark. But there was a genuine quality about this Portuguese girl that Markita liked.

Mark was very pleased to return to the patio to find that Sebastian and Elena seemed at ease with his younger sister. It was obvious that Markita had warmed to them.

A servant followed Mark with crystal goblets on a silver tray. The four of them enjoyed the wine and light conversation before Mano and Aimée joined them.

Descending the stairs, the couple heard laughter and a deep bass voice echoing from the side patio. A smile came to Mano's face as he told his wife, "Perhaps, it is Mark's friends from Half Moon Bay who have arrived a little early."

Sebastian was the first of the four to see the middle-aged

man and woman coming through the double doors that led to the patio. He was thinking what a striking pair they made, and he knew instinctively that they had to be Mateo's parents. He graciously rose from his chair ready to greet them, and at that moment Mark turned to see his parents. He stood to make the introductions.

Mano seated his wife as he told Sebastian, "It is a pleasure to meet you and your charming daughter, señor. We are honored that you've come to Golden Splendor to celebrate our Festival of the Grapes. It is a special occasion for me and my wife Aimée."

"Ah, señor, it is Elena and I who are honored to have been invited. It is a grand estate you have here, Señor Mateo," Sebastian replied with gusto.

Just as Markita had formed a hasty opinion about Elena Fernandes, her father found Sebastian Fernandes a fascinating character. He was a man that Mano wanted to know more about and talk with at length. He was certain that this Portuguese fisherman could have many tales to tell him.

Aimée's all-knowing eyes observed her son and how he looked at Sebastian's daughter. She had to confess that she had not been prepared to meet a young lady with Elena's rare beauty. It was also apparent to Aimée that Elena had made a favorable impression on Markita, who chattered away with the pretty girl from Half Moon Bay.

It was also interesting to Aimée that little Elena seemed perfectly at ease with the gathering of Mark's family. Some young ladies he'd brought here had been nervous. But not Elena Fernandes.

Sebastian was not a shy fellow. He was an exuberant person whether he was working his fishing boat or enjoying himself leisurely as he was this afternoon. Mano found him intriguing. His deep voice was almost melodious, but Mano could also imagine that he could roar like a fierce lion.

He was enjoying his conversation so much with Sebastian that he was almost sorry when the servant announced to him that other guests were arriving. Reluctantly, he and Aimée excused themselves to greet the Renaldos. Francisco immediately went in search of Markita when Aimée told him where he would find her and whisked Markita away from the patio.

Markita, atwitter about the Fernandes, exclaimed, "Oh, Francisco, isn't she gorgeous? I think my brother must think so, too."

"She's very beautiful, Markita, but not as beautiful as you," he told her, his soft, warm eyes gazing down at her. Like the Mateo men, Francisco was as tall as Markita was tiny.

Mark decided that it was the perfect time to take Sebastian and Elena for a stroll in the courtyard gardens before it became too crowded with guests. So he guided the two of them down the flagstone pathway amid the majestic palms and tropical plants. Both Sebastian and Elena gasped in awe.

When they came to the fountain with its bubbling waters spraying down into a fish pond with huge goldfish swimming amid clusters of water lilies, Elena sank down on the bench to absorb the loveliness of the spot. She was entranced.

The two men exchanged glances. Sebastian smiled. "Mateo, I thank you again for inviting us here. My Elena will never forget this occasion as long as she lives. I don't have to tell you that she's never been at such a grand place as this before."

Mark gave him a warm pat on his broad shoulders and told him, "But you gave her the grandest gift of all—you gave her so much love, sir. I saw that the first night I was at your cottage." He offered Sebastian a cheroot and took one for himself, lighting up both of them.

"You sincerely believe this, Mateo, that love is the grandest gift one can give?" Sebastian asked, a serious expression on his rugged face.

"I do. Money does not buy happiness. I was lucky. My parents could give me this luxury, but they gave me a lot of love, and that was far more important to me," Mark told him.

"I like your thinking, Mateo. I would say that you have been a most lucky fellow."

When Elena was finally ready to leave the bench and this area of the garden, the three of them strolled around the courtyard. The first guests they encountered were Alonso and Lola, who had just left Alonso's quarters for the Mateo house.

By now, Mark had also developed a close friendship with Lola, and she adored the young señor, who was so devoted to her brother. He called out to them, "Hello, you two." He saw that old Alonso had his best pants and shirt on. What really pleased Mark was how much better he looked.

He loved to tease Lola, and he had come to realize that she rather liked it. "My, my, my! Look at you, Lola. You look mighty spiffy. We're going to have to watch her this afternoon and evening, Alonso." He grinned deviously.

Alonso chuckled. "Not me. I'm not going to watch her, Mark. She's a big girl now. I'm going to let her paddle her own boat."

"Shame on you, Señor Mark. You're going to give your friends the wrong impression of me," she chided him lightheartedly.

They all laughed, and once again Mark made the introductions. When Lola learned that they were from Half Moon Bay, she told them that that was where she'd lived for many years before she'd come to Golden Splendor to stay with her brother Alonso.

"I can't imagine that you'd ever want to go back there after living here. A place like this could spoil a person," Sebastian told her.

"Oh, no, Señor Fernandes, I'd never wish to go back there now," Lola confessed.

Sebastian smiled. "Well, Half Moon Bay just flows along in the usual way. We fishermen go out daily to make our catch. It's just a simple life there as you must know."

"I know, señor. I know very well the long, hard working days I put in," Lola declared.

Sebastian urged the two young people to run on and enjoy themselves. "Alonso, Lola, and I will talk about Half Moon Bay for awhile."

Mark could not have been more delighted to finally have the opportunity to get Elena alone. He considered that Sebastian had done him a great favor.

Sebastian understood Mateo's eagerness. He could remember how it was to be young. He figured that he could linger for awhile with the elderly Alonso and his sister. Lola, he judged, was about his age, and he'd taken an immediate liking to her. He admired her saucy response to Mateo; she had spice and ginger, qualities he'd found so lacking in women since he'd lost his Miranda.

It would have probably surprised Lola if she had known that Sebastian didn't consider her plump. He found her figure most voluptuous, and her lady-like attire impressed him. He disliked the popular style of necklines cut too low and bosoms half-exposed. It was too gaudy, he thought.

So the three of them sat by the fountain for the next half-hour to talk about Half Moon Bay, Golden Splendor, and the generous Mateo family.

Mark could not fight the urge to pull Elena behind a huge

oleander bush to plant a kiss on her luscious lips as he'd been wanting to do since the minute he'd helped her off the wagon.

"I've never seen a woman more beautiful than you, Elena. I swear I'll not leave you for a minute the whole afternoon or evening." He grinned.

"Oh, Mateo." She giggled. "Why should you worry, eh? I'm with the most handsome man who will be here today."

His violet eyes looked deep into hers as they resumed their walk on the pathway. "I might as well confess that I'm a damned possessive man, Elena, and I consider you my girl."

Nothing could have pleased her more than to hear him say that and a twinkle came into her dark eyes as she, too, enlightened him. "And I, too, am possessive, Mateo. I take nothing lightly. That is my nature, so you'd best know that. I come from a Portuguese father and a Latin mother, so need I say more?"

He roared with laughter. "No, *chiquita*. That tells me all I need to know."

He found her the most bewitching of creatures. His two hands could have spanned that tiny waist of hers, but he had no doubt that she could have fought him like a tiger if she were angry with him.

He took one more kiss before they left the seclusion of the garden, noting sadly that it was probably going to be the last private moment they'd have. He also declared to her, "I care very much for you, Elena."

"And I care for you, Mateo, or I'd have not welcomed your kisses," she admitted honestly.

To Mateo, she was so utterly refreshing. She played no silly games with a man. That was what set her apart from other young ladies he'd met who attempted to use their wiles on him.

He'd found them boring and dull. But Elena was not boring

or dull, and she'd not hesitated for a minute to tell him how she felt about him.

He loved the way those luminous black eyes of hers had looked directly up at him to confess that she, too, cared for him. She was a rare jewel.

Ten

Elena had never seen such a multitude of people gathered at one home. The courtyard gardens were filled with the milling guests and the elegant parlor was also occupied with couples.

She had no idea where her father was by now in this sea of faces, but she was certain that he had to be enjoying himself.

Sebastian had spent a long time after he'd parted company with Elena and Mark talking with Lola and Alonso. Now he was enjoying a conversation with a friendly gentleman about his own age. It was amazing how swiftly the afternoon had gone by, and the sun was now sinking low in the western sky.

By this time Elena had met Mateo's older brother, Carlos. He was very nice, but he wasn't as warm and outgoing as his sister or Mateo.

Mateo had not left her side for a minute, and she feared he was depriving himself of mingling with his own friends just to keep her from being alone. So she told him, "Mateo, I know you must have many friends here. I would be fine if you wish to go to speak to some of them. Please don't feel restrained from doing so."

"*Chiquita,* I wish to be right here with you. Don't you know that? But I am going to seat you right there on that bench and I don't want you to move an inch until I get back with some punch. God, I might not find you the rest of the evening as tiny as you are." He chuckled.

She gave a lighthearted laugh. "I promise. Not seeing you the rest of the evening would be terrible."

Reluctantly, he left her to go to the long table draped in a frosty white tablecloth where fruit punch was being served from four huge cut-crystal bowls. He took two cups and started back to Elena.

Three young Mexican lads were lighting torches around the courtyard now that twilight was descending. Lanterns hanging on iron rods already glowed brightly.

As impatient as he was to get back to Elena, he had to stop to chat with some of the workers. Before he could get back to her, he'd paused three or four times to speak to the workers and their wives.

But he had no reason to be concerned about Elena, for she was in the company of his mother, who had chanced to be walking down the flagstone path and spotted Elena sitting alone. So she took advantage of the moment to have a few words with the pretty girl. Long ago, Aimée and her husband had realized that it was impossible for them to be able to greet and speak briefly with each of their guests if they strolled around the gardens together, so she would go in one direction while he roamed the other side of the courtyard. They made a point of trying to get back together just before the buffet line formed for the feast.

It was always easier for Aimée to spot her tall husband than it was for him to spy her, for she was so petite.

Few young ladies were as beautiful as Elena Fernandes and one's eyes were drawn to her like a magnet. Aimée was surprised that she was sitting alone.

She walked up to greet her, for Elena had not noticed her approach. "Well, Elena, I trust you are enjoying our festival? May I sit with you awhile to catch my breath?"

"Of course, señora, please do. To answer your question, I must tell you that I'm having a wonderful time. I've met so many people. Oh, I met your son, Carlos," Elena told her.

"So now you have met all of our family. By the way, where is Mark?"

"He has gone to get some punch, and I was doing as Mateo told me. He told me not to move an inch." She laughed.

"I can see why he'd not want you venturing too far away, Elena. We share something in common. We are both very short ladies. We would be swallowed up and not be seen for hours."

"Oh, señora, I've never seen so many people at one gathering before," Elena declared.

"Yes, it seems to get larger every year. I confess that I don't know how many more harvests I'll be able to manage this," Aimée told her.

"I—I don't see how you manage it, what with all the food and everything," Elena said to her.

"Well, I have good servants and an excellent cook, or I'd never be able to do it. But it is Mano's way to thank his workers and their families for the hard work they do in the vineyards and winery. We both worked very hard to make Golden Splendor what we envisioned it could be, and we could not continue without our loyal employees," Aimée explained.

"Well, you've seen your visions and dreams come true, señora, for this is a most beautiful place. I know I shall never forget this day, and I thank you for inviting my father and me," Elena told her.

"Well, you're very sweet, Elena. I wanted to meet the Fernandes family who was so gracious to my son, inviting him to dinner. He came home raving about your father's *paella*."

Elena chortled. "Ah, yes—Papa and his *paella*! He is very conceited about that, swearing that no one can make it quite as well as he does. I am the cook usually, except on the evenings when Papa wishes to prepare his *paella*. Then I only chop up the vegetables for him to throw in that big iron pot of his. Papa takes full charge of that."

Aimée listened to her and watched her lovely face as she spoke. What a delightful change she was with her straight-forward manner. Some young ladies would not have admitted to her that they cooked or labored in a kitchen, for they would have been too anxious to try to impress her. Oh, Aimée had never been fooled when Mark or Carlos had brought such girls to Golden Splendor. They were superficial and shallow, and Aimée could see right through them.

So she could understand why Carlos and Mark had yet to find someone they wished to marry. The chances were that her younger son would take himself a bride before Carlos. Now that she had met Elena Fernandes she was sure of it.

"You'll have to give me your Papa's recipe for his *paella*," Aimée said.

Elena laughed. "I could try, señora, but I'm not sure it would be right. Papa measures nothing."

For Mark, it was a grand sight to see his mother and Elena sitting together laughing and enjoying one another's company. He'd felt that the two of them would get along just fine and obviously they did.

Once he joined them, Aimée excused herself to go in search of her husband since it was time for the buffet line to form. But Mark knew how long that line would be, and he didn't make any effort to escort Elena there just yet. So they lingered, enjoying their fruit punch.

For the first time in the last two hours, Elena finally saw her papa. Sitting at one of the many little tables in the court-yard gardens, he, Alonso, and Lola were already enjoying a plate of the good food.

Markita and Francisco had also waited, and the four young
people shared a table.

Mark was happy to see his young sister in a gay mood.
He had wondered if she'd noticed that Roberto had come
alone with just his family. But she had definitely made a
point of seeing if he'd brought that red-headed girl. And
Roberta had had only a brief conversation with her, for Francisco was devotedly by her side. Markita found herself rather
liking it. The truth be told, she was having the best festival
ever!

An hour later when the music began to play, Francisco
immediately asked Markita to dance with him. But what really surprised Elena was seeing her papa lead Lola up on
the platform to dance. Wide-eyed, she turned to Mark to
declare, "I've never seen Papa dance before, Mateo!"

He laughed. "Well, let's you and I just get up there and
show them up." He held out his hand to her.

It was their first time together on the floor, but it was as
if they'd danced dozens of times before. Her petite body
molded into his arms, and they glided around the floor.
Markita's keen eyes didn't miss anything even though Francisco was whirling her around the floor. She saw how her
brother was looking down at Elena, his eyes adoring her. If
they weren't lovers already, they certainly were going to be,
she thought.

Elena's black eyes were looking up at him as though she
were entranced and they were the only ones on the floor.
They both had the look of love on their faces, the romantic
Markita observed.

Francisco was a fabulous dancer and Markita had to admit
that he could make any young lady look grand. She thoroughly enjoyed having him guide her around the platform,
for she knew they were being watched by the guests because
they danced so smoothly.

By the time Mark led Elena back to their table, he was stirred by her petite, curvy body that had swayed against him when they'd danced. Elena was equally shaken at being so close to his firm-muscled body and having his arms enclose her.

Aimée had observed the two of them dancing together and she'd gently nudged her husband. "Look! Look at them. They're in love, Mano, I would swear it."

Mano laughed. "Brings back old memories, eh *querida?* Of course, they're in love, but I knew that when Mark described her to me weeks ago. I was reminded of myself when I was talking to my old *amigo* Pablo about you."

She laughed. "I never knew that."

"A man has a few secrets, *mi vida,*" he whispered, leaning over to kiss her cheek.

For Mark, this glorious night was coming to an end too quickly and he'd had only one private moment with Elena, when he'd guided her behind the oleander bush to steal a kiss from her honeyed lips.

He was determined that before this evening ended he would spend more time with her and her alone, away from this crowd of people that surrounded them.

He chose the moment when his parents, Francisco, and Markita were up on the platform dancing and Sebastian and Lola were returning for a second dance.

"Come with me, Elena," he whispered in her ear. She got up from the table and Mark led her away. They left the music and noise of the guests behind them as they slipped through the darkened area of the courtyard. She had no idea where he was taking her, but she didn't care as long as she was with him. He stopped at a gazebo at the far end of the gardens in an isolated spot. One small lantern was lit, hanging on a post. It was like an enclosed room with long benches built into the walls. Bright green pads covered the wooden seats.

"It's lovely, Mateo!" she exclaimed as she turned around to survey it.

"Damn, Elena, I was determined to have a moment with you and you alone. The only place I could think of was this gazebo," he told her. "To be sure no one spies us out here I'm blowing out that lantern."

He pulled her into his arms and together they sank down on a bench. "This is what I've been yearning to do all night Elena. I've wanted to hold you in my arms," he murmured softly in her ear.

His lips were quickly and hungrily searing hers with his passionate kisses. Elena was just as hungry for his lips as he was for hers. But kisses were not enough to satisfy these two hot-blooded individuals. Dancing together had inflamed both of them.

His nimble fingers began to fumble with the front of her bodice. He wanted to caress the full round breasts he'd felt pressed against his chest as they'd danced. She had only to feel his touch to be ignited with such a fire of passion as she'd never known before. Mark heard her soft gasps and he knew the sensation he was stirring within her. Her supple body pressed closer to him.

When he bent his head down to let his lips tease the tips of her breasts, Elena felt as if a liquid fire were flowing through her body. She sighed. "Oh, Mateo—Mateo! Kiss me more!"

He didn't have to be urged to do that as he pushed her gown below her tiny waist, at the same time frantically removing his shirt.

With his bare chest pressing against her bared breasts, the flame of their passions became a wildfire spreading over them. He wasted no time in relieving himself of his pants and removing her gown. In a husky voice he told her, "I'm going to make love to you. Nothing can stop me but you."

Her hands were on the back of his neck. She stammered breathlessly, "I want you to, Mateo. I want you to make love to me."

He wasn't sure he could have stopped himself had she protested, for he'd reached such a peak of desire. She could feel the heat of his firm-muscled thighs as he burrowed between her legs. Quite suddenly, she felt his mighty thrust as he entered her, and he felt her just as suddenly stiffen. But he soothed her. "Just hold on to me, *querida,* and I'll make you forget that little hurt you just felt. Trust me, Elena *mía.*"

What he had told her was true for he made her quickly forget that second of pain as she soared with him to a grander height of ecstasy. She felt as if she were ascending to the heavens higher than the tall pines surrounding the gazebo.

Mark wished the moment never had to end. He'd never had a woman excite him as Elena had when she had abandoned herself to sweet surrender in his arms.

He had no inkling of how long they remained quietly in one another's arms. It was Elena who first began to stir when she found herself feeling as if she were going to fall asleep. She wriggled in his arms. "Mateo, I'd better get my gown back on. What if someone else were to come out to the gazebo?"

Reluctantly, he roused himself from his languor. "I never thought about that possibility," he mumbled. There were other young lovers who might be seeking an isolated spot as they had.

She yanked and pulled on her gown, but she couldn't get it up. Mateo's foot rested on the flounce, restraining it. "Mateo, move your foot. It's on my flounce." She giggled.

"Sorry, *chiquita.*" He laughed as he got up to get into his pants and shirt.

A few minutes later they were going back to the torch-lit area of the gardens. But as they drew closer, Mark realized that they'd spent more time out at the gazebo than he'd thought. The music had stopped playing and the courtyard was deserted.

Mark was glad that the festivities were over and all the people were gone as he escorted Elena inside the house. At the base of the stairs, she realized that her hair was falling over her face and the comb with the lovely flowers was no longer at the side of her head. "Oh, Mateo, I lost my hair ornament," she told him, a stricken look on her lovely face.

He assured her that he'd go out to the gazebo to look for the comb so she'd have it before she left for Half Moon Bay in the morning.

He kissed her goodnight. "Sweet dreams, *querida*. I'll see you in the morning," he told her as he watched her start up the stairs.

Mano, who had come out of his study to walk down the hall, came upon the intimate scene. Quickly he retreated down the hall, an amused grin on his face.

Eleven

For the longest time after Elena had closed the door of the bedroom where she was to sleep, she roamed the room thinking about what had happened since the time she and her father had arrived at Golden Splendor. To her, they'd entered a magical world when they had rolled through those double iron gates at the entrance.

She was still in a bedazzled state. This fabulous home was like a palace with its courtyard gardens. Aimée and Mano Mateo were the king and queen. Mark and Markita were prince and princess. She was still unsure of how she felt about Carlos.

The next morning when she finally woke up, she packed away her lovely gown and her pretty slippers. For the journey home she put on a bright floral skirt and a yellow drawstring tunic which she tucked inside the waistband of her skirt. On her feet she wore her leather sandals.

She had only to look outside the windows to see a gusting breeze blowing through the trees, so she went over to the dressing table to plait her thick hair into one long braid to fall down her back. This was the way she always wore her hair when she was out on her father's fishing boat to keep it away from her face. There was always a breeze out on the bay.

Most young ladies would have found her ensemble unacceptable as proper attire at Golden Splendor, but for Elena it was the natural garb she should wear to be comfortable to travel back to her home. She'd worn her fancy gown last night to the festival. Today, she was to board the flatbedded wagon to go home.

The first person she met when she went downstairs was Aimée Mateo, and Aimée found her just as impressive in her simple daily costume. The two of them shared a cup of coffee on the patio before Aimée was forced to leave her to say farewell to some of her other overnight guests.

But she was not left alone too long, for Carlos strolled out to the south patio to have his morning coffee after his morning constitutional.

He spied the beautiful Elena and stood for a minute before moving toward her table. Like all of his family, Carlos was favorably impressed by this young lady from Half Moon Bay. She was nature's child, unpretentious and guileless.

He was used to the gowns his mother and sister wore as their morning and afternoon frocks, but to see this girl sitting complacently in her tunic and gathered skirt told Carlos many things about Elena Fernandes. He found himself admiring her.

"May I join you?" he asked her as he ambled up to the table.

"Of course, Carlos, please do." She smiled up at him. "Your mother just left to say goodbye to some of her guests."

He took a seat and motioned the servant to bring his coffee. "It was a grand night, wasn't it? So very special to my parents. I trust you've had a good time?"

She smiled again. "I had a glorious time, Carlos. I go back to Half Moon Bay with very fond memories of Golden Splendor." She confessed that she'd never before ventured out of her village.

"So you've lived there all your life?" Carlos asked her.

She nodded. "Mateo tells me that you are a lawyer in Sacramento. It must be a very big place."

"Oh, it is," he agreed. He found her innocence infectious. It would have been impossible not to have liked her.

"I can't imagine such a place." Her eyes grew wide as she tried.

She was not prepared for his next move when he dug into the pocket of his coat to pull out the hair ornament she'd lost in the gazebo the night before. He laid it on the table and told her that he believed it belonged to her.

It took all the willpower she could muster to casually reply, "Ah, thank you, Carlos. I was so disappointed when I found I'd lost it."

"I found it when I was taking my walk this morning," he told her as he began to sip his coffee.

She amazed herself by the cool, calm manner she had even though she was feeling very embarrassed. She knew where Carlos had found the hair ornament and he would assume— correctly—that she'd been in the gazebo with Mateo.

She gave him a sweet, serene smile. "How lucky I am that you found it, Carlos. It was so very nice to spend a moment with you this morning, but I must go now. Papa will be wanting to leave for home very soon."

He rose and bid her goodbye. Suddenly she disappeared through the double doors and Carlos was left alone to muse about this intriguing young lady.

She was no ordinary young woman—not Elena Fernandes! She hadn't seemed the least bit flustered when he'd laid the flowered hair ornament on the table. As a lawyer, he found her an interesting study. Her black eyes had looked directly into his without flinching throughout their conversation.

Carlos finished his coffee quickly, for he didn't plan to linger much longer before starting back to Sacramento. Two nights was all he could stay, for he had cases requiring his attention.

Suddenly, Mark rushed onto the patio. He'd just encountered his mother and she'd told him she'd left Elena there.

"Elena just left, Mark," Carlos told him. "I think she went upstairs to finish packing."

Mark turned hastily to go back into the house. Dejected, he lamented that he and Elena would not have another private moment before she and Sebastian would board the flatbedded wagon to go back to Half Moon Bay.

Had he not been hunting for that hair ornament of hers in the gazebo, he would have been on the patio when Elena was there. So now, he decided to station himself in the hallway to wait for her and Sebastian to come downstairs.

But he was not going to be able to present her with her hair ornament for he had not been able to find it. He'd looked all over the gazebo and checked the path they'd taken back to the house, but he had not found the flowered comb.

He arranged himself on the velvet settee in the hallway to wait for Elena to descend the stairs. He expected that Sebastian would be planning to depart by midday so they could get home long before the dinner hour. Tomorrow, he'd board his fishing boat and go out in the bay.

Shortly, he spied the huge Sebastian at the top of the steps, but Elena wasn't with him. Mark greeted him. "I trust you had a good night's sleep last night, sir." He saw the valise in his hand. "Are you and Elena getting ready to head for Half Moon Bay?"

"Well, I did sleep like a baby and yes, we've got to be getting home, Mateo. It was a grand time we had here and I wish to bid your dear parents goodbye if you could tell me where I would find them."

Mark told him that his parents were in the parlor. "And Elena—where would I find her?"

"With that little sister of yours. They're having themselves some girl talk." He turned toward the parlor, leaving Mark in the hall.

Mark sank down on the settee, impatiently waiting for Elena and Markita to appear. That inquisitive sister of his was probably questioning Elena about last night and where they'd disappeared to while the dancing was going on. Markita was a curious little cat! Oh, he knew her so well.

But knowing Elena as he was beginning to know her, he figured Elena would only tell her as much as she wanted her to know.

Soft gales of feminine laughter alerted Mark to glance up at the second landing, and he saw his lovely Elena and his sister Markita.

Once they descended the stairs and Mark and Elena met, Markita knew that she should excuse herself for they had eyes for only one another. She said a farewell to Elena. "Come back to Golden Splendor very soon," she urged her.

"Thank you, Markita," Elena replied as she quickly turned her attention back to Mateo.

Mark took Elena's arm to whisk her out the front door to find some private place for the two of them before they were to say goodbye and Elena was to leave him. "I thought I was not going to have a moment alone with you," he confessed.

As he guided her around the corner of the entranceway, she admitted the same fear.

"I searched, Elena, but I could not find your hair ornament," he told her.

She smiled. "I know. Your brother found it before you got there. He gave it to me this morning on the patio."

A frown etched his brow. "Carlos? Carlos found your comb?"

"Yes. He said he came across it when he was taking his constitutional," she told him.

"Well, at least you have it again." He reached for her hand.

Mark heard Sebastian's deep bass voice echoing through the hallway as he walked along with Mano. So Mark had time for only one hasty kiss before they were joined by their respective fathers. "That kiss has got to keep me warm until I see you again, *querida*. Miss me as I will be missing you," he murmured softly in her ear.

"I will miss you desperately, Mateo. Come to Half Moon Bay very soon," she urged him.

Before long, Mark was standing with his father watching the flatbedded wagon roll out of the drive. Mano turned to his son and gave him a paternal pat on the back. "I like your friends very much, Mark. Elena Fernandes is a most charming young lady."

"She's the most beautiful woman I've ever seen," Mark declared impulsively. Mano wondered if Mark realized just how much he'd revealed to him with that remark.

Mark chanced to turn in his father's direction and saw an amused smile on his face. Mark grinned sheepishly, but neither father nor son said anything as they walked back into the house. But Mano draped his arm around Mark's shoulders in a comradely fashion.

Aimée observed their return, pleased. She'd always liked that her husband had always been as affectionate with his sons as with their only daughter. Aimée's own father, Paul, had always been a demonstrative man not restraining himself from giving her brothers Emile and Armand a warm embrace whenever the notion struck him.

But Aimée had noticed that many fathers affected a formality and reserve with their sons. Old Carlos was that way with Mano. As strange as it might seem, old Carlos was more affectionate with her than he was with his own son.

Aimée was beginning to wonder if *her* son was going to be like his grandfather in more ways than one. She had hoped that he might bring a pretty young lady to their festival this year, but that had not happened. She worried that he might end up a bachelor and prayed that wouldn't be. She wanted him to find himself a good wife and know the joys of being a husband and father.

She had had a chance to observe Carlos during the festivities last night. Oh, he was very gracious and dignified as he spoke with the young women attending the affair. But she had not seen him dancing once during the festival.

As soon as he had shared a light lunch, he would get into his buggy and start back to Sacramento. When Aimée had gently protested his hasty departure, he had told her, "I've been away from my office for two days. I'm going to have work piled up when I get back, Mother."

"I understand, dear," Aimée had told him.

"I'm glad you do, Mother. The festival is over. I've got to get back home and attend to business," he had told her.

Aimée had given him a nod of her head, but in her heart she was feeling a little sad as all mothers do when their child no longer considers their parents' house home. But she was not faulting Carlos for that. It was the way life was.

Carlos now felt that Sacramento was his home, not Golden Splendor.

The truth was Carlos was happy to leave. He had enjoyed the quiet dinner with his family the night he'd arrived at Golden Splendor and he had visited with everyone. But the milling crowd of people gathered in the courtyard gardens the next afternoon and evening had bored him. He'd slipped away to go up to his old room and close the door to block out all the noise, but the noise still permeated the air.

Then he'd slipped down the back stairs and walked to the far end of the gardens. Finally, the music and the buzzing of people talking seemed far in the distance.

Carlos had sat down on one of the benches to enjoy the

peace and darkness. But Mark and Elena Fernandes pierced his solitude as they sought the privacy of the gazebo. He watched his younger brother dim the lantern and had no doubt what Mark had on his mind.

He heard their laughter and he felt like an intruder, so he slipped silently from the bench and returned to the house. He was glad to find that the music had ceased and the horde of people were spilling out the courtyard gate. Unnoticed, he entered the back of the house and mounted the back stairs.

Once he got to his room he closed the door, and the evening had finally ended!

As he undressed and sought the comfort of his bed, Carlos thought about Mark and Elena, still back in the gazebo. He could hardly fault his brother, the little Portuguese girl was an utterly beautiful lady. She wasn't one of those silly twittering girls who drove him crazy. He also had to credit her with being very natural with no pretenses about her. And she seemed completely unaware of her rare beauty.

His admiration had mounted even more this morning when he'd sat with her no longer than fifteen minutes. She had a practical head on her shoulders. She didn't wish to be traveling back to her fishing village in a fancy gown just to make an impression. Carlos had been favorably impressed by her, for she was the most genuine woman he'd met in a long time.

Perhaps Mark had at last found someone who could capture his reckless, restless heart. Any lady that could do that had to be most unusual.

When he finally guided his buggy up the drive at his little two-story house and saw the lamplight glowing from his parlor windows, a surge of serenity engulfed him.

His devoted cat greeted him the minute he walked through the door, meowing and brushing himself against Carlos's leg as if to tell him how happy he was to have him back home.

Carlos reached down to pat his head affectionately and tell him, "I know, Amigo! I'm glad to be home, too."

It was long past the dinner hour, but when he and Amigo went into the kitchen he found a platter of fried chicken, a loaf of fresh-baked bread, and an apple pie. That with a glass of milk was enough to fill Carlos's empty belly. Of course, Amigo got a share of the four pieces of chicken before Carlos devoured the rest.

The hour was late when Carlos dimmed the lamps left burning and he and Amigo climbed the stairs to his bedroom. Stella had probably been in her room and sleeping soundly for two hours or more.

It was a good feeling to crawl into his bed tonight and feel Amigo curled up at his feet.

Twelve

It was not easy for Elena to adapt back to the routine of her days once she returned to Half Moon Bay. Their first night home, Vasco sat at the kitchen table entranced by all the things she and Sebastian told him about Golden Splendor.

The next morning, her father and Vasco left the house to go out on their fishing boats. For Sebastian, normal life had resumed.

But Elena was left at the cottage with her vivid memories of Mateo making passionate love to her in the gazebo.

While she cleaned, she found herself envying Mateo and Markita. How wonderful it must have been to be raised in a place like Golden Splendor!

Never had she found the cottage as lacking as she did now. It was shabby compared to the Mateo estate.

That one magnificent day and night at Golden Splendor had changed everything for Elena Fernandes. She could find no contentment now for she could not help comparing how the Mateo family lived to her own existence in Half Moon Bay.

She could clean the cottage every day; but to her, it now looked shabby. In the late afternoon as she worked in the kitchen peeling the vegetables and cooking the meat for their supper, she knew it was not going to compare to the delectable foods she'd tasted at the Mateo feast.

She thought about the long hours she spent preparing and

baking three or four loaves of bread which would only last two days the way Vasco and her father devoured it. Then she would be spending another afternoon doing the same thing again.

Oh, yes, she envied Markita Mateo! She would love to live in that fine old mansion surrounded by courtyard gardens. She could have contented herself for a long time just sitting by that magical fish pond to watch the fish swimming and the lacy spray of the waters of the fountain.

She had to admit that she had had a wrong impression about wealthy people. They were not all snobs as she'd assumed. The Mateo family had been warm and friendly. Even Carlos was nice.

Oh, she would never forget the Festival of the Grapes! Like any young girl, she would never forget the first time and place a handsome young man had made love to her.

Now, she had to cling to the hope that he'd meant the words of endearment he'd whispered in her ear and that he would be coming to Half Moon Bay very soon.

More than ever she knew that she was not going to settle for one of the young Portuguese men to be her husband. She would not live in this fishing village the rest of her life. She did not wish to have a baby every year and live her entire life in a four-room cottage.

Maybe it was enough to content her Papa and Vasco, but it was not enough for her. As far as she knew, her big, bashful brother had never had a girl for himself. Just to go out on his fishing boat daily and come home to eat and sleep seemed enough for Vasco. Yet, Elena knew that many of the pretty Portuguese girls found Vasco attractive; they were always quizzing her about him and whom he was courting. But a devious streak kept her from telling them the truth and she played coy.

When he wasn't on his fishing boat, he was at the cottage.

On the weekends, Vasco liked to go roaming with the over-sized, reddish-brown dog he called Rojo. The two of them would go into the nearby woods and walk aimlessly for hours. Often he'd bring her a big handful of wildflowers he'd picked.

That first week back, Elena would retire to her bedroom in the evening and lie on her bed, staring out the window at the starlit sky. That same starlit sky was shining down on Mateo, and she wondered if he lay on his bed thinking of her, too.

The week after the festival was a busy week for Mano and Mark because the processing of the grapes had begun in the winery. Both of them put in very long hours.

Once he'd put away a hefty evening meal, Mark would quickly go up to his room to seek the sweet comfort of his bed. But the beautiful image of Elena Fernandes was etched deeply in his memories. Just as soon as things were running smoothly in the winery, he was determined to make a trip to Half Moon Bay to see her.

That tiny little miss who barely came to his shoulders could make him go weak with wild desire. He wanted to make love to her again. Just remembering that night in the gazebo was enough to make him hunger for her sweet lips. No woman had ever cast a spell on him as Elena Fernandes had!

Now that he had finally possessed her, he was left with a raging fever in his blood.

Although he'd made love to several young ladies, he'd felt that when the right girl came along he'd know it instantly. He was convinced that Elena Fernandes had to be that girl.

Just the thought of some other man kissing her or holding her sent him into a jealous rage. He had to hope that his searing kisses would keep her warm until he could be with her again.

Was this how a man felt about the lady he asked to be his wife? The question startled him, for he'd always told himself that marriage was a long way away for him. A wife and babies were not for him right now.

But Elena Fernandes had changed his thinking.

The second week after the festival, Mano and Mark were still getting up at the crack of dawn to get to the winery. Aimée was asleep when Mano left their bed, and it wasn't until two hours later that she finally propped herself on the pillows to get herself awake. Only then did she get into her dressing gown to go downstairs to sit in the kitchen with Celia and have her coffee and croissant. This was when she went over her plans with Celia for the family's evening meal and the wine she wished served. If there were to be any guests for dinner, she would tell her cook.

Markita was the sleepyhead of the family and she often slept two hours longer than her mother. Like Aimée, she never sat at the dining room table in the morning. She sipped her coffee and roamed around Celia's kitchen, sampling the food Celia was preparing for the Mateo's lunch.

Celia adored the daughter of Señora Aimée, who had first invaded her kitchen as a toddler. She was always calling her "her little taster." "But you are a pest, little Markita. One of these days you and I are going to collide, and I'm going to burn you real bad with one of my hot pans," she was always telling Markita.

Markita would just giggle. "I'll take my chances, Celia. Look at all the goodies I get to taste before the rest of my family."

Markita dearly loved this old Mexican cook and she could well recall those days when she was only five or six and spent her time in the kitchen pestering Celia. Celia would give her hands a sharp slap when Markita would reach up to touch a pan just out of the oven. She'd harshly caution her not to do that for she'd burn her fingers.

But one day it had happened that Celia had not seen her in time and Markita had touched the hot pan. Shrieking, Markita had burst into tears, and Celia had gathered her up in her arms and placed a cold cloth around her little finger. "Ah, *niña,* now you know why Celia didn't want you touching those pans." For the longest time Celia had held her in her lap and kept wrapping a cold cloth around her stinging finger, but never again had little Markita reached up to the table to help herself to one of the fruit turnovers or tarts.

Perhaps, of all the Mateo children, Celia adored the little Markita the most. The two Mateo boys, Carlos and Mark, had not been underfoot in her kitchen as they were growing up.

The feelings Celia had for Markita were the same close feelings Alonso had for the young Mark. He had been at the estate before Celia. When Alonso was hired to work for Señor Mano, Carlos was just a young lad and Mark was a toddler of three. Little Markita had yet to make an appearance. He had been so happy for the señora when, finally, she had herself a daughter. He saw Markita take her first steps and a few years later he was there when Mano placed her on her new pony. He could recall how she took to that pony and sat in the little saddle Mano had bought especially for her. Mano had told her that she'd have to give her new pony a name, and without hesitation she'd told him that she was naming the pony Poco.

Alonso had also been at Mano's side when he'd led out a magnificent thoroughbred to present to his middle son, Mark, on his eighteenth birthday.

Alonso could never forget the wide-eyed young man when Mano had told him that the handsome stallion was his. "Happy birthday, Mark. He's yours. I turn the reins over to you. Now you and your stallion go and get acquainted," Mano had told his eighteen-year-old son.

Mano understood his children, for he took the time to know them despite the long, hard hours he worked in his winery and vineyards.

Carlos's birthday gift had not been a fine thoroughbred, because Mano knew he didn't care to ride horses. When he'd tried to sit Carlos as a youngster on a pony, the boy had protested, screaming and yelling. So Mano had lifted him off, set him back on the ground, and sold the pony the next week.

So for Carlos, Mano had bought a nice little gig and a fine bay to pull it and Carlos had been as thrilled as Mark had later been with the stallion.

The same gig and bay were with Carlos in Sacramento. Carlos took great pride in his carriage and kept it highly polished and properly repaired. Alonso had to say that it looked as fine as it had when Mano presented it to him almost seven years before. The little bay was still feisty and Carlos gave her special care.

Celia and Alonso, who had been with the Mateos and shared so many happenings with them, felt a part of this grand family. They didn't consider themselves hired help.

Even Lola was beginning to understand the magic of Golden Splendor. She and little Markita had formed their special bond of friendship and now that she'd been a part of the Festival of the Grapes, she understood why Alonso felt that the Mateo family was his family, too.

She felt that way herself!

Part Two

Mateo Magic

Thirteen

Elena was impatient. Mateo had not appeared at her door after two weeks, and although she reminded herself that he had not made any promise about when he would be coming to Half Moon Bay, he had said that he'd be seeing her very soon.

Sebastian sensed her restlessness and questioned whether he'd been wise after all to have accepted the invitation to Golden Splendor. After having been exposed to such grandeur, Elena was finding things back at their cottage and in Half Moon Bay very dull. Sebastian could see why she was feeling that way, but he didn't know what to do to help her. Had he never taken her there, she would not have known about that strange wonderful world so different from theirs.

He'd seen how she and Mateo's sister had laughed and talked, enjoying one another's company. That was what his beautiful seventeen-year-old daughter should be doing at her age.

Elena was not the only one to have a new awareness about things since that visit to Golden Splendor. Sebastian had had his share of private musings as he'd gone about his days on the fishing boat. All the years of his life he'd never been around such fancy folks as the Mateo family. He realized that he probably never would have been so privileged had it not been for Mateo's meeting Elena. Now, he didn't try to fool himself at all. It was Elena that had made all this happen for the Fernandes family. His beautiful little daughter had caught the fancy of Mark Mateo.

But Mateo lived in a different world than Elena. This bothered Sebastian; he was a simple fisherman and had been all his life. His Portuguese father and mother had died within four months of one another, and he'd been fending for himself since he was seventeen. He'd had to work hard for the money he'd made. There had been times when he'd slept on the wharf because he couldn't afford the price of lodging.

His lucky break had come when a wharf manager, Alfredo Alvarado, had offered him the apartment over his carriage house in exchange for chores. Alfredo was slightly impaired so he couldn't keep the grounds in proper order by himself.

Alfredo lived with his daughter Miranda in a nice little frame house. Sebastian was delighted to have the quarters above the carriage house, along with the luxury of a cot and some blankets, and happily chopped wood to stack on the back porch, weeded the flowerbeds, and pruned the shrubs.

Since Alfredo managed the wharf office, Sebastian had a ride every morning to the wharf where he boarded the fishing boat he was working on.

It was also a pleasant arrangement for Alfredo, for the husky young man was a hard worker. When he got in from his day out on the bay, he worked another hour chopping wood. On Sundays, he spent most of the day in the yard.

In those days, Sebastian ate a lot of fish, for he was always able to bring home a couple of the catches of the day. He had only one skillet and one pot, but he could conjure himself up a very tasty supper.

Sebastian felt he was living luxuriously. The vendors were always ready to sell their vegetables cheap in the late afternoon when Sebastian left the trawler, not wanting to cart them back home. Sebastian had all the potatoes, turnips, and cabbage he needed to make a most tasty meal. One of his fishing pals had a garden and kept Sebastian well-supplied with onions and peppers.

Once a week he stopped by a little bakery to buy himself two large loaves of their fresh-baked bread, and that would last him for a week.

Sebastian was frugal, and he put as much of his pay as he could spare in a tin can. It was exciting to see how the tin began to fill up. He vowed that one day he'd own his own fishing boat.

He'd been living at Alfredo's place for awhile before he first saw the beautiful Miranda. Never had he seen a creature as lovely as she.

He worshipped her from afar and often dreamed about her. But he knew that this would be all it could ever be between the two of them. She didn't act as if she knew he existed. When she stepped on the back porch to gather up the kindling he'd cut the night before, Sebastian knew that she had to see him, less than fifty feet away, chopping the wood for her cookstove. He was too huge to miss.

The pretty Miranda had noticed him but she was too shy to let her eyes glance in his direction when she was out on the porch. In the privacy of her house she stared out the window to watch him swagger up the drive after his day of fishing.

At night when she was in her bedroom, she could see his lamps burning in the carriage-house quarters. Since he had no curtains, she often could tell that he was moving around the room with just his pants on, his huge chest bare.

She found him sensuous with his thick black hair and firm-muscled, strong arms. For a man who had such a massive chest, he had a trim waist and narrow, firm hips. He towered well over six feet.

It was apparent that there was not a lazy bone in Sebastian

and her father was always talking about what a hard-working young fellow he was.

That he put in a long day on the fishing boat and then worked for her father for another hour or two increased her admiration for him. Yet, Sebastian's day did not end when he stacked her kindling. He could not rest his tired body as her father did in the early evening as she prepared dinner for them. Sebastian had to prepare his own dinner and clean up his dishes.

She found that she was falling in love with Sebastian Fernandes even though they'd never had five minutes of conversation.

Both of her parents were very strict with her so she'd never had a suitor. Since her mother's death, she'd been left to take charge of the house and the cooking and she hadn't even found time to spend with her best friend, Consuela.

But she did begin to ponder how she could manage to meet Sebastian as the weeks went by, and she continued to watch him daily. When her father was gone from the house, so was Sebastian. When Sebastian arrived in the late afternoon, Alfredo was already home.

The hand of fate finally played into her hands though. She'd put in a busy day preparing the two nice roasting hens Alfredo had brought home the day before. While the oven was fired up, she made two peach pies and placed them in to bake.

That afternoon Alfredo did not feel well and went upstairs to rest before dinner.

Knowing that her father was upstairs, she watched out the kitchen window. When Sebastian walked to the back porch with an armful of wood, she went boldly to the door, not knowing that the sight of her left Sebastian weak.

She introduced herself and learned his name. "It is nice to finally meet you, Sebastian," she said. "May I offer you a peach pie for your dinner tonight? I baked two hens today; perhaps you might like one of them, too."

Sebastian was overwhelmed by her kindness. "I—I hardly know what to say, miss." He felt awkward in her presence.

She laughed. "Just enjoy them, Sebastian." She turned to go into the kitchen to bring out the pie and a platter holding the baked hen.

"Ah, the hen smells wonderful. Enjoy it, I certainly will," he told her as he began to back down the steps. "I'll make some of my *paella* for you and your papa one night soon."

"Paella, Sebastian? What is that?" she asked him.

"Do you like seafood, miss?"

"Oh, yes, I love it," she told him.

"Then you'll like my *paella,"* he told her with a twinkle in his black eyes as he turned to go.

Miranda stood on the back porch to watch him walk away. She liked his cocky swagger when he walked toward his quarters. Now that she had finally met him, she had had the full impact of his dancing black eyes and warm smile. She found him extraordinarily virile.

She told herself that her father need never know that she'd given him one of her peach pies or one of the baked hens.

During the next two months, Miranda managed to arrange several more brief encounters. She timed going out to the yard to pick a bouquet from the flowerbeds when Sebastian was working there. She took her little dog out for a romp while her dinner was simmering and Alfredo was napping in his chair after getting in from his job.

When Sebastian returned the platter, he gave her a generous serving of his *paella* which she praised the next day when she saw him. Sebastian's chest swelled with pride for he'd put a special effort into that pot of *paella.*

For two years he worked for Alfredo, and he filled several tins with the wages of his work on the fishing boat. The first small boat he could afford to purchase was in need of repairs before he could run it into the bay, so he continued to work to draw wages. Little by little, he readied his boat for the water. He did well on his own, for he didn't mind putting in long hours and hard work, and he sold his first little boat to buy a larger, better boat.

But his tins were empty. This didn't bother Sebastian, though; he had the trawler he wanted. He'd just keep working as long and hard as he had the last two years. He'd have those little tins filled again, he promised himself.

All the pretty Miranda and he got to share were brief, stolen moments, but Sebastian was content. They were young, and he was a patient man.

He was convinced that he and Miranda would one day be able to be together as he felt they were destined to be. So now that he had his fine new fishing boat and his business was flourishing as he brought in good loads of fish daily, he set himself a new goal. He wanted a little place to call his own. It was important to him to own his own plot of ground and have his own cottage.

Meanwhile, Alfredo had taken ill and died, leaving Miranda alone with no close relatives to come to her aid. So Sebastian began to do much more for her than just chop the wood and tend the flower gardens.

It was nice to have Sebastian's strong shoulders to support her. He helped her face many problems that she encountered when her father died.

Nightly he'd dine with her after he came in from his fishing boat and they'd talk for hours, Miranda asking questions, Sebastian advising her.

She didn't hesitate a minute when Sebastian asked her to marry him just two months after Alfredo's death. They had a quiet, simple wedding. They sold Alfredo's house and bought their own cottage, which was their home for the rest of Miranda's life. It was the cottage where their son Vasco and their daughter Elena were born, and it was Sebastian's home still.

Two months after Sebastian and his Miranda celebrated their first wedding anniversary, Miranda gave birth to their son Vasco. The Portuguese fisherman strutted around the fishing village like a proud peacock.

Miranda regained her strength quickly after Vasco's birth, but Sebastian played the doting husband since her labor had been long and painful. She was such a tiny little thing, and Vasco had been a huge baby. Having gone through those endless, tedious hours of labor, he didn't wish his wife to become pregnant again for a long, long time, although his fishing pals welcomed their wives' having a new baby every year.

But his Miranda was more delicate, and Sebastian kept this in mind when they were making passionate love after Vasco was born.

He was glad that the next few years passed without Miranda's becoming pregnant. Vasco was a rambunctious tot who proved to be a handful for Miranda. While she never voiced her feelings to Sebastian, she had decided that she would not have another baby for awhile, even if she had to go to Mama Leone, who helped the women rid themselves of babies unwanted.

Miranda kept herself aloof from most of the fishermen's wives, who constantly gathered together to chat and gossip in the afternoons when their husbands were out on the bay. Somehow, she never found herself fitting into their little clique.

With each year that passed after Vasco's birth that she didn't find herself pregnant, she was thrilled. Never was it a question that her Sebastian's arms holding her didn't excite her and she adored to have him make love to her, but she could never forget the anguish and agony those moments of ecstasy could create months later.

The next few years were prosperous for Sebastian, and he did much better than the other Portuguese fishermen. They added two rooms to their cottage. Miranda had made their home attractive with her special little touches and she dressed much better than most of the other wives. They labeled her a snob because she didn't wish to fritter away her afternoons gossiping with them.

Miranda knew the rumors circulating around the group about her, but she shrugged them aside. She confessed to herself that she did feel on a higher level than most of them. It wasn't hard for her to figure out why Sebastian had more money than most of the other fishermen. One night she told Sebastian what she thought, and he roared with laughter. "You are exactly right, my Miranda! Since we've had Vasco, my old friend José has had five new babes."

"So he has five more mouths to feed." She laughed.

Marriage to Miranda had only enhanced his adoration of her. He adored his husky little son and it was a pleasure to come home every night to his clean, neat cottage to be greeted by his pretty wife.

Miranda's announcement that she was going to have another baby filled him with mixed emotions. He was elated that they would have another child, but he feared for her well-being. But little Elena proved to be no laborious delivery, for she was a wee one. Sebastian swore that no baby was more beautiful than his daughter, who had the delicate features of her mother. Vasco had been the image of him. Elena surely had to be Miranda reborn.

Miranda's recovery was amazingly quick. But dealing with young Vasco and the new baby took its toll on his wife, and Sebastian saw this when he came in from his day on the bay. She looked weary and worn. For months, she had no desire to return to Sebastian's arms, for she was too exhausted and tired to make fierce love with him.

When she sank into the bed at night, there was only one thing on her mind and that was to get some rest to meet the next day to cope with her two children. She was ready for sleep.

Sebastian, being the understanding husband he was, never tried to force his attentions on her. He decided to take his son with him in the mornings. Vasco loved accompanying his papa on the fishing jaunts. For Miranda, it was a blessing to have only her little Elena to tend during the day.

After a month of this routine, Sebastian saw a vast change in his wife. She was not so bone-weary tired. He realized that he'd had a very clever idea.

It was a most wonderful night for Sebastian when he held her in his arms once again. But she was quick to tell him, "As much as I love you, Sebastian, I'll never have another baby. I wish to have no more children. Elena will be my last child. She is so special, Sebastian. I feel it deeply here in my heart, and I am very happy I had her."

After Elena's arrival and Sebastian started taking Vasco with him, Miranda began to glow with new loveliness. She had never been more sensuously beautiful. Jealous Portuguese wives like Juanita Moreno were irked when they heard their husbands talking about Sebastian Fernandes' Mexican wife. A fury of gossip about Miranda exploded around the village.

When Sebastian heard the rumors, he didn't take them lightly. The next day on the wharf, he warned his pal Moreno to tend to his big mouth of a wife. "She tells lies, Moreno, about my wife and I'll not allow it," he growled. Moreno promised he'd take care of Juanita that evening. He knew Juanita and that mouth of hers, so he never doubted Sebastian was telling him the truth.

Next, the rumor circulated around the village that Juanita and her friend Gloria had both received a beating from their husbands. The women stayed inside their houses for several days because of their bruises.

Miranda had no inkling that Sebastian had spoken with Moreno about his gossipy wife and her foul tongue. But then she didn't realize just how jealous Juanita had always been of her or that Moreno ogled her when she'd walked by their house.

It didn't make her feel kindly toward Miranda after she'd received a beating from her husband, so Juanita only harbored more hatred for Sebastian's wife.

Fourteen

Miranda might have shrugged the evil gossip aside and Sebastian might have got his sweet revenge, but it whetted the curiosity and interest of some of the fishermen who'd viewed the sultry Miranda when she'd been on the wharf to greet her husband in the late afternoon.

Her simple frocks were ones she'd made, but she was always neatly dressed and all her dresses displayed her trim figure. Never were the necklines of her dresses revealing, but some were scooped enough to tempt a man. Miranda's firm breasts pressed against the cotton material.

She always wore her thick, glossy hair loose and free. Never did she wear it in coils like some of the ladies her age. The only way she ever restrained it was to put it back and tie a colorful ribbon around it.

As far as Sebastian was concerned, Miranda had never been as beautiful as she was now that she was the mother of two.

One of his new fishermen was titillated by the sight of Miranda. In the month he'd worked for Sebastian he'd seen her twice, and he wondered how a man like Sebastian could have been so lucky to win her.

Sebastian was such a huge bear of a man that José Martinez could not possibly understand how the petite Miranda could have found him attractive.

José was conceited about his own fine male body. He, too,

had firm-muscled arms and legs. But his broad chest tapered down to a trim waist and rounded hips. He believed he had as fine a physique as the bullfighters he'd watched in the rings in Mexico.

He'd only been in California for a few weeks before he'd ventured northward to Half Moon Bay. Back in Mexico, he'd left a wife, Lucia, and two small children. Five years of marriage had been a bore to José, who was a lady's man. Being married strangled him, so he decided to do a little wandering. He'd left Mexico, promising Lucia he would send for her and the babies as soon as he found a good job.

But those were not his intentions at all, for José was ready to resume his bachelor days. He'd done just that after he'd crossed the border to travel up the coastline of California.

He found that women surrendered to his tall, dark, handsome charms, and he almost always received lodgings and good meals from generous, eager ladies as he made his way to Half Moon Bay.

Some places he would stay only one night, but then there were times he would linger two or three days in one spot.

It was a long distance from the border to his destination which was San Francisco where his older brother lived. From the letters he had received it sounded as if he were living a very good life, so José figured that he might be able to stay with him for awhile.

It had been slow going for him, though, since he'd left Mexico with very little money in his pocket. He had to credit the lovely ladies along the way now that he'd arrived in Half Moon Bay, for he now had a fuller valise than it was when he'd left his home.

He had three nice shirts, some silk neckscarves, and a black twill jacket, which were all gifts from ladies. The grandest little trophy he'd received was a gold pocket watch

José was at a high peak by the time he got to Half Moon Bay.

It was by chance that he met Sebastian on the wharf and the fishing boat captain just happened to need a new man for his crew. So José was hired. The good-hearted Sebastian had taken him home that late afternoon to have dinner with his family and spend the night until he could get lodging at the inn the next day.

The first night José slept on a cot in Vasco's bedroom. It was one fine-looking family Sebastian had and, of course, his eyes instantly appraised the beautiful, sultry Miranda. Lying on the cot, he promised himself that he was going to have her—one way or the other.

José discovered that a man earned his wages when he worked for Fernandes. They put in a long day, but Sebastian worked just as hard as his crew. That evening the two men went in different directions, José toward a cheap inn near the wharf and Sebastian toward his cottage.

José had rather expected Sebastian to invite him to his house again for dinner, and José had anticipated seeing the fisherman's pretty wife and enjoying a good home-cooked meal for free. But the offer hadn't been made.

Some days Sebastian brought his son Vasco along with him. Sebastian's son was large for his age and looked just like his husky father. The little daughter, Elena, was the image of her beautiful mother.

José had been working for Sebastian almost two weeks when he spied Miranda and her daughter standing on the wharf when Sebastian's fishing boat pulled in one late afternoon. It was one of those days when Vasco had accompanied his father on the trawler.

José was fired immediately by the sight of her as she waved at her husband, the breeze blowing her long hair back from her face. How he envied Fernandes!

When the crew left the boat to move hastily on their way to their homes and Sebastian joined his wife and daughter, José stayed behind and watched them begin to walk back to their cottage. Sebastian held Vasco's hand, his free arm snaked around Miranda's tiny waist. José's eyes studied the slow, sensuous sway of her round hips, and he was enflamed with a wild desire to possess her.

But as much as Miranda Fernandes intrigued him, he was more than ready to get out of Half Moon Bay and head for San Francisco. Since the time he'd left Mexico and made his way this far up the California coast, he'd not put in such hard days of working as he had here for Sebastian. He had no time for courting. By the time he got into the inn, he was too exhausted to go out to hunt himself a woman.

So José knew he was not cut out to be a fisherman. He had a different lifestyle in mind for himself. He'd found out that he didn't have to be too ambitious or hard-working when a nice woman was willing to furnish a roof over his head, cook him good meals, and buy him nice clothes to wear. This was more to his liking and he hardly called it work when all he had to do was make passionate love to earn his keep.

In two days, he would be getting his second weekly wages from Sebastian, and he planned to leave for San Francisco when he got his pay. He'd even decided that to possess the beautiful Miranda was not worth putting in any more long, exhausting days working on her husband's boat. But José did not tell Sebastian that he'd not be with him on Monday morning.

By chance, he overheard Sebastian tell his son to go on home and tell his momma that he'd be a couple of hours late for he had a repair to make on the boat.

"Can I come back here and help you, Papa?" Vasco had asked him before he rushed down the wharf.

"I suppose so—if you hurry home and get back here before dark." Sebastian smiled.

"I'll be back, Papa," Vasco called as he darted hastily toward the cottage.

Had José not heard the conversation between Sebastian and his son, he would not have impulsively changed his plans. He turned his steps away from the direction of the inn.

He stayed some twenty or thirty feet behind young Vasco as he made his way home. Vasco found his mother puttering in her kitchen preparing their evening meal when he rushed into the kitchen to give her Sebastian's message. Before she could stop him, he breathlessly explained that his papa had told him he could come back to the wharf to help him and raced out the door. She called out to him, but he didn't hear her. She noticed that storm clouds were gathering over the bay. As fast as her Vasco was running down the road, she figured that he would be back with his papa before the storm broke.

Elena was taking a nap, so Miranda realized that she had plenty of time to relax and wait for Sebastian and Vasco to get home for supper. She locked her front door, and then she went back to Elena's room to check on her. She was glad that she was sleeping peacefully, for she had been running a slight fever that afternoon.

But Miranda was not too pleased to touch little Elena's forehead and find that she felt warmer than she had when she'd put her down for a nap about an hour ago. Miranda was a worrying mother, and she went back to the front room to wait for her husband and son.

She picked up the little dress she was stitching for Elena, hoping to calm her concern over her daughter's fever.

José had hidden in the bushes until Vasco ran past him on his way back to the levee. Then he came back to the road that led to the cottage. Lightning flashed across the sky in the southwest, and there was a distant rumbling of thunder.

His decision to come to the cottage had been such a spur of the moment reaction that he had no idea what he was going to say to Miranda when he arrived at her door. Usually he had a well-planned plot for every occasion. Tonight he did not.

When Miranda answered the rap on her door and saw José, she felt no apprehensions. It was only after he had entered the front room that she wondered why he would come to the cottage when he must know that Sebastian was at the wharf working on his boat.

An uneasiness washed over her. She didn't like the way he sauntered into the room or the lusty leer in his eyes. She didn't hesitate to question him, and his flippant response made her nervous and ill-at-ease.

"I must ask you to leave, José. I've a sick daughter tonight, so I've no time to visit with you." Deciding it was the time to put him in his proper place, she added, "I don't appreciate your coming here, José, when you know that my husband is not home."

Instinct told her to move farther away from him. She'd not invited him to sit down, and he stood beside her, glaring down at her.

Nothing had prepared Miranda for the next half-hour of her life. An evil smirk came to his face at the moment his two strong hands grabbed her. "Scream," he snarled, "and you'll only wake up your daughter." She cursed him as he tore at the front of her dress. When her breasts were bared, he sucked at them so viciously that she had to restrain her screams. But she fought him like a wildcat. This only made him more abusive. He bit her nipples, and she screamed in pain. His massive hands squeezed her throat.

"Sebastian will kill you, *bastardo!*" Her black eyes reflected her contempt and disgust. She turned and twisted so that he could not burrow himself between her thighs. José was not used to a woman resisting him.

"Lie still, bitch," he panted huskily.

"No, I will not. You sicken me. You're less than a man. A real man would not have to do this," she hissed at him.

That was more than José's ego could tolerate. He held her throat in a vise-like clasp.

Her black eyes had a startled look in that moment just before her head suddenly went limp. Miranda Fernandes had uttered her last words. José had choked the life out of her. Now it was José who had a stunned look on his face as he rose slowly from her limp body, knowing that she was dead.

Now he was the one trembling and afraid, for he'd not planned on murder. He'd never met a woman like Miranda Fernandes, who'd resisted his advances so fiercely.

Shaken, he backed toward the front door. Faster than young Vasco, he ran down the dirt road all the way to the inn. Frantically, he gathered up his belongings and threw them into his valise. Just as quickly, he left the inn to start northward, for he was not about to wait until morning to catch a boat traveling up the bay.

He walked that night until exhaustion forced him to seek out a wooded area where he fell on the ground and slept. He didn't begin to relax and quit trembling until he reached Salinas. Half Moon Bay was far back in the distance.

Back in Half Moon Bay, the village was stunned by the news of Miranda Fernandes' murder. There was already speculation that Sebastian had done it in a jealous rage. He was known to be volatile.

The authorities might have suspected Sebastian if it hadn't been for the alibi young Vasco supplied. He told the police that he'd gone home to tell his mother they'd be late for supper and then he went back to the wharf to help his papa.

They'd returned home together to find his mama on the front room floor. His little sister was still asleep in her room, not knowing what had happened to her mother.

Never for a minute did the authorities doubt the young Vasco who'd told them with tears streaming down his face, "I wish now I'd stayed home with mama. I could have been there to help her." So while others might have questioned Sebastian's guilt, the police never did.

He tried to help them in every way he could. He told Sheriff Fischer, "Whoever came to our door and Miranda allowed in that house she knew, sheriff. I can tell you. She would have never invited a stranger into our house."

"Well, whoever came through that door, Sebastian, was a man, not a woman. Two very strong hands choked your wife," Burt Fischer told him.

Dazed, Sebastian moved in a nightmare that would not end. Not even when he watched Miranda being lowered into her grave could he accept that his beloved wife was dead.

Realization hit him between the eyes when Monday morning arrived and he had no mother to leave at the house with Vasco and Elena. There was nothing he could do but leave Vasco in charge of his younger sister with some very strict rules laid down to his son. Vasco took his new responsibility seriously.

He was met that Monday morning by a compassionate crew. They admired him for showing up on the wharf, for they knew the depth of his sorrow. But as the fishing boat pulled away from the docks, Sebastian suddenly realized that Martinez was not on deck. Now that he thought about it, he hadn't been at the funeral. He quizzed his crew. No one had seen or talked to José in the last two days.

His oldest fisherman remarked, "You know José. He's sort

of a loner, but then he's a young hombre and not married. He don't have family like the rest of us do."

"That's right, Lorenzo," Sebastian mumbled, but his mind was whirling with suspicion.

He already knew what he was going to do as soon as his day was over on the fishing boat. He would walk over to Mrs. Kershaw's boardinghouse to see if José were still there. If he weren't, then Sebastian felt he would know the bastard who'd killed Miranda. He'd make a point of going to the authorities the first thing in the morning.

It didn't take but a moment's conversation with Ida Kershaw to confirm what he'd expected to hear. "He skipped out of here sometime in the early evening, Sebastian. The rascal went off without paying me what he owed me," she grumbled.

Sebastian assured her that she'd get paid, for he knew that Ida had rented José a room because he was working for Sebastian.

"It ain't your fault he cheated me," she told him.

"Well, I feel responsible to you, Ida. Like me, you work hard for your money. I'm going to take this information to the police first thing in the morning, but I've got to get on home now. My kids are there alone," he told her.

A pained expression came to her face as she told him how sorry she was to hear about Miranda. "God forgive me, Sebastian, for judging, but the first thing that crossed my mind was that José had killed Miranda and was hightailing it away from here fast."

"God forgive us both then, Ida, but I'm convinced of it— especially now that I've had my talk with you. If it weren't for my kids, I'd search until I found the bastard," Sebastian declared.

"You've got a big load to carry, Sebastian, but you'll do it. I've got no doubts about that," she assured him.

"I'm sure going to try, Ida. Right now my world is sorta shattered." A mist of tears welled in his eyes, and he quickly turned to leave the inn.

Ida Kershaw once again realized how unfair life could be to take a life of one so young and pretty as Miranda Fernandes, who left a loving husband behind and two sweet kids.

Fifteen

As he'd told Ida Kershaw he was going to do, he went to the authorities the very next morning, but nothing ever came of it. Weeks had gone by and now it had been years, but for Sebastian those terrible days still seemed as though they'd just happened yesterday.

Now his son and daughter were grown up, but back then he'd had to leave them alone, worry gnawing at him when he was out in the bay and they were at the cottage alone.

Vasco had done a fine job of taking care of his sister, Sebastian had to admit. He did finally accept the arrangement and relax more about everything.

He sat tonight in his favorite chair, puffing on one of the long slender cigarettes that Gusstavo had given to him and pondering where all the years had gone so quickly. He recalled how suddenly it had happened that his pretty little daughter was thirteen, declaring to him that she could handle the cottage on her own and Vasco could accompany him on his fishing boat as she knew her brother was yearning to do.

So Sebastian had given in to her, allowing Vasco to go out daily with him. In a few short weeks it was apparent that Vasco was going to be a fine fisherman.

So life did become kinder to Sebastian, but always in the back of his mind were thoughts of meeting up with José Martinez. He believed their paths would cross again, and when that happened, he vowed that he would be the judge and the jury. Justice would be done.

It seemed everyone in the fishing village had forgotten Miranda except for him, Vasco, and Elena. The older his little Elena grew, the more she became like her lovely mother. She even had Miranda's feisty, saucy walk. His wife would never be gone as long as Elena lived.

As old Ida Kershaw had predicted, Sebastian had not done too bad a job at raising his children.

Vasco worked hard for him and flatly refused to take full wages, pointing out that he lived at the cottage and ate from his father's table. "I don't need that much money, Pa," he said. "I'd not feel right about it."

So Sebastian respected his wishes and gave him no more argument about it. But when Vasco was eighteen, he bought a second fishing boat and put Vasco in charge of it. In a month's time Sebastian knew that he had made a smart move, for their business was thriving from their doubled catch.

The Fernandes were definitely the most prosperous Portuguese fishermen at Half Moon Bay.

By the time Elena was sixteen, she realized that a lot of the other jealous young Portuguese girls gossiped about her as their mothers had about Miranda.

Like her mother, Elena shrugged it all aside when she sashayed around the wharf or village. She found she didn't have much in common with most of them anyway.

She also felt the same way about their older brothers when they approached her with their sweet talk and eager smiles. None of them had whetted her interest.

So instead of clustering with the young girls or their brothers in the early evenings, Elena stayed in the cottage sewing a new floral skirt for herself. Elena loved the pretty new clothes she was able to make for herself.

So Sebastian was a very happy man and a very proud

father by the time Mateo had come into their lives and they'd received their invitation to Golden Splendor.

But lately he'd sensed a discontent in Elena which disturbed him, and he had no idea what to do about it.

Sebastian could certainly understand why his little Elena was feeling in low spirits after all the splendor she'd discovered on the fancy country estate of the Mateo family. So one night he offered her some money to buy herself a pretty frock.

"Oh, Papa, I don't need another dress. You just bought me that yellow one a month ago," she told him.

"Well, then get yourself some new sandals, eh?"

"My sandals are fine, Papa. You keep your money," she said. It wasn't a new frock or new sandals that she needed to brighten her spirits. It was the sight of Mateo at her door she wanted. But she could not fool her papa, who knew her so well. She had thought she had successfully disguised her feelings, but obviously she hadn't.

Two nights later, when Sebastian suggested that she come out on the boat with him, she accepted. She tried to show an enthusiasm that she truly wasn't feeling when she told him, "I'll come, Papa, and I'll fix us a picnic basket. We'll have ourselves a feast right on your boat."

A broad smile covered Sebastian's face. "Ah, that sounds like a wonderful idea, honey."

It did prove to be a wonderful day for Elena. It was perfect on the bay. She'd dug out her old fishing garb the night before. The next morning she'd gotten up early. Vasco and her father were already in the kitchen eating a hearty breakfast. She gathered up the half-dozen boiled eggs she'd fixed the night before and the little fried fruit pies. She sliced off some of the fresh-baked loaf of bread and generous slices of ham to put in her wicker basket.

Sebastian watched her putting the food in the basket and told her, "Honey, you don't have to feed the crew."

She giggled, "I know, Papa. But I want to be prepared in case Vasco pulls up beside your boat and I have to feed him, too."

A short time later the three of them were walking toward the docks, the two huge men on either side of her. She looked like a mere child in her fishing garb, a long black braid hanging down her back.

Just the sight of her boarding the fishing boat stirred up excitement among the crew. Some of them had not seen Elena for awhile and mercy, how she'd changed! The older members of Sebastian's crew felt as he did that she looked more and more like Miranda.

Long ago, Sebastian had laid down very strict rules for her to obey when he'd taken her on the boat and she always remembered them. Now she could understand why he'd been so stern with her, so today she observed his laws and went directly to his cabin. When she was a wee one, she'd been allowed more liberties than Sebastian would allow after she turned ten.

They enjoyed their picnic lunch at midday, and Sebastian chuckled. "I feel the need for a nap, but I guess that will have to wait until I get home. You spoil me, honey."

But nothing prevented *her* from taking a nap after Sebastian went back to the deck. When she awoke, they were already heading in to shore. The day was coming to an end, but it had been a pleasant day.

But the next morning, she was left at the cottage alone as her father and Vasco went off to their fishing boats. They both threw themselves into their work, but she no longer enjoyed her life in Half Moon Bay.

She'd blamed her discontent on going to Golden Splendor

and feeling a letdown after the festivities, but it was more than that.

Maybe meeting the handsome Mateo had ignited her restlessness. All she knew for certain was that she wanted more out of life. She was determined to see more of the outside world, but how could she possibly speak about her feelings to her father or Vasco? Neither of them could understand.

She had no way of knowing that her feelings mirrored those of her mother. As much as she'd loved her husky Portuguese husband, Miranda knew frequent periods of loneliness and depression. Even Vasco had not been able to fill the void. Had Elena had her mother to speak with, she could have understood herself better now.

Miranda could have told Elena so much. She could have told her why she'd so willingly surrendered to the handsome Mateo, for Miranda had been a passionate, sensuous woman.

Elena knew that she was not a lady of low station who gave her heart away easily. When she'd surrendered to Mateo, she'd believed that she loved him and that he loved her. It was not a frivolous affair to be twittered about by promiscuous girls. Elena found the actions and the giggled whispers of such girls disgusting.

To her the interlude she'd spent with Mateo was private, not a memory to be shared with other friends. But she was now beginning to wonder if Mateo had taken that moment as seriously as she had. For she still waited for him to come to her. Didn't he realize how much she needed his assurance that he cared for her?

If she had acted foolhardy and assumed too much, Elena knew one thing for sure: She'd never settle for the likes of Emilio.

There were other worlds outside Half Moon Bay, Elena realized now that she'd been to Golden Splendor.

* * *

It took Elena very little time to put the cottage in neat order and have herself dressed during the morning hours. It was the long afternoons that hung heavy on her. A proficient cook, she'd already made up enough loaves of bread to take care of her family for two days. She'd also baked pies to have for the next two evening meals. When her oven was fired, she always baked two hens instead of one. She never just fried one pullet, she had two cast iron skillets on the stove for her chickens. What was left over from the first evening was warmed up the second night.

It was one of those afternoons that Elena had plenty of time on her hands before Vasco and Sebastian were due home. Bored, she decided to take a stroll on the wharf, something she had not done for a long time.

Actually, the last time she'd walked on the wharf was the afternoon Emilio had rushed up to her and grabbed her arm. Suddenly, the handsome Mateo had been there at her side playing the role of her protector. She would never forget that she'd gazed up at his face and thought he was the handsomest man she'd ever seen.

Taking a stroll that afternoon did her good, for she was tired by the time she got back to the cottage. Just being among the crowd of milling people eased her *ennui*.

The following afternoon, she went for another walk and met a most interesting lady. Everything about the woman intrigued her.

The fancy lavender parasol she held to shade her face from the sun matched her lavender gown. She wore a pair of earrings with stones of a deep purple hue. She nodded to Elena with a warm friendly smile. The next day, Elena saw her again.

The woman called out to her. "Young lady, may I speak

with you a moment?" Elena didn't hesitate a minute. She joined her.

"I am spending a few days here in your quaint little village and I'm finding it a most fascinating place. Do you live here?" the woman asked her.

"Oh, yes, I've lived here all my life. I've seen you here on the wharf the last three days," Elena told her as she sat down on the bench beside her.

Delores Delgardo saw that the girl was more beautiful than she'd realized. "May I ask what your name is, dear?" Delores asked her.

"Elena Fernandes," she told the woman.

"Well, Elena, I'm Delores Delgardo from Sacramento. I'm here with my son for a few days of rest from my business. I own a dress salon."

Suddenly Elena understood why she looked so elegant. She figured that it must be a very fancy salon from the look of her gowns.

"Sacramento, you said? I've never been there." She gave a soft laugh. "But then, I've never been anywhere except here at Half Moon Bay."

"Ah, as beautiful as you are, Elena, you must not bury yourself. Give yourself a chance to see more of the world."

"One day I probably will, Señora Delgardo." Elena smiled.

Delores Delgardo had a particular charm about her that made people warm to her instantly and Elena was no exception. She had a manner that encouraged people to talk freely and by the time the two of them parted company that late afternoon Delores knew that Elena was seventeen and the daughter of a Portuguese fisherman. Although her mother was dead, she had a protective older brother. She was a sweet, naive girl who had no inkling of the rare beauty she possessed.

Delores was very excited when she left the wharf to meet

her son. No young lady she had working for her right now modeling her expensive gowns was as striking as this little miss she'd chanced to meet in an obscure fishing village.

Delores's head was whirling crazily, plotting how to persuade this lovely child to go back to Sacramento with her and enter her employ.

She rushed into the room at the inn where she and Miguel were staying and announced, "Oh, Miguel, I have just met the most beautiful young lady. I've not seen anything like her for a long, long time. Remember Mignon? Well, Elena Fernandes is as beautiful as she was!"

"Are you going to offer her a job?" Miguel asked.

"I wouldn't hesitate a minute to ask her. The question is whether or not she'd accept and come with us. I've some thinking to do tonight. She's to meet me down on the wharf tomorrow afternoon. I've got to convince her then to come with us, for the next day we'll be leaving."

Miguel shrugged his shoulders and casually remarked, "You'll manage, Mama dear. You always do."

She gave him a look of disdain which he didn't see for he was too busy sipping his drink. But she asked him to go downstairs and order her a dinner tray. She didn't wish to put in an appearance again tonight in the stuffy dining room amid a group of chattering, dull guests.

She slipped out of her gown and into a loose, full dressing gown. She didn't need the distraction of Miguel around her tonight. He could dine by himself; she wished to be alone to think.

As she was undressing she considered Miguel's idle remark that she'd manage as she always did. What a mouthful he'd said! Her twenty-five-year-old son had contributed nothing to help her along the way. He had yet to find any direction in his life, and if he didn't work for her he would probably be out on the streets starving.

He was as shiftless as the man who'd fathered him when she'd been young and foolish. For that mistake she'd paid dearly all the rest of her life.

Miguel was not a smart young man with a shrewd mind like hers. He had no winning ways so she could understand why the people around her dress salon or her hotel found him obnoxious. He was tolerated only because he was her son.

Elena's spirits were lighthearted and gay so Sebastian did not question why. He was just glad to see her in a happier mood than she'd been in for the last few weeks.

She made no mention to her father about the very exciting lady she'd met on the wharf or that she planned to meet her again tomorrow. But that evening, after she'd cleaned the kitchen and gone to her bedroom, she picked out with special care what she'd wear tomorrow. It was her brown-challis gathered skirt splashed with brightly colored flowers and with it she'd wear the drawstring yellow-batiste tunic. In her hair she was going to pin the pretty cluster of yellow flowers she'd worn at the festival.

She could not exactly explain to herself why she was so thrilled about her upcoming meeting with Delores Delgardo. All Elena knew was that being around her was like being back at Golden Splendor; she had a touch of class and elegance.

The next morning her father and Vasco left at their usual early morning hour and she got busy putting the cottage in proper order.

When she had dressed and put the finishing touches to her hair, she stood before the mirror, pleased with the way she looked. This skirt and tunic were her prettiest ensemble.

Delores Delgardo would have been delighted if she had

known how vulnerable and receptive Elena was. She would not have been as nervous about the outcome of their meeting. But she couldn't know that this pretty young girl was disillusioned and disappointed because weeks had gone by and Mateo had not come from Golden Splendor to see her. She could not know the boredom that had sunk deep inside Elena since she'd returned from Golden Splendor where she'd briefly tasted a different lifestyle.

Promptly at the appointed hour, Elena was on the wharf, looking even more attractive than she had the day before. But Elena was not the only one who had dressed with special care.

When Elena exclaimed how beautiful Delores's ensemble was, Delores gave her a smile. "Well, dear," she said, "that's my business. I design gowns and my seamstress makes them. I have three very beautiful young ladies about your age who wear them to the grand balls and social affairs around the city. The elegant ladies who attend these galas are impressed so they come to my salon to order a gown like the ones they see my girls wearing. It's a very exciting life."

Elena was wide-eyed with excitement, and her interest was whetted. Delores sensed it so she kept up her tales of the glamourous life she and her girls enjoyed.

"My girls live at my hotel, which is near my dress salon, and they have the privilege of my dining room in the hotel or room service. All that, and I pay them a generous wage. They even have the opportunity to buy any of the gowns they model at a reduced price. They live a very good life and meet all kinds of exciting people. I know it sounds like boasting when I tell you that the wealthiest ladies of Sacramento come to my salon, but it is true."

The look on Elena's face was enough to tell Delores that she had been impressed by everything she'd heard. "You—you also own a hotel, señora?"

"Yes, I own the Towers Hotel and have for a few years now." Delores felt the time was right to make her offer to Elena. "You could be one of my girls, Elena," she told her, "and mind you I'm very discriminating when I offer a girl a position. She has to be very special with charm as well as beauty. You have that, Elena."

"You're—you're offering me a job, señora?" Elena's black eyes were flashing brightly.

Delores laughed. "I leave tomorrow to go back to Sacramento. I'll take you with me if you are interested."

"Oh, Papa would never hear of it," Elena declared.

"Papas are like that. I well remember how mine was when I was your age. Sons are different; they can go venturing. Well, I must confess that I ran away, but I never regretted it." She smiled.

"You ran away from your home, señora?" Elena asked.

"I did; and if I hadn't, I would never have acquired my dress salon and hotel," she said. Delores was a cunning woman, and she played Elena perfectly.

"I must go now, Elena. As I told you, I leave tomorrow at five. I will come to the wharf at three. If you meet me here, I will buy your passage also. If you are not happy in Sacramento, then I will provide your return fare. The decision has to be yours, dear," Delores told her.

The two of them departed to go their separate ways, Elena promising to think seriously about Delores's offer. Elena was in a very thoughtful mood as she walked toward her father's cottage.

She had a lot of things to think about before this night was over. Her head was whirling with all that Delores Delgardo had told her, and she knew that she was going to have to put on an act to cover up the things hanging heavily on her mind. This wasn't easy for Elena, for she was honest and did not easily play frivolous games.

By the time she'd walked all the way back to the cottage, she had to admit that the golden opportunity Señora Delgardo had offered to her seemed like the answer to everything. Weeks had gone by since the festival, and Mateo had not brightened her door.

Had that silly little Portuguese heart of hers played her false? Had she dreamed of a love that would never be?

Sixteen

Elena noticed a strange smell the minute she entered the cottage, and it suddenly dawned on her that she'd not pulled the pot to the back of the stove when she'd left the house at mid-afternoon. That morning she'd put on a big pot of beans. They were cooked by mid-afternoon when she'd left to go to the wharf to meet Señora Delgardo. She'd intended to pull the cast-iron pot over to the far end of the stove away from the heat, but she hadn't.

So she smelled scorched beans. In hopes of salvaging them, she poured some water in the pot. She stirred them vigorously and added more wood to the still-glowing embers.

It wasn't long before Vasco and Sebastian would be coming home as hungry as wolves, and she set the table and boiled water for corn.

In a madcap rush she baked a pan of cornbread, but her attention wasn't on preparing dinner tonight. Other thoughts were parading through Elena's mind.

It had not been a good day for Sebastian or Vasco. Two of Sebastian's crew had not shown up; and Vasco had caught few fish for the long day he'd put in, and he'd got a deep, nasty cut on his finger. He was like an angry old bear when Elena tried to tend to the cut and bandage it properly.

When they sat down at the table, the two men each took a generous helping of beans, a huge piece of the cornbread, and an ear of corn. Ravenously, they started to eat, but they suddenly paused and exchanged disgruntled glances.

Elena realized instantly that the beans tasted scorched. Rarely did Sebastian snap at her as he did this evening. "What did you do, Elena—go to sleep this afternoon and let your beans burn? They are terrible."

"I'm sorry, Papa. I guess I must plead guilty to taking a nap and letting my beans go dry," she told him. She watched the two of them shove the beans to the side of their plates and devour the ham, corn, and cornbread. She gave a shrug of her shoulders and started to eat the food on her plate.

Both of them seemed to be in a foul mood tonight as they got up from the table and left her with the job of cleaning the kitchen.

When her dishes were stacked and the hot water was poured in her dishpan, she picked up the huge pot of beans, took them to the backyard, and poured them onto the ground. She called to Vasco's old dog Rojo, thinking that he could at least have himself a feast. But when he came up to sniff at the beans and turned his back on them, that was the ultimate insult. She sat down on the back steps and broke into tears. Her feelings had already been hurt enough by her father and Vasco.

But once the tears had flowed for awhile she found herself feeling angry with all of them—her father, Vasco, and old Rojo. She wiped her eyes with the bottom of her apron.

As she went back into the kitchen she was grumbling under her breath that she'd just let them see how they'd manage without her. She'd just go to Sacramento and wear those fancy gowns of Señora Delgardo's and there would be no cooking or cleaning for her to do. Dear Lord, she'd be living in luxury compared to her life here!

By the time she was dimming the lamps in the kitchen she was telling herself that another year could go by in her life and nothing would change in Half Moon Bay. Vasco would surely grow old and live in the cottage the rest of his life. Well, she was not going to do that!

She walked through the front room, but neither Vasco nor Sebastian looked up from their papers as she went on out the front door to sit down on the front step. Sitting there, she thought about Mateo. She was convinced Mateo was not coming to her as he'd promised. How could she possibly have thought a man like him would offer her marriage? They lived in two different worlds. She'd allowed herself to dwell in foolish folly. His wife would be from a wealthy family in his own valley. The daughter of a Portuguese fisherman did not fit into the world of the Mateo family.

By the time she went back into the house, Elena had decided to accept Señora Delgardo's offer. She would go to Sacramento with her tomorrow.

So she didn't linger in the parlor with her father and brother, instead, she bade the two of them goodnight. Sebastian was feeling rather guilty about his harsh manner with her during the dinner so he rose from his chair and gave her a bear hug. "I'm sorry. I was in a foul mood tonight, honey. It was a bad day out on the bay, but that wasn't your fault. Your beans weren't all that bad."

"Oh, yes, they were, Papa. Rojo even turned up his nose at them when I tried to feed them to him." She smiled.

They all exploded into laughter, and Elena was glad the evening had ended with all of them in a happy mood. She told both of them that she loved them for she wanted them to remember that tomorrow night when they came home to find her gone.

She did love both of them dearly, but she could not allow her emotions to stop her from seeking a future outside Half Moon Bay.

She was convinced that a better life awaited her in Sacramento or she'd not have dared plot such a daring adventure. She had a great need to have her *own* life—without the two of them hovering over her. There were times when she felt smothered.

The next morning when Sebastian and Vasco left the cottage, she told them both that she loved them. But neither man gave her declarations a second thought. Elena was an unrestrained young girl who was very affectionate and never sought to hide her true feelings.

Sebastian and Vasco made their way to the docks with the hopes that it was going to be a more profitable day today. Elena got busy in the cottage to put it in perfect order. She made the beds and cleaned the kitchen. She even took the time to sweep the floors and water the pots of flowers.

Only then did she go to her room to start packing her valise. She didn't take the fancy gown she'd worn to the festival. She had only one gown which had been bought at a shop. It was a simple frock with a white collar and cuffs, and the black material was sprinkled with delicate white flowers. By the time she had stuffed the old valise with two nightgowns, a cotton wrapper, two gathered skirts, two tunics, and her undergarments, it was bulging. But she couldn't resist putting in the little leather sandals which were always so comfortable to slip into.

She placed the little black frock and her best slippers on her bed, for this was what she was going to wear to travel to Sacramento.

Packing her valise had not taken long at all, but the letter she wrote sitting at the kitchen table took a lot of time. She wanted her father to understand why she was making this venture. She explained to him why she'd not discussed her plans with him. It would have only ended in a horrible fuss, for she had known that he would have never agreed to let her go to Sacramento. At the end of the letter, she pointed out that many girls her age were married and away from their families. She told him she had the need to be free to seek out life away from Half Moon Bay. She wrote that she now knew that there were other worlds besides the one she'd lived in all her life.

She left her letter on the table and went to her room to dress.

When the kitchen clock chimed two, Elena was ready to leave. She wished her departure could have been after dark so that their nosy neighbor would not be sitting by her front window to see her leave with her valise.

But she couldn't fret about that. By the time her father and Vasco got home, she would be traveling with Señora Delgardo toward Sacramento.

Before she went out the front door, she took one long, lingering look around the little cottage that had been her home all the days of her life. She prayed that she was doing the right thing. But once she went out the door and began to walk toward the dirt road that went by the front of the cottage, she didn't look back. She didn't dare.

She just kept walking.

A short time later, Delores had her son take her to the wharf. She told him to sit in the buggy back in the distance.

"Will she show up, Mother dear?" Miguel taunted.

"She will come," Delores told him, sure of herself. Without her natural conceit she could never have succeeded with her salon. She'd done it all on her own with stubborn determination and a lot of guts.

As Miguel turned to go back to the buggy, he sought to prick her once more. "I bet she doesn't show up."

"Don't bet on it. That's your problem. If you wish to make things happen, then you must believe that you can. *You* never try to make anything happen, Miguel. You're too lazy." Delores dismissed him peremptorily.

There was no great love between this mother and son. Miguel had never done anything in his whole life to garner any admiration from Delores. Without guilt and remorse, Miguel took greedily all the funds his wealthy mother gave him for the meager lackey jobs he did for her. As long as he could remember, Delores had not lived up to a motherly image. She'd been a businesswoman who was completely absorbed in her own life. He was just a bother that she wished she hadn't been saddled with.

Yet, there was no woman he'd ever met that he admired more. They lived lavishly, so Miguel knew her income was vast.

When he wasn't angry with her, he also had to admit that she was a most striking lady. She didn't look forty-two.

His taunting of her had not dented Delores's spirits, but then Miguel had learned a long time ago that he never won when he tried to parry with her. He went back to the buggy and, settled in the seat, closed his eyes to take a nap.

His mother must have felt very sure the girl would be accompanying them, for she'd sent him this morning to buy passage for her. When Miguel had pointed out that Elena might not show up and she would have wasted that money, Delores quipped, "So I lose it, Miguel. I've been a gambler all my life. Haven't you realized that yet?"

A smug smile came to Delores Delgardo's face when she saw the feisty Portuguese girl coming up the wharf. Her gut instinct had been right again. She appraised the natural, sensuous sway of her body. Some young ladies practiced hours to learn to walk that way. What a jewel she was going to be! What a fortune she was going to make from all the expensive gowns this young lady would sell for her!

"I made my decision last night, señora," Elena said. "I am going to go to Sacramento with you."

"I felt you would come, Elena. In fact, I felt it so strongly that I sent Miguel to buy your passage this morning," Delores said.

Elena gave a soft gale of laughter. "You must have known more than I knew when I left you yesterday."

"Well, young lady, there is no reason for us to tarry here any longer. Come, my son is waiting for us in our buggy. We can go to the inn and have some refreshments before we board the boat," Delores suggested. She well-remembered that Elena had told her that her father was a fisherman, and she didn't wish him to encounter them. She would have wagered that Elena had not received his permission to go to Sacramento.

There was a cocky air about Delores when she and the young lady arrived at the buggy. Her dark eyes met the gaze of her sleepy-eyed son, dispatching a message to him: *You would have lost your bet!*

As he was expected to do, he jumped down to help his mother and Elena into the buggy and took charge of Elena's old valise. It was a rather pathetic piece of luggage, he noticed.

They arrived at the inn and spent a very pleasant hour there. Delores sent Miguel downstairs to get them a carafe of coffee. He brought the tray back to his mother's room himself, for there were no luxury services at this little inn. Then he had left the two of them alone.

His mother busily informed Elena that they would have dinner on board the *Moonlight Bay.* "We travel up the bay to a place called Rio Vista. Then we go to the livery to get my buggy and we'll make the rest of the trip to Sacramento overland, Elena."

An hour later, Elena was traveling away from Half Moon Bay aboard the *Moonlight Bay.* The boat plowed through the San Pablo Bay before veering into Suison Bay. They traveled the outlet of the bay until they reached Rio Vista.

The late afternoon and evening was an adventure for Elena, and Delores had only to watch her face to know that. Excitement sparkled in her black eyes as she observed everything around her.

By the time they arrived in Rio Vista, darkness had descended over the coast. Delores and Elena waited at the dock for Miguel to walk to the livery and bring back the buggy. He had far more luggage to load into the carriage for him and his mother than he did for Elena.

For the last three hours, Elena had been so entranced by this venture northward toward the big city that she'd not thought about her papa and Vasco back in Half Moon Bay.

By the time the buggy entered Sacramento, her pretty head was whirling with excitement. She did not doubt that she'd made a wise decision to leave home and seek her future.

Seventeen

Sebastian had a strange feeling as he and Vasco approached the house. No smoke came out of the chimney as it usually did at this time of the day. There should have been a fire burning in the cookstove. Elena always had pots of food on the stove for their supper when they came in from their long day.

He said nothing to Vasco, but he was wondering if she'd taken ill. He grew more concerned when they turned off the main road and he saw Mateo's buggy at the side of the house. Mark was slumped over, taking himself a nap.

"Mateo, my friend," he called out, "why are you sitting out here, eh?"

Mark, roused from his sleep, told him no one was home to answer his rapping on the door. "So I decided to wait. I figured that Elena had gone out on the boat with you today." But since she wasn't with her father, a look of puzzlement creased his face.

"As you can see, Mateo, she is not with us. I—I don't like this at all. Come, let's go inside," the older man urged. Following Sebastian and Vasco up the front steps, Mark muttered his agreement. "I arrived over an hour ago."

Horrible memories of the past washed over Sebastian when he opened the door. If he should find his little Elena murdered as her mother had been, he didn't know if he could stand it.

The house was ghostly quiet, and when he called out to her, she made no appearance.

"Where is that little imp at this time of the day?" Sebastian questioned, checking each room of the little house. Vasco had gone on to the kitchen with the bundle of fish he'd brought home, so he was the first one to spy Elena's letter lying on the table.

He picked it up and called to his father, "Pa, you'd better read this." He handed the paper to Sebastian, who quickly scanned the carefully composed page and passed it on to Mark. Rage contorted the old fisherman's face, but all Mark could utter was, "Oh, God!"

"Oh, God is right, Mateo! I can't believe my Elena would be so foolish! She is too young and innocent to go out on her own, especially to a place like Sacramento. Oh, yes, I will pray many prayers for my Elena, Mateo." He sank into the kitchen chair dejectedly. Vasco, stunned, walked out of the kitchen. Devastated by what Elena had done, he sought comfort from old Rojo. He patted the dog's head, asking over and over why she'd left like this and hurt her papa so painfully.

He finally got up and told the old dog, "I'll fix you something to eat, Rojo. No need for you to go hungry."

By the time Vasco came back into the kitchen, Sebastian was brewing a pot of coffee. "Well, at least, she put the house in order before she left," he was saying sarcastically to Mateo.

Mark sensed the bitterness in his deep voice. He himself felt guilty, wondering if Elena had thought he'd betrayed her since so many weeks had passed and he'd not come to her. It wasn't because he'd not wanted to see her. He'd not made love to her and forgotten her; but she hadn't known that. He agonized, but couldn't share these concerns with Sebastian. But what he did tell Sebastian was the truth. He would have been here much sooner had his father not taken a bad fall and been laid up.

"I've had to handle everything for father the last three weeks around the vineyards and winery," Mark told him.

Vasco, putting together a meal for his old dog, listened. He sensed that Mateo was as shocked as he and his father.

"I'm sorry to hear about your pa, Mateo. I hope he's going to be all right. He's one fine man," Sebastian said.

"Oh, yes, sir. He's doing better all the time. Is—is there anything we could do, sir?" Mark asked him.

"What, Mateo? I ask you what? I'd not know where to start looking in a place as big as Sacramento. She gave me no hint as to where she'll be working. No, I'll not go searching for her as much as I love her. She chose to leave. I've my living to earn." There was indignation and impatience in his voice. He was finding it very hard to accept that Elena had left.

"I guess you're right." There was nothing he could do here now, and Mark announced that he'd better leave for Golden Splendor.

Sebastian urged him to stay and have dinner with them. But Mark told him he couldn't, for he had to get up early in the morning.

"Send word to me if you hear anything from Elena, sir. You know I'll be anxious to hear from you." He didn't hesitate for a minute to honestly admit to Sebastian, "I care very much about your daughter. I, too, share your concern about her."

"Yes, Mateo—I understand. I will send word to you," Sebastian assured him as he walked with him to the front door.

The two of them gave each other a warm embrace and said their goodbyes. Mark told him, "I'll try to get back up here in a week. I shall hope you've had word from her by then."

Sebastian watched him get into his buggy and disappear into the darkness. Had Elena not acted so impulsively, she might have had herself a suitor in Mark Mateo. Sebastian would have approved of him wholeheartedly. Elena had been a very foolish girl.

Perhaps, he should have tried more to understand her discontent, he chided himself as he went back into his kitchen.

His dutiful son had been busy preparing supper, and four fish fillets lay ready for the skillet. The kitchen table was set with two plates instead of the usual three.

In his quiet, simple way, Vasco declared, "We've got to eat, Pa. I'm hungry."

"So am I, Vasco. You slice us a couple potatoes to fry, and I'll whip us up some cornbread cakes. We'll have ourselves a good feast, eh?"

A big broad smile lit Vasco's face. "We sure will, Pa. We sure will."

An hour later they had eaten everything. The cornbread, fish, and fried potatoes were all gone. Vasco washed the dishes and straightened the kitchen. He'd had to do the housework years ago when he was left with the responsibility of little Elena.

While Vasco was busy in the kitchen, Sebastian made a careful survey of his daughter's bedroom for some clue. He found nothing. But he also found that she had taken precious little with her. Sebastian could only pray that she'd get very homesick and come rushing back where she belonged.

He walked out of her room and closed the door. He planned on keeping it closed as long as she was gone. Later, when Vasco saw the closed door, he understood the depth of his father's pain. When he went to his own room, he wasn't feeling kindly toward the little sister he'd always adored.

* * *

Mark had time to think as he drove back to his own home. Many thoughts rushed through his head. The most troublesome worry had gnawed at him throughout the past three weeks: What if Elena were pregnant? He had a simple solution that he was sure would ease her mind: They'd get married immediately. His beautiful Elena would not be shamed because of him. Never would he have not assumed his responsibility for his child.

He now feared that she had found herself pregnant and, when he didn't come to Half Moon Bay as soon as he'd promised, she had made a desperate flight away from her home. Fearing her father's reaction, she had left in a panic.

Did she really have a job to go to in Sacramento or had she just told Sebastian that so he wouldn't worry about her?

By the time he arrived back at his father's estate, he had decided on a course of action. He would investigate on his own, and the first places he would look were the two inns in the village. Their ledgers would have the register of guests. If one of those guests were from Sacramento, then he would have something to go on. He was already plotting a visit with Carlos so that he could check around the city for Elena.

As soon as Mano was up and able to assume his duties, Mark would head for Sacramento if Elena had not returned to Half Moon Bay by then.

He knew the boat she must have left on. Old Raymond at the ticket office would be more than willing to supply him with the passenger list.

The Mateo family had had their dinner by the time Mark arrived back home, but Celia had kept some food warmed for him. He didn't want to discuss Elena's sudden disappearance with his family, so he just told them that the Fernandes family was fine and they didn't prod him for more news. But that wasn't enough to satisfy Markita, who kept quizzing him. Mark shrugged her questions aside. "Will you let me eat my dinner, Markita? I'm starved. For once and for all, I will tell you that Elena is fine and she sends her regards to you. Now, leave me be." He rapidly devoured the food on his plate and went directly to his room.

Mark was a man in torment for the next two days, for he couldn't do what he yearned to do. He had an obligation to his father, so he couldn't just strike out to go to Sacramento to track down Elena Fernandes.

But three days later, Mano joined him at the dining table for the hearty breakfast Celia had prepared. When he announced that he was ready to accompany Mark to the winery, Mark could not have been more pleased.

When Mark saw for himself that his father was moving with his usual vigor, he asked, "Do you think Golden Splendor could do without me for a few days, Father?"

Mano gave him a sly grin. "I think we could. I was wondering when you'd be asking me this, Mark. I think it's time you went calling on that pretty little Portuguese girl before she forgets you. Absence does not make a heart grow fonder, son."

"I can't fool you, can I, Father?" Mark laughed, a sheepish grin on his face.

"No, we're too much alike, *hijo mío*," Mano told him.

That was all the two of them had to say to one another to have an understanding.

The next morning Mark left for Half Moon Bay and began his investigation.

His family name opened doors for him, and he interrogated the innkeepers and Raymond at the ticket office.

By the time Sebastian and Vasco finished their work day, Mark had the name of the woman who, with her son, had stayed in the village and had left with Elena.

Dorothy Dansworth and her son Marshall were from Sacramento, and they were the only guests registered on the day

Elena had disappeared. She had to be the one who'd enticed Elena away.

Once he'd talked with old Raymond, Mark was convinced he was on the right track. The Dansworths had taken the five o'clock boat. They had also booked passage that morning for an Elena Fernandes.

That was all Mark had to know for him to guide his buggy to Sebastian's cottage that late afternoon and wait for Sebastian and Vasco to arrive.

Sebastian greeted Mark, but, shrugging his broad shoulders, he told him, "I wish I had some good news to tell you, Mateo, but I've had no word from Elena."

"Well, I've some news to tell you, sir. I've been in the village for a few hours, and I've done some snooping around," Mark said.

"Come in and tell me what you've learned," the old man invited.

Mark followed the two of them through the front door of the cottage and took a seat while Sebastian went to get them some wine.

Vasco sank down in one of the chairs and asked Mark, "Do you mean you've heard something about Elena, Mateo?"

"I think so, Vasco. I think I know the name of the woman your sister left here with. It's something to start with at least." By then Sebastian had returned with the wine, eager to hear Mark's news.

Sebastian shook his head when Mark recounted all that he'd learned. "Damn, Mateo," he muttered, "why didn't I think to do what you've done today? This brain of mine isn't as sharp as yours."

That evening Mark did remain to share the evening meal with them. But the cottage wasn't the same without Elena, and he left soon after the dinner.

When he bade Sebastian good night, he told him that he was going to go to Sacramento and try to track down Dorothy Dansworth. If he could find her, he was sure that he'd find Elena.

They shook hands and Sebastian told him, "You are a good man, Mateo, and the Fernandes family is lucky to have you for their friend. God go with you to Sacramento!"

"I'll find her, sir." He turned and left.

Vasco and Sebastian stood on the porch to watch his buggy go out to the main road and head for the inn. Vasco remarked, "I like that Mateo, Pa. He's got to be very much in love with my sister to do all he's done."

"Yes, Vasco, he loves her, and that is why she's played the little fool to have done what she's done. Had she only been a little patient," he sighed dejectedly.

"Elena has never been patient, Papa. You know that," Vasco said.

"This time she may regret her impulsive action. A man like Mateo is worth waiting for. But then, Elena will have to find out something about life for herself—as we all do," Sebastian told his son and turned to go back inside his house.

It had been over a week since Elena had left Half Moon Bay, and she had to confess she'd not regretted her decision to accompany Señora Delgardo. Everything in Sacramento was exciting to her. She had her own bedroom, which was lavishly furnished. She went down each evening to the hotel's dining room wearing one of the pretty gowns Señora Delgardo had given her. Delores had taken her to her fashionable dress salon, and that had been quite an adventure for Elena. She'd never been anywhere like it and had never seen so many gorgeous gowns hanging on racks. She had her first fitting, and Delores instructed her about the selection of appropriate slippers and accessories. She learned that she could enhance or distract from her gown and that this knowledge was very important.

At the Towers Hotel, Delores employed a woman named Colette who apparently did nothing but style the models' hair when they attended an elegant party or social affair.

During that first week, Colette arranged Elena's thick, glossy hair in many different styles and Elena marveled how a different coiffure completely changed her image. Once Colette twisted it into a daring upsweep, but the next time she pulled it back severely into one massive coil at the back of her head, leaving teasing wisps at Elena's temples.

Colette exclaimed, "Oh, Elena, you've got such a perfect face that no hairstyle would not be flattering to you! Your lovely thick mane is a joy to work with. I have much trouble with Babette's hair. It is so fine and silky."

"I think you create miracles, señora." Elena smiled up at her.

Of the three young ladies living at the Towers Hotel, Elena had warmed immediately to the green-eyed Deirdre. She had the most beautiful golden-blonde hair that Elena had ever seen. Camilla had jet-black hair like Elena's, but it was much coarser and frizzy. Babette had the silky, light copper-colored hair that Colette had remarked was so hard to style. Babette was a tall, willowy young lady who towered four or five inches over Camilla and Deirdre. Elena wondered if that were why she was so bossy with the others. She'd taken an instant disliking to her and determined that she'd not boss her around. The señora was her boss, not Babette!

Elena felt giddy, for she could not believe how generous Señora Delgardo had been to her since she'd arrived. She'd been given four lovely gowns to wear during the day and evening when she went down to the dining room to eat her meals. But there had also been an array of lacy undergarments, three nightgowns, and a lovely silk wrapper.

She'd told Elena, "Now these things are yours, dear, to wear whenever you wish."

It was the finest wardrobe Elena had ever owned, and she took a special pride in dressing each day. What Elena didn't realize was that Delores didn't want her going down to the dining room in her simple floral skirt and tunics.

Since she couldn't hurt the girl's feelings by telling her that, she furnished her with a suitable wardrobe. Elena was going to earn far more for her than the cost of anything she'd given to her that first week. Delores Delgardo was sure of that.

Elena Fernandes was a young lady of such rare beauty that she was bound to capture the attention of women as well as gentlemen.

Eighteen

Colette Charboneau and Delores Delgardo went back a lot of years with one another. Both of them had had ill-fated marriages and had been left to fend for themselves. Colette was luckier than Delores, for she had had no children.

For over ten years, Colette had gone her own way. She had earned herself a living by dressing wealthy ladies' hair and managed to make enough to provide herself with a nice apartment, but she'd lived modestly.

The very striking Delores had lived a most flamboyant lifestyle. Wearing one of the gowns she'd stitched for herself, she'd chanced to catch the eye of a very wealthy gentleman, Travis Terherne. For eight years she was his mistress. He knew that they would never be married, but he adored Delores. But he was very much a married man—with five children.

To make it up to Delores, he set her up in her dress salon and deeded her one of the hotels he owned in Sacramento.

Travis never tried to hide her as his backstreet mistress. He took her to many galas in the city. His friends knew that Travis could never be a free man because his wife was a devout Catholic.

Most of his gentlemen friends admired Travis for his open, honest approach to life. None of them could find fault with his charming companion Delores. She was an elegant lady.

Over the years, Delores was given a fortune in jewelry.

Her salon prospered as did the hotel, and Travis was very proud of her. The stolen moments they spent together were the most wonderful part of his life.

But Travis had had warnings about his health for over five years. A massive heart attack struck him one evening after he and his wife Violet had had a violent argument.

One of Travis' good friends brought the shocking news to Delores. The day of the funeral Delores had not gone to the services at the church but she had gone to the cemetery to see him lowered into the grave. She stood back from the crowd shrouded in black and her lovely face was concealed by a black veil draped over her black bonnet.

When everyone else had left, she walked up to the grave to place her yellow rosebuds on Travis' grave. Yellow rosebuds were what he'd always brought her.

Then she got back in the buggy which Travis had bought for her and left the burial ground. But she still made trips to the cemetery to place yellow rosebuds on Travis' grave.

Delores had never allowed any other men to enter her life. There had been many who'd tried, for she was a very attractive lady, but the relationship she'd shared with Travis had been so perfect that she couldn't settle for less.

After Travis' death, she met Colette and urged her old friend to join her employ. Delores's offer was too generous for Colette to turn down. She was to be furnished a suite of rooms on the same floor of the hotel as Delores. She had a free ticket to eat in the dining room anytime she wished. All that plus a nice salary far surpassed what she was making now, so she didn't hesitate a minute.

She never regretted accepting Delores's offer. She and Delores got along just fine, and it always amazed her when she heard other employees complain about how difficult she was.

But she would be the first to admit that Delores was a shrewd, demanding business lady.

It didn't surprise her when Delores came to her one evening to ask her opinion of Elena Fernandes after she'd been working with her for ten days.

"Sheer perfection, Delores! The girl is exquisite," Colette declared.

Delores smiled. "Tell me more, Colette."

"Well, Elena will love wearing the fancy gowns and going to the *soirées*. Now a Babette or a Camilla, she isn't. She'd never have the finesse to handle an overly bold gentleman. Her fiery temper would explode and she'd tell him off. It would not matter to her who he happened to be."

Delores smiled. "You see, Colette, what you've told me has been very helpful, for you and she have these leisurely talks and you get insights that aren't open to me."

Delores had reasons to believe that both Babette and Camilla sold more than the gowns at the *soirées,* and she didn't approve of this. However, she could not regiment them when they were on their own free time.

"I will pair Elena with Deirdre. What do you think, Colette?" Delores asked.

"Oh, no question about it!" Colette quickly responded.

"I hear Babette is chafing with a big dose of jealousy." Delores laughed.

"Oh, I know. I found that out the other night when I was styling her hair. She's calling Elena *Little Miss Innocence.*" Colette chuckled.

"Babette would have trouble recalling when she was a sweet innocent thing like Elena," Delores commented.

A short time later the two of them said goodnight and Delores left Colette's suite to go to her own.

The next night Elena witnessed an exciting flurry when Babette, Camilla, and Señora Delgardo prepared to go to a grand affair at one of the estates on the outskirts of the city. There were times when Delores wished to accompany her girls to see that everything went off to her liking. Usually, the girls went to the parties on their own. While Delores rarely attended the smaller dinners, she tried to choose the girl best-suited for the occasion. She had not been pleased with Babette lately.

Miguel drove the ladies to the estate, and then he had three hours to do as he wished. Tonight he wished to spend an hour or two with Lucia, who eagerly gave him pleasures as long as he paid her fee. That was never a problem for Miguel; he always had plenty of money. Delores was a generous mother.

Had she not been so busy running her salon and going to so many social functions in Sacramento and had she consulted with her bookkeeper more often, she would have known just how much money her shiftless son was taking out of her account. She would have been startled.

That evening after Babette, Camilla, and Delores left the Towers Hotel, Elena and Deirdre went down to dinner together. It was a pleasant evening for Elena. She liked Deirdre.

"It might not be the biggest hotel in Sacramento, but it has the best food, Elena. I've dined in the so-called best hotels in the city," she told Elena.

There was enough time during the leisurely dinner for Elena to learn more about Deirdre. She felt free to speak with her, but she was still reluctant to talk to Babette or Camilla. Babette was a snob, and Camilla seemed to be so under Babette's influence that she did and said little on her own.

"How long have you worked for Señora Delgardo, Deirdre?" Elena asked her.

"A year now, Elena. Like you I came here with one valise stuffed full and I had very little money in my reticule. Of course I didn't accompany Señora Delgardo here as you did. I'd run away from my aunt in New Orleans, so I'd made a long, long journey to land in Sacramento. I'm sure she was glad to be rid of me, for I'd been forced on her when my mother died. Dear God, I don't know how I ever made it this far." Deirdre smiled ruefully.

"Oh, I would hate to think of coming that far. I can't say I would have been as daring as you, Deirdre," Elena confessed.

"You might have. I was disillusioned about the young man I was in love with. Philippe kept postponing our wedding date after he'd had his way with me, so I thought to myself that I'd just show him," Deirdre admitted.

Elena questioned if this were also the main drive within her—to show Mateo that she didn't need him after he'd made love to her and never come to Half Moon Bay to see her. Yes, she, too, had been disappointed by the man she loved with all her heart.

Long after the two of them had parted company and Elena was in bed in her room, the memories of Golden Splendor and Mateo came flooding back to her. She ached for the warmth of those strong arms and the sensuous, searing kisses of his lips. For the first time since she'd arrived in Sacramento, she found herself thinking of the people back in Half Moon Bay.

For hours she tossed and turned, also thinking of her papa and Vasco.

When morning came, Delores announced that she wished her to accompany her to the salon. Elena had only an hour to get dressed. That didn't give her much time.

As she and the señora traveled to the salon, Delores surprised her. "You are going out to your first dinner party tonight," she said. "Deirdre will be going with you. It is at the home of the most respected lawyers in the city. Ricardo Gomez and his wife Margarita are a charming couple. Señora

Gomez is a tiny lady like you, so the gowns I've designed for you should interest her."

Margarita Gomez was one of her best clients and a woman with a definite taste for exquisite gowns. She was also a lady who spoke her mind freely and she had let Delores know she had not been pleased with Babette.

Delores felt that she would warm more to little Elena, and Deirdre had met with her approval, which made them the perfect choice for this dinner party.

Elena tried on three gowns before Delores made her decision and sent Elena back to the hotel. Delores told her, "I'll bring your ensemble when I leave the salon this evening. I want you to rest so you'll be fresh for this evening."

Miguel was waiting for her when she came out of the salon, for his mother had already given him instructions to get Elena back to the Towers before he delivered two finished gowns to the palatial homes of her clients. Besides her driver, Miguel was also her delivery boy.

By five that afternoon, he was back at the salon in the buggy seat waiting for Delores.

When he didn't immediately leap down to help her, she snapped impatiently at him. "Do you think you could stretch yourself and give me some assistance?" Her arms were laden with the gorgeous scarlet gown with the black lace flounces that Elena would wear that evening and a lovely emerald-green taffeta for Deirdre. From her safe, she'd pulled out her emeralds for Deirdre to wear and had chosen the black-jet dangling earrings and necklace for Elena.

Miguel said nothing, but a sneer was on his face as he took the gowns from his mother and placed them in the buggy. She waited by the side of the buggy for him to boost her up to the seat.

There was no conversation between the two of them as they went to the hotel. Delores was preoccupied and slightly nervous, but the Gomez dinner party seemed ideal for Elena's first appearance.

There was no question in Delores's mind that the girl was going to look stunning. Colette had already told her how she was going to style both young ladies' hair. Deirdre's hair would be fashioned in a sophisticated upswept hairdo which seemed perfect to display Delores's exquisite emerald teardrop earrings. Elena's thick long hair was going to be pulled back from her face to lie in soft cascading curls.

Miguel was disgruntled to find that he was hardly going to have time for dinner before he'd have to take the girls to the Gomez home. His mother had kept him hopping all day long, and his whole evening was going to be spent carting her girls around.

Two hours later, Delores was more than pleased with the appearance of the two young ladies. They both looked breathtakingly beautiful. There was a proud look on her face when she and Colette settled down in her sitting room to have dinner.

Colette had never known anyone with such a flair of fashion as Delores Delgardo. It was truly a God-given talent, Colette felt. Delores was just as pleased about Elena's manner, for she'd seemed not the least bit nervous about the evening.

"She gave me no hint of nerves," Colette concurred. "Not at all! I don't think you're going to have a thing to worry about tonight."

So Delores relaxed and enjoyed the dinner she shared with her old friend.

Elena was in the grandest spirits as she and Deirdre entered the two-story mansion. She was curiously excited as she stepped onto the plush carpeting in the foyer and was greeted by a myriad of twinkling candles. One had only to enter the home of Ricardo Gomez to see the opulence and grandeur, so Deirdre knew Elena had to be awestruck by all that her eyes beheld. Yet, Elena didn't seem ill-at-ease or nervous in the least about her first party at the Gomez's home.

Like Delores, Deirdre had been apprehensive about this evening since it was to be Elena's first night on an assignment. But she realized shortly after they entered the hall that she had no reason to feel concerned. Elena seemed perfectly at ease in the elegant foyer.

Deirdre had to admit that this little girl from Half Moon Bay amazed her and garnered her respect and admiration.

Nineteen

Margarita was so intrigued by the beautiful Elena that she personally took her around the spacious parlor to greet her guests. Later, Delores would be pleased to learn that Margarita had been impressed by girl and gown.

Deirdre and Elena moved in different areas of the room, answering the questions of ladies who wanted to know who had fashioned their gorgeous gowns.

When they entered the elegant dining room to be served a most delicious feast, Deirdre was seated at one end of the table and Elena at the other. Often during the meal Deirdre glanced across the room to see if Elena were handling herself well and was pleased to see that she was.

It was crystal clear to Deirdre that Elena had found herself a champion in Margarita Gomez. She had made a point of placing her close to her own seat.

Elena seemed to be enjoying herself for she was laughing and talking to the people on either side of her. Her relaxed air amazed Deirdre.

The smaller dinner parties were usually more sedate and dignified, lasting about another hour past coffee and dessert. There would be no music and dancing as there had been at the *soirées* Babette and Camilla had attended last night. They had not returned to the hotel until past midnight.

Elena spied Deirdre and gave her a big smile to let her know that she was doing just fine. But when she'd glanced down the long length of the table, a face looked very familiar to her. And that face was regarding her quizzically.

It was Carlos Mateo, sitting just a short distance from Deirdre. Elena hardly touched her dessert, and as soon as the group began to leave the table, she rushed to get to Deirdre. The model could see the rush of panic in Elena's eyes as they stood in a secluded corner of the long hallway. "What's the matter, Elena? You've been doing so well all evening."

"I've got to get out of here," she said. "I'll tell you later. Can Miguel take me to the hotel right now? I'll have him come back for you."

"Sure, honey. You do just that. Have him come right back, though, because this party will be over shortly," Deirdre told her.

Elena rushed for the front entrance, taking no time to say good night to her host or hostess. She boarded the carriage and told Miguel to take her to the hotel and then return to pick up Deirdre.

Miguel asked no questions. He was very aware that his mother had a different attitude toward the girl from Half Moon Bay than she had toward any of her other models. Elena seemed to be receiving special privileges and pampering.

To see Carlos Mateo had been very upsetting to her. How could she explain to him how she happened to be at this dinner party? She had no desire to face Mateo's brother this evening. She did not want to answer his questions. When she had met him at Golden Splendor a few weeks ago, she had been a guest invited to the festival, the daughter of a Portuguese fisherman. Now he had come upon her at the elegant Gomez party.

Elena rushed into the hotel and went directly to her room, and Delores had no inkling that she had arrived for she was still with Colette. She did not expect her girls for another two hours.

Deirdre had covered for Elena with their hostess, and Margarita had accepted her explanation that Elena had not been feeling well all day. Margarita had told her, "Oh, she was charming, Deirdre! I liked her very much. Tell Señora Delgardo I will be coming to her salon in a day or two, for I loved both her gown and yours."

Deirdre knew this would make Delores happy. The two gowns cost several hundred dollars. The señora told Deirdre, "Tell Elena that I hope she is feeling better and that I'm looking forward to seeing her again. I found her most delightful."

"I will, señora. I will tell you good night now and, as always, it was a wonderful evening," Deirdre told her graciously and turned to go out the door. Miguel was waiting for her in the carriage, and she was most anxious to get to the hotel and talk to Elena. She wanted to find out what had set her into such a panic when she'd been having such a grand time all evening.

She rushed through the lobby and up the stairs to the second landing. She would have knocked at Elena's door, but Delores came around the corner. Delores assumed that Elena had already gone into her room and that was just as well, for she preferred to talk to Deirdre alone about how the evening had gone.

"Come to my suite, Deirdre, and tell me how the dinner party went," she urged. So the younger woman followed her and sat on the settee.

"Was Elena a little shy around Señora Gomez's guests?" Delores inquired.

"Quite the contrary, señora. Margarita Gomez warmed to her from the minute she met her and took her around the parlor to introduce her to everyone. Elena has charm and grace," Deirdre told her.

"Ah, wonderful!" Delores smiled. "Well, you go get your beauty sleep. I will see you tomorrow."

"Yes, I think I will. Good night, señora," Deirdre told her, rising from the settee to leave. On her way to Elena's room, she realized that she should have told Delores about Elena's early departure, but this would have displeased the designer. She realized she'd protected Elena from a harsh reprimand, for Delores could be hateful when crossed. All the girls had experienced her tonguelashings at one time or another. Sooner or later, Elena would, too. But Deirdre wanted to spare her for awhile, if she could.

Oh, she had no doubt that the señora would find out about it. Miguel would mention it or Margarita Gomez would make an innocent comment. But Deirdre shrugged that aside for tonight. She'd face that later.

She knocked, and Elena opened the door. She was in her nightgown and robe. "Were you already in bed and asleep, Elena?"

"Oh, no, come on in. I was hoping you'd stop by. I felt bad about what I did. I know it was rude, but I just had to get out of there," Elena told her as she closed the door.

"You seemed to be having such a good time, Elena. What happened so suddenly to change that? Did you feel ill? That's what I told Señora Gomez when she asked about you. She liked you very much, I must tell you."

"I liked her, too, Deirdre. I'm not ill, nor was I earlier. I saw a man I knew. I realized that he also recognized me, I didn't wish to have to encounter him," Elena confessed.

"Would it have caused problems for you, Elena?"

"It could have. This man knows I'm from Half Moon Bay. I see no reason why I shouldn't tell you, Deirdre, for I consider you my friend. I ran away from home to come here with Señora Delgardo. My father would never have approved, so I just left him a note. But I didn't tell him whom I was going to be working for when I got here. I just told him in the letter that I had a job in Sacramento."

"I can understand now why you made your hasty departure, honey. Do you mind telling me who the man was?" Deirdre asked her.

"Carlos Mateo. Do you remember my telling you about Golden Splendor and the festival I attended there? He is the oldest son of the family who owns Golden Splendor."

There was a twinkle in Deirdre's green eyes as she asked her if this Carlos was the one she had spoken so fondly of. "Is the Mateo you talk about this Carlos? Is he the fire that sparks those black eyes of yours?"

Elena giggled. "No, not Carlos! It is Carlos's younger brother that I told you about."

"Well, chances are, Elena, you probably won't run into him at the next party," Deirdre told her.

"I can't be too sure about that. He is a lawyer here in Sacramento," Elena told her.

Deirdre explained to her that a lot of the gentlemen there tonight were lawyers because Ricardo Gomez was one of the most prestigious attorneys in the city. Before she left Elena to go to her own bedroom, she told her about meeting the señora in the hallway. "I didn't tell her that you left early this evening. Hopefully, she'll not find out, Elena."

But the amazing little Elena had a very simple solution. With a shrug of her dainty shoulders, she told Deirdre, "If she does, then I will tell her the truth."

Deirdre left for her own room with a smile on her face. She wondered if Delores Delgardo realized that she did not intimidate this fiery Portuguese girl from Half Moon Bay.

The señora was accustomed to having all of those who worked for her be in awe of her.

She had no doubt that Elena admired the señora and was excited by this strange new world she found herself in. But Elena was a spirited little thing who'd not allow the arrogant Delores to intimidate her. The following days could be most interesting, Deirdre thought, closing her bedroom door.

Seeing Carlos had jolted Elena, and she realized by the time she got back to the hotel that she'd been very inconsiderate of her father. She should have written a letter to him days ago. She'd been just too absorbed in what was happening to her.

She had been writing to him when Deirdre had knocked on her door. After Deirdre left, she got back on the bed, propped herself on the pillows and didn't dim her lamp until the letter was finished.

Delores left the hotel hours before Deirdre or Elena roused from their beds. By the time Delores closed her salon that afternoon she was a most happy lady. Margarita Gomez had come to her salon to order the gowns that Elena and Deirdre had worn the night before. She was also singing Elena Fernandes' praises. Before she could inquire about Elena and how she was feeling, another lady who had attended the party last night arrived wishing to order the lovely emerald-green gown Deirdre had modeled.

When Miguel drove his mother home that late afternoon, he could tell she was in a very gay mood and feeling generously disposed toward him. Giving him the evening off, she told him that she'd get Domino to take Babette and Camilla on their assignment for the night. This affair would probably have twice as many guests as the Gomez couple had had last night, but she doubted that as many gowns would be ordered tomorrow as she'd taken orders for today.

When his mother was this cheerful, Miguel could almost bring himself to like her.

Twenty

Carlos Mateo knew that he was not hallucinating when he sat at the opposite end of that long dining table and saw the beautiful Elena Fernandes close to Señora Margarita. What puzzled him was that she had been invited to the Gomez dinner and he wondered what had brought her to Sacramento. She was moving in an elite circle for the daughter of a Portuguese fisherman.

For the longest time after he returned home he pondered what might have brought about this turn of events. How could a young girl like Elena afford the exquisite gown she had worn? No lady had outshined Elena Fernandes at the Gomez dinner party tonight!

The Golden Splendor festival had been relaxed and carefree, very different from tonight. But Elena seemed to be perfectly at ease. He saw a grace and charm he admired in her. At the festival, she had impressed him as being a breezy, vivacious little señorita. She seemed lively and gay in the courtyard gardens at his folks' estate.

Tonight, she was more sedate and sophisticated. The Elena he saw beside Margarita Gomez he would be proud to escort to any social occasion.

Long after he'd crawled into his bed and his cat Amigo was curled up at the end of the bed, he thought about the Elena Fernandes he'd seen tonight. He'd always considered his mother Aimée the most beautiful lady he'd ever laid eyes on. But he had to honestly admit to himself that he'd seen a beauty whose loveliness matched his mother's.

He knew that one way or the other he was going to try to find out what Elena was doing here in the city. He hoped one of the young lawyers he'd become friends with might be able to enlighten him, for he could hardly inquire about her from Ricardo Gomez. He didn't know him that well and that was why he'd been so elated to be invited to their dinner party.

Tomorrow he was going to start trying to track her down.

If her mother and father had not noticed it, Markita Mateo had certainly been aware of the short-fused manner of her brother. Mark was not usually like this at all. For days, he'd not had a smile on his face. She had noticed it especially when the family had gathered around the dinner table in the evening. Oh, he was courteous with their parents, but he did not tease her as he usually did. This just wasn't like him. He was acting more like Carlos. Quiet and reserved was not Mark's usual manner.

She was convinced she was right that something was bothering him when they encountered one another in the stables the next afternoon. She was preparing to go for her usual daily ride as he was mounting his stallion to go to the vineyards. As she walked toward the stall where his horse was quartered, she teased him. "Boy, you're in a sour mood lately! Did you and pretty Elena have a lovers' spat?"

"Shut up, Markita," he snapped at her, fire blazing in his eyes. His harsh tone was so startling that she whirled around to look up at him as he sat on his horse.

"You're being presumptuous calling me and Elena lovers, Markita," he told her and spurred his stallion out of the stable.

Markita stood there, still stunned, for a moment before she moved on to the stall; but she was even more convinced now that it had something to do with Elena Fernandes. She'd definitely hit a sore nerve.

When she returned from her ride, Mark was leading his horse back into the stall. When she turned her horse over to the young stableboy, he called out to her, "Wait up, Markita, I want to talk to you before you leave." She knew one thing and that was that she wasn't going to endure any more harsh remarks from him. She'd just walk away.

Markita didn't know what to expect of Mark since he was in such a strange mood lately, but since he'd asked, she waited for him.

When he had his stallion secured in his stall, he came to join her and urged that they go to the other end of the stable. The two of them sat down on an old wooden bench and Mark apologized. "You didn't deserve my acid tongue, honey, and I'm sorry. It's not your fault that I'm in a foul mood. I wish to hell Elena and I had had a lovers' quarrel as you suggested. At least I'd know where she was."

A frown came to Markita's face and she stammered, "Where is she, Mark? Isn't she in Half Moon Bay?"

He felt free to talk to his younger sister. Probably it was because he knew that she so genuinely like Elena. There was a serious look on his face as he confessed to her that he'd not seen Elena on the last two trips he'd made to Half Moon Bay. "The first time I went there, I learned that Elena had gone to Sacramento. She left her father a letter saying she had a job there. He knows nothing else."

"No wonder you've been in such a black mood! I find all this hard to believe. Elena seemed so devoted to her family. I also got the impression that she was very taken with you. Why—what would have urged her to do something so foolhardy?" Markita pondered.

"I wish I knew, honey. And I wish I knew where in Sacramento she'd gone to work," Mark said.

His younger sister had only to look at the expression on his face to know that Elena Fernandes obviously meant much more to him than any other young lady he had courted. Her black eyes locked with his as she told him, "Mark, I think Elena was in love with you. So I speak now not as your sister but as a woman. I know we didn't get to spend much time together, but we talked openly with one another. She liked me and I liked her. So I ask you one question: Did you make promises to her that you didn't keep?"

"No, Markita. No, I didn't. I just didn't get to Half Moon Bay as soon as I told her I would—but damn it, you know why I didn't. I had to take over for father," he told her.

A parade of thoughts rushed through Markita's head but she didn't dare prod him. She appreciated that he had confided in her. Now she understood the torment he had been enduring.

"Take a few days off, Mark, and go to Sacramento. Maybe you could find her. You could always stay with Carlos," she suggested.

He smiled and bent over to kiss her on the forehead. "You are exactly right, and that is exactly what I have in mind. By the way, little sister, thanks for letting me talk to you. I needed to talk to someone."

"Anytime, big brother." She smiled up at him. But she turned very serious as she told him, "Mark, I always knew the girl you'd fall in love with would be exceptional. That's why I guess the first time I met Elena I thought to myself that she had to be the one. Don't let her slip away, Mark. Go to Sacramento right away. Father's fine now."

"You'll know what I'm up to, but I don't intend to be as frank with Father and Mother about this trip," he confessed.

Together they walked to the house and parted company at

the base of the stairs. Mark headed for his father's study, where he expected to find him, and Markita mounted the stairs.

It didn't surprise her when Mark was not at the dining room table the next evening, but she played her role as the inquisitive little sister. "Where's Mark?" she asked.

"He's gone to Sacramento for a few days, Markita," Mano told her.

"To see Carlos?"

"Yes, dear, that was what he said," Aimée told her daughter, but Aimée knew that something else was calling Mark to Sacramento. Mano shared her feelings.

Mark didn't linger long in Half Moon Bay or at Sebastian's cottage. It really didn't surprise him to learn that there was still no word from Elena.

"I'm going to Sacramento and I hope to bring you back some news. Maybe, if I'm lucky, I could be bringing your daughter back with me," he told Sebastian.

"God go with you, Mateo," Sebastian told him as they parted company.

Mark stayed the night in Half Moon Bay, but he was up at the break of dawn to start for Stockton. The second night he spent in Stockton. The next afternoon he arrived in Sacramento and went directly to his brother's home. Carlos was still at his office when Mark arrived, but Amigo obligingly kept him company in Carlos's comfortable parlor.

Carlos had a very nice home, Mark had to admit. His housekeeper seemed pleasant, and it was apparent that she kept his brother's house in a neat and perfect order, which he knew Carlos would demand.

Mark had been there about an hour when Carlos came

through the front door with his briefcase and saw his younger brother relaxing in his parlor.

"Well, Mark, this is a nice surprise. I trust everything is fine back at Golden Splendor and this is just a pleasure trip to the city," Carlos greeted him.

"Everything is fine, Carlos. Father is up now and back to his usual routine, so I felt free to have a few days away from home. I also have a little personal business to attend to. I hope you don't mind my impromptu visit."

"My family is always welcome in my home, Mark. Need I tell you that?" Carlos assured him. He laid his briefcase in one of the overstuffed chairs before going over to the teakwood liquor chest to pour them each a drink.

Once the drinks were poured, he sat down to have a leisurely talk with his brother.

"You've got yourself a really nice place, Carlos. I've had a chance to look around the house. Stella has already settled me into your guest bedroom, and I took a stroll around the grounds before old Amigo and I got cozy here in the chair," Mark told him.

"It's the perfect setting for me, Mark. I like it. Stella runs my house and has a good dinner prepared when I come home from the office. I enjoy her fine meal and then go upstairs to go over my legal papers."

Mark smiled. "It sounds like an ideal arrangement for a man getting himself established in his law practice."

"It's an all-consuming profession, Mark, but I love it. I know Mother and Father feel that it's time I thought about getting married. But I've no time for a wife right now, and I'd certainly not want the distraction of a crying baby in the evenings when I come home from the office." He laughed.

"No, that could distract a man from the quiet solitude you must need right now. Better stay a bachelor for a few more years, Carlos," he teased his brother.

"At least you seem to understand what I'm saying, Mark. Thanks for that." Carlos laughed.

The two Mateo brothers shared a pleasant evening that first night. Stella fixed a scrumptious dinner for them, and both Carlos and Mark raved about it when she served them dessert.

She had already sensed that Señor Carlos' brother had a bit more of the devil in him than the señor.

After dinner, they went back to the parlor to have an after-dinner liqueur and talk some more. That next hour was enlightening to both of them.

Carlos explained to his brother, "You know, Mark, it pained me not to step into father's shoes as I'm sure he wanted, but Golden Splendor was his dream and he realized its fulfillment. I could not pretend to be enthused about the vineyards or winery for the feeling was not there. I wasn't interested in growing grapes, so I would have been no good at it."

"Then you have nothing to fault yourself for, Carlos," Mark told him.

"Yet there is no man I admire as much as I do our father."

Mark told him that he shared his feeling, but he also confessed, "I can't tell you, Carlos, that I will be able to settle for just the winery and vineyards. I don't feel that strongly about them right now even though I'm working there with father to help out where I can. I've yet to find my calling," he admitted.

Remembering that Carlos usually went upstairs to work at his desk after dinner, Mark concluded their talk. He certainly didn't wish to disrupt his brother's routine, and they had already sat in the parlor long over an hour since leaving the dining table.

So Mark suggested that Carlos work on his papers, for he had had a long day coming all the way from Stockton. "I've the need to get to the comfort of a bed. Stella's good dinner and your fine liquor have made me ready for a good night's rest. I'm going to tell you good night."

"I hope you sleep well, Mark. I'm glad that we had this opportunity to have a private time to talk. I don't think we've ever really talked before. It was long overdue, Mark," Carlos declared.

Mark, who had always been able to display his feelings and emotions more easily than Carlos, gave his older brother a warm embrace as he told him, "I agree. I think we both understand one another much better after tonight." Carlos dimmed the parlor lamps as Mark headed for the stairs.

But Mark didn't dim the lamps in his room or go to bed for over an hour. He sat plotting where he would start his hunt for Elena in the morning. It was going to be like hunting for a needle in a haystack.

Twenty-one

Had Carlos known that Mark's reason for coming to Sacramento was to search for Elena Fernandes, he could have saved him the futility of the next day. But although their conversation that evening had revealed their most intimate feelings about themselves and their desires in their lives, the subject of Elena Fernandes never came up. Carlos never thought about mentioning that he had seen her. At least, he could have sworn it was Elena sitting at the opposite end of the table.

A few days after the dinner party, Carlos had inquired of his lawyer friends about the striking young lady that all of them remembered but none of them knew anything about. So Carlos's very practical nature deemed that he put the idea of tracking her down aside. His analytical mind told him that she spotted him and recognized him just as he'd recognized her. But she'd not sought him out after dinner.

Everything he had observed that evening had convinced him that Señora Gomez was very fond of little Elena. It appeared that a warm friendly relationship existed between them, but Carlos questioned how this could have come about. He even speculated that Elena could be Margarita's relative, for they both possessed the same dark, sultry beauty.

It was only after he'd been in his bedroom at his desk working for about an hour that he remembered the strange incident, so he promised himself that he'd mention it tomorrow to Mark.

Carlos had left the house just a short time before Mark emerged from his bedroom to go downstairs. As soon as he'd enjoyed the hearty breakfast Stella had fixed for him, he embarked on his impossible quest.

For the next eight hours, Mark hit boardinghouses and hotels. He also went into the shops and stores lining either side of the streets, but no one seemed to know anything about the girl Mark Mateo described to them.

He was tired and angry, for he knew he could do this for days and still not find her. His first stop had been at the courthouse, where he learned that there was no Dorothy Dansworth listed as owning property in the city. That bothered him. Although he still believed she was the woman who'd promised Elena a job, no lady by that name owned a shop or store in the city.

Traveling down the street toward Carlos's house, he thought that if he should spy Elena right then, he'd yank her into the buggy, turn her over his lap, and spank her soundly. That was what the little minx deserved!

Carlos hadn't had as hectic a day at his office, so he managed to go home earlier. He was already there when Mark returned from his futile search.

As they had the night before, the two Mateo brothers had an enjoyable prelude to dinner. Carlos said, "I trust you took care of the business you came to Sacramento to attend to."

"It is all taken care of, Carlos, so I'll probably be heading back to Golden Splendor the day after tomorrow. Do you think you could put up with me for that long, big brother?"

Carlos laughed. "I'm going to try my darnedest!" In a more serious tone, he told his brother that he had enjoyed the time they'd had together. "The truth is, I wish you'd come up to Sacramento way more often, Mark. We weren't very close when we were growing up, but maybe that could change now."

By the time they'd shared the dinner that night, indulging themselves on the delicious roast beef Stella had prepared, Mark was telling himself that he'd never really given himself a chance to get to know his older brother.

Mark was amused by Carlos's devotion to his furry cat. He watched Carlos place some of his roast beef in a saucer to set beside his chair so Amigo could enjoy it, too.

"I don't recall your having such a fancy for cats when we were growing up, Carlos," Mark remarked.

"I didn't. Amigo was just an accident that happened when I least expected it, shall we say. It was right after I'd gotten settled here in Sacramento. One of the lawyers in my firm had a wealthy client who died, and her Persian cat had three of the cutest kittens. So Edmund had to place this family of cats. Like me, he's a bachelor, but his mother took the mother and one of the kittens. His lady friend took another kitten, and he talked me into taking old Amigo here. I can't say I've ever regretted it."

Mark realized that Carlos had a far more generous nature than he'd imagined. He could also be caring and loving, for it was obvious that he loved Amigo.

Amigo accompanied them to the parlor after dinner. There was no doubt that the cat considered himself a member of the family.

When Carlos had served him an after-dinner liqueur and settled down in his chair, Mark asked him if he ever took a night away from his cozy nest to go to any of the social affairs in the city. "I've always heard that Sacramento has some grand balls and elegant events. After all these months you've surely been to a few, being the up-and-coming young lawyer you are, Carlos."

"I go to a few." He smiled. "You've got to remember that

I was never the charmer you were at social events around the estate. I never had your way with women." It was at that moment that he remembered Elena Fernandes.

"I don't know that I was that much of a charmer," Mark was commenting when Carlos interrupted him.

"I must tell you that I got quite a shock at the last social affair I attended. Señor Ricardo Gomez is one of the most respected lawyers in the city and certainly the wealthiest. He and his wife had a dinner party, and I felt very honored to be invited. I've been told they have a very select list of guests."

"You have a right to feel smug, Carlos. Obviously, your name had been mentioned in most glowing terms to this respected lawyer, Gomez, for you to have received an invitation to his home for a dinner party," Mark reasoned.

"But that was not my surprise, Mark. The surprise was to see Elena Fernandes there. I remembered her as the little Portuguese girl, the daughter of the fisherman in Half Moon Bay. But there she sat at the long table in the most exquisite gown you've ever seen. She was stunning, Mark! She and Margarita Gomez seemed to know one another. Señora Gomez was talking with her constantly, and Elena seemed completely at ease in this very sophisticated setting. So you can see why I was stunned," Carlos told him.

Now it was Mark who sat in a state of shock as he listened to his brother. In a hesitant voice, he asked, "Are you sure it was Elena, Carlos?"

"As sure as a man could be, but I have to admit I didn't speak to her. I meant to, but when the dinner was over and the guests were leaving the table, I lost sight of Elena. I didn't see her the rest of the evening, and I didn't know Señora Gomez well enough to inquire about her," Carlos told him.

Like Carlos, Mark's head was whirling with questions.

How would Elena know a woman like Margarita Gomez, the wife of a wealthy lawyer in the city? How would she possibly have acquired such a fancy gown as Carlos had described? The Elena Carlos had seen at the elegant dining table was sophisticated and assured. The Elena he knew and loved was a delightfully innocent, naive girl, the daughter of a Portuguese fisherman who didn't move in Sacramento's social circles.

Carlos told him, "Well, I could not go to the Gomez home and inquire of Señora Gomez about Elena."

"I understand your position, Carlos," he said, but he was thinking that there was nothing to prevent him from calling on Margarita Gomez.

Sleep didn't come easily for Mark that night for he sat in his room planning to seek out Margarita Gomez and make discreet inquiries about Elena Fernandes. When his shrewd, cunning mind sparked with a good idea, he was finally ready to dim his lamp and go to bed. Then sleep came swiftly.

Carlos had already left his house the next morning by the time Mark crawled out of his bed. But once he was up, he moved hastily.

He'd not wanted to ask Carlos last night where the Gomezes lived, but he knew if he were a prominent lawyer in the city then he'd have no problem obtaining that information.

A half-hour after he'd left Carlos's home, his high-stepping bay was pulling his gig up the long drive of the Gomez's palatial estate. He had only to observe the grounds and the impressive two-story mansion to know that the family lived luxuriously. It was also obvious to Mark that Ricardo Gomez was as proud of his Latin heritage as his father, Mano, was.

He saw the magnificent courtyard gardens and the lavish grilled iron railings on the second-floor balconies and the entranceway.

He had thought he knew how to approach Margarita Gomez, but now that he had arrived, he was no longer sure. It was going to depend on his impression of the lady when he met her. Once he met her, he'd make that decision.

He was ushered into the house by one of the servants and guided into the elegant parlor. The young servant-girl excused herself to summon the señora, who had not come downstairs yet. Her dark eyes had taken time to survey the finely attired young man and note that he was very good-looking. She had never seen a more handsome hombre in her life, she thought as she left the parlor.

The sight of him had set butterflies fluttering in her stomach, and her heart beat faster as she climbed the winding stairway.

Margarita Gomez was not a lady who roused from her bed early in the morning. Ricardo left the house to go to his office long before she left the bed. So when the servant girl announced to her that she had a young gentleman in her parlor wishing to speak to her, Margarita went downstairs dressed in her satin dressing gown of jade green. Her thick hair was pulled into a huge coil atop her head. On her ears were the earrings she always wore except when she and Ricardo were having a special party. They were the gold hoops that Ricardo had bought for her when they were a young married couple struggling to earn enough money to keep a roof over their head. She cherished those earrings.

Often they laughed about the luxury they now enjoyed, for the two of them had never forgotten those lean, hungry years. Margarita had always felt that those memories kept the two of them thinking properly as Ricardo climbed the ladder of success in Sacramento. She had known Ricardo when he was an uncertain young man about to begin his career.

When she descended the stairs and came to the parlor

door, she hesitated for a minute to scrutinize her guest. She could understand why little Rosa's eyes had twinkled; he was a very handsome young gentleman, but she didn't know him.

But she certainly recognized the name, Mateo. Who in California would not know that name and the fine wines from Golden Splendor?

For years, their cellar had housed Mateo wines. Her husband had been intrigued to learn that Mano Mateo's son was now practicing law in Sacramento and that was why he had been invited to their dinner party. Ricardo wanted to meet him. The reports he had received on him were glowing. Now Margarita was about to meet another Mateo. She had to say that Mateo men were very handsome.

When Margarita Gomez made her appearance in her parlor, Mark rose from his chair to greet her. Her dignity demanded respect.

"Señor Mateo, please be seated," she urged him.

"Señora Gomez, I appreciate your seeing me. I know that it is presumptuous of me to call on you when you don't know me, but I have to talk with you."

Margarita ordered the young servant girl to bring them some coffee. "Will you join me?" She motioned for him to sit down.

"I never turn down a cup of hot coffee." He smiled at her. "As I told your servant, my name is Mark Mateo and I come from the Valley of the Moon region. Are you familiar with that part of the state, señora?"

"Oh, *sí,* I am. It is very picturesque. And I recognize the name Mateo, señor," Margarita declared, but she was still not too alert and needed a cup of coffee.

"My father owns Golden Splendor. He is a vintner. Perhaps, you may have drunk some of his fine wines, señora," Mark said.

"My husband has several bottles of Mateo wines in his

cellar right now." The servant served the coffee, and Margarita took a couple of sips before she asked, "Now, you have me most curious as to why you wished to talk with me. Please, tell me señor."

"I seek information about a young lady who attended your dinner party a few nights ago. My brother Carlos was one of your guests that evening, and he told me that he saw Elena Fernandes here."

"Ah, so Carlos is your brother! It was my first time to meet him, but I hear from my husband that he is a very impressive young lawyer. Ricardo is always interested in young men like your brother who show promise."

Margarita had a talent for making people around her relax and Mark was no exception, although he had been apprehensive about encountering her this morning.

Mark smiled. "I hear that Señor Gomez is the best lawyer in Sacramento."

Margarita gave a soft laugh. "Well, I naturally think so. But now let us talk about Elena. I trust she is in no trouble, for I found her a little charmer and liked her instantly. I met her the night of the party, but I liked Elena very much. Unfortunately, I can tell you little about her."

Mark warmed to Margarita as she'd warmed to Elena. He decided to be frank.

"As far as I know, Elena is in no trouble," he quickly assured her. "She just has a father who is very concerned about her, señora. You see, I am a friend of the Fernandes family and Sebastian has not heard from her since she left Half Moon Bay. I don't have to tell you that she is very young to be away from her family. I promised him I would see what I could find out while I was here in Sacramento visiting my brother."

Margarita told him, "I think that is very nice of you, señor.

So am I to assume that her father didn't know she was leaving Half Moon Bay?"

"No, he did not know. She left only a note saying she was coming here for she had a job," Mark told her.

"Well, then I *can* help you. She works for a Señora Delores Delgardo, who owns a fashionable dress salon and has very beautiful young ladies like Elena wear her exquisite gowns and attend parties like mine the other night. For Señora Delgardo, it proves to be profitable, for she always gets orders for her lovely gowns. She is a grand designer. Her gowns are outstanding. As a matter of fact, I ordered both of the gowns Elena and Deirdre modeled," she confessed.

Mark laughed. "I know how ladies love their fancy gowns, for I have a mother and a sister."

"I trust that now you will be able to go back to Elena's father with some news to lighten his heart. I can understand a parent's concern about a daughter. Elena is so young and so beautiful. Now I can't tell you where Elena lives, but you will be able to find Delores Delgardo at her dress salon every day. She can certainly tell you."

"Oh, señora, I am so beholden to you. You've given me something to go on. I was wondering how I was possibly ever going to find her. I looked all over this city for eight hours yesterday."

A few minutes later, Mark rose and thanked her graciously again for her hospitality and time. She walked with him to the door. She told him, "It is a pleasure to have met you. Tell your father how much we enjoy his fine wines."

"I shall, señora. I hope we meet again," he told her, his violet eyes looking deep into hers.

"Oh, I think we will, Señor Mateo." She smiled up at him.

She remained at the entrance until he had boarded his gig and left. She was pondering as she went back inside if this young man was inquiring out of duty to her father or was his concern for himself and the beautiful Elena?

One thing she did know and that was that she'd never met as handsome a young man as Mark Mateo since the day she'd first laid eyes on Ricardo Gomez when he was this young man's age.

She couldn't wait to tell Ricardo about her visit with Mark Mateo.

Twenty-two

From the Gomez home, Mark went in search of the Delgardo salon. It took only two inquiries to get the directions he needed. The first gentleman he asked didn't know the location of the salon, but the first lady he stopped knew exactly how to direct him.

The minute he entered the salon he was approached by Selina, a very attractive young lady who quickly learned that he wished to purchase nothing. She was so spellbound by the gentleman towering so close to her that she committed the unpardonable sin as far as Delores Delgardo was concerned: She told him where Elena resided.

Delores had a strict rule about letting the public know where her girls lived. Selina had been told that, but she'd only been working for Delores for two weeks. She became a babbling idiot when she was face to face with Mark Mateo.

After the handsome Mark Mateo went out the door of the salon and Selina was no longer under the spell he cast with those devastating violet eyes, she realized she had given him information she'd been forbidden to divulge. The rest of that afternoon she was a nervous wreck; if the señora found out, she would surely lose this job she needed so badly.

That late afternoon she walked home distraught, and all the rest of the evening she wondered if she'd be met at the salon by a very irate Señora Delgardo.

* * *

Mark entered the lobby of the Towers Hotel and walked directly over to the desk clerk to inquire about the room number of Elena Fernandes. He was hardly prepared for the clerk's indignant manner. In a sharp retort, he was informed, "I don't give that information out, sir."

Mark was not accustomed to such resistance and he bristled. But the firm, determined look on the clerk's face told him that nothing was going to make this young man waver.

"I am an old friend of Elena's. I didn't realize that she was denied visitors. Apparently, this hotel has strange rules," he snapped, turning on his booted heels, and walking away as if he were going to the front door.

But he didn't leave the lobby. He moved discreetly into a secluded corner to take a seat and light up one of his cheroots.

Miguel had chanced to be close enough to hear Mark's inquiry and the clerk's refusal. He wondered why the man did not leave. Elena's "old friend," he noted, was a formidable figure with an unmistakable arrogance. To Miguel, this man spelled trouble. His face reflected his irritation at being refused Elena's number.

Miguel watched him for awhile before he started to saunter around the lobby like a strutting peacock. With his robust physique, Miguel Delgardo could also intimidate.

But he made no such impression on Mark, who merely took a deep puff on his cheroot and smirked. So warned, Miguel decided to let his mother worry about this man. It meant nothing to him one way or the other, and he saw no reason to fret about it.

So he walked past Mark and went to the back of the hotel. After all, this hotel and the salon was his mother's domain. He merely worked for her.

The longer Mark sat, the angrier he got. He wasn't going to let some little desk clerk deny him the opportunity to see Elena now that he'd gotten this far.

So he marched back to the desk to inquire of the desk clerk when Señora Delgardo was expected back. He was told that she usually arrived at six. Giving a shrug of his broad shoulders, he remarked to the clerk, "I guess I'll just have to speak with Señora Delgardo if Señorita Fernandes can't receive a guest. I didn't know she was kept a prisoner here at the Towers."

The clerk became flustered by his accusation. "What are you saying, sir? Señorita Elena is no prisoner here."

"Well, perhaps I got a wrong impression. Señora Delgardo will be able to enlighten me, for if I leave this hotel right now then I'm going to wonder what kind of hotel this is," Mark declared. His deep voice could clearly be heard by the other guests sitting in the lobby.

The desk clerk was getting more upset by the minute. He stammered, "I just carry out Señora Delgardo's orders, sir."

"Well, you tell Señora Delgardo that I'm sitting right over there when she comes in, because I intend to talk to her," he said, and he turned to take a seat very near the desk clerk's counter.

The clerk noticed that Mark had a perfect view of the front entrance as well as the desk clerk's counter. But there were those late afternoons and early evenings when Delores Delgardo came through the back entrance of the hotel. Clarence, the clerk, wondered if this was what she'd done tonight.

Mark was not a man who gave up easily, and he sat there idly for another hour. But the only people who came through the front entrance were some gentlemen and a couple of ladies. He was certain that neither of these little ladies was Delores Delgardo.

By the time Mark guided his buggy into Carlos's drive it

was almost eight. He knew his brother would be wondering what in the hell had happened to him. Mark knew one thing and that was that he was famished. Carlos had had his dinner well over an hour before and was probably already up in his bedroom looking over legal papers.

But when Mark went through the front door, Carlos and Amigo were sitting in the parlor. "God, Mark, where—what caused you to be so late?"

"It's a long story, brother, and I'll tell you all about it as soon as I've eaten. Do you suppose I could invade your kitchen to get some food to put in my belly?"

Carlos told him he'd have Stella warm something up, but Mark insisted that he not disturb her and followed Carlos into the kitchen. Stella was no longer there.

Carlos smiled. "Hey, the coffee is still hot. Let's see what's left on her cupboard shelves." Two pieces of peach pie, four pieces of fried chicken, and a half-loaf of baked bread looked like a feast to the starving Mark. He poured himself a cup of the hot coffee and filled his plate with the chicken. He spread two pieces of the sliced bread generously with butter.

Ravenous, Mark began to eat. Amigo's nose had smelled the impromptu meal, and Mark felt two paws on his leg, so he pleased the cat by dropping him a little piece of the chicken. By the time he'd eaten the peach pie he was sated.

He and Carlos went back into the parlor to share a nightcap, and Mark told him about his long and puzzling day. He still didn't have the answers, but he vowed that he would before tomorrow was over.

He told Carlos about the visit he paid to Señora Gomez and he quickly noted the stunned look on Carlos's face. He realized that Carlos would probably not have been so bold, but he quickly soothed his apprehensions. "She was most gracious and kind. We had a very nice chat. She told me where I could find out about Elena." He told Carlos that Elena worked for Señora Delgardo.

"So that was how little Elena was welcomed into the Gomez home," Carlos remarked.

"That's right. This Señora Delgardo's lovely girls model her creations at fancy dinner parties like the one Señora Gomez had. The ladies see and admire her exquisite designs, and she reaps a harvest," Mark told him.

"So that also explains the expensive gown I saw Elena wearing. It wasn't hers at all. It was the property of the salon," Carlos commented. He'd finished his drink and decided to have another, for he sensed that Mark had much more to tell him.

Carlos was as perplexed as his brother about the unconventional procedure at the Towers Hotel. He didn't like the smell of it if he had to be honest, but he said nothing to his impulsive brother. Carlos could tell from the way Mark was talking that he wasn't about to be denied an audience with Elena before he left to go back to Golden Splendor.

"Do you know anything about the Towers, Carlos?" Mark asked.

"There was a time when it was considered one of the grander establishments in the city; but, of course, that is not true today. Finer accommodations have been built, but I think it is still considered a nice hotel in a good part of the city. I have to admit that I find the situation you encountered very strange," Carlos told his brother.

"I've got a lot of question marks where this Delores Delgardo is concerned. I have to ask why she used a false name in Half Moon Bay," Mark remarked.

"There is only one reason for any person to use an alias, Mark, and that's because they don't want their true identity known. Now, what are you planning for tomorrow?" Carlos quizzed him for he knew his brother well enough to know he had something in mind.

"I'm going to that salon, and I'll see Delores Delgardo one way or the other. Before I get back here tomorrow, I will see Elena, too," Mark vowed, and Carlos never doubted that he would. Mark was a stubborn hombre when he set his mind to a task.

The two of them said good night, and Carlos wished him good luck tomorrow.

It was a busy day for Delores Delgardo. She had to get to her salon and gather the accessories to complement the gowns Elena and Deirdre would be wearing to the garden party at the Crauthers' country estate. Since this was early compared to most of the affairs her girls attended, Delores couldn't wait until five-thirty but had to send everything to the hotel by Miguel no later than one this afternoon.

Delores didn't really care for Clarise Crauthers, but the woman did spend money lavishly in the salon. She was a pain to work with. Delores had the feeling that she was vying with Margarita Gomez to establish herself as the grand hostess in the city, and her husband was probably the wealthiest gentleman in Sacramento.

But Margarita Gomez had a grace and charm that came naturally and Clarise had to work to project that same image. She still didn't manage to do it even with all the money her husband spent on her fancy gowns and their lavish country estate.

When Clarise had come to the salon, she had specifically asked that the two young ladies who'd been at Margarita's dinner come to her garden party. Delores had assured her that this could be arranged.

Delores chose dainty little white slippers to go with the

lovely lavender gown she'd selected for Elena. It had a low-scooped neckline edged with white lace and Delores chose pearls for her jewelry.

For Deirdre with her fair hair, she picked a robin's-egg-blue gown. That seemed to be a very popular color this season. Deirdre had such enchanting eyes. When she wore green, her eyes were like emeralds; in this gown, they would take on a bluish-green hue.

At mid-morning she had Miguel load the finery in her buggy to take to the hotel. She told her clerk Meredith, "I don't care who comes in this morning asking for me, Meredith; I'm not in the salon. Do you understand?"

"I understand, señora," Meredith told her. She had been with Delores the longest of any of her clerks. She often played the role of buffer for the señora.

Delores went directly to her office and closed the door to spend the next two hours at her desk.

When Mark Mateo entered the salon, he was graciously greeted by Meredith, who had only to survey his expensive attire to know he was a wealthy young gentleman.

"I'll talk with Señora Delgardo about what I wish to purchase," he announced to the woman.

"The señora will not be back to the salon until one, señor. If you would tell me what you wish, then maybe I could help you," she offered.

"No, I must speak with the señora. I wish to order three gowns and a variety of accessories for my lady, and I was told by my good friend Margarita Gomez that the señora would be most accommodating. I leave the city this afternoon, so I have no time to waste. I'll just have to go to another dress salon and tell Margarita that I didn't find Señora Delgardo available to help me," Mark lied convincingly. Meredith's eyes brightened, and she told him in a syrupy, sweet voice, "Oh, señor, you be here at one and the señora will see you immediately, I assure you."

It was interesting to Mark how the clerk's attitude had changed when he'd mentioned Señora Gomez's name. He felt no qualm of conscience, for he was weary about getting the runaround. Being a Mateo, Mark was not used to this kind of treatment.

He wasn't in the best mood when he came back to the salon at one. The first person he encountered was the young lady who'd been so talkative the day before, but she acted a little reserved this afternoon. He'd arrived a few minutes before one.

But the young clerk let her guard down when Mark purchased two reticules and three soft, wool shawls. Once again, the girl became enchanted by the handsome man who spent his money so freely and he learned from her that Elena was to attend a tea at the Crauthers' estate this afternoon at three.

He could have left then, but he wanted to meet the señora to satisfy himself about other things which were troubling him.

While he was paying for his purchases, a nervous Meredith came rushing up to him. "Señor, I did not see you come in. I trust Selina took good care of you."

"She did. Now may I see Señora Delgardo, for I've no more time to waste here," he told her with a most arrogant air.

"Come with me, señor," Meredith urged him.

Mark found himself being led to the back of the salon to Delores Delgardo's office. She was just finishing the lunch she'd had brought to her so she wouldn't have to interrupt her work.

Delores was curious about the young man Meredith had told her would be coming back this afternoon at one. Meredith had described him in glowing terms as a most aristocratic-looking gentleman. Meredith's expert eyes recognized fine materials when she saw them, and she told Delores, "His attire was fine-tailored, señora, and he wore a white, linen shirt. He had class, señora."

When Meredith ushered Mark into her office, Delores found that Meredith's description had not prepared her for the man she now saw standing before her. He had the busiest eyes, and she knew they were scrutinizing her carefully. Those eyes were not black; nor were they a deep blue. They were violet. He had a proud, self-assured manner.

"Please, sit down, señor, and tell me what I can do to help you make a selection of gowns for your lady," Delores said in her most charming way. Mark had to admit that she was a particularly attractive middle-aged lady. She was fashionably dressed—as he had expected her to be.

He sat in the chair in front of her desk, and his piercing eyes looked straight into hers. A devious grin spread across his face. "I've no gowns to buy, señora. It is a young lady I seek. That young lady is working for you, and I intend to see her come hell or high water for her father is very concerned about her."

His manner and intimidating air were enough to unnerve the sophisticated Delores. "I've several young ladies working for me, señor. Which young lady do you wish to see? I'm sure it can be arranged," she told him.

"Oh, I will see her, señora, and I'm sure you must know it is Elena Fernandes. She didn't have her father's permission to come here to work for you, and I need not tell you that Elena is very young."

Everything about this young man cried out that he was trouble, Delores told herself. "I—I assumed that she had her father's permission when she left Half Moon Bay to come with me, señor. How could I have known otherwise?"

The woman lied and Mark knew it. He also knew that he

had made her very nervous, for her eyelashes fluttered and her hand was fidgeting with the papers on her desk. "I am very protective of the girls working for me, señor, and I think you will find that Elena is very happy here."

"So is that why I was denied the chance to see her at the Towers Hotel yesterday, señora? Is she not allowed to see a friend if she wishes?"

"I do not allow the girls to have young men come to their rooms at the hotel. That is for their protection."

"That I can understand, señora. But I'm not *any* young man. I am Elena's friend, as well as her father's, so I shall see her one way or the other. Where is she this afternoon? My time in Sacramento grows short."

Delores was not used to the inquisition he was putting her through. "She is on an assignment, señor, and she won't be back at the hotel until late afternoon."

"Then there is nothing to stop me from coming to the hotel this evening to take her out to dinner. I intend some private time with her, and I'm a little too old for a chaperon."

By now, Delores had become vexed by his arrogance. "That will have to be Elena's decision, señor. I will leave word with my desk clerk that you are to be sent to my suite at seven," Delores said.

Mark rose from the chair and smiled down at her. "I'll see you at seven, Señora Delgardo, but I'll not accept that Elena will refuse to see me. You might as well know that right now."

She watched him leave her office; and, even though he'd pressed her to the limit of her patience, she found herself admiring his forceful, masterful way.

She knew that there was nothing she could do to stop this young man from meeting Elena, for he meant exactly what he said. He was going to see his lady.

Part Three
Fernandes' Fury

Twenty-three

Delores sat at her desk for the longest time thinking about her encounter with Mark Mateo. She was asking a lot of questions about some of the things he'd said to her. She had to wonder just how intimate his friendship was with the beautiful little Elena. He was a most compelling man; and, since he'd stated that he and Elena were *very* good friends, the experienced Delores wondered if Elena were as innocent as she looked.

The other question prodding her was how he'd found out so much in such a short time. How had he known to go to the Towers? Delores was curious about this shrewd young man; he had surely charmed someone who'd revealed all this information about her.

She would never have suspected Margarita Gomez, and if she had known that her own clerk had been indiscreet, Selina would have been without a job that afternoon.

Miguel's carriage was taking Deirdre and Elena out to the Crauthers' estate about the same time Mark finally had his audience with Delores Delgardo. The girls would change into the gowns they were to wear for the tea after they arrived at the estate, and they had an hour before the tea was scheduled to begin.

As the carriage rolled along the countryside, Deirdre

sighed, "God, I'll be glad to get this over with this afternoon. I detest this woman. Be prepared, you'll not be meeting a lovely Margarita Gomez. Clarise Crauthers is a haughty bitch who treats you like her hired help. But she spends a lot of money with Delores so that's all that matters to her."

"I don't imagine it will last long since it's an afternoon tea, will it?" Elena asked.

"No, and thank goodness for that. We should be getting back to the city by five."

"And we will have time to prepare ourselves once we arrive?" Elena asked.

"Ah, yes. We'll be shown to guest bedrooms to don our pretty gowns before we start our little stroll in Clarise's gardens to mingle with her guests."

Elena laughed. "I can tell you aren't looking forward to this afternoon."

Deirdre told her she'd done these little teas before for Clarise. "She is the worst snob, Elena; yet her husband is the nicest gentleman. You might have met them at the señora's party. But the difference between the two ladies is simple. Clarise was from the poor part of town when she married Carter Crauthers. All his wealth and power went straight to that frizzy red head of hers. What in the world attracted him to her, I'll never figure out."

She told Elena that Carter Crauthers might well be the wealthiest man in Sacramento. But Clarise's frustration had always been that she could not manage to be the Grand Dame of Sacramento's elite society. Deirdre declared, "And she'll never be able to dethrone Margarita Gomez."

"Why would that be so important to a lady?" Elena asked her.

"To Clarise it is, but it really isn't to Señora Gomez and that is why she is so relaxed and more charming. Should you meet her in the salon, she would be as warm and friendly as she was at her dinner party. But Clarise Crauthers might look right through you if she passes by you," Deirdre told her.

So Elena had a vivid description of the lady she would be meeting this afternoon. She strongly suspected that she would be of the same opinion as Deirdre.

When they arrived at the estate, a servant ushered them into the house and they met with Clarise Crauthers for a brief moment before they were dismissed and shown to their rooms to change.

That brief meeting with their hostess was enough for Elena to see what Deirdre had been talking about. She found her a plain woman. Her only pretty feature was her flawless, gardenia-white complexion, but her frizzy red hair would have driven Colette crazy. Her blue eyes had no sparkle in them.

She had a pear-shaped figure which her fancy garden party frock couldn't conceal. The few weeks she'd been with the señora had taught Elena something about fashion and color. She saw that Clarise Crauthers' gown did not flatter her.

A servant guided them to one of the guest bedrooms upstairs; and as soon as the door was closed, Elena told Deirdre, "Señora Crauthers should never wear that color with her bright red hair!"

Deirdre giggled. "So, you see what I was talking about."

By the time the two of them were dabbing toilet water behind their ears and on their wrists, several carriages were rolling up the drive of the country estate.

Looking out the window, Elena exclaimed, "It looks like the whole city is coming out here! It must be a grand affair."

"Oh, you can bet anyone who is anyone will be here this afternoon. At least, they will have been invited," Deirdre told her.

Elena noted the sarcasm in Deirdre's voice when she said, "Well, come on, honey, let's go perform our little act."

"I'm ready if you are," Elena replied. Deirdre didn't have much zest this afternoon. She seemed preoccupied.

While they were going down the carpeted hallway toward the stairs, Elena told her how beautiful she looked. "I bet that gown gets lots of orders once the ladies see it this afternoon."

Deirdre shrugged her shoulders. "The truth be told, Elena, I couldn't care whether it sells or not, for it makes me no more money. Señora Delgardo is the only one who reaps that reward. Remember that, honey."

Elena was sure now that something was bothering her and she wondered if she and the señora had had a disagreement.

That clash had not happened yet, but Deirdre knew it was coming soon. She was sick of this life she'd been living for a little over a year now. She was tired of never having any time for a life of her own. She was young, and yet she saw her youth slipping away without any time for courtship.

You could hardly have a beau, for you were always at the beck and call of Delores Delgardo. You weren't a prisoner at the Towers Hotel, but in a way you were.

Unlike Camilla and Babette, she'd rarely taken advantage of the discount on ensembles she'd worn, and the two gowns she'd bought had not been flamboyant. She must warn Elena about this so she wouldn't end up spending a whole week's wages on one of these so-called discounted designs she was wearing.

Deirdre had convinced herself that if she worked in a bakery or shop she would have regular hours with her evenings free. The entire Sunday would be hers to do as she wished.

But when Elena arrived and Deirdre saw how sweet and innocent she was, she delayed her departure. The more she'd gotten to know Elena and they'd talked for endless hours, the more she felt the need to protect her a little longer.

Elena had told her about her life and history in Half Moon

Bay. So Deirdre also understood why Elena would have been very receptive and vulnerable to Delores's persuasive charms.

Because of Elena, Deirdre had decided to give Delores one more month of her life. But Deirdre knew that sooner or later Elena would start to feel as she was feeling lately—that she was wasting her life here. She was too young and beautiful to want to settle for this life week after week and month after month.

Today during that very brief period she had for some time to do as she pleased, she had dropped in at a little hat shop. She and the owner, Lisette Simone, got to talking and before she left, Deirdre had been offered a job. Lisette had told her that her shop was doing a thriving business and the ladies were clamoring for her unique chapeaus. "I need a hclper, Deirdre. I can't keep ahead of my orders lately. If it would be any incentive to you, there are living quarters at the back of the shop. I occupied them myself when I first opened the business."

To Deirdre, it was the answer to everything she was looking for. She wanted to say yes right then and there, but she asked Lisette if she could have until the end of the week.

"I will hold the job open for you, Deirdre, because I like you and your appearance. I could have hired two or three young ladies, but they weren't what I was looking for," Lisette had told her.

Deirdre had walked back to the Towers Hotel in the highest of spirits that afternoon. But she had had less than an hour to rest before the Crauthers' affair. So her mind was not really on the event; her head was whirling about the possibility of the job at the little hat shop.

* * *

At the appointed time, Deirdre and Elena descended the stairs to the gardens.

Some of the gallant gentlemen accompanied their wives, but a lot of them hadn't come. Men usually didn't enjoy these afternoon teas as they did the dinner parties in the evening. So there were always more women at Clarise Crauthers' social gatherings than men.

Deirdre had come to the conclusion that Clarise chose the afternoon instead of the evening to have her social gatherings because pre-dinner events didn't last as long. This was to her liking. Actually, parties were ordeals that Clarise would have preferred to not have to endure but was forced to for her husband's sake.

The beautiful sight of Deirdre and Elena descending the stairs was observed by Clarise's son, Carter Junior, and his guest, Tyler Lee Barton. Carter Junior's eyes were focused in on the beautiful Elena, but Tyler Lee swore that Deirdre had to be the golden-haired goddess he constantly dreamed about meeting one day.

Deirdre spotted Carter Junior and his ogling friend, and she whispered to Elena, "Be prepared, Elena. You're going to be meeting Clarise's son. I guess he's home from his college back East. Looks like he's brought a friend." She'd met Carter Junior before, and she found him as obnoxious as his mother.

Carter Junior's father was a dignified gentleman, well-mannered and quiet. Deirdre deduced that it wasn't from his father that Carter Junior had inherited his manners. It was from Clarise.

Deirdre and Elena were escorted around the gardens for the next half-hour by Carter Junior and Tyler Lee. Deirdre was growing very irritated by Tyler Lee, for she knew exactly what he had on his mind and he was preventing her from speaking with the ladies about her gown. She had to get away from him. "You'll have to excuse me, Tyler Lee," she said, "but I see a couple over there I must speak with." She didn't wait for his response, quickly dashing into the milling crowd. She didn't stop moving until she reached the opposite side of the vast gardens.

She knew that she'd left Elena at the mercy of Carter Junior, but if she were to keep working for Delores Delgardo she was going to have to learn to shift on her own. This afternoon was a good time for her to start.

The tea had been going on an hour and Elena had not been free of Carter Junior at all. Clarise sat at a table with her friends, smiling proudly when they asked about the lovely lady Carter Junior was with. But she mentioned nothing about Elena being there to model her gown. She just casually commented, "Yes, Elena is a very lovely young lady." Without any further explanation, Clarise moved on to the next table.

Elena kept searching the garden area for some sign of Deirdre, but she saw only a sea of faces unknown to her. So she endured Carter Junior and prayed the next hour would quickly pass.

She was a little riled that Deirdre had left her with two such boring young men as Carter Junior and Tyler Lee. She had reached the limit of her patience, so she rose from the wrought-iron bench to announce to Carter Junior, "It was very nice to meet you and you, too, Tyler Lee, but I must leave you now. I was sent here to display this gown. I fear the two of you have been a distraction." She smiled so sweetly down at them that they couldn't be offended, and they watched her petite figure disappear into the throng.

In the next few minutes, Elena stopped and talked to three ladies who were generous with their compliments about her lovely, lavender gown.

A short distance away, Deirdre saw that Elena had finally freed herself from the two leaches.

As Deirdre had done when she had left the three of them, Elena went to the other side of the garden. She was pleased to see some people get up from the tables to leave. The long dull afternoon was finally coming to an end.

Elena sank onto a bench. She was feeling disappointed that she'd not seen Señora Margarita. She'd surely been invited, but she'd not seen her lovely face in this sea of people.

Twenty-four

Mark Mateo had no intentions of waiting until seven that evening and going first to Señora Delgardo before he could see Elena. Who the hell did this woman think she was? It was insulting, and he'd not tolerate her laying down such rules to him.

He had all the information he needed to find Elena, so he got into his buggy and tossed the purchases he'd bought into the seat beside him. He had no problem in getting directions to the Crauthers' country estate. He had time to stop at a tearoom and have a leisurely late lunch.

While he ate, he thought about Elena. He could understand that her pretty head would be whirling in this new, glamourous world. Life back in Half Moon Bay must seem very dull compared to this. There was no question in his mind that Señora Delgardo wanted to control Elena's life. His innocent Elena would not be aware of her manipulation, for the lady was cunning!

He'd watched her face as they'd talked and knew she resented very much that he was determined to see Elena alone. No, she didn't like him at all.

When he pulled his gig up the drive of the Crauthers' country estate, he could see that a vast crowd had gathered. But he also noted that a couple of the carriages were leaving.

Some of the ladies observing him entering the gardens wondered why they'd not seen this finely-attired gentleman earlier. He drew many admiring glances. But Mark's eyes were busy scanning the crowd for the sight of Elena.

Deirdre had seen Elena finally sitting alone and was preparing to join her when her green eyes noticed Mark Mateo entering the garden. She, too, stared and appraised this paragon arrogantly swaggering over the grounds.

She had no way of knowing that this was Mark Mateo, but she knew he was one handsome devil so she stopped just to watch his fine male body move along the walkway. He seemed to know exactly where he was going, and he marched up to the bench where Elena was sitting. His hands reached out to Elena, and she took them. Suddenly he whisked Elena out of the gardens, his right arm snaking around her waist and his other hand holding hers, guiding her through the crowd.

Instinctively, Deirdre knew that he had to be the one Elena had talked to her about. That had to be Mateo. She smiled, for once again she knew she was going to be left to finish up another party by herself.

He'd merely told her when he held out his hands to her, "You're coming with me, Elena. We've some talking to do."

Elena had been so stunned by the sight of him that she could not find her tongue to speak or protest. Breathlessly, she discovered herself being rushed to his gig. She could hardly keep pace with his long striding steps. Twice she stumbled on her lavender gown, but Mark's strong arm was around her waist.

Finally, she found her voice and glared at him. "Mateo, you're acting like a madman. I'm going to tear this gown."

He scooped her into his arms. "I can remedy that, *chiquita.* Yes, I am a little mad, for I've had a devil of a time getting to you. You've not been easy to track down, Elena Fernandes," he told her as he put her on the seat of his gig. Then, he wasted no time leaving the estate.

Her heart was pounding wildly at the sight of him and secretly she was more than pleased that he had been trying to track her down.

Once he had the gig rolling down the dirt road, his deep violet eyes darted angrily toward her and he asked, "Do you realize, Elena, that you are a prisoner at the Towers? I wasn't allowed to see you yesterday. Señora Delgardo controls your life."

Elena looked at him, perplexed and puzzled. She stammered, "I—I do not understand what you are saying, Mateo. You—you came to see me at the hotel and were not allowed to come to my room?"

He saw the confusion on her lovely face and he mellowed. His arm went out to pull her closer to him and he told her, "We'll talk later, *chiquita.* I'm taking you to the hotel and no one will tell me I can't take you to your room—neither that wimp of a desk clerk, nor the lordly Señora Delgardo."

Right now, nothing mattered to Elena, for his strong arm was around her and she was content to snuggle close to him and let him talk. He told her how he'd promised Sebastian he would try to find her when he came to Sacramento. "He's been very concerned about you—as any father would have been."

"I wasn't happy about leaving as I did, Mateo, but I knew Papa would never approve and I didn't want to tell him where I would be working. Knowing Papa, I was afraid that he would come here and cause trouble. I—I felt I had a right to do this for myself. I figured if it didn't work out, then I could always go back home. Was there anything so wrong in that?"

"I suppose not, Elena. But what about me? Didn't I deserve more from you? Did the night of the festival mean so little to you?" His deep violet eyes pierced her reserve and she saw his anger.

But her own temper flared. "I had to assume that it meant nothing to you, Mateo, and you'd forgotten about me. I waited and waited, but you never came as you had promised," she snapped back at him.

"Oh, Elena, it wasn't that I didn't want to. My father was injured and I had to take over for him at the winery and vineyards for the next three weeks. When I was finally able to leave Golden Splendor to come to you, it was the very day that you ran off with Señora Delgardo. I was waiting at the cottage when your father and Vasco got home. I thought maybe you'd gone out on your father's fishing boat for the day."

He told her that he'd been in the kitchen when her father had read the note she'd left on the kitchen table. Elena began to feel like a small child who was being reprimanded for being naughty.

There was a very sober look on his face. "You should have had more faith in me, Elena," he told her. "I meant every word at Golden Splendor. Remember that from now on."

She sighed. "Oh, Mateo! I'm glad you found me."

He mellowed when she snuggled closer to him on the buggy seat. "I'm glad I found you, too, little Elena."

She was about to ask him how he had found her, but they were entering the city and a short time later they pulled up to the Towers Hotel.

He grinned at her. "This time I'll take you to your room."

"Of course, you will come with me. I wish to know all the news about Papa and Vasco. I wish to hear about your family. I—I think about that glorious festival more than you might realize," she told him while he leaped to help her out of his buggy.

His hand was still holding hers when they walked into the lobby and passed Clarence at the counter. When he saw the two of them heading for the stairway, he called out to her, "Señorita Elena, you know you're not allowed to take a gentleman to your room."

She gave him a pretty smile and shrugged her dainty shoulders. "It's all right, Clarence. Señor Mateo is an old friend of mine."

Mark didn't say a word, but he couldn't resist giving the fidgeting Clarence a smug smile when his pretty Elena kept going toward the base of the stairs with him striding by her side.

Clarence returned to his counter shaking his head in despair for he knew the señora was not going to like this. But there was nothing he could do to stop that big strong fellow.

As she and Mark climbed the steps, she asked him, "And Papa—is he all right?"

"He seems to be, Elena. He still makes his daily runs out on the bay. I guess I can't tell you anything more than I already have. He has been anxious about you—as he had a right to be," he told her.

By the time they'd reached the second landing and entered Elena's bedroom, Mark had no desire to talk about his family or hers. He flipped the lock to insure their privacy.

She had moved slightly ahead of him as they'd entered the room, and he called her with a luminous glint in his deep violet eyes, "Come to me, Elena *mía*."

Quickly, his strong arms enclosed her and his head bent down to capture her lips. She responded to his kisses with such fervor that Mark knew she was as hungry for him as he was for her.

"I've missed you—missed you so much," he murmured huskily in her ear.

The two of them were intoxicated by the same magic

they'd discovered on the night of the festival. There was no night's darkness, but the drapes of her windows were pulled and her bedroom provided as much privacy as the gazebo had.

With a sheepish grin on his face, Mark told her not to worry about anyone coming in the room for he'd secured the door. Elena laughed. "Oh, Mateo, what a devil you are!"

"I know, but tell me you love me anyway." He smiled at her.

"I surely must, Mateo," she murmured. His hands caressed her, causing a liquid fire to move through her petite body.

He scooped her up in his arms and carried her to the bed, removing the fancy lavender gown. Mark ridded himself of his clothing, and she felt his body searing her flesh. Her arms reached up to encircle his neck, urging him to make love to her for she was flaming with passion.

His eyes danced over her face, impassioned now by her wild desires, and he heard her gasps as she pressed even closer to him. Now they were fused together, and a blazing inferno consumed them.

She could feel the fierce pounding of his heart in his broad chest as he cried, "Oh, yes, *mi vida!* Oh God!"

It took some moments for the two of them to calm from the ecstasy they'd shared. Mark was the first to rouse from the bed, for he wasn't sure how long they'd get to enjoy their private paradise. He had no doubt that that beady-eyed desk clerk had run as fast as he could to Señora Delgardo.

As soon as he had his shirt and pants on, he sat down to yank on his boots. Elena lay languorously on the bed, but Mark gave her a gentle nudge. "Come on, you little minx, don't lie there to tempt me again, for I've a need to talk to you."

She rolled over to look at him. Her eyes were as soft as

black velvet. "Wasn't making love better than talking, Mateo?"

He smiled. "I could hold you in my arms forever, Elena, and never tire of it."

She finally left the bed to gather up her undergarments and the lavender gown, hanging it up as she told him, "I like you to hold me in your arms."

"And that is one of the reasons we must talk, *mi vida*. I must leave for Golden Splendor tomorrow by midday. Do you think you can be ready to leave by then?"

She had taken one of the gowns from her personal wardrobe out of the armoire and was fastening the bodice. He reminded her that she had no loose ends to take care of here. All she had to do was pack up her belongings; he'd pick her up in his gig the next day at noon.

Elena didn't answer him for a minute, for she had to be sure what he was proposing, so she sat on the chair to slip her feet into her leather slippers.

She laughed. "Just a minute, Mateo, you're hitting me too fast. You say you're leaving for Golden Splendor tomorrow. Are you asking me to go with you?" His answer meant everything to Elena. If he said he wanted to take her back there to become his wife, she would eagerly accept his proposal immediately.

Her back was turned to him as she picked up a slipper. She was glad.

"Of course, honey, I want you to come with me tomorrow. Why do you think I tracked you down? I want to get you back to Half Moon Bay where you'll be with your father where you belong. This place isn't for you, Elena."

At first, she'd grimaced, dejected, but that feeling was quickly replaced by resentment. She managed to conceal her disappointment when she turned in the chair to look up at him and said, "I—I do not wish to return to Half Moon Bay and my father's cottage yet, Mateo. I—I like working for Delores Delgardo."

Her declaration stunned him. He had assumed that after their passionate lovemaking she would agree to accompany him back to Half Moon Bay. His usual clever thinking was clouded or he would have realized what she was trying, in her simple way, to tell him; but he stood there baffled.

Then he became indignant. "Well, Elena, this lady you say you like working for is a fraud and sooner or later you will find that out. For your information, she registered under a fake name when she was staying at Half Moon Bay and enticed you to leave there. You think about that."

She saw the anger on his face. "I'll remember all you've told me, Mateo," she told him in a calm, cool voice.

"I'll be at Carlos's home until midday if you should change your mind, Elena, but I'll be damned if I'll come back here. It goes against my nature to put up with what I've endured at this hotel and from Señora Delgardo," he told her as he moved away. But before he got to the door, there was a sharp rap and Elena heard herself being summoned. She knew the voice; it was the señora. So she rushed ahead of Mark to turn the lock.

Delores Delgardo marched into the room, her eyes glaring at Mark Mateo. He'd outfoxed her, and Delores didn't like that at all. Like a snake she hissed at him, "A little early, aren't you, señor?"

He smirked, seeing before him a woman who was trying her damnest to stay in control and not doing a very good job of it. "I didn't wish to wait that long, señora. I'm an impatient man who doesn't like being told when I can do something." He turned to Elena. "You see," he said, "the señora told me I'd have to check with her at seven before I could see you. So don't tell me you're not kept a prisoner here at the Towers."

His intense eyes darted back to Señora Delgardo, and he went through the doorway. He turned a deaf ear to Delores's shriek, demanding that he wait just a minute.

Too much was happening too fast for Elena. She was suddenly left alone with Delores Delgardo, and Mateo was gone.

But Elena was not as shaken as Delores was. That arrogant young man had made accusations about her, and she worried about their impact on Elena.

Yet, she was completely out of patience with Elena, who had dared to disobey her strict rules about men in her room.

She turned her rage on Elena, and Elena discovered a different woman from the one she'd thought was so nice. "You know my rules, Elena, and you disobeyed them."

"I know your rules, señora, but Mateo is no ordinary man. He is a family friend and he brought me news of my father."

Delores was in a very irate state. "Family friend or not, Elena, I am the boss at the Towers and my rules will be obeyed."

"Mateo lives by no one's rules but his own, señora. He is the son of Mano Mateo. You surely have heard of the winery of Golden Splendor. Mateo's father owns that," Elena told her calmly.

Now it was Delores who was confused, wondering how the daughter of a simple Portuguese fisherman had managed to capture the eye of the son of one of the wealthiest men in California. Obviously she had. That young man had been hellbent to see Elena, and he'd succeeded.

Common sense told her that she'd best drop any further discussions with Elena tonight. She had some thinking to do. The Mateo family was far too powerful for her to do battle with.

"We'll talk tomorrow, Elena," Delores told her and abruptly left the room.

The whole fiasco had taken its toll on Elena, and she flung

herself across the bed to allow her tears to flow. Her mind was a muddled mess, and she was feeling very uncertain about everything.

Twenty-five

From the far end of the garden Deirdre had seen the handsome, dashing man whisk Elena away. She'd flown to the front entranceway to see the two of them in a buggy, rolling down the country road.

For the second time, Deirdre realized that Elena had done a disappearing act. Once again she was left alone to finish the party.

When she had said her farewells to the Crauthers and was ready to board the carriage, she had to wake the sleeping Miguel who'd been napping.

"Where's Elena?" he wanted to know.

"She left early," Deirdre said, offering no more information. She didn't care for Miguel. He gave her a chill anytime she was around him.

"Mother is not going to like that," he muttered.

"Well, that's between your mother and Elena, isn't it?" Deirdre remarked.

To her great delight, she was not forced to have any more conversation with Miguel as they traveled back into the city, for it was a very short trip from the Crauthers' estate.

She reminded herself that she'd have to tell Elena that after her departure the tea became very dull for Carter Junior so he and Tyler Lee suddenly disappeared from the gardens.

The closer they got to the hotel, the more anxious she was

to seek out Elena to learn what had happened at the Crauthers' tea party.

When they arrived at the front entrance of the hotel, Deirdre did not wait for Miguel to help her out of the carriage. That arrogant bastard was too lazy to make the effort. None of Delores's polished grace and charm had rubbed off on him during the years he was growing up, Deirdre had decided long ago.

She gave Clarence a fast nod as she made her way to the stairway. Once on the second landing she went directly to Elena's room before she went to her own. She gave a rap on the door and called out. Elena told her to come in for the door was unlocked.

Elena wiped the tears from her eyes, but Deirdre knew instantly that she had been crying. Her heart went out to her, for she looked so childlike sitting on the side of the bed. Deirdre rushed over to her to give her a sisterly embrace. "What's the matter, honey? You've been crying. I saw that good looking son-of-a-gun dragging you out of the garden. Did he hurt you?"

"Oh, no, Deirdre, Mateo would not hurt me. He—he was just mad at me for leaving Half Moon Bay without telling him I was coming here. He's a family friend," Elena informed her.

"Well, aren't you the lucky one! God, he is a handsome devil! I think I envy you, Elena Fernandes." She laughed, bringing a weak smile to Elena's face.

"So why the tears, sweetie?" Deirdre quizzed her.

"He was determined we were going to talk, and so he brought me back to the hotel. Clarence tried to stop us, but Mateo is not a man who takes orders from a desk clerk."

"I think I like this man, but go ahead. What happened, then?"

Elena did not mention the sweet interlude they'd shared

making love. "I told him I wasn't ready to go back yet, Deirdre," she said. "I like what I'm doing here. There's not much to do back there, and I've lived there all my life. I've enjoyed being in this completely different world of Sacramento. Do you know what I mean?"

"I understand. I really do, Elena," Deirdre told her. But she also knew that Elena would have been wiser to have left with the handsome young man who wanted to take her back to her father's home in Half Moon Bay. Then, Elena described the scene that had taken place with Delores. "Oh, she was very angry with me for bringing Mateo to my room and because I left the tea early. It didn't seem to make any difference to her that Mateo was a family friend who'd come here from the valley to look for me. He promised my father he would try to find me, for Papa was concerned."

"You are a lucky girl, Elena, to have a father who worries and a good friend like Mateo. Remember that, honey. Most of us don't have anyone who gives a damn," Deirdre pointed out.

"I guess I am lucky, Deirdre. Tonight I'm not in good favor with Señora Delgardo, though." Elena sighed.

"Don't worry about her. All of us have had the sting of her wrath. Sooner or later, it was bound to happen to you, too. Now you know that she can be a bitch when she doesn't get her way. Always remember that," she warned Elena. She had very definite reasons for trying to make an impact. Since Elena had not wished to leave with her friend, she was going to be left to deal with the señora on her own. Deirdre had prolonged her departure as long as she could if she wanted to take that job at the hat shop.

"I'll tell you what, honey. You go wash those red eyes of yours while I get out of this fancy gown. I'll go down to the dining room and have a dinner tray sent up to the room. How does that sound to you?"

Elena was most agreeable to Deirdre's suggestion. She had no desire to go downstairs tonight.

Elena's remarks haunted Deirdre as she rushed down the hallway to her room. She'd told her that she didn't know what she'd do without her, but Elena was going to have to learn.

Deirdre cared very much for Elena and she felt a deep concern for her, but she had to get on with her own life. She could not pass up this job at the hat shop to remain with Elena.

Later, when the two of them had shared their dinner trays, she prodded Elena to talk about Mateo. To Deirdre, he had seemed like a shining knight coming to rescue his lady love.

Had she known that evening that he had given Elena an ultimatum, she would have encouraged her little friend to forget this silly, shallow existence and go back with him to her Half Moon Bay home. But Elena didn't tell her that.

It was almost midnight when they said good night, but Elena was in better spirits. That late night, had Elena known of Deirdre's plans to leave the Towers Hotel and Señora Delgardo to go to work at the hat shop, it might have influenced her to go to Carlos's home the next day to leave for Half Moon Bay. But Deirdre didn't tell her of her own plans.

Deirdre was hardly ready to face Delores Delgardo the next morning at such an early hour to be quizzed about the Crauthers' tea party.

Deirdre knew exactly why she was asking certain questions, and she tried to protect Elena. "I'm sure you'll be receiving some orders for gowns, señora. Señor Mateo did not appear until the party was almost over, so Elena was not gone that long. Now the real distractions were that pest of a son of Clarise's, Carter Junior, and his friend Tyler. Elena and I had to tolerate the two of them for the first hour. We couldn't rid ourselves of them." Deirdre did not care that Delores might be hearing things she didn't want to hear.

Knowing that she had a new job to go to, Deirdre was feeling very free to express herself as she'd yearned to do often in the past.

Deirdre's frank, straightforward manner left Delores with no more questions to ask her. Long ago, Delores had determined that Deirdre had a touch of class that Camilla and Babette didn't have.

She also found herself curious when Deirdre mentioned to her, "I found it surprising that Señora Margarita Gomez did not attend the affair."

"Margarita doesn't find afternoon teas that interesting, and she and Clarise have nothing in common. If it were not for Carter, they would never be invited to the Gomez's dinner parties," Delores told her.

Delores left her room in a seemingly good mood and Deirdre was glad of that. Deirdre felt that she had probably protected her little friend for the last time.

Mark and Carlos had said their farewells that morning before Carlos left for his office. Carlos understood his brother's black mood, for he was not used to being refused by young ladies. Obviously, Elena Fernandes had a mind of her own and was just as headstrong and stubborn as Mark. While he didn't agree with Elena's decision to remain with Señora Delgardo after all Mark had told him about her, he had to admire the spirit of this young lady. His younger brother had finally met a woman who would not bend so easily to his will, and that was probably what intrigued Mark so much.

That last evening after dinner, Carlos felt that it was not a night for conversation. He excused himself shortly after dinner to go to his bedroom, leaving Mark with his troubling thoughts. They'd had some nice, chatty evenings during Mark's visit and Carlos was grateful for those talks.

Amigo also seemed to sense his unpleasant mood that last evening, and he followed Carlos up the stairs to stay with him. For the next hour, Mark drank his brother's fine cognac and thought. It was as if Elena had firmly slapped him across the face this late afternoon when she'd announced that she was not leaving with him.

He was cussing himself and Elena as well. He'd never allowed any woman to get to him as she had. This whole thing was very confusing to Mark Mateo. It still had not dawned on him that all the words of endearment he'd whispered in her ear had not included marriage and that she would have been going back to the same life she'd left behind. She wasn't ready to settle for that.

For the beautiful Elena, the dull quiet solitude at her father's cottage hung too heavily on her. She cared nothing about associating with the other fishermen's wives to listen to their endless chatter or hear their screaming babies. She didn't want any of the Portuguese fishermen's sons coming to call on her. She'd known all these young men all her life, and none of them interested her. They never had.

No man until Mateo had ever excited and titillated her.

The next morning was a tense one for Mark. After Carlos left, Mark went up to the guest bedroom to pack his bag.

He'd gone into Stella's kitchen to tell her goodbye and thank her for all the good meals she'd fed him. Stella had told him, "You come again soon to see your brother, Señor Mark. It was a pleasure to have you here."

"Thank you, Stella. I will be here to pester you again one of these days." He grinned.

The clock struck twelve, and Mark knew that he should get in his buggy to leave. Elena knew the hour he'd told her.

But he paced the parlor, delaying his departure another half-hour. Fierce Mateo pride demanded that he wait no longer. She was not going to come, he told himself.

So he climbed into his buggy and guided it down the drive onto the main road.

But his heart was heavy as he traveled to the outskirts of the city. Although he could tell Sebastian Fernandes that he had seen her, he was disappointed that she wasn't sitting on the buggy seat beside him.

He had time to think as he drove to Half Moon Bay. He recalled the tales about his Grandfather Mateo and his wife, who was also Portuguese like Elena. Theirs had been a most tempestuous courtship. Was this the way his and Elena's love affair was destined to be?

Once he arrived at Half Moon Bay, he took Sebastian the news of his daughter, but he didn't linger at the cottage.

He was still in a foul mood. His patience had been taxed to the limit and his male ego had been dented, but he tried not to show it when he told Sebastian that he had seen her and that she was fine.

"She would not come with me, sir. It seems she doesn't wish to return here yet, so that's about all I can tell you," Mark confessed.

Sebastian smiled weakly. "So I guess we wait, eh?"

Mark gave him no answer. He was not a man to wait for anything or anybody. As much as he adored her, he'd not wait endlessly for her to suddenly decide to return.

A sadness washed over both Vasco and Sebastian as they watched Mark leave their cottage. Vasco remarked to his father, "I've got a feeling we may not be seeing Mateo for awhile, Pa."

"I fear you're right. Your sister is a fool!" Sebastian told his son. He turned to go back into the house. More than ever, he was baffled by Elena's actions. She'd always been such a levelheaded girl. Now she'd taken leave of her senses.

Sebastian and his husky son went into their kitchen to prepare their dinner. Vasco was not a person to express his innermost feelings. He usually kept them to himself. But tonight he seemed to feel the need to speak to his father. "Papa, I still find it very hard to understand what Elena did. I thought I knew her so well, for I took care of her after our mama's death. But I find it hard to forgive her for what she's done, leaving us as she did. It—it hurt me, Papa."

Sebastian had only to look up at Vasco's rugged face to see the sincerity there and the hurt he felt. "I know, Vasco. Believe me, I know." Vasco was as wounded as Mateo was, Sebastian suspected.

He feared that Elena would be paying for her impulsive, irresponsible ways.

Deirdre could not delay any longer telling Elena about her plans to leave, for she wanted her to hear it from her and no one else. She'd kept a very careful tally, and as of tonight she owed Delores Delgardo nothing. She had one week's wages to collect from the señora. This afternoon she had walked over to the hat shop to be sure the position was still open before she had her talk with Delores.

Lisette was thrilled and announced that she could move in tomorrow if she wished. That was all Deirdre had to hear to go forward with her plans.

Elena was devastated by Deirdre's announcement. "Oh, no, Deirdre! I can't imagine going out with anyone but you. I've never gone out with Camilla or Babette," Elena moaned.

"Oh, Elena, honey, I know. I put this off for over a month after you arrived because I like you. This has not been a hasty decision. I've been plotting this for over two months.

I want more out of life than I've gotten here. Maybe you'll start feeling the same way, Elena. My life was not my own. It belonged to Delores Delgardo."

She told Elena where she would work and live. "I'll have Saturdays and Sundays off to do what I wish, and this sounds wonderful to me, Elena. I might even find time to have myself a beau." She laughed.

Elena was quiet and thoughtful for a few minutes while she listened to Deirdre. "Perhaps, I was a fool, Deirdre, to have not gone home with Mateo. He gave me until noon the next day to make up my mind. He let me know that he would not be coming back to the Towers. He told me to come to his brother's house if I wished to go home with him. Now, I wonder if I should have gone to Carlos's the next morning," Elena confessed.

"Oh, Elena! I wish I had known this. I would have urged you to pack up that night and go over there the next morning," Deirdre told her.

"Well, it's too late for that now. Mateo is on his way back to Golden Splendor, and I am here," Elena replied.

"If you ever get desperate about leaving here, you can always come to me, honey," Deirdre tried to comfort her.

"I'll remember that, Deirdre," Elena said.

Nothing was the same after Deirdre left the Towers Hotel. Delores Delgardo was in a foul mood because she needed to replace Deirdre. She was forced to pair Elena with either Camilla or Babette, and this arrangement was not working at all.

It became obvious to Elena that Babette and Camilla made dates with gentlemen they met at the *soirées* for late night rendezvouses. Elena realized that neither of them liked her. But neither did she care for their ways, so it was very strained when Elena and Camilla were sent out together. However, when Camilla was away from Babette and her influence, her manner was different.

As days went by, Elena became more miserable and especially lonely with Deirdre not there to talk with. But she did remember what Deirdre had warned her about, and she didn't buy any of the gowns. She spent very little of her wages and put her money in one of her reticules in the drawer.

As the holiday season approached, Elena's depression deepened and she found her thoughts straying back more and more to Half Moon Bay. She'd never been away from her family at Christmas. She couldn't imagine not being at the cottage with Vasco and her father.

Elena wasn't her usual vivacious self when she attended the social affairs, and she was in a blue mood the night she was assigned by Delores to accompany Babette. After they'd returned to the hotel, Babette smirked as they walked down the hallway toward their rooms. "Did the cat get your tongue tonight? I don't think I saw you talking with anyone. You acted bored to tears. Señora Delgardo isn't going to be pleased. If she gets one order for your gown, she and you are both going to be lucky."

"And I'm sure you will delight in telling her, eh Babette?" Elena asked her curtly.

But she didn't wait to see what Babette would reply, for she had reached her door. She turned to go in and locked the door behind her.

As Elena expected, Babette tattled to the señora. But Babette didn't have to tell her anything for Delores to know that Elena's gowns had not been selling well. But Delores needed Elena far more than Elena could have realized. She had yet to replace Deirdre and without Elena to model her gowns, sales would surely have decreased even more.

She knew she'd been cold and aloof with the girl lately

so, being the shrewd cunning businesswoman she was, Delores decided that she might try being sweeter to her.

When Babette noticed how syrupy sweet the señora was around Elena the next day, she was shocked. She didn't understand Delores at all. She had expected an opposite reaction.

But Delores had more than one reason to be nice to Elena. Señora Gomez had come to the shop to request Elena and Deirdre for a holiday party she was going to be having at her home in two weeks.

When Delores told her that Deirdre was no longer working for her, Margarita chose Camilla to accompany Elena.

"It is a shame that you lost Deirdre. She seemed to be a very nice young lady. I can tell you right now, señora, that I don't care for your girl Babette," Margarita told her candidly.

"I understand, señora, so it will be Elena and Camilla I'll assign to your party," Delores assured her.

Delores went to work immediately on the gowns for the two girls. For Camilla with her dark, sultry coloring, she decided on a bright scarlet dress. Elena would wear a brilliant emerald-green gown and with it she would wear Delores's treasured teardrop emerald-and-diamond earrings.

For the first time in days, Elena seemed excited about her assignment, which pleased Delores.

When Elena went into the salon for the final fitting, Delores was elated. She swore this had to be the most beautiful gown she'd ever designed. On Elena's tiny figure it was sheer perfection!

Elena exclaimed, "This is the loveliest ensemble yet!"

That was enough to make Delores swell with pride. She knew of no one more honest than Elena, so her ego soared. Almost childlike and gushing, she declared, "Oh, Elena, I'm so delighted to hear you say that. I thought it to be an out-standing gown."

"And it is, señora."

Elena did not realize it, but she had won Señora Delgardo back to her side and was once more in her good graces. Delores was as sweet as honey when she and Elena were together, as she had been when Elena first arrived in the city.

Seeing this, Babette was incensed and her resentment for the little Portuguese girl heightened. She was infuriated when Camilla innocently remarked that she and Elena had been assigned to Señora Gomez's dinner party.

Poor Camilla was perplexed when Babette directed her fury at her. She couldn't understand why her friend was so angry with her, but when she asked why, Babette's response was a cold glare. Turning her back on Camilla, she walked out of the room.

Camilla, puzzled, had no inkling what she'd done wrong.

Twenty-six

It had been a very happy time for Deirdre at the hat shop. Lisette spent a lot of time teaching her how to trim the merchandise with flowers, ribbons, and veils; and Deirdre liked the challenge each little hat represented when she prepared to go to work on it.

Lisette told her, "I will teach you how to trim them, but I want you to create your own lovely hat. That's what makes this so satisfying and special, Deirdre; it is your creation, not mine. Don't be afraid to be a little daring if you wish."

She was restrained at first and tried to pattern her trimming after Lisette. But lately she had been stretching herself and Lisette was praising her work.

Deirdre liked the routine of the day at the shop. Sometimes she helped customers, and Lisette continued to work in the back room.

It wasn't a constant flow of ladies, so there was always time for her or Lisette to go back into the kitchen to brew a fresh pot of coffee. Sometimes they sat at the little wooden table to share lunch together, and other times they had to eat in shifts.

No day was ever the same. Some mornings Lisette would bring a pie or cake she'd baked the evening before. At least a couple of mornings during the week, Lisette would drop into the bakery down the same street to pick up a half-dozen cinnamon rolls for them to munch on.

Lisette was an easy-going person, the atmosphere at the shop was relaxed. She was not tense like Delores Delgardo or fiery.

When they'd finished their day's work on Saturday, Lisette went to her own apartment to enjoy her next day puttering around her place catching up on things like cleaning. She'd been tempted to invite Deirdre over the first weekend for dinner on Sunday evening, but she thought maybe it was better that she allow Deirdre to have a day away from her to do whatever she wanted.

That first weekend was rather strange to Deirdre and yet, it turned out to be a very pleasant afternoon. She wore a simple long-sleeved, sprigged-muslin frock. Atop her head, she wore a wide-brimmed hat with a band and streamers of deep green which matched the deep-green background of her muslin gown.

For over an hour she roamed first one street and then another. To her surprise, she came upon a lovely park just a few blocks away from Lisette's shop.

It was a dear place with little walkways and benches. Many young couples strolled in the mild California weather, and flowers still bloomed profusely. Elderly people seemed to enjoy sitting on the benches to watch the squirrels scampering around. One old gentleman had brought a bag of breadcrumbs to feed to the birds flying down from the branches of the many trees.

Deirdre told herself that next Sunday she was going to come back here and she, too, would bring some crumbs for the animals.

She took a seat beside a fish pond to watch the large goldfish swimming and flipping in the water.

She sat there for the longest time feeling perfectly content; and she realized that she'd been here in Sacramento for more than a year, but she had actually seen very little of the city.

It was really a small world you lived in when you worked for Delores Delgardo.

When she finally rose from the bench to start back to the shop, a hump-shouldered man came along pushing a wooden cart with buckets filled with small bouquets of flowers tied with bright-colored ribbons around the stems. Pulling some change out of her reticule, she purchased a bouquet for herself.

Then she started walking down the flagstone walkway to go back to the shop. She was beginning to feel hungry and planned to fix herself a good dinner.

She smiled as she walked out of the park. Funny as it might seem in such a short time, she already considered those two little rooms at the back of the shop home. Never had she thought of her bedroom in the Towers Hotel, as elegant as it had been, as her home.

She'd been at the shop for a month, and she'd added a lot of personal touches to the two little rooms. About a block away from the hat shop there was a marketplace that sold vegetables, fruits, and a variety of odds and ends. Deirdre had purchased a wooden rocker for her bedroom, for there was nothing to sit on except the two kitchen chairs. Oh, how very comfortable that little old rocker was to sit in and rock back and forth.

One stall had a mountain of ruffled pillows covered in chintz, and Deirdre had purchased four of them. They'd done wonders to brighten up her bedroom.

She couldn't refuse herself the darling little footstool covered in a lovely needlepoint, and she'd shined the cherry wood of the legs and frame until it glowed.

Deirdre could honestly say that she had no regrets about leaving her job with the señora, but she often wondered about Elena and how she'd fared in the last four weeks.

* * *

The night Camilla and Elena left the Towers Hotel to travel by carriage to the Gomez's home, there was a slight chill to the night air. Anticipating this, Delores had designed a short cape of emerald-green lined in satin for Elena's ensemble.

To complement Camilla's scarlet gown, she'd had the seamstress make up a soft-wool black cape lined in scarlet satin. Both young ladies looked quite stunning when they left the hotel.

As Elena and Camilla went downstairs together in their finery, they were both rather lighthearted and gay. Camilla realized that Elena could be fun to be around when Babette wasn't along. Elena decided that Camilla could be warm and friendly now that she had gotten to know her better.

She told Camilla as they were jauntily walking across the lobby, "I'm glad we've finally had a chance to spend some time together. I guess I had the impression you didn't like me, so I didn't try to get to know you."

"Oh, no, Elena, I do like you. Please don't think I don't," Camilla stammered as she gave Elena a warm smile. Privately, she was thinking to herself that Elena was very nice and she'd just allowed Babette to influence her too much all the time she'd been here.

But lately, Camilla had observed the little Elena standing up to Babette and putting her firmly in her place. She had to admit that she admired Elena's spunk. "The señora is the only one who will boss me, Babette—not you!" Elena had declared to the statuesque Babette, who towered over her.

Unaware of how Elena was influencing her, Camilla had not been as intimidated by Babette as she always had been in the past. Babette was seeing the change in Camilla and how she could not influence her as she once had. Elena could charm everyone, she pouted.

As for Delores Delgardo, she could go to hell as far as Babette was concerned, and she'd never go to her again to

MORE PASSION AND ADVENTURE AWAIT... YOUR TRIP TO A BIG ADVENTUROUS WORLD BEGINS WHEN YOU ACCEPT YOUR FIRST 4 NOVELS ABSOLUTELY *FREE* (AN $18.00 VALUE)

Accept your Free gift and start to experience more of the passion and adventure you like in a historical romance novel. Each Zebra novel is filled with proud men, spirited women and tempestuous love that you'll remember long after you turn the last page.

Zebra Historical Romances are the finest novels of their kind. They are written by authors who really know how to weave tales of romance and adventure in the historical settings you love. You'll feel like you've actually gone back in time with the thrilling stories that each Zebra novel offers.

GET YOUR FREE GIFT WITH THE START OF YOUR HOME SUBSCRIPTION

Our readers tell us that these books sell out very fast in book stores and often they miss the newest titles. So Zebra has made arrangements for you to receive the four newest novels published each month.

You'll be guaranteed that you'll never miss a title, and home delivery is so convenient. And to show you just how easy it is to get Zebra Historical Romances, we'll send you your first 4 books absolutely FREE! Our gift to you just for trying our home subscription service.

BIG SAVINGS AND FREE HOME DELIVERY

Each month, you'll receive the four newest titles as soon as they are published. You'll probably receive them even before the bookstores do. What's more, you may preview these exciting novels free for 10 days. If you like them as much as we think you will, just pay the low preferred subscriber's price of just $3.75 each. *You'll save $3.00 each month off the publisher's price.* AND, your savings are even greater because there are never any shipping, handling or other hidden charges—FREE Home Delivery. Of course you can return any shipment within 10 days for full credit, no questions asked. There is no minimum number of books you must buy.

4 FREE BOOKS

FREE BOOK CERTIFICATE

4 FREE BOOKS

ZEBRA HOME SUBSCRIPTION SERVICE, INC.

ZB0594

NAME

ADDRESS _____ APT _____

CITY _____ STATE _____ ZIP _____

TELEPHONE ( )

SIGNATURE _____ (if under 18, parent or guardian must sign)

GET
FOUR
FREE
BOOKS
(AN $18.00 VALUE)

tell her anything about Elena Fernandes. A lot of good it had done the last time she'd informed the señora about Elena's lackluster manner the night of the party they'd attended together.

She sat in her room and sulked. Then she suddenly got up and began to dress. She didn't need Delores Delgardo to have herself a fancy party to go to. There was a nice gent who'd welcome her company, and she'd return to the hotel late tonight with more money in her reticule than she could make for a week working for Delores.

Dressed in one of her fancy gowns, Babette left the Towers Hotel an hour later.

It was like a sparkling wonderland with lit torches lighting the winding drive of the Gomez estate. Ricardo Gomez and his beautiful Margarita were there at the front entrance greeting their guests.

Camilla watched the lovely Margarita Gomez affectionately embrace Elena Fernandes. Neither she nor Babette had ever been so warmly embraced by any hostess of parties she'd gone out on. A special relationship existed between this lady and Elena, Camilla concluded.

Camilla could see why Margarita Gomez was considered the queen of the city's social scene. She was the picture of elegance and charm. She was so very gracious without a hint of being haughty.

Her white satin gown was adorned with tiny seed pearls and around her throat she wore a pearl necklace with a magnificent emerald clasp. On her finger she wore the largest emerald Camilla had ever seen.

The parlor was aglow with candlelight, with the most majestic Christmas tree standing in one corner. The top of the tree almost reached the high ceiling.

The women servants carrying silver trays around the parlor to serve champagne were all dressed in rich scarlet frocks with frosty white aprons edged with lace ruffling. It was not hard to understand why Señora Gomez was considered the queen, for she entertained regally.

Elena had only to enter the parlor for many eyes to turn in her direction, and she assumed it was the gorgeous gown she had on. But many of the ladies just liked her as Margarita did. They found she possessed certain qualities in common with their hostess. She had a grace and charm.

One of the lovely ladies came up to her to tell her it was good to see her again. "You just get more beautiful all the time, and your gown is glorious."

"How sweet you are, Señora Montera! It's good to see you again." Elena smiled.

"Well, how sweet of you to remember my name when you meet so many people," Olivia Montera remarked.

"I always remember someone as nice as you were when I met you at the señora's last party," Elena told her.

"Well, I must have a gown like that, but I don't fool myself that it's going to look as good on me as it looks on you. But I'll pretend it does." She laughed.

Camilla found that these elegant ladies warmed to her this evening, and she believed it was because she'd accompanied Elena instead of Babette. She also conducted herself like Elena instead of imitating Babette's bold ways.

A short time before dinner was announced Carlos Mateo approached her. "Good evening, Elena. You are looking most charming. I wondered if I might see you here tonight, for you're apparently Señora Gomez's favorite model."

She smiled. "I'd like to think so, Carlos. I like the señora very much. I might say that obviously the two of them must like you, too, for you've been invited to another of their parties." She yearned to ask him about Mateo, but she didn't dare. She feared what he might tell her.

Seeing her in this elegant setting, Carlos could understand why she'd not wish to give all this up to return to Half Moon Bay and her dull existence there.

Any of Margarita's guests who were expecting to feast on the traditional Christmas dinner were in for a delightful surprise. They were served delectable roast ducklings drizzled with a sauce flavored with orange juices. An herbed rice was served with it. For the dessert, Margarita had broken away from the traditional puddings and fruitcakes and had chosen a delicious strawberry mousse.

Ricardo had playfully teased her about the menu for her party, but he never questioned her judgment.

She'd just laughed. "You wait, *querido*. So I dare to be different! You of all people know that I've never fit into a mold."

He loved his wife's self-assured air, and he would have never wanted her to be any other way than the way she was, for that was what had always made her such an interesting, exciting woman to him.

He had only to observe their guests around the dining table thoroughly enjoying the ducklings to know that Margarita had been right.

He was also impressed with one of their guests tonight. The more he heard about him, the more interested he became. Only one thing kept him from offering young Carlos Mateo a position in his prestigious law firm: He was now working for his best friend.

He could never do that to Marcus.

Twenty-seven

Margarita Gomez had an inquisitive nature. She always had been a most curious lady, which had intrigued Ricardo for he, too, as a lawyer, had an inquiring mind.

Tonight, she sat at her dining room table observing Elena sitting beside Carlos Mateo. But she was also intrigued by the other Mateo brother, who'd come to her for information about Elena.

She hoped to have a private moment with the girl before the evening was over. She had been very impressed by young Mark Mateo; he had an honesty she liked. She liked that he was so earnestly determined to find Elena that he dared to be turned away from her door since he wasn't expected that morning. Yet, he had chanced that!

But somehow that private moment with Elena never came and before Margarita realized it the guests were leaving and she was to tell Elena and Camilla good night. So she told Elena as she was preparing to go out the door, "Come have lunch with me."

"I would be delighted, señora," Elena told her.

"I will send my driver to the hotel to pick you up. Just let me know," Margarita told her.

"I will let you know, señora, and it will be soon, I promise," Elena said, following Camilla outside.

As the two of them were boarding the carriage to go back to the hotel, Camilla remarked, "Señora Gomez sure has taken a liking to you, Elena! How did you manage that? I'm just curious, I guess."

Elena laughed. "I can't really tell you, Camilla. I honestly can't. I know that I liked her the first time I met her and I guess the same was true for her when she met me. That's all I can really tell you."

Camilla shook her head as she declared, "Never has any hostess treated me—or Babette—as grandly as she treats you. You have some kind of charm that neither Babette nor I apparently have."

"Oh, Camilla, I don't know about that," Elena demurred.

"I think you do, but you might not realize it," Camilla declared. She was thinking that Elena was very different from Babette. Babette would have been gloating had she been in Elena's place this evening.

They returned to the hotel, and both young ladies went to their own bedrooms. But Camilla had a completely different opinion about Elena after tonight, and nothing Babette could tell her was going to change that, Camilla decided.

Camilla still had her gown and cape on when Babette came rushing in her door. "Well, Camilla, do you think that fancy gown might have made some sales for old Delores tonight?" Babette asked her. It was obvious to Camilla that Babette had been sitting in her room drinking since she didn't have to work this evening.

But Babette hadn't been in her room until just a few minutes before when she, too, had returned to the hotel. She'd gone to see a gentleman friend shortly after Elena and Camilla had left for the *soirée*. Arnold Parkinson had greeted the sensuous Babette with a smile when she'd knocked on the door of his luxurious apartment. Parkinson was a bachelor who frequented most of the social affairs, usually playing the escort to very wealthy widows.

He was in his dressing robe, holding a drink in his hand,

and he ushered the willowy Babette into his apartment. He invited her to join him with a drink. They had one drink and then another. Soon they were in his boudoir and Arnold was taking his pleasure with her. Once he was sated, he rose from the bed to go into his dressing room and Babette picked up her gown.

Arnold was a fastidious person and was always impeccably attired. Since he took awhile to get dressed, Babette fastened her bodice and petticoats, and brushed her hair. Then, in his parlor, she helped herself to another drink.

When Arnold emerged from his dressing room looking dapper in his fine-tailored coat and pants, she immediately assumed that he was taking her out to dinner.

But instead he dropped her off at the Towers Hotel, for he was on his way to a fancy holiday party. So Babette found herself back at the front entrance while Arnold and his gig disappeared into the darkness. She had not been rewarded with dinner or a roll of bills placed in the palm of her hand.

So she was in a very disgruntled mood when she went to Camilla's room and learned that the Gomez party had been wonderful.

The last thing Babette needed to hear from Camilla as she removed her cape and greeted her was her next words, "Call her naive if you like, Babette, but Elena has something you and I don't have."

Babette threw her head back and laughed. "You've had too much champagne, Camilla."

"No, no, Babette, I've not had that much to drink. I know what I saw and heard tonight. I'll not look down my nose anymore at Elena Fernandes. You and I never got an invitation for lunch from a lady like Señora Gomez. No, you laugh all you like, but I won't be laughing with you," Camilla told her.

Babette quickly whirled around and went out the door, slamming it with a mighty blow.

Carlos Mateo returned to his home late able to understand his brother's frustrations when Elena refused to go with him when he left Sacramento.

Elena could bewitch any man. He had even found himself falling under her spell tonight for she had been the most beautiful lady at the party. Despite her loveliness and sensuous figure, Elena seemed not to be aware of it. She had a childlike quality that made a man want to protect her. Yet, she could appear sophisticated and sultry when she looked at you.

It was no wonder she'd caught the eye of his younger brother, whose restless heart had never been tamed by any woman.

He'd had no word from Golden Splendor since Mark had left Sacramento, but he had not written to them either for he'd been too busy. His schedule became more demanding day by day.

He knew Aimée was going to be disappointed that he'd not be staying a week when he came for the holiday festivities, but two days were all he could possibly allow himself.

When Mark returned home from Sacramento, he was pleased to see that his father was managing just fine at the winery. But Mano told him that his grandfather had been ailing. "He wants you to come and see him, Mark."

So the next afternoon, Mark rode over to La Casa Grande to see his ill grandfather. That visit was to change all of Mark's plans.

As a youngster, Mark had always liked being around his Grandfather Paul Aragon, for he was a jovial little Frenchman who laughed easily and was fun-loving.

Grandfather Mateo was reserved and sedate and walked around with such dignity that Mark was always afraid he was going to do or say the wrong thing. But when he was sixteen, he didn't care whether he pleased his stern-faced grandfather or not. Nor did it bother him if Grandfather Mateo approved of his behavior.

But things changed between them when Mark returned from Mexico and old Carlos saw his enthusiasm for the bulls. He liked nothing better than talking about his own prized Mateo bulls. After that, the two of them spent time together and formed a closer bond. Mark's brother Carlos had no more interest in his grandfather's bulls than he did for his father's winery and vineyards.

Mark found old Carlos in a cantankerous mood because his housekeeper and cook, Estellita, had insisted that he stay in his room and let her bring his breakfast up to him.

But she'd met Mark before he'd gone upstairs to see the old man and told him, "He doesn't need to tax himself, Señor Mark, walking up and down those steps. *Madre de Dios,* I fear he could fall!"

"You did exactly right, Estellita. You just keep being as stubborn as he is," Mark said, patting her shoulder before he left her to go upstairs.

The first thing he heard from his grandfather was a complaint. "She is worse than a nagging wife, *nieto,*" he barked.

"Grandfather, you should be glad Estellita cares about you the way she does. I'll give you no sympathy, for I think she's right. Save your strength today and maybe you'll feel stronger tomorrow."

"So, you are going to start bossing me, too, eh?" he remarked, but a slow smile emerged on his face.

Mark grinned. "Just a little, Grandfather. I took the liberty of asking Estellita to send up some coffee for us."

"Well, that is good. Maybe it is just as well that we visit

here in the privacy of my bedroom where there are no servants snooping around, for I have some things to speak with you about. It's good you came this afternoon, *nieto.*"

When the young Mexican servant had served them and closed the door, old Carlos began to ramble about the past. He spoke once again to Mark about his disappointment that Mano had no interest in his bulls and La Casa Grande. "Oh, don't take me wrong, Mark. No father could be prouder of a son than I am of Mano. But it has always been my great desire that a Mateo should run La Casa Grande."

"But that might not be possible, Grandfather," Mark pointed out.

"Maybe, but maybe it is possible, *nieto.* There is always you, and I know that your heart is not in the vineyards. We've talked enough the last six months for me to be sure of that," old Carlos told him.

That old man was so shrewd that Mark didn't even try to lie to him. What he'd said was true. So he confessed this.

There was a very serious look on old Carlos's face as he raised in his chair to look at his grandson. "I want you to listen to me and not say a word. I want you to absorb all I'm going to say to you for the next few days and give it some thought. Believe me, it could be the most important decision you'll ever make."

He told Mark that as much as Aimée and Mano had hated to see Carlos move away from Golden Splendor, it had been the right decision for him. He projected that young Carlos would be a most successful lawyer.

"Mano and Aimée will live at Golden Splendor the rest of their lives and be very happy. If Mano is lucky, maybe his little Markita will marry a young man who loves the grapes as much as Mano does," Carlos said.

Mark laughed. "That would be perfect, wouldn't it, Grandfather?"

"I think so. Now we come to you, *nieto.* I know you love the bulls, so I made out a new will two weeks ago. You will inherit La Casa Grande, and I challenge you to breed a finer bull than I did. I want you to take charge of my ranchero, for I am an old man and my days are numbered."

Mark was stunned by his grandfather's revelation. It was a well-thought-out plan, and Mano knew—and approved—of his decision, he told Mark. Mano was not a young man anymore and could never have run the ranch as well as he did his vineyards.

"It is yours, Mark, to do with as you wish. I'm weary and ready to step down. It's yours to take charge of right now, if you would. You go home and think about it. I'm not going anywhere, and La Casa Grande is going to be here."

Mark stammered, "I—I'll think about everything you've said. Right now, I'm in a bit of a daze."

"I understand, *nieto.*" They talked a little while longer but Mark could tell his grandfather was tiring so he prepared to leave.

He rode back to Golden Splendor, still stunned that his grandfather had willed his vast ranch to him. That evening he was very quiet and thoughtful during dinner, but Mano understood the reason why. When Mark excused himself early to go to his room, Mano was certain that his father had told him about changing his will.

Mark had a lot of thinking to do and he could not concentrate in the parlor. To take charge of running Carlos Mateo's huge ranch was overwhelming. He would have so much to learn.

That night as he lay on his bed, he realized that his grandfather was offering him the sun, moon, and stars! That cunning old fox had whetted his interest, challenging him to breed a better bull than his. Could he possibly do it? Did he dare try?

He was a young man dwelling in daydreams that late night. His thoughts flew to Sacramento, and he envisioned Elena as his beautiful bride and La Casa Grande as their home.

He considered his grandfather's challenge for two days. On the third day, he rode to La Casa Grande to accept.

"But you must guide me, Grandfather," he said, "if I'm to run La Casa Grande as you have."

"I will teach you, Mark, and you will end up being much smarter than I was at your age. I had to struggle on my own and I made many mistakes. I can spare you some of that," old Carlos assured him. He was elated that Mark would be his heir.

Old Carlos wasted no time in instructing his grandson, for he had no time to waste. Each day Mark went over to La Casa Grande to spend at least two or three hours, and the two of them would sequester themselves in the study or his grandfather's bedroom.

In the study there were journals stored on shelves. Old Carlos had recorded everything. Mark studied those journals and learned about the early days at La Casa Grande and its growth and prosperity. It was a slow, tedious process to go over each and every book, but Carlos was there to answer any of his questions. The entries reflected the heights of joy Carlos had felt about a bull he'd bred and the great disappointments.

The more Mark read, the more fascinated he became about the ranchero. Carlos had anticipated this response, which was why he had wanted Mark to absorb some history before he started riding out on the range with his foreman, Orlando.

At the end of two long weeks of daily visits, Mark was convinced that his grandfather was wiser than he'd realized. Perhaps, he had been destined to run La Casa Grande and that was why he had yet to get something going with his life as his brother had.

"Your days with Orlando are going to be much longer than they have been with me. It's going to be early rising and you're going to be bone-tired by the time you finish the day with Orlando Fuentes. It's probably time you moved here, *nieto*."

Although old Carlos realized that his foreman would have to step down soon, too, he was glad that Orlando was there right now to take Mark under his wing. The time had come for younger men to run the ranch.

Mark had not thought about moving to La Casa Grande this soon, but he saw the logic of it and in the end it would be much simpler for him. He wondered how his parents would take this news.

But they were both very understanding about it. Mano knew the long day Mark would be putting in and Aimée told him that he could have dinner with them anytime he could manage it.

When he went to his room after dinner, he gathered pants and shirts to get him through the next few days.

He found himself getting more and more excited about this ranch that was to be his. He was looking forward to riding over every acre of it with Orlando in the days to follow.

The impact had finally hit him, and it was staggering. But when he was gathering his few belongings to take with him, he realized that after tonight La Casa Grande would truly be his new home.

As Carlos had left Golden Splendor to establish his new home in Sacramento, he would be leaving in the morning to establish his new life and home at La Casa Grande.

Twenty-eight

Elena was delighted to find out that Lisette's hat shop was close to the Towers Hotel. It was just a fifteen minute stroll.

Deirdre was thrilled to see her come through the door. She had just finished waiting on a customer and Lisette was in the back of the shop working on a new hat which had to be ready in the morning.

Deirdre gave a shriek of delight and rushed around the counter, grabbing Elena in a warm embrace. "It's good to see you!" she cried.

"I've missed you, Deirdre," Elena told her.

"I've missed you, too, honey. I've Sundays off and I've been tempted to come to the Towers to see you, but I didn't want to cause you any trouble with Delores. She wasn't pleased with me when I told her I was leaving."

From the back of the shop, Lisette could overhear the two young ladies talking and she'd had a fleeting glance of the young lady who'd entered the shop. She kept working on the hat, allowing them some private moments to talk to one another.

Deirdre led Elena to the far corner of the shop where there were two chairs and a small table placed by the front window. Deirdre asked how things were going for her.

"It hasn't been so bad, but need I say I wish it were you I was going on assignments with instead of Camilla? I think the señora knows she'd best not put me with Babette. We don't get along well together."

"Has Babette tried to give you a bad time?" Deirdre asked, for she knew how overbearing she could be.

"Only once, and I told her off. I let her know that she couldn't give me orders," Elena said.

"Well, good for you! Did it work?"

"It must have, for she's not tried that again. We meet in the hallway occasionally, and that's about it."

Luckily, no customers came into the shop for almost a half-hour, so the two of them chatted like magpies before Lisette finally came through the draped doorway to greet Elena.

Deirdre introduced Lisette to Elena. Lisette smiled. "Well, it is nice to finally meet you, Elena. Your name has been mentioned many times by Deirdre." She turned to Deirdre to suggest, "It seems slow out here, so why don't you and Elena go back to your quarters? I'll tend the shop."

"Thanks, Lisette," Deirdre told her as she urged Elena to come with her. She led her through the two small, cozy rooms which were now her home. "It isn't the fancy bedroom I had at the Towers Hotel; but oh, Elena, it is so much nicer to me. I love cooking in my little kitchen and going out to shop for things to brighten it up."

"You look content and happy, and you have a cozy little place back here. I'm happy for you, Deirdre. But I do miss you terribly," Elena confessed.

"And I miss you, too, and I think of you often, Elena. I'm so glad you came today. I've discovered the nicest little park and I go there on Sunday afternoons. It's so serene and peaceful. You will have to come with me some Sunday."

"It sounds wonderful to me, Deirdre."

"It's wonderful to be able to do things I'd not done since

I started to work for Delores Delgardo. Oh, Elena, don't let her use up too many of your days and nights."

"I won't, Deirdre. As you told me, I've not bought any of the gowns and I've been holding onto my wages."

"Good for you, honey. Oh, Elena working for someone like Lisette is nothing like working for the señora."

"Well, I must not stay much longer. After all, this is a working day for you," Elena remarked.

But Deirdre told her, "Lisette knows that I'll work this evening after the shop is closed and I've had some dinner to make up for the time I've spent visiting with you."

"I do have to get started back to the hotel now, Deirdre, but I promise to not wait so long to come see you again," Elena said, rising from the chair.

"You'd better not. I've got a great idea. You come here Sunday afternoon. We'll go to the little park I told you about, and then we'll come back here. I'll fix dinner for the two of us," Deirdre suggested.

"I'll be here," Elena declared as the two of them walked to the front of the shop. Elena paused to tell Lisette goodbye and that it was nice to have met her.

"It was nice to meet you, too, Elena. Come to the shop again." Lisette looked up from the bonnet she was trimming.

A few minutes after Elena had left, Lisette told Deirdre to pull down the shade and lock the door for the clock was striking five. She went to the back of the shop to get her reticule before she left to go to her own apartment.

"Your friend is very nice, Deirdre, and most beautiful," she remarked.

"She certainly is, and I was so happy to see her."

They said good night, and Deirdre secured the front door, turning to go back to her rooms. Every evening, the minute she got back to her quarters and before she started preparing her meal, she kicked off her slippers to pad around the kitchen in her stocking feet.

She'd usually slip out of the simple gown she'd worn during the day and get into her loose dressing gown. This evening, having seen Elena, she was in a good mood. But there was so much that she'd not told her, she realized while she puttered in her cubicle of a kitchen. She'd forgotten to tell her about the nice young man she'd seen at the park the last time she was there. She hadn't known how long he'd been sitting in his carriage observing her when she happened to turn to see him staring in her direction. But as he'd put his buggy into motion, he'd given her a wave of his hand and a friendly smile.

Deirdre could not deny that she was anticipating seeing him the next time she was at the park. Even though a distance had separated them, Deirdre had known he was very good looking. He was finely attired, but he wore no hat. There was an aristocratic air about him. He sat erect in his fancy buggy behind a prancing roan bay.

She hoped that the next time he came to the park he would introduce himself.

For Deirdre, it was nice to once again have girlish daydreams. It had been a long time since she'd felt so carefree and young.

As many times as she and Lisette had talked, the older woman had never mentioned her age; but Deirdre knew that she had to be flirting with thirty. She had been married once, she'd told Deirdre, but there had been no children. Lisette had never mentioned what had happened to her husband. Deirdre didn't know if he'd died or they'd just gone separate ways. All she had been told was that Lisette had been forced to earn a living for herself.

Something about Lisette's manner when she spoke about

her husband led Deirdre to believe that the marriage had ended in bitterness.

Lisette never ever spoke of her family.

Elena had left the hat shop and sprinted down the avenue toward the Towers Hotel. She crossed the carriage path to go down a busier street which led directly to the hotel, when she was struck without any warning by the strangest sensation. Her head seemed to be whirling, and her blood rushed to her face. She leaned against the building and took off her wide-brimmed hat, fanning herself.

What in the world was the matter with her? She had felt wonderful all day—until now.

The only previous experience she could relate this to was once when Vasco had innocently run into her, slamming her to the ground. When she'd tried to get up, her legs had been weak and she had gasped for breath.

She rested for a few minutes before she gathered the courage to continue. The closer she got to the hotel, the happier she was for she still felt weak and flushed.

She heaved a deep sigh of relief when she finally entered the lobby. When she walked past the counter, Clarence greeted her. "Miss Elena, are you all right? You look as pale as a ghost."

"No, I'm not feeling well at all," she told him with a weak smile. He watched her go toward the stairway, and then he moved to watch her slowly climb to the second landing. She wasn't mounting the stairs as spritely as she usually did, and Clarence knew that she certainly wasn't feeling well.

By the time she reached her room, she was feeling so weak that she flung her hat and reticule on the chair and sank down on the bed to kick off her slippers.

But when she was about to lie back, the strange malaise

disappeared as swiftly as it had struck her and she felt like her old self.

Later, she joined Camilla in the dining room and ate voraciously, concluding that she'd felt faint because she hadn't eaten all day.

The next morning she felt great. Convinced that she had to be more careful about her diet, she ordered a breakfast tray before she dressed to go to the salon for a fitting.

It was a miserable day outside, and Elena chose her light-wool, bottle-green gown which had a matching cape she could drape around her shoulders. There was a chill in the air, and a dense fog and drizzle moved in over the coast.

The cape covering her shoulders felt good as she got into the buggy to go to the salon. Like Deirdre, she'd learned never to expect Miguel to assist her. The only time he stretched himself to do that was when Delores was along.

Elena wondered why Delores Delgardo tolerated a worthless son like Miguel when she demanded so much from the others around her. He never pestered her, but Elena knew he was a nuisance to some of the other girls. They were afraid to complain to the señora because they didn't want to lose their job.

Elena had let him know that he dare not try to trifle with her from the minute she got to Sacramento, and she'd not had to say another word. The attitude she projected warned Miguel that he'd better leave this Portuguese girl alone.

The chill in the air matched the chill in Miguel's eyes, for he figured that it might be Elena's fault that his mother had given him some harsh warnings about the way he'd been pushing his weight around with a girl in the dining room. Now, he knew that pretty Marietta would not have complained to his mother, but he suspected that she had confided in Elena for Elena always dined at her assigned table. The two of them were always talking together as Marietta served Elena.

Elena would be bold enough to approach his mother. Camilla or Babette would not have concerned themselves with the matter, but Elena would have. Like Elena, Marietta was of Portuguese descent.

The same pelting mist was falling when Miguel came to the salon to pick Elena up to take her back to the hotel. Elena was thinking that the rich red-velvet gown would feel comfortable this cool winter night.

Delores had been pleased when she'd viewed Elena during the final fitting. The dress was perfect for the holiday season. She'd told Elena that she would bring the ruby earrings with her this afternoon. "You'll need no other jewelry, Elena. Oh, what a dream you are going to be! Don't forget to get Meredith to give you the red-velvet slippers with the silver buckles before you leave. I'll bring everything else," she told Elena as the seamstress helped Elena out of the gown.

The assignment Elena was going on tonight was unique, for she would not have Camilla or Babette with her. Delores had told her it was one of the grandest affairs of the holiday season.

"I prefer that you go to this one alone, Elena. Margarita Gomez will be there, so that should make you feel better," she reassured Elena.

She told Elena about the Barringers. Bernard Barringer was the publisher of the newspaper and the president of the biggest bank in the city. His wife, Eugenia, was some years younger than he, and they had just recently married. His previous wife, Matilda, had died two years before.

"She is new to the elite social circle here in Sacramento. She and Bernard met when he was visiting in Paris. They say she is a very beautiful woman, which might explain why so many of the ladies are jealous of her."

It was comforting to Elena to know Margarita would be there this evening. The thought of going to a grand party alone petrified her.

But a strange transformation came over her when she was dressed in the deep-red velvet gown, which was so exquisite. Her jet-black hair was styled in a sophisticated hairdo which displayed Delores's expensive ruby earrings. She calmed as she looked at her own reflection in the full-length mirror. She didn't look like the little girl from Half Moon Bay. She looked like a sophisticated, self-assured young lady and that was the way she was feeling when old Domino gallantly assisted her into the carriage. She was glad it was Domino taking her to the Barringers this evening instead of Miguel.

When Domino pulled the carriage up to the front entrance of the Barringer home, Elena was awestruck. If the Gomez house was a mansion, the Barringers' home had to be a castle, she concluded.

She was feeling like Cinderella when Domino helped her down from the carriage. Her slippers were not glass, but red-velvet. She didn't expect to meet her handsome Prince Charming here tonight, for he was many miles away back at Golden Splendor.

She was greeted by a dignified white-haired gentleman who introduced himself as Bernard Barringer. At his side stood his very beautiful wife clad in a most exquisite green gown with emeralds adorning her wrists, ears, and throat.

To Elena, Eugenia could have been a queen for she looked so regal.

Elena received a warm, friendly welcome from Eugenia Barringer, whose eyes were already scrutinizing Elena's gorgeous velvet gown. It was the most outstanding gown she'd seen this evening and she didn't hesitate to tell Elena this.

There was a spontaneity about Eugenia Barringer that was very much like Elena's free-spirited nature, and Elena felt very much at ease around this lovely lady so recently arrived from France.

Eugenia found Elena warm and refreshing compared to some of the stuffy ladies she'd met since her arrival in Sacramento. There was no question about it that Elena Fernandes was certainly the most beautiful young lady she'd seen here.

As Elena moved on toward the parlor, Eugenia leaned over to whisper to Bernard, *"Charmante!* She is a beauty."

Twenty-nine

It had been a wonderful evening at the Barringers and Elena had had a grand time. She was really glad that Delores had not sent Camilla along with her. Margarita Gomez had spotted her and immediately rushed to introduce her to two of her good friends.

All too swiftly, the evening had come to an end. Elena, Ricardo, and Margarita left at the same time, and Margarita reminded her of their lunch date. So Elena suggested the next Wednesday.

"That would be perfect, dear," Señora Gomez told her as the three of them prepared to go down the steps. Suddenly Elena swayed against her. Margarita thought at first she'd missed her footing on the top step.

She clasped Elena's arm. "Elena dear, what's the matter?"

"I—I don't know, señora," Elena stammered, embarrassed. She certainly didn't want Margarita to think that she'd had too much to drink, for actually she'd drunk very little this evening. She'd spent so much time talking. But Margarita did not blame the champagne.

She urged Ricardo to take hold of Elena's other arm. "You almost fainted on us, Elena. We're going to see you to your carriage. You get Domino to take you into the lobby of the hotel. I trust you are not coming down with some illness. Were you not feeling well tonight, Elena?"

"I was feeling fine, señora, but this is the second time

I've had this happen. I was walking back to the hotel, and all of a sudden I felt faint. But it passed quickly."

"If this happens again, you should see a doctor," Margarita cautioned her.

The couple helped Elena into the carriage, and Margarita asked her to send word to her how she was feeling tomorrow. Elena promised that she would and that she would still plan on seeing her on Wednesday.

Elena was glad that the hour was apparently late enough that she wouldn't be bothered by Delores's usual post-party quizzing.

She wasted no time getting out of the velvet gown, thinking that she could not blame her swooning tonight on an empty stomach. She had taken her fill of all the delectable foods on the massive table. Some of the foods she'd eaten she'd never had before, like the truffles and the *foie gras,* which Margarita had explained was goose liver chopped and pressed with truffles and seasonings.

"Is it not delicious, Elena? Eugenia enjoys serving her native French delicacies," Margarita had told her.

"It's wonderful! I've never eaten anything like it before," Elena had exclaimed.

Margarita rejoiced in her openness and honesty. The more she saw her, the more she genuinely liked the young girl. How many would have confessed that they'd never eaten truffles or *foie gras?*

No, it wasn't the lack of food that she could put the blame on this time, so what was it? She was too young to be too ill, she told herself once she was in her nightgown and crawling into her bed.

She'd always been healthy. She thought back to the past, pulling the coverlet up to her chin. Childhood illnesses had never kept her in bed for long.

But since this was the second time it had happened, in

exactly the same way, so swift and unexpected, Elena was disturbed. Would it strike her again?

It was a long time before she finally drifted off to sleep, and Elena was not happy to hear the rapping on her door early in the morning. She knew who it was and she wondered why the señora could not have waited to get her report instead of disturbing her at this ungodly hour.

Sleepyheaded, Elena opened the door to Delores. She could not muster any lively morning greeting to her as Delores anxiously rushed into the room to ask about the party. "I just had to find out how the evening went before I left for the salon," Delores said, her face glowing with excited anticipation since this was the first party Elena had gone on alone.

"You'll have to forgive me, señora, but I'm still half-asleep. It was a grand party and ran very late. Everything went fine and I would suspect that you'll have an order or two for the red-velvet gown for the holidays. That is about all I can tell you." Elena shrugged her shoulders.

Delores, realizing that she was being dismissed by Elena so she could get back into her bed, found herself resenting the saucy Portuguese girl this morning.

However, Miguel noticed that his mother's manner changed completely between morning and late afternoon when he picked her up. There was a simple explanation. Eugenia Barringer came into her salon to order not only one of the gowns in the brilliant red-velvet, but another stitched in a deep, rich green.

Two other ladies who'd attended Eugenia's party also came in at mid-afternoon to order the velvet gown for their Christmas Day celebrations.

Delores was soaring to the heavens. Elena had definitely impressed the ladies at the party. Delores could not have been more pleased knowing the hundreds of dollars the model had earned for her last night.

But she realized as well that she would be devastated if she lost Elena. It would be a disaster for the salon, especially since she was still working with only three girls instead of four.

She'd interviewed three young ladies this last week, but none of them would have worked out. Delores had instinctively known it after talking to them for five minutes.

She was considering another jaunt outside Sacramento to some of the villages. Maybe she'd spy another little marvel like Elena.

But she could not be away from her salon right now. That expedition would have to wait until after the holidays. Camilla and Babette had a holiday party to attend, but Delores knew already that they'd never sell four gowns in one evening. If she were lucky, they'd sell two.

The next day, Elena sent a message to Margarita Gomez that she was feeling just fine and that she'd be able to come to her home for lunch on Wednesday. Elena had sought out Domino to take her message to the Gomez's residence.

Miguel complained to his mother that Elena took too many liberties, like the errand she'd sent Domino on today.

"Don't worry about it, Miguel. You don't bite the hand that is feeding you. Right now, Elena Fernandes is enriching my coffers, my dear son, and that's enabling you to get your allowance. I know why Elena sent Domino to the Gomez home. She told me that Señora Gomez invited her to lunch on Wednesday. She has my permission to have Domino take her there, Miguel."

Miguel said nothing more about Elena in the days to come. He also understood why his mother catered to her.

* * *

Elena was excited about going to Margarita's for lunch and she went to a little dress shop about a block away from Delores's salon to purchase herself a new frock which she knew she would find far less expensive than a Delgardo gown. She found what she thought was the perfect ensemble to wear to Margarita's for their luncheon date. The full-gathered skirt was a red-and-green plaid with a high-necked, long-sleeved white top. With it was a short, deep-green jacket which was just perfect for these cooler December days in Sacramento.

She walked back to the hotel feeling quite pleased that she'd purchased herself an attractive outfit to wear to Margarita Gomez's home and that the price had been so reasonable. She'd also purchased a gift for Señora Gomez. She had spied a dainty pair of white lace gloves which she thought looked perfect for Señora Gomez. She wanted to bring a present since Christmas was just a few days away. The señora had been so kind to her.

Elena was feeling very encouraged that she'd not had any more fainting spells. But Margarita had thought of her often since they'd last parted that late night at the Barringer's home. Elena's message had pleased Margarita, and she was glad the girl was feeling fine.

However, Margarita recalled the one and only time in her life that she'd had fainting spells. It had been when she and Ricardo were expecting their only child. She wondered if it were possible that little Elena could be pregnant. If so, Margarita would have wagered it would be that handsome Mark Mateo's baby.

When Elena boarded the buggy to go to the Gomez's home, she looked exactly right. Old Domino even told her how pretty she looked as he assisted her up to the seat.

When she arrived, Margarita greeted her. Her dress was

simpler than the gowns that Elena had always seen her wearing to the fancy parties. But she was just as striking.

"At last, Elena, we are to have our long-overdue lunch together." Margarita smiled, leading Elena back to her sitting room so they could talk before their meal.

Elena had never seen this room before. But like Señora Gomez, the room was sheer perfection. It reflected the personality of Margarita Gomez with its bright floral settees and chairs. Sunshine streamed through the many windows, and huge urns of palms and ferns flourished in the bright light.

Elena told her how beautiful the room was. Margarita laughed. "Ricardo swears I spend more time here than in any other room in the house. He is right."

She complimented Elena on her ensemble. "Oh, Elena, I was so glad you were not going to be laid low with some malady. The holiday season is a terrible time to be ill. I remember when I went through little spells of fainting similar to yours the other night. I never had the vapors except when I was expecting our son. I think I scared Ricardo to death." She laughed.

"And did you experience that all the time you carried your child, Señora Gomez?"

"Oh, no, Elena. Thank goodness for that. Ricardo would have been a nervous wreck for nine months." She laughed again.

Their talk was interrupted by a servant who announced that the midday meal was ready.

It was a tasty light lunch. The steaming crocks of thick fish chowder were laced with small-diced fresh vegetables served with thin slices of fresh bread buttered and toasted in the oven. Herbs were sprinkled over the buttered bread.

A dessert of fruits was served in small bowls lavishly topped with a thick, sweet cream.

"Oh, señora, the chowder was absolutely delicious," she declared. With a warm twinkle in her eyes, she added, "My papa would surely enjoy it, too. We always had fish on our dinner table, and my papa swears he makes the best *paella*."

Margarita saw the warm expression on her face as she spoke of her father. There surely had to be a great love in her heart for him. "And I bet he tells the truth, Elena. I would love to taste his *paella*. What does he put in it?"

"Everything, señora," she told Margarita, naming the many ingredients he put in his big cast iron pot.

"I used to enjoy puttering in the kitchen when Ricardo and I were first married," the señora told her.

"You cooked, señora?" Elena asked. She could not imagine Margarita Gomez at a stove.

"I did. Our first house was very small. Ricardo and I speak about that little place quite often, Elena, for we were just as happy there as we are in this fine old mansion," Margarita declared.

Elena realized that she'd assumed that Ricardo Gomez had always been the wealthy man he was today.

"You really mean that, don't you?"

"I do. We enjoy this grand life we live now, but it was our devoted love for one another that truly brought us our greatest happiness."

"I hope to feel that way about someone someday," Elena remarked.

"And I will wish that for you, too, my dear. But we've spoken enough about me. I wish to know more about you while we're to have this nice private time. Tell me about your family and your life at Half Moon Bay. I'm curious. Why did you leave your home back there?" Margarita prompted her.

So Elena told her about her father and Vasco and that her mother had been killed when she was very young. She spoke about her father being a fisherman with two fishing boats that sailed out on the bay daily. She described the little cottage they lived in and the small fishing village.

She told the señora that it had just been a chance meeting with Delores Delgardo on the wharf that led to her coming to the city.

"I'm surprised that your father allowed you to leave, for he seems like such a doting man. How did you ever persuade him, Elena?"

"I didn't try, señora. I had a need to see more of the world than just that little village. So I left a note when I caught the boat with Señora Delgardo," Elena confessed.

"Oh, Elena—how worried he must be about you!"

Elena lowered her eyes and nodded her head. "I know, señora. I'm not proud about that. I hope to make it up to him one day."

Margarita Gomez was such an easy person for Elena to talk with that Elena made another confession to her. "I would have never thought about leaving before Papa and I went to Golden Splendor for their Festival of the Grapes. There I discovered a world I'd never seen before. It was all so exciting—that magnificent house and grounds, Mateo's nice family, and the exciting afternoon and evening we spent there as their guests. I came back to our little cottage and—I'm ashamed to say this to you—I found it shabby. Life after that seemed very dull and boring."

Margarita reached over to pat her hand and assure her that she had no reason to feel guilty. "As you said, you entered a strange, wonderful world you'd never known before. It was only natural for you to be impressed." She didn't comment on but privately noted the tremendous impact Mark Mateo had had on her life.

Elena thanked her for being so understanding. But now Margarita understood many things. This little Portuguese girl had also made a strong impact on Mark Mateo's life or he'd not have come to her to seek information about Elena.

She didn't have such a pleasant taste in her mouth for Delores Delgardo. A sophisticated woman like her had to know she was persuading a naive, innocent girl to leave her home to come with her so she could profit from Elena's breathtaking beauty and freshness. It was far too cosmopolitan a world for Elena to have been thrust into.

Knowing the whole story made Margarita all the more protective toward her.

They returned to the sitting room after lunch, and Margarita said again how glad she was that they'd been able to have this private talk.

Margarita's dark eyes looked deep into Elena's as she told her, "You know I have your best interest at heart, Elena. So I feel free to give you some advice. Go home for the holidays. Go home to your papa. It would be the greatest gift you could give the dear man."

With a smile on her face, Elena exclaimed, "Oh, señora, I'm going home. I couldn't imagine spending Christmas anywhere but that cottage with Papa and Vasco. I couldn't imagine a more lonely Christmas than being in that hotel room."

"That's wonderful! I am so very happy to hear you say that. But I would have insisted, had you remained here in Sacramento, that you spend Christmas Eve and Christmas Day with me and Ricardo," she said. She rose from the floral settee to go over to her desk to pick up a small package.

She handed the box to Elena and wished her a happy holiday. In turn, Elena reached down to pick up the small package beside her reticule. She handed Margarita her gift.

The two of them opened their presents. Margarita saw the dainty, white-lace gloves. "You have such exquisite taste. They're lovely, and I thank you so much, dear."

"I hoped you'd like them. I saw them and thought of you,"

the girl told her as she began to raise the lid of the small box Margarita had handed her.

When Elena lifted the lid of the box and saw the delicate gold cross nestled inside, she was reminded of her mother Miranda, who had always worn a cross around her neck. Hers had been larger, but Elena could remember that her mama had told her the reason she always wore it was because it made her feel safe.

"I shall wear this always around my neck, señora. It is just beautiful! It will make me feel safe." Elena immediately fastened the clasp of the gold chain.

What Elena didn't know was that Margarita Gomez had not gone out to purchase the cross. It came from her own cherished pieces of jewelry that she'd owned for many years.

Margarita had given to her impulse to give this cross to Elena some very serious thought. She'd even discussed it with Ricardo. He'd told her, *"Querida,* if you wish to give the cross to Elena, then do so."

Elena could have been her daughter had she been blessed with one, but she hadn't been. She'd kept the cross to give to her daughter-in-law when her son married. But her only son had died, unmarried, at a very young age.

Ricardo knew the devastating blow the boy's death had been to his lovely wife, and he understood the sudden attachment she felt for Elena Fernandes. He also knew his Margarita and that she'd probably not tell Elena that the cross had been given to her when she was fifteen.

When Ricardo got home that evening, he didn't have to ask Margarita if she'd had a nice day for her lovely face was glowing. Excitedly, she displayed the pair of white-lace gloves Elena had given her. "Aren't they lovely, Ricardo?"

"They're gorgeous, *querida.* There is a touch of class about Elena as young as she is," Ricardo remarked as he bent to kiss her cheek. Ricardo knew why these little lace gloves meant so much to this lady of his who had a drawer filled with gloves. Elena had chosen these for her, so to Margarita they would always be special.

This was the Margarita he adored so much. But he of all people knew that his wife had known heartaches and devastating despair when she'd lost their son. So they'd clung together to share that grief and then they'd picked themselves up to go on with their life.

Elena Fernandes was very special to his wife, and Elena was obviously just as fond of his Margarita. That was all that mattered to Ricardo.

Thirty

Deirdre waited for Elena to come to the shop that Sunday afternoon until a few minutes after two. Obviously, she wasn't coming or she'd have been there by now. So Deirdre draped the short blue-velvet cape around her shoulders and adjusted the bow of her blue-velvet bonnet before she left with her basket filled with the breadcrumbs she'd saved for the last three days.

It was another beautiful Sunday, and she made a very fetching sight as she walked down the street and entered the park swinging her basket back and forth. She went directly to the bench that she now claimed as hers since she had been coming there every Sunday.

The same young man who'd been there last Sunday admired her once again from his buggy. Why, he wondered was such a lovely young lady always alone? He would have expected her to have a beau escorting her to the park and keeping her company. But she seemed to be enjoying her solitude and shortly after she'd tossed her first handful of crumbs on the ground, the birds flew down from the tree branches to enjoy the feast.

He knew that it was certainly not because she couldn't attract a man, for she had a most delicate loveliness, fair hair, and a trim, shapely figure. She dressed fashionably, looking very attractive every time he'd seen her.

Today, he was determined to get a closer view of her, and

he inched his buggy closer to the bench where she sat. Deirdre was still unaware that she was being scrutinized; she was completely absorbed in watching the birds.

The closer he guided his buggy toward her, the more beautiful she looked to him. Entranced by the sight of her, he found himself bringing the buggy within twenty feet of her bench. He leaped down and walked toward her.

Deirdre recognized him immediately as the handsome young man who'd waved to her a week ago.

Her heart started pounding crazily as if she were a schoolgirl as he came up behind her. He asked her, "May I join you? I saw you here last week."

"Yes—yes I saw you, too," she stammered. What was the matter with her that she felt so unsure of herself now when she'd been to all those very sophisticated affairs when she worked for Delores?

He took a seat beside her. "It's so lovely and peaceful here, isn't it? Obviously, you enjoy it here as much as I do."

"I love to come here on my day off. I work all week, so it's nice on Sunday afternoons to just sit and feed the birds," she told him, feeling calmer now. He looked at her with the most gentle, warm dark eyes. He wasn't like most handsome men. There was no arrogance and conceit about him, and Deirdre liked that.

"I, like you, have only Sunday afternoons to indulge myself with a leisurely drive through the park. Forgive me, I've not introduced myself. My name is Carlos Mateo," he told her.

The name hit her like a thunderbolt, for that was the name of the young man Elena had seen at the Gomez party and who had caused her hasty exit. Apparently, he'd not seen her there that night, and she certainly couldn't recall seeing him.

Somehow she managed to keep her composure. "It's nice to meet you, Carlos. My name is Deirdre Deverone."

Carlos was thinking that she had the most brilliant green eyes he'd ever seen. Her name suggested a French heritage like his mother, Aimée. French ladies surely had to be the most beautiful women in the world.

They found themselves talking to one another with ease, but Deirdre didn't wish to mention the Gomez party or that she'd worked for Delores Delgardo, so she spoke about her job at the hat shop and Carlos spoke about his profession. He'd never been able to talk with young ladies the way his brother could, but he found Deirdre different.

Deirdre also realized that of all the handsome, debonair gentlemen she'd met at parties, she'd not sat and really talked to them as she was talking to Carlos. He was as interested in her, and she told him about her job and her quarters in the back of the hat shop.

It suddenly dawned on Deirdre that the sun was sinking low in the sky. There was no longer any couples strolling in the park.

She laughed. "My goodness, Carlos, the sun is setting on us. I guess I was just enjoying talking with you so much that I didn't realize how late it was getting. I hate to say goodbye."

Carlos was impressed by her honest admission. He, too, had enjoyed her company. "I've enjoyed our time together, Deirdre."

"I don't have anything fancy to offer for dinner, but I do have a beef roast cooked. You're welcome to share it with me, Carlos," she told him, realizing how impulsive she was being.

"I've got a better idea for a young lady who has got to go back to work in the morning. Give me the honor of taking you to my home for dinner this evening. My housekeeper and cook will have a good dinner prepared when I get home. Come and enjoy it with me. Stella takes very good care of me and my house—along with my cat, Amigo."

Deirdre laughed. "You have a cat named Amigo?"

"Yes, and he is very much my amigo. He is there to greet me every evening when I come home from the office. I don't know what I'd do without old Amigo."

"You tempt me, Carlos, but your cook might not find an unexpected guest to her liking," she demurred.

"Stella always fixes too much for just me. Please, Deirdre, I don't wish to say farewell to you yet," he told her. His hand reached out to cover hers, and Deirdre found it impossible to refuse him. As if he sensed that she was going to accept his invitation, he told her, "Get your wicker basket and we will be on our way, eh?"

She laughed. "Oh, Carlos, you are going to be a grand lawyer. See how you've swayed me! You have a very persuasive way about you."

Carlos could not recall a time when he'd felt so lighthearted and gay as he was when he assisted Deirdre up into his buggy. She brought out a boldness in him that amazed him.

Deirdre Deverone brought out certain traits in him that he'd never known he possessed, and he could not have been more pleased to discover them.

When they arrived at Carlos's two-story, stone house and went through the front door, Amigo was right there to greet them. Carlos bent down to give him a couple of gentle pats on the top of his head. Amigo, curious about this strange lady he'd brought home, sniffed the hem of her gown.

Deirdre chuckled. "Are you checking me out, Amigo?"

Carlos told her to make herself at home while he went to the kitchen to tell Stella to set another plate at the table. "I'm sure Amigo will keep you company while I'm in the kitchen."

Deirdre removed her cape and her bonnet to lay them on the chair. Amigo swayed at her feet as she moved around the parlor before finally taking a seat in one of the overstuffed chairs by the hearth. She was already putting together a picture of Carlos. He was a bachelor who lived in his very nice comfortable home with a housekeeper and his cat Amigo as he pursued his law practice in Sacramento. She was quite certain he wasn't a married man.

Often when she'd chanced to meet young men at parties she'd attended for Delores, they'd tried to make dinner dates with her. But she had had no way of knowing if they were married or not, so she'd always refused. That had never stopped Babette or Camilla. But she knew that Elena never made dates with men she met at these affairs.

The minute she'd taken a seat in the overstuffed chair, Amigo had jumped onto Deirdre's lap. "You're a friendly fellow, aren't you?" She stroked his head, and Amigo swished his big fuzzy tail, purring contentedly.

Carlos watched them. Amigo didn't always cater to some people who came to the house.

"I see that the two of you are getting acquainted," Carlos commented. Before he took a seat, he asked her if she'd like a glass of wine.

"Of course, Carlos. I'd love a glass of wine."

They sat together, falling into a lighthearted conversation and sipping their wine, until Stella announced that dinner was ready.

Stella got her first glance at the young lady and she approved of what she saw. She was a pretty little thing with all that golden hair falling down her back. Stella's scrutinizing eyes also approved of the long-sleeved, high-necked blue gown. To Stella's way of thinking, too many young ladies wore their gowns with necklines cut too low. She was also thinking that Deirdre and Señor Carlos made a fine looking pair. This was the kind of young lady he should squire. She had no doubt that this was the perfect little miss for the señor.

She was mannerly and gracious. Stella liked her warm, friendly smile.

Señor Carlos seemed to thoroughly enjoy her company. He spent so much time alone; Stella would like to see him take himself a wife. A man needed a woman by his side to make his life complete.

It naturally pleased Stella when she heard Deirdre raving about her meal. Dinner had not been over long before Deirdre requested that Carlos take her home. "It's a work day for both of us in the morning, so I dare not linger any later for both of our sakes." She smiled up at him.

So he helped her drape the cape around her shoulders and went to the kitchen to tell Stella that he was going to be taking Deirdre home now.

When she heard them leave, she nodded approvingly. "Yes, sir, that's a proper young lady. She went home when a proper young lady should."

She was a religious, straitlaced woman who didn't approve of the frivolous, flirtatious girls she observed on the streets of the city.

For both Deirdre and Carlos it had been a wonderful afternoon and evening. He hated to see it end when he took her back to the hat shop, but he'd already decided that he was going to see her again if she were willing for him to call on her.

He'd never met a young lady like Deirdre Deverone before, and his interest was whetted. He wanted to get to know her much better. So when he had walked Deirdre to her door, he didn't hesitate to tell her that he'd like very much to see her again.

"I'd love to see you again, Carlos. It was a glorious day and evening for me," she told him.

A pleased smile came to his face, for she was so genuine and he liked the way her green eyes looked directly into his.

He didn't try to kiss her as he was yearning to do. He told her, "Well, now that I know where you work and live, don't be surprised to see me coming through the door."

"Nothing would please me more, Carlos," she said.

Carlos finally brought himself to say good night and Deirdre went through the front door as Carlos went to his buggy.

That night he found it hard to concentrate on the papers at his desk. A lovely face framed with golden hair and flashing emerald-green eyes kept haunting him.

As he was going home in his buggy the next afternoon, he fought the urge to stop by the hat shop just to see her for a few brief moments.

Things moved at a slow pace at the hat shop on Monday and Tuesday; the ladies were not interested in buying bonnets right now. Fancy gowns and other accessories had their attention.

Even at the Delgardo Salon, the demand for models had ceased. The last party was on Tuesday, and nothing else was booked for the rest of the week.

Elena had done as she'd told Señora Gomez she was going to do. She'd booked her passage to go to Half Moon Bay. The same afternoon she'd gone shopping for gifts for her family and Deirdre.

On Wednesday afternoon, she planned to go to the hat shop before she left for Half Moon Bay.

Like Elena, Deirdre had gone out on Monday afternoon to do some shopping. Lisette had told her to do whatever she wished for a couple of hours that afternoon. "It's a ghost town around here. You take off early this afternoon, and I'll do the same in the morning, Deirdre."

So Deirdre had left the hat shop around two-thirty and gone directly to the market square. She thought she might be able to find something to give Lisette for Christmas. She'd made Elena a hat which would be perfect with her dark hair.

Everything from handicrafts, paintings, and furniture, to foods could be found in the open square. She roamed aimlessly around the different booths and tables in hopes of seeing something to purchase for Lisette. She also planned to stop at the food vendors' before she left, for they had very good buys on fresh vegetables.

At one of the booths, she found an old, leather-bound book. Etched in gold was the word *law,* and that was enough to make her pick up the book. Even the binding was in magnificent condition, and the price was so reasonable that she couldn't resist buying it for Carlos even though she didn't know whether she'd even see him again before Christmas.

She tucked the book into her large wicker basket to move on and was beginning to feel discouraged that she wasn't going to find anything for Lisette. But she had to buy *something,* she told herself.

She was almost at the end of the booths, so she decided to buy Lisette a crocheted shawl from an elderly lady. It wasn't exactly what she'd had in mind, but she only had this afternoon to shop. So she paid the old woman and went on to the food vendors' carts.

But then she saw exactly the gift she'd had in mind for Lisette, who adored her pet canary. It was a brass bird cage. She couldn't resist asking the woman what she wanted for it.

Deirdre didn't have much money left in her reticule once she'd purchased the fancy bird cage and arrived at the long row of food vendors.

She bought only a few of each of her favorite vegetables—potatoes, onions, and carrots. She would have loved to have purchased one of the fine-looking cured hams hanging across the rack, but the price was too high. She bought some apples, thinking that she'd make herself an apple pie.

She couldn't afford anything more, and she picked up her

basket filled with the vegetables, the book she'd bought for Carlos, and the shawl for Lisette.

Suddenly, she heard someone summoning her. She turned to see a man closing up his booth. "I've got two fine pullets left, missy. Do you want them real cheap?"

"I—I don't know if I've got enough left to buy them, mister," she told him.

"What you got, eh?"

She fumbled in her reticule and looked at him with a weak smile on her face when she confessed the small amount of coins that remained.

"Give me that, and the pullets are yours. I'm ready to go home," the shriveled fellow told her. He handed her the two young hens and took her coins. "A merry Christmas to you, missy!"

"A merry Christmas to you, too," Deirdre told him as she took the shawl out of the basket to place the two pullets inside. She draped the shawl around the bird cage to conceal it before she headed for the hat shop.

She rushed into the hat shop and told Lisette that she had to get back to her quarters quickly before she dropped something. Lisette laughed for it appeared Deirdre had bought more than she could handle.

Deirdre chuckled, too, when she came back to the front of the shop a few minutes later. "My shopping is done, Lisette. Enjoy yourself in the morning, and I'll be glad to handle things here," she told her.

"Well, shall we call it a day? It's close enough to five. I've had no one in all the time you've been gone, Deirdre. Our customers are occupied right now with their upcoming family gatherings. Hats can wait. I expect it will be this way until after New Year's Day."

Lisette got her reticule and prepared to leave the shop. But she paused at the door. "You've been such a help to me here, Deirdre. I can depend on you, and it's been nice to have someone like you to take over to give me some free time."

"It has worked out well for both of us, Lisette," Deirdre agreed, and they said good night.

Now that the door of the shop was locked, Deirdre went back to her quarters. As she usually did, she kicked off her slippers and got out of her sprigged-muslin gown. She slipped on her dressing gown as she always did in the late afternoon.

But this evening when she sat down at her little kitchen table to eat her dinner, she felt lonely and she knew why. Last night she'd shared dinner with Carlos Mateo.

Carlos was engulfed by the same feelings when he sat alone at his own dining table with Stella serving his dinner as she did nightly. Stella noticed how quiet and thoughtful he was tonight compared to the way he had been last night when he had had his pretty lady at the table with him.

He realized the change Deirdre Deverone had already had on his life. By the time he had gone upstairs with Amigo slowly trailing behind him and sat down at his desk, he'd made a decision which for him was out of character and quite impulsive.

He was to leave for Golden Splendor in a couple of days for the holidays, but he was going to invite Deirdre to accompany him. It was the first time he'd ever wanted to bring a young lady home.

He desired very much for her to be with him for the holidays, and this told him just how intense his feelings were for her.

Thirty-one

When Carlos made a firm decision about something he could be a man of action. The time was growing short if he were to approach Deirdre about accompanying him to Golden Splendor, so he guided his buggy to the hat shop before he went to his office.

Deirdre was raising the window shades and unlocking the door when she saw his buggy pull up in front of the shop.

She could not have been more excited when she saw him leap down and stride toward the door. She rushed to greet him. "Carlos, what a nice surprise!"

"I just couldn't wait to see you again, Deirdre. Sunday was a long time ago." He grinned.

"Oh, Carlos, how sweet you are!"

His hands reached out to take hers. "I want you to go home with me for the holidays. You told me you have no family here and I want you to meet my parents and share Christmas with me and them. Say you'll go, Deirdre. I want that so much."

Deirdre was not prepared for his forcefulness. Her pretty head was whirling as she tried to absorb what he'd just said. He wanted her to go with him to Golden Splendor to spend the holidays at his parents' home. She could not take that lightly, for he was telling her more than he might realize.

"Oh, Carlos, are you sure?" she stammered. "Are you sure

your parents would approve? After all, the holiday is a family time."

"My parents will be delighted, Deirdre. Trust me. Just say you'll come. We'll be there two days, and then I have to return to Sacramento."

Trust him. She did. So she accepted his invitation to spend the holidays with him and his family.

There was a boyish exuberance about Carlos when he left the hat shop once she'd agreed to go to Golden Splendor with him. Deirdre was as giddy as he was. Everything was suddenly changed. She'd had no particular plans, except that she and Lisette might get together.

Now, she was going to the country estate of Golden Splendor. She began to think about what she would wear. She didn't have to worry. Clothes were something she had plenty of for any occasion.

She remembered that Lisette had told her that business would be slow until the new year, so she had no qualms about asking for a few days off.

It was so quiet during the morning hours that Deirdre had time to go back to her quarters to check out her wardrobe to start choosing the gowns she would take with her for the two nights and days she would be a guest at Golden Splendor. She chose carefully. She didn't have Delores's exquisite jewelry to enhance the gowns, but she had acquired a few nice pieces.

She decided that she should give Lisette her gift this afternoon when she left the shop, for she'd not be here on Christmas Eve to give her the bird cage and shawl.

When Elena came back to the hotel from Margarita Gomez's house, she took off her gown and jacket and hung them up. This was to be her traveling ensemble when she left for Half Moon Bay.

That evening she ate dinner early and returned to her room. She was glad that she'd not encountered the señora in the dining room, but she hadn't expected to see her, knowing she was probably checking out Babette and Camilla before they left for their party.

A part of Elena's evening was spent packing for the trip to Half Moon Bay. Tomorrow she was going to have to tell Señora Delgardo that she was leaving to spend a few days with her father.

She put Deirdre's gift on her dressing table. She was very pleased with all the gifts she'd bought. For her papa, she'd selected a pearl-grey silk shirt and as she was packing it into the valise she recalled a time when she and he had been strolling down the wharf. A dapper gent passed them, and Sebastian had remarked to his daughter that one day he was going to have himself a silk shirt. She smiled, thinking that now he was to have one.

For Vasco, she'd purchased a black-leather vest which she knew that he would surely like. But she'd returned to the hotel with very little money left after buying gifts and her passage on the *Bay Queen*.

All the money she'd been saving from her wages was practically gone.

She slept later than she'd intended to. She'd decided that when she was dressed she was going to go down to the dining room for a light breakfast before she walked to the hat shop. She didn't want another fainting spell. This time she wasn't going to start out on an empty stomach.

But as she was sitting at one of the dining tables, a couple took the table next to hers. The lady removed her damp cape. The young man took it to hang it on one of the coat racks. The young lady dabbed her face with her handkerchief and noticed Elena studying her. "It's raining cats and dogs outside just in case you've not been out of the hotel yet," she said.

"Oh, no!" Elena moaned.

"I know. My friend and I were caught out in his buggy. It came on quite suddenly," the young lady told her.

A short time later Elena left the dining room and went to the front entrance of the hotel. The rain was coming down so heavily that Elena could hardly see down the street. So she went up to her room to wait out the storm before she dared to start for the hat shop.

But the noon hour went by and the clouds seemed to get darker. At two, the rains still fell over the city. Elena began to pace the room impatiently for she wanted to see Deirdre so much before she left for Half Moon Bay. But she knew if this kept up throughout the afternoon she would not be able to go. She'd be drenched to the skin before she'd walked a block.

A few blocks away, Lisette returned to the hat shop. She had gotten caught in the downpour. By the time she arrived at the shop, her gown and undergarments were damp.

So she wasn't in the best of moods as she stomped into the shop. Deirdre looked up to see her wet hair streaming around her face. "Oh, Lisette, get back to my room and let's get you some dry clothes. I bet you are wet to your skin."

Lisette's slippers made a swishing sound with each step she took.

Deirdre took Lisette's cape and her slippers. She handed a large towel to Lisette. She put another towel under the rack where she hung Lisette's cape and placed her slippers.

She and Lisette were about the same size, and while Lisette ridded herself of her damp clothes, Deirdre laid out everything from undergarments and stockings to one of her muslin gowns on the bed.

"Thanks. I've never seen it rain so hard, and it came on so suddenly," Lisette told her, brushing her wet hair back from her face.

"I hadn't even noticed that it was cloudy until I heard the rain hitting the windows," Deirdre told her as she picked up Lisette's wet garments and went to hang them on another rack.

"While you get dressed and get that wet hair of yours tended to, I'm going to brew us a pot of fresh coffee. I think you could use some," Deirdre called, going into her little kitchen.

Lisette knew she could use some coffee, but she suddenly thought about the articles in her large, leather shopping bag. Somehow, they were dry. At least, she was grateful for that.

In Deirdre's dry clothes, with her hair twisted in a coil at the top of her head, she relaxed in the kitchen to enjoy the coffee.

By now they'd been sitting for some time, and Lisette could laugh about the mess she'd been in.

Deirdre laughed. "You looked like a drowned rat, Lisette."

"I didn't think I'd ever hear myself saying this, but I'm glad we've had no one come into the shop the last hour," Lisette confessed.

"I'd venture to say that we'll not have anyone if this keeps up for another couple of hours," Deirdre remarked.

"Was it this quiet all morning?"

"No one, Lisette."

"Well, it will be like this for awhile. Another week I would say, judging from last year," Lisette told her.

"Well, now I did have one person come to the shop. My friend Carlos stopped by. Remember I told you about meeting him? Well, Lisette, I've been asked to share the holiday with him and his family. I am so thrilled! I accepted his invitation remembering what you'd told me about the shop," Deirdre said excitedly.

"So you're going to be spending the holidays with them?"

"You don't mind if I take off a few days, do you?" Deirdre asked her.

"No—no, that's all right, Deirdre," she drawled, but Deirdre noticed a changed expression on her face.

"Well, I remembered that you had told me that you were going to close the shop on Christmas Eve and Christmas Day. Since the next day is Sunday, I figured if I were off three or four days it would be all right with you," Deirdre continued quickly.

Lisette tried to mask her feeling of disappointment when she once again told her that it was fine for her to take off three or four days. It was not that Deirdre would not be here to help her in the shop that disappointed Lisette. She had been anticipating that the two of them would spend the holidays together, for she knew Deirdre had no family in town. The same was true for her.

Lisette realized that she'd been too presumptuous where Deirdre was concerned. When she'd come here to work several weeks ago, it had seemed like an ideal situation for both of them. Deirdre took a lot of the load and responsibility off her shoulders. There was no question about it; Deirdre was a hard worker. Lisette had been impressed by how neat she'd kept her living quarters and bought things to make it more attractive.

They worked well together. But Lisette had failed to realize that Deirdre was a most beautiful young lady who was bound to attract some young gentleman. She had obviously done just that and would spend the holiday with Carlos Mateo instead of as Lisette's companion.

Lisette was disappointed; it was lonely being alone at Christmas time.

Lisette gave Deirdre no hints that she was displeased with her decision to go with Carlos for the holidays. How could she have done that when Deirdre had presented her with the lovely shawl and the brass bird cage for her beloved little canary?

Despite her excitement about leaving in the morning with Carlos to go to Golden Splendor, Deirdre was sorry that she wasn't going to be able to give Elena the gift she'd made for her.

Night came early that evening. The skies were still heavy with clouds, but the rains had dwindled to a light sprinkle by the time Lisette said good night, the bird cage in one hand and her leather bag in the other hand. Deirdre knew that she had pleased her with the gifts she'd chosen for her. She knew how much she adored her little canary Tippi.

Deirdre had thanked her for the lovely blue-velvet reticule Lisette had given to her. It was a perfect match for her blue cape and the velvet bonnet she wore so often. Inside the reticule had been a pair of blue gloves in a soft cloth that was lighter than wool.

As she went back to her quarters, Deirdre was thinking about Carlos and wondering if he were as filled with anticipation as she was this evening. She prayed that all this foul weather would pass and they would have a pleasant day to travel to Golden Splendor.

Elena dismissed all thoughts of getting to see Deirdre by the time the clock in her room had chimed four that afternoon. But she couldn't avoid seeking out Delores to tell her that she was going home for the holidays.

Like Lisette, Delores was totally unprepared for Elena's announcement. A stunned expression came to Delores's face, for the Christmas holidays meant nothing to her. She was hardly the type of mother who'd ever prepared a special dinner or trimmed a Christmas tree even when her son was growing up. The truth was she found the whole holiday scene a nuisance.

"You—you mean you're going back to Half Moon Bay, Elena?" Delores asked her.

"I'm going home to my family, señora. I can't imagine spending a Christmas holiday in a lonely hotel room. How sad that would be!"

Delores was no fool and she would have been very foolish to have dared to try to discourage Elena from going to her family. The young lady would have defied her. She had only to look at Elena's face to see that nothing would have stopped her.

Delores tried to mask her feelings and told her to enjoy her visit. "When can I expect you back, Elena?" she asked.

"I'll spend just a few days, señora," Elena told her, leaving Delores's suite.

But Delores sat in a quandary the rest of the evening. Once Elena got back to Half Moon Bay, she would be under the influence of her father and the handsome Mark Mateo.

There was no Christmas spirit sparking in Delores Delgardo that evening. If she lost Elena, she could lose everything. But something else plagued Delores. When and how had she lost touch with reality? For the first time in more years than she cared to remember, she recalled the simple, humble surroundings she had been reared in. Her mother and father had made it a special time for her and her brothers and sisters.

Elena's words kept ringing in her ears: She could not imagine any place being more lonely at Christmas time than a hotel room.

Delores could only vaguely remember when she'd not spent her Christmas holiday in a hotel room. She couldn't recall when she'd last bought Miguel a Christmas gift, and as far back as she could remember he'd never given her a present.

Her parents had observed the holidays. She could remember the simple little gifts her mother would make for her because her father was too poor to buy them presents from a store.

She could certainly not recall any sentimental holidays with Diego when she'd married him. When, she wondered, disturbed, had she lost her awareness of Christmas? She honestly could not recall when she'd stopped purchasing gifts for Miguel.

She felt so depressed sitting alone in her suite that she decided to go down the hallway to Colette's. Colette had a way of comforting her when she was feeling low.

Colette greeted her with a smile. To see her friend standing before her in her colorful dressing gown with a glass of wine in her hand was enough to lift Delores's spirits. "Come in, Delores," Colette urged.

The first thing Delores noticed was the festive air in Colette's sitting room. Little evergreen wreaths were hung on the three windows and a small two-foot tree was decorated with a dozen small gifts around its base. The sweet aroma of bayberry and pine permeated the room. Candles were burning and twinkling.

"Colette, you are a sentimental soul, aren't you? You seem to be very much in the holiday spirit," Delores remarked as she sat on the settee.

"Oh, I always am, Delores! I went down to the hotel kitchen and got over in an isolated corner to make up my special pâté. I often go down there, Delores, to concoct a dish I love. I've some finger sandwiches made up. Let me bring us a tray of them and get you a glass of wine. We'll get your spirits lifted," Colette promised.

Colette had had no need of a two-bedroom suite as Delores had, so when she'd come to the Towers Hotel she'd insisted that one of the bedrooms of the suite be made into a small kitchen. She loved to cook and didn't want to have to go down to the dining room nightly or have a tray sent up. Delores had been generous enough to oblige her.

It pleased Colette to see Delores devour two small sandwiches with relish. "They're delicious, Colette. Imagine! We've known each other all these years, and I'm just now finding out what an excellent cook you are. You've kept secrets from me."

Colette gave one of her infectious laughs. "Not really, Delores. You're busy with your salon and your girls. Fixing your pretty ladies' hair still leaves me a lot of time on my hands. So while you are busy with your work, I have a very nice life of my own. I have you to thank for it. I enjoy making up your pretty ladies, and it still leaves me time to go to the quaint shops I love to browse in and cook—which I've always loved to do. I made my pâté this afternoon because your cook wanted to watch me make it."

Delores was so impressed with Colette's sandwiches that she reached for a third one. Colette refilled her glass. She had sensed that Delores was upset about something tonight, and it pleased her that she seemed to be enjoying herself now.

While Colette was in the kitchen, Delores roamed the room and took a closer look at the Christmas tree. One of the small packages had Miguel's name on it.

She had a rather perplexed look on her face when Colette returned. "You—you have a gift for Miguel?" she asked.

"But of course, Delores. I have always had a gift for your son since the first year I came here. Christmas is a time of joy. I give all my friends some little gift. I have no family, but I have many friends." She smiled.

Delores realized when she went back to her own suite that her old friend Colette and Elena Fernandes had a mutual feeling about the holidays: It was a time for friends and family. Now she understood why she was so lonely and depressed at Christmastime. She also realized something else this evening: Colette was a much happier woman than she was.

Thirty-two

The *Bay Queen* made a very early departure the next morning. Elena was up and dressing while it was still dark outside her windows. The sun was rising by the time Elena was boarding the boat.

Even though Delores knew it would be a quiet day she had Miguel drive her to the salon; but before she left the hotel, she stopped at Elena's room to check out her armoire. None of the fancy gowns were missing from the armoire, and the toiletries were still on the dressing table. She decided that she was just going to have to wait to see if Elena returned. She'd apparently taken nothing except what she'd brought with her when she'd come from Half Moon Bay.

By midday, the *Bay Queen* had turned into San Pablo Bay to travel southward. By then, the sights began to look familiar to Elena and she had to confess that she was excited to get back to Half Moon Bay. This was where her roots were. It was where Papa and Vasco were. Nothing could ever change that. All the glamour and glitter of Sacramento was only a moment's pleasure. It was not long-lasting. It was only filling a void.

She took three jaunts around the boat because the small cubicle which was her compartment was too confining. She was observing the countryside, for she could judge now just how far away they were from Half Moon Bay. On her last trip around the deck, she saw how low the sun was sinking and she knew that her papa and Vasco would be veering their fishing boats around to head for the docks.

She also knew that they'd not go out tomorrow. It was Christmas Eve, and Sebastian never worked on Christmas Eve. He would not go back to work until the day after Christmas. It dawned on her that she was going to have difficulty carrying the two heavy valises on the walk from the wharf to the cottage in the slippers she had on. Oh, how she wished that she'd left her little leather sandals at the top of her valise instead of at the bottom!

She hoped that it wasn't going to be dark, but the *Bay Queen* was scheduled to arrive at dusk and she would still have an overland trip of ten miles.

As she had figured, darkness was shrouding the village by the time she arrived. It was going to be a long, laborious walk with those two large valises to carry up the road to the cottage; and yet, she'd packed very little to bring home with her except for the gifts for her papa and Vasco.

Luckily for her, a twelve-year-old Portuguese boy she knew was still roaming the street and he rushed to her side. "I'll carry your bags for you, Elena," he offered.

"Oh, Chico, I'll let you carry one. I can manage the other." She smiled down at him.

"I can handle both of them without any trouble," he boasted, a big grin on his face.

"I've no doubt that you could. My goodness, you have grown since I last saw you, Chico," she declared, noticing how tall he was now.

"I know," he said with a cocky air as he sauntered beside her. "I'm almost as tall as you."

"You sure are!"

"And you've gotten prettier, Elena," he declared.

Elena laughed. "Oh, Chico, that's awfully nice of you.

Right now, I'm feeling very tired so I don't feel very pretty. I'm just tired."

"Yeah. I heard tell you had gone way up to Sacramento. That's a real big place, eh?"

"Oh, yes, Chico—a very big place," she told him, fumbling in her reticule for some coins to give to him when they arrived at the cottage. She could see the cottage up ahead and it was a welcome sight for the slippers she was wearing were hurting her feet. Had Chico not carried one of those valises she would not have been arriving at the cottage this soon.

The glowing lamplight streamed out the front room windows, and Elena dismissed Chico once he had placed her valise beside the door. "Here, Chico, take this and get yourself something," she told him as she took his hand to place the coins in his palm.

"Thanks, Elena. Thanks a lot! Merry Christmas," he exclaimed as he dashed down the steps and disappeared into the darkness.

Sebastian's cottage lacked the woman's touch that Elena always gave it at the holiday season, but he had made an effort to put up a tree and decorate it. Vasco had tried to discourage him from even doing that. "It ain't going to seem like Christmas this year anyway, Pa, without Elena here," Vasco had told him.

"Well, we're still going to have our Christmas tree and we're going to have ourselves a Christmas dinner. Pedro brought me that nice pork roast. He never forgets me when he butchers his hogs," Sebastian retorted.

There was no question about it. It took a longer time for their dinner to be ready now that Elena was no longer home.

This afternoon they'd arrived back at the docks early so the crew could have a nice long holiday with their families. Sebastian considered that his gift to all of them.

Vasco had gone straight home to start chopping wood and to get a fire going in the cookstove, but Sebastian had stopped at the grocery store so he could get a few things he needed for the next two days. Tonight he was going to make his *paella*.

For Christmas Eve they'd feast on the huge pork roast, which would last through Christmas Day. His old buddy Pedro had supplied him with almost everything he and Vasco would need for their Christmas feast. He had brought a basket of sweet potatoes and other fresh vegetables he'd grown in his fall garden.

Vasco was having a qualm of conscience this evening as he chopped the wood. There were only two packages under their tree. One was for Elena and the other one was for him, but nothing was under the tree for his Papa. Now Vasco was wishing he'd gone out to purchase something for Pa. But he'd just not felt in the spirit to do so this year. He still could not understand what had possessed his sister to leave home.

By the time Sebastian returned, Vasco had a supply of wood chopped and the fire blazing in the cookstove. He knew this was to be one of their *paella* dinners, so he started chopping up the ingredients for Pa to toss into his big cast-iron kettle.

Sebastian came through the front door, his arms laden with purchases. When he had laid everything on the kitchen table, he went into the front room to light the candles he'd placed around the room as Elena always did.

"You see? I light all the candles like Elena. It does make the room look pretty, eh Vasco?" Sebastian remarked as he came back to the kitchen.

He wasted no time yanking his apron from the peg to tie around his wide middle. He hummed a tune as he always did when he was puttering and cooking in his kitchen.

When he saw that the water was simmering, he sprinkled

in his various herbs and all the ingredients Vasco had chopped up for him.

A few minutes later, everything was in the pot, so Sebastian told his son, "Now we let the kettle and the fire do their job and we will have ourselves a glass of wine, eh?"

It was now dark outside and the two of them were ready to seek the comfort of the chairs in the front room after the long day they'd put in.

Vasco's big heart went out to his father tonight, for he knew how hard he was trying to salvage something of past holidays when Elena had been there to share them. He knew how his father was hurting, but he was putting up a brave front. Never had he loved his father more, but never had he felt so angry with his little sister.

Sebastian turned to Vasco. "Did you hear something?" he asked.

"I heard nothing, Pa. Do you hear something?" Vasco asked in return.

Elena felt strange knocking on the front door. She would have normally opened the door to walk in, but she didn't feel free to do that tonight.

Sebastian heard her rap and rose from his chair to go to the front door. To open the door and see the sparkling black eyes of his daughter with an uneasy smile on her face told him his prayers had been answered. It was the grandest Christmas gift he could have received—just as Margarita Gomez had told Elena.

He gathered his daughter in his two huge arms and held her, too overcome with emotion to speak. Tears streamed down her cheeks when he finally was able to stammer, "Oh, Elena, my little Elena, you came home for Christmas!"

"Oh, Papa, Christmas would not be Christmas without you and Vasco," she told him as his two huge arms held her close.

But as her father folded her in a warm embrace, Elena's dark eyes met Vasco's, and she saw nothing but coldness. He hated her for what she'd done. A deep pain stabbed at her.

Enthusiastically, Sebastian exclaimed to Vasco when he finally released his daughter, "You see, Vasco, she did come home!"

Elena was determined that Vasco was not going to spoil her homecoming. If he would not come to her, then she would go to him. She walked over to plant a kiss on his cheek and tell him, "Oh, Vasco, I missed you and Papa more than you could possibly know."

He had only to feel her tiny hands patting his shoulder and her black eyes looking down at him to feel himself mellowing as angry as he was with her. "Good to see you too, little sister," he told her.

Rising from the chair, he went over to pick up the valise on the floor to take it to her room. Elena announced that there was another valise out on the porch, and he went out on the porch to get that one, too.

Vasco asked her how she'd managed to carry these two valises up to the cottage and she laughed, telling him that she'd gotten lucky when young Chico had come along.

While Vasco was taking the two valises to her old room, Sebastian had time to carefully scrutinize his daughter. He could not fault anything he saw. She was more beautiful and her gown and cape were finer attire than she'd ever worn in Half Moon Bay. She'd certainly not returned to him looking downtrodden and weary. She looked like a fine lady, as elegant as Señora Aimée Mateo. His eyes missed nothing about her as he surveyed her from head to toe. He saw the delicate, dainty gold cross around her throat and the gold earrings on her dainty ears. But it was the look on her pretty face that told him that his Elena was pleased and happy with her new life.

He gave her a warm smile and told her, "I did not approve of what you did, Elena, but you look wonderful—so what can I say?"

"Thank you, Papa, for saying that. It means very much to me to hear you say that. I knew you'd never approve; and yet, I knew it was something I must do. I've no regrets except that I caused you worry. I trust you'll forgive me for that," she told him.

"You know me too well, my Elena. No, I'd never have agreed to let you leave here; but if you are happy, then I am happy," he told her.

The three of them spent a wonderful evening together feasting on Sebastian's *paella* and Portuguese wine. Elena told them about the city of Sacramento, the elegant parties she attended, and the many people she'd met. She described the grand old mansions and the special friends she'd made, like Señora Margarita Gomez and Deirdre Deverone.

Sebastian and Vasco sat spellbound by her tales. She told them that just one of Señora Delgardo's gowns cost more than they earned in a week's catch from their fishing boats.

Sebastian was beginning to understand why Elena was not willing to return to Half Moon Bay with him when she was living such a fine life in Sacramento. He also knew that Half Moon Bay would never content her anymore. This little cottage would seem dull in comparison to what she had now been accustomed to.

He and Vasco had insisted that they clean up while she got herself settled in her old room. By the time they dimmed the lamps in the kitchen, Elena had unpacked her valises and had her two gifts under the Christmas tree.

Vasco noticed the extra packages when he came into the front room. Elena had bought each of them a gift from Sacramento. He decided right then that he had to get to a store in the morning, before they closed for the holidays, and get a gift for his Pa and little sister.

It had been a very long day for Elena and she fell asleep almost as soon as her head hit the pillow. She'd not known just how exhausted she was until after she'd eaten dinner and gone to her old bedroom to get the two packages out to place under the tree.

She slept long after her father and brother had gotten up and had their breakfast. But Vasco immediately rose from his chair. With a boyish smile on his face, he announced, "I've got some errands to do, Pa. I suddenly got the Christmas spirit!"

Sebastian gave a chuckle. "I'm glad to hear that. Go do your errands."

For Sebastian, it was a glorious sight to see Elena's door slightly ajar as it always used to be. He couldn't resist peeking to assure himself she was there in her bed.

Once Elena awoke, she was a busy young lady the rest of the morning and afternoon. While Sebastian prepared the huge pork roast to put in the oven, Elena worked in the kitchen. The old cookstove's oven was fired up for hours, for Elena baked two pies and a cake for their dinner tonight and tomorrow.

Once her baking was finished, she left the cottage to gather up cones and greenery to decorate the mantel in the front room. She wanted to smell the pungent scents of pine and cedar.

By mid-afternoon, Elena had the cottage looking very festive, permeated with the wonderful aromas of the holiday season.

Vasco returned with his purchases, and now he had some packages to place under the tree. He had had no trouble choosing a present for his father, but he had been rather embarrassed when he sought to purchase a gift for his sister. She was such a fancy little lady now.

But he had luckily encountered a very nice clerk in the mercantile store who suggested toilet water and scented soaps. "All young ladies adore toilet water and scented soaps, sir," she'd told him. Vasco had felt rather foolish sniffing the various fragrances she'd displayed to him. He'd picked the jasmine, for he recalled how Elena was always picking the wild jasmine blossoms when she went strolling in the woods.

"Your sister will love this, sir," the clerk had told him.

Vasco started for home with what he considered a nice gift for his sister and he knew his Pa would be very pleased with the black hat he'd purchased for him. He was feeling much better now for he, too, had gifts to place under the tree.

When he walked through the door he noticed the difference in the front room immediately. Elena's touches were everywhere as they had been in the past. With the fresh smells of pine and cedar and the scents from her jars of dried flower petals, the house smelled like Christmas. The mantel was lined with a garland of evergreen and red berries. As he placed his gifts under the tree, he could hear Elena's lilting laughter echoing from the kitchen as she and their father worked over the feast they were preparing.

It was a gay evening the three of them spent, and Elena put on one of the prettier gowns she'd brought from Sacramento. Sebastian's pork roast was utterly delicious. Vasco helped Elena clean up the kitchen. He told her she was looking too pretty in her fancy gown to do dishes, so he washed them and she dried them and put them away.

They all gathered in the front room to sit around the Christmas tree to exchange their gifts. Once Vasco had opened Elena's gift, he put on the black leather vest and wore it the rest of the evening. Elena knew that her father was more than pleased with his pearl-grey shirt from the way he kept caressing the soft material. He looked at her with warmth in his eyes, for he knew that she'd remembered his boast to have a silk shirt.

When Sebastian opened Vasco's gift to find the fine felt hat, he placed it atop his head, where it remained the rest of the evening.

Elena loved the sweet-smelling toilet water Vasco had bought for her. "Oh, Vasco, thank you! You must have remembered how I was always picking the wild jasmine when I went walking in the woods. No blossom smells sweeter than jasmine."

"Yes, I remembered, Elena." He smiled at her.

When she opened her father's gift to her, she was hardly expecting the exquisite strand of pearls in a velvet case. She gasped, "Oh, Papa! Papa, they are beautiful!" She realized now, as she could not have known a year ago, what a piece of jewelry like this cost.

"I've gotten to give to you, Elena, what I never had the opportunity to give to your mother. She always wanted a strand of perfectly matched pearls," he told his daughter.

"I'll cherish them forever, Papa," she promised, rushing to kiss him.

It couldn't have been a happier night for the Fernandes family this Christmas Eve.

Christmas Day was just as festive. Sebastian wore his grey silk shirt and strutted around the cottage like a proud peacock. Vasco wore his leather vest over his blue shirt. Elena wore her father's pearls around her neck.

Elena was thinking as the three of them were sitting down to Christmas dinner that she wouldn't have missed this occasion for anything in the world. Had Señora Delgardo said she couldn't have these few days off, she would have come to Half Moon Bay anyway.

She went to her room late that night, knowing she could not possibly leave tomorrow afternoon as she should do to keep her promise to the señora.

Papa and Vasco would be shattered, and she couldn't do that to them after the last two wonderful days they'd shared.

Whatever she faced when she returned to Sacramento, she'd face it. But she would never hurt her father and Vasco again as she had several months ago when she'd left with Señora Delgardo.

Another day or two should make no difference, Elena told herself to justify her decision to remain a little longer.

Thirty-three

Carlos swore that Amigo could always sense when he was going to leave to go on one of his three or four days jaunts to Golden Splendor. He became very testy and protested with loud meows.

When he picked Deirdre up at the hat shop, he told her about his very unhappy Amigo.

"Poor Amigo—he will have a lonely Christmas," Deirdre sympathized.

"Oh, hardly. My housekeeper will see that Amigo gets his share of her turkey. The chances are he will be curling up on her bed instead of mine. I understand that's what he does when I'm gone."

He lifted her luggage into the buggy and went around to leap up in the seat. Quite hastily, Deirdre found herself traveling with this handsome young man to spend a three-day holiday with his parents at Golden Splendor.

She was very excited to be going to the wine country she'd heard about but never seen. Yet, she was also in awe of Carlos's family. How would they accept this strange young lady they'd never met who would be intruding on their family gathering at Christmas time? What if they didn't approve of her?

Everything had been going so wonderfully for her and Carlos. She wanted nothing to spoil it. She liked Carlos very much, although she couldn't swear it was love she felt right now. But she trusted him, and that was more than she could say for most of the men she'd met in the last few years.

Had she not felt that she could trust Carlos, she would never have agreed to leave Sacramento to go so far away alone with him.

She'd worn her most elegant traveling ensemble. The blue outfit consisted of a long-sleeved, demure gown of very light wool and had a matching cape. She wore the same brilliant-blue bonnet she often wore to the park.

She'd brought one fancy gown of emerald-green and a more casual dress in a shade of purple. Deirdre thought it very feminine; it had a white-lace collar and cuffs.

With as much care as she'd chosen her gowns, she'd picked out her jewelry. Since she owned no exquisite emeralds, she'd chosen her pearls.

She did have a very beautiful amethyst broach and earrings that she'd bought to wear with the purple gown.

Wanting to feel that she'd look just perfect for Carlos and his family, she'd taken a long time deciding which of her gowns to bring and she was pleased with her choices.

She was also pleased about the weather. After the miserable day yesterday, it was wonderful to be greeted by the bright sun this morning. They'd stopped at a quaint little inn for a midday meal, for Carlos knew they had a long afternoon of traveling ahead of them.

It was a long five-hour drive in his buggy to get to Stockton where they'd be staying the night. By the time they had checked in at the hotel and he was escorting her to her room, he knew she was weary although she wasn't complaining.

When they got to the room, which was directly across the hall from his, he told her, "Go inside and rest, Deirdre. I'm going to order baths for us, and we'll have dinner in my room at seven. We won't have to worry about making the effort to go downstairs. Tomorrow the day won't have to be this long."

She sighed. "That sounds wonderful to me, Carlos."

The luxury of an hour of rest on the comfortable bed and a nice relaxing bath did wonders for her. But she wasn't in the mood to get back into the gown she'd traveled in all day today and would wear again tomorrow, so she slipped into the jade satin dressing gown with long, flaring sleeves.

It flowed full from the shoulders and Deirdre could see nothing improper about walking across the hall to dine with Carlos. The truth was it was more concealing than the gown she'd worn today.

She was sure Carlos would understand. As soon as they had dinner, she was going to return to her room to seek her bed, for she didn't wish to arrive at Golden Splendor in an exhausted state.

She wore her long fair hair loose and flowing over her shoulders. As Carlos greeted her, he thought she looked absolutely beautiful and he recognized that she had on a lovely dressing gown. Aimée wore her dressing gowns downstairs in the mornings to have her coffee.

He understood that she just felt the need for comfort, for Deirdre was not a woman to flaunt herself at a man. He realized that she was tired from the day of traveling when, after they finished their dinner, she politely refused another glass of wine. Smiling across the table at him, she told him, "Oh, Carlos, I must bid you goodnight or you'll be carrying me across the hall."

He rose from the chair and helped her up. A devious twinkle was in his eyes as he told her, "I would not mind that at all, Deirdre." He took her arm and led her across the hall to see her safely inside her door, telling her good night and telling her to rest well.

As he returned to his own room, he was thinking that he'd

never expected to find a woman like Deirdre Deverone. She had all the qualities he had sought in a woman. He liked the comfortable feeling he had when she was with him, and he had the impression that she felt the same way about him.

Everything had happened so fast that he found himself bedazzled. He had thought when he bought his little home in the city and settled in at the law firm that he was going to be a bachelor for a few more years at least. Now he wasn't so sure.

The Sunday afternoon when he'd spotted Deirdre in the park everything had changed.

By the time he had made his impulsive decision to invite her to accompany him to Golden Splendor, Carlos had already admitted to himself that he was helplessly in love with her. Now he was anxious to see if his parents approved of her, for this was very important to Carlos. But he really didn't have a shadow of a doubt about what their feelings would be. His mother would adore her, for Deirdre reminded him of Aimée in many ways.

He wanted Deirdre to be his wife! It wasn't going to be long before he would ask her to marry him.

It was almost four in the afternoon when they arrived in the valley of the wine country. Carlos pointed out the fertile vineyards on the right side of the road. "That's my father's vineyards, Deirdre," he said proudly.

Excitement was now churning within her. The long rows seemed to go on endlessly. "Oh, Carlos, this is a first for me. I've never seen a vineyard before. I came from sugarcane and cotton country."

They'd soon be arriving at his family's country estate if they were now going by the vineyards. Deirdre was getting anxious and nervous about meeting Carlos's family. She wouldn't even have a chance to look in a mirror to straighten straying wisps of hair before she'd be standing before them.

Carlos guided the buggy into the grounds that were surrounded by a five-foot-tall stone wall, and he turned in her direction to give her a warm smile. He sensed her apprehension.

Deirdre saw the perfectly manicured lawn surrounding the sprawling two-story stone mansion. She was intrigued as they drew closer to the house. She could see the French influence at the front entrance and in the front gardens, but she had only to look at the side of the estate to see the Spanish influence in the courtyard garden.

Carlos had told her that his father, Mano, was of Latin descent and his mother was French.

As he brought the buggy to a stop, he told her, "Welcome to Golden Splendor, Deirdre!"

"Oh, Carlos, it takes my breath away. It is such a beautiful place!" She sighed. It was truly a place of splendor.

Upstairs, Markita glanced out her bedroom window and saw Carlos's buggy rolling up the long drive to the entranceway. She couldn't believe what she saw. There was a lady with Carlos—and a very beautiful one, too! She dashed like a gazelle down the stairs to tell her parents that Carlos was home. "And he's brought a woman with him. I can't believe it!" she exclaimed excitedly.

A slow smile came to Aimée's lovely face as she gazed up at her husband. "Do we dare to hope that Carlos has found himself a lady, Mano?"

He smiled down at her. "Ah, *querida,* you're such a romantic! She may just be a good friend that Carlos has invited to share the holidays with us. She might not have had a family in Sacramento to spend Christmas with so Carlos brought her with him."

Aimée was as excited and curious as her daughter. The

three of them left the sitting room to greet Carlos and his guest.

A servant had just opened the door, and Carlos and Deirdre were entering the hall. Deirdre caught her first glimpse of the Mateo family. They made a striking trio. The tall, trim gentleman who was still very handsome, his jet-black hair slightly streaked with grey, had to be Carlos's father. The young girl with hair and eyes as black as night must be the younger sister Carlos had spoken about. But the person Deirdre's eyes lingered on was the dainty, petite lady who hardly came to the top of her husband's shoulders. Her golden hair was sprinkled with silver.

She rushed up to them, and Carlos embraced her. Deirdre saw how beautiful she was with her delicate features and brilliant, violet eyes.

Carlos released his mother to introduce Deirdre. "I'd like you and father to meet Deirdre Deverone." He grinned at Markita, teasing her. "Now, Markita, I've not forgotten you. Deirdre, this is my sister Markita."

Deirdre could not have wished for a warmer welcome. She was telling them how nice it was to meet Carlos's family, when Aimée took her by the arm to guide her to the parlor. Mano, Carlos, and Markita trailed behind.

"I am so very happy that you will be spending the holiday here with us at Golden Splendor, Deirdre," Aimée told her as they entered the elegant parlor.

While Aimée summoned a servant to serve some refreshments, Markita's curious eyes studied her brother's attentive manner toward this pretty lady. She could see why, for she was fair of face and figure.

Carlos had always been gracious, but his manner around Deirdre Deverone was different. Mano was amused to note that his little Markita was as curious as her beautiful mother.

Aimée had only to be in the company of Deirdre for the

next half-hour to know why her son had invited her for the holidays. Deirdre had an air of sophistication and possessed grace and charm. This was the type of young woman Carlos would choose to share his life with.

Mano took notice of their relaxed manner as they'd turned to look at one another and exchanged smiles as they chatted in the parlor.

Markita could not ever remember seeing her older brother so lighthearted and gay. There was nothing stiff and reserved about him this late afternoon. She had to credit Deirdre Deverone for the change in Carlos.

It suddenly dawned on Aimée that it had been a long journey from Stockton to Golden Splendor, so she told Deirdre, "Please, dear, forgive me for not showing you to your room sooner so you can relax and refresh yourself before dinner. You've had a long trip today."

But Markita jumped up from her chair to declare, "I'll show Deirdre to her room, Mother."

"Well, all right, Markita. Take Deirdre to the room across the hall from yours," Aimée told her daughter.

Carlos raised a skeptical brow for he knew his nosy little sister would be quizzing Deirdre about the two of them. However, he had no doubt that Deirdre would be able to handle the situation for she was no dumb Dora. She was a smart, clever young lady.

That was another of the many things he admired about Deirdre. She wasn't one of those empty-headed little idiots he'd so often found himself cornered with.

Deirdre rose to leave with Markita, and Carlos told her that he'd see her at dinner. He smiled. "Get some rest, Deirdre, and don't let Markita talk your ears off."

Deirdre smiled down at him. "Don't worry, Carlos. Markita and I will get along just fine." She turned to follow Markita out of the room.

"You see, Carlos," Markita snapped back at her older brother as she took Deirdre's arm. "Older brothers can be so bossy," she told Deirdre as she led her out of the parlor.

The remaining adults overheard Markita, and they exchanged smiles.

Aimée rose from her chair but turned to her son to tell him, "She is utterly charming, Carlos. I'm so happy you brought her here. Now, I leave you and your father to visit, for I must talk with my cook." She quickly left the parlor to go to the kitchen.

Mano suggested the two of them go to his study to have a drink and a father-son talk.

"That sounds like a good idea to me, Father," Carlos replied. "What did you think of Deirdre?"

"Well, son, you must know I have always had an eye for beautiful ladies, for I wooed and won your mother, who is still the most beautiful woman in the world to me. I think Deirdre is also a beautiful young lady."

Thirty-four

By the time Mano and Carlos went to the study at the end of the hallway, the sun was setting and there was a slight chill to the air. Mano went over to the liquor chest to pour Carlos and himself a drink.

"Where is Mark?" Carlos asked.

"That was what I was going to speak to you about before dinner, for he is due to be over here tonight. Mark is now living at La Casa Grande, Carlos. Your grandfather has been ailing for well over a month now."

"Oh?"

He handed his son a drink and took his glass to sit in the leather chair at his desk. He lit up one of his cheroots. Carlos had never enjoyed a cheroot as he and Mark did. He began to tell Carlos what had transpired since he'd last been home. He hoped that his oldest son would not resent his grandfather's decision and in turn resent his younger brother.

Mano could assure him that Mark's smooth tongue had not influenced old Carlos's decision. Long before he'd approached Mark, old Carlos had discussed it at length with him, and Mano had put his stamp of approval on the plan.

"Mark is now the owner of La Casa Grande," he told Carlos. "He lives there now instead of here."

"I think Grandfather Carlos made a wise decision. I'm happy for Mark, for he is exactly the one who should take over the ranch. But I'm sorry to hear that Grandfather Carlos is failing. What is it?" Carlos asked his father.

"Just old age and a heart that is wearing out, Carlos. I was over there a few days ago, and I could see how weak he has become in just a few weeks' time," Mano told him.

"Then he will not be coming over here tonight?" Carlos asked.

"Oh, no, Carlos. And not tomorrow either, I'm sad to say."

"Then I will go over there to see him tomorrow, Father."

"I think that would be very nice, Carlos, and may I suggest that you take Deirdre with you. Your grandfather would enjoy meeting her."

"I was planning to take her with me. Grandfather Carlos will like Deirdre," Carlos told him with an assured tone.

"I'm sure he will," Mano agreed.

The clock on the wall of the study was chiming six when the two of them emerged from Mano's study. But Mano could not have been a happier man as the two of them climbed the stairs to their bedrooms. Carlos had taken the news about Mark as he'd prayed he would; Mano wanted no hard feelings between his sons.

Carlos didn't have much time to relax by the time he took a bath and changed into a fresh, white-linen shirt and a pair of black pants. Carlos had left a few pairs of pants and some shirts in his old bedroom so he never had to pack a lot when he came back to Golden Splendor on visits.

The minute he'd walked in the front door he'd noticed the magnificent wreaths hanging on all the doors of the parlor and dining room. Garlands draped the railings of the stairway. Everything looked as festive as it always did this time of the year.

Tonight they would enjoy a grand feast before they returned to the parlor to exchange their gifts. It would be late before the house was quiet. Everyone would sleep late and a brunch would be served in the dining room. Members of the family would eat at various times between eleven in the morning and one in the afternoon.

On Christmas Day, the family would gather once again for dinner, and Grandfather and Grandmother Aragon would come from Chateau L'Aragon to join the festive evening. On Christmas Eve, the Aragons went to their two married sons' homes to share the evening with their families.

Christmas Day would end the holiday for Carlos. This year he was not going to be able to stay on at Golden Splendor to see the New Year in as he had last year. He and Deirdre had to start to Sacramento the day after Christmas. She had to get back to her job, and he needed desperately to get back to his office. His mother was going to protest, but he knew she would understand when he explained that Deirdre also worked and was only allowed a few days off.

No one could have had a more intriguing family as Carlos felt he had. Their holiday feasts were like everything else in Mano and Aimée Mateo's lives: A magnificent blending of two cultures and cuisines. His mother had perfected it so both families enjoyed their feasts.

But Carlos could never acquire a taste for his Grandmother Mateo's New Year's Day dinners. She was a southern-born lady who insisted on black-eyed peas; Carlos choked on them. He liked the thick-sliced cured ham and the pans of cornbread, but he had never learned to like those awful peas. He much preferred to go to his Grandmother Aragon's for dinner on New Year's Day.

Deirdre found Carlos's younger sister a little charmer, but she refused to give her any clue as to her and Carlos's relationship. Markita left the guest room flustered without her curiosity satisfied. But Markita found Deirdre just as charming.

Markita, like Carlos, had inherited their father's dark Latin handsomeness, Deirdre thought. And Carlos's mother was absolutely gorgeous!

After Markita had left the room, she took the gifts she'd brought for Carlos's family from her valise. It hadn't been easy to pick out gifts for the Mateo family with her limited funds. But she'd done the best she could afford to do. Lisette had suggested two lovely clusters of her velvet flowers which ladies could wear in their hair or on their hats. She had taken Lisette's suggestions of dainty lace-edged handkerchiefs and the clusters of velvet flowers. She'd chosen a pink cluster for Markita and white ones for Carlos's mother.

For his father, she had bought a brown leather journal he could use in his study. Somehow, she felt that Carlos would be very pleased with the old law book she'd purchased for him since it was in such excellent condition.

She placed her gifts on the velvet chair until she could put them under the massive Christmas tree in the elegant parlor.

She had plenty of time for a leisurely perfume-scented bath and an entire hour to lie across the bed to relax before she had to start getting dressed to go downstairs. As she lay there, she was thinking that she would never forget this holiday. This place was fabulous, and Carlos's family were just wonderful. She was curious if she would be seeing his brother tonight. It was strange how life had entangled her and Elena's lives. Here she was at the Golden Splendor that Elena had spoken about so glowingly when she told her about the Festival of the Grapes.

Elena was in love with Mark Mateo whether she was willing to admit it or not, Deirdre was convinced. Now she found herself falling in love with Mark's older brother, Carlos. She wondered what the future held for both her and Elena and if their lives would be bound together in the years to come.

The relaxing bath and the rest on the bed did wonders for her. She felt very refreshed when she fashioned her hair before slipping into her lovely emerald-green gown. By the time she had fastened the pearl necklace around her neck and had the pearl earrings on her ears, she was very pleased with the reflection she saw in the mirror.

She was dabbing toilet water behind her ears and at her throat when there was a knock on her door. She suspected it was Markita and went to open it.

Markita stood before her in the loveliest pink gown. Deirdre was glad that she'd chosen the cluster of pink flowers for her gift.

Markita was animated like her mother, Aimée. As she viewed the lovely Deirdre, she exclaimed with gusto, "You are gorgeous! That gown is stunning!"

"Thank you, Markita. May I say that you look most beautiful in your pink gown?" Deirdre responded.

"Pink is my favorite color. That is why I picked this gown for this evening," she told Deirdre as she gathered her gifts from the chair.

"Pink is very flattering to you. I bet you look lovely in jonquil-yellow, too," Deirdre remarked as she and Markita went out the door. Markita commented that she did like yellow for her gowns.

While they descended the stairway, Markita chatted away, telling her that she would be meeting Mark this evening and that tomorrow evening she would meet her Grandfather and Grandmother Aragon. "But my Grandfather Mateo is too ill to come this Christmas. Carlos is named for him. Grandfather Mateo raises bulls. Do you like bulls, Deirdre? I think they are ugly," she declared.

Deirdre laughed and confessed that she didn't know

whether she liked them or not. "I guess I can't give you an honest answer about that," she admitted. One thing about Markita, Deirdre had already decided, was that she was an open book. There was no mystery about how she felt on any subject.

Markita was already forming her own, definite opinion about Deirdre: Carlos was a fool if he didn't marry this charming lady.

When they approached the archway of the parlor, they found Carlos anxiously awaiting them.

The sight of Deirdre was enough to take his breath away, and he rushed to greet her and take the packages she was carrying. He had a brief moment as Markita left them to whisper, "Oh, how beautiful you look tonight, Deirdre!"

He took her to the settee where Aimée was sitting. Mano had already poured her a glass of his chilled white wine.

When Carlos was placing Deirdre's gifts under the Christmas tree, he couldn't have been happier that he'd given way to the impulse to invite her to share the holidays with him and his family. It meant a great deal to Carlos that his family was impressed with this young lady who'd so swiftly won his heart.

Mark had not yet arrived at Golden Splendor from La Casa Grande. The truth was he wasn't in much of a holiday mood this evening. He'd put in a long day and Grandfather Mateo had had a bad day, so he was reluctant to leave La Casa Grande. But Estellita had urged him to go to Golden Splendor to share the evening with his family. "I'll keep a close eye on him, Señor Mark, and if the least little thing goes wrong, I'll send one of the men to get you back here," she'd told him.

Mark had seen a definite decline in old Carlos in the past week. It had been about that long since Mano had last been over to the ranch, so he had decided that tonight he'd prepare his father for the changes in his grandfather. Mark knew that Grandfather Mateo would never live to see another Christmas. The truth was he might not live to see the New Year in.

At Golden Splendor, Mano kept glancing at the mantel. The hands of the clock were getting close to the dinner hour, and he knew his Aimée would not delay their meal. He wondered if things were not going well this evening at La Casa Grande and if that was why Mark was late.

In the morning while Aimée still slept, he planned to go see his father.

At Aimée's appointed hour, Celia announced that dinner was ready to be served. Mano escorted his wife, and Carlos took Deirdre's arm with one hand and his sister's arm with the other. At that moment, Mark dashed through the front door.

He came empty-handed, for he'd had no time to go into town to purchase gifts, but Mano and Aimée were elated that he had finally arrived. Markita chided him. "It's about time you got here to escort me into the dining room," she scolded.

Mark wasn't prepared to meet the fair-haired guest holding Carlos's arm. Carlos introduced Deirdre to his younger brother, but Deirdre had recognized the handsome young man immediately. She'd seen him at the Crauthers' garden party when he had lured Elena away. He had not seen her, however, hidden as she'd been in the gardens.

But as Carlos made the introduction, Mark's deep violet eyes connected with her bright green eyes and he had a strange feeling that they knew one another. Deirdre realized that he was far more handsome now that she was seeing him close than he'd looked from a distance. His violet eyes were devastating. He'd inherited his mother's eyes, but his hair was as black as a raven's wing—just like his father's, Carlos's, and Markita's.

Throughout dinner, Mark probed his brain, trying to remember if he'd met this lovely lady before. Something about the look in her eyes told him that she knew him, but he couldn't recall meeting her. If he'd met her, he would have remembered her. She wasn't the kind of lady a man met and forgot.

While the Mateo family enjoyed their Christmas Eve feast, Mark concluded that his family approved of this beautiful lady Carlos had brought to Golden Splendor for the holidays. It was also apparent to Mark that Carlos was very enamored with Deirdre Deverone. He could see why.

Carlos was more lighthearted and gay than he'd remembered ever seeing him. Mark's keen, experienced eyes saw how the pretty Deirdre looked at Carlos. He could tell that she was equally attracted to Carlos.

Madre de Dios, if he weren't going to be wrong about Carlos! He might not end up being a bachelor after all.

As they returned to the parlor, Mano went to Mark to seek a private conversation with him before the two of them rejoined the rest of the family. Once they were in the study behind closed doors, Mark told his father that old Carlos was fading fast.

"Estellita urged me to come tonight, but I'll not stay late, Father," Mark told him.

"I'll be there in the morning," Mano said. "I'm glad you've been with him the last several weeks. I know that this has meant a lot to him. I might tell you while we're alone that I told your brother this afternoon about your grandfather's will. He approves, too. I thought you should know."

"Yes, I am glad to know that, Father. I'd never want Carlos to resent me or Grandfather Mateo's decision," Mark declared as the two men took the last sip of the brandy Mano had poured.

Mark told him that old Carlos's lawyer had come to La

Casa Grande last week. "That old fellow tied up all the loose ends. He amazed me, Father. He's gone over everything with me. He told me that he'd already given Mother a generous gift of Grandmother's jewelry and that the rest of her gems are mine to give to my bride, Carlos, and Markita. I think Grandfather had grave doubts that Carlos would ever take a bride, but after tonight I'm not too sure about that."

Mano laughed. "Yes, I'd agree with you about that. I think Deirdre would make a perfect bride for Carlos."

Mark's violet eyes sparkled deviously as he commented, "Oh, so you noticed, eh?"

"Of course, my son. I've always had an admiring eye for a charming, beautiful lady. Did I not pick your mother to be my bride?"

Mark grinned. "Well, that was enough to tell me that you are a connoisseur where ladies are concerned, Father."

A glint came to Mano's dark eyes as he confessed to his son, "I can't deny that when I was wild and reckless I had my fair share of pretty ladies, but after I met your mother I never desired any other woman."

Mark smiled and nodded his head. He understood that feeling. It was the way he felt about Elena Fernandes. Mark realized a few moments later that his father was perceptive when he took his arm and said, "It would have been nice if that little Elena could have been here with us tonight, Mark. I liked her—liked her very much."

"I would have liked that, too, Father; but she wished to remain in Sacramento," Mark replied.

A devious grin came to Mano's face as he pointed out to Mark, "Sometimes, son, when a lady tells you *no,* she doesn't really mean it. She just wants you to use a little sweet persuasion. It would amaze you how often a lady can change her mind."

Mark roared with laughter. "Father, I bet you were a rascal when you were young."

"But I got the woman I loved, and that was all that mattered to me," he told his son.

Thirty-five

It was a strange Christmas Eve for Aimée Aragon Mateo, for Grandfather Mateo was not there as he usually was. Her son Carlos had not seemed happier than he was tonight for as many Christmas Eves as she could remember. Her Markita was her usual vivacious self, but Mark was trying so hard to be his happy-go-lucky self that Aimée knew it was forced. She'd seen Mano and Mark slip away after dinner and assumed that his sober mood had to do with his grandfather's condition.

She knew her generous son always bought lavish gifts for all the family, but tonight he'd arrived empty-handed. She surmised he'd had no time away from La Casa Grande for anything as frivolous as shopping. Her younger son was carrying a heavy load on his shoulders right now, and she admired him tremendously.

When the dinner was over and the family had settled back in the parlor, it was time for the gifts to be handed out. Mark made his apologies to his family that he had no gifts under the tree. "I'll make it up to all of you later," he promised.

Mano quickly dismissed his concerns by telling him, "You're taking care of Father, son, and that and the ranch is a full-time job. We understand."

Mark tried to spend a little time with each member of his family as the evening went on. He'd left his father's side to spend some private moments with his mother. She was elated, having just opened her gift from her husband. Usually, Mano's gift to Aimée was an exquisite piece of jewelry.

Markita was anxiously opening her three gifts from her parents, Carlos, and Deirdre. She sighed and gasped over her parents' gift to her, but she was just as exuberant over the little pink cluster of velvet flowers and the lace-edged handkerchiefs Deirdre had brought to her.

Mark moved closer to see Deirdre open her gift from Carlos: A delicate gold bracelet for her dainty wrist. She was more than pleased with it. Mark realized that Carlos had very deep feelings for this young lady or he'd not have spent that much money on a gift.

"Very pretty, Deirdre," Mark remarked as he came up behind her. He grinned at his brother. "You have Father's fine taste in jewelry, Carlos."

"Thank you, Mark," Carlos replied. He noticed that Mark was carrying an empty wine glass. He also sensed that Mark was not in a holiday mood tonight. He looked tired, and the festive air he was trying to display for the benefit of his family wasn't fooling Carlos.

"Sit down and keep Deirdre company, Mark, while I get all of us another glass of wine," Carlos urged him.

"A man could get no better offer than that. I will always be willing to keep a beautiful woman like Deirdre company," he jested with his older brother.

Lighthearted, Carlos grinned at Deirdre. "Beware of this younger brother of mine," he warned. "He has a silken tongue where pretty ladies are concerned."

Deirdre laughed. "I've met that kind before. Don't worry, Carlos. Mark and I will be fine."

Mark's deep violet eyes had a glint in them when he told her she'd been a great tonic for his older brother. "I've never seen Carlos in such high spirits, and I think it has to be you that's performed this miracle," Mark told her.

"I'd like to think that, Mark," she told him softly.

A very serious look crossed Mark's face then, and he asked her, "Deirdre, tell me while Carlos is gone if we've met before. It's been driving me crazy all night. Something in the way you looked at me made me wonder if we'd met."

"I've seen you before," she explained, "but you couldn't have known. I recognized you immediately. You see, I saw you come into the Crauthers' garden party and whisk Elena Fernandes away. But you didn't see me."

"You were there that afternoon?" he asked her.

"Yes, you see Elena and I were sent out on assignment to that garden party. I used to work for Señora Delgardo. I left and went to work at a hat shop before I met Carlos."

"I see," he mumbled thoughtfully. "And Elena—have you seen her since you left the salon?"

"I have and she is fine, Mark, but I am sure there is going to come a day when Elena will discover that she has no life of her own. Then she will want to leave as I did. There is no time for your own life when you work for Señora Delgardo. Your entire life revolves around society parties, modeling Delgardo gowns, and enriching the señora's coffers."

"I don't have a very high opinion of Señora Delgardo, Deirdre. I was not allowed to see Elena or take her a message from her concerned father. It seems to me that you and Elena were prisoners at the Towers Hotel."

Deirdre smiled. "Delores Delgardo claims her rules are for her girls' protection. But the truth is Señora Delgardo wants to be the dominating force in her girls' lives."

"Well, that was why you saw me make my rude appearance at the Crauthers' party. I was determined to see Elena while I was in Sacramento. My only disappointment was that she would not return to Half Moon Bay with me. I was concerned about her, and her father is, too. Damn it, I care about her, Deirdre," he confessed.

Her green eyes warmed as she looked at him. "That is obvious, Mark. Be patient with her, for she will tire of the glitter—probably sooner than I did. You see, Elena has a loving family. I had no one to care about me."

Mark smiled. "I think you do now, Deirdre."

"I only know that I've never been happier, and that is all that matters to me. Working in a hat shop drawing meager wages might not appeal to some, but I have my living quarters furnished at the back of the shop. I have the freedom of Sundays off, and I spend them in a nearby park. That is where I met your brother, Mark. This would have never happened if I'd still been working for the demanding Señora Delgardo and living at the Towers Hotel."

"I'm very happy for you and Carlos, Deirdre. Tell Elena when you see her that she is constantly in my thoughts. When I can, I will try to come to Sacramento again; but I can make no promises right now," Mark told her. He saw that his brother was coming toward them and knew he would not have been allowed to have this lengthy conversation with Deirdre if Carlos had not stopped to talk to his father.

Mano had told him about his grandfather. When Carlos finally returned to Deirdre and Mark with the wine, it didn't surprise him that Mark announced, "I will share one more glass with the two of you, and then I will be leaving for La Casa Grande. I won't be able to come back tomorrow, Carlos. I know you understand, so I will say my farewells for the Christmas holiday tonight."

"Deirdre and I will be coming over tomorrow to see Grandfather Mateo," Carlos informed him.

"Wonderful! He will be happy about that, Carlos. And I will get to see the two of you tomorrow," Mark said as he prepared to leave them.

He said goodbye to his mother and father. Markita accompanied him to the front door. She gave him a big kiss on his cheek as she told him, "It's not going to seem right tomorrow without you with us, Mark. I'll—I'll miss you."

He gave her a brotherly hug. "Are my ears deceiving me, little sister? You'll miss me?"

"Yes, I will. As obnoxious as you can be at times, I'll miss you." She grinned impishly. But just as quickly that elfin smile changed to a more serious expression. She took hold of his arm to restrain him from going down the front steps. In a most solemn tone she asked him, "Why do we think that our lives will remain the same and never change, Mark? Carlos no longer lives here, and now you are gone. That leaves only me at Golden Splendor."

"I guess that's just the way it is, Markita. I would not have imagined living at La Casa Grande six months ago, but it would seem destiny directs our lives for us. There will come a day when you, too, will leave Golden Splendor."

"I don't know, Mark. I—I might just end up being an old maid," she replied dejectedly.

Mark threw his head back with a roar of laughter. "An old maid, Markita—you an old maid? Never in a million years will that happen."

Mark got into his buggy and gave a wave of his hand to his sister as he guided the buggy down the drive. Markita stood on the front porch until he disappeared in the darkness. Then she returned to the parlor.

Markita could not have known that she and her mother were sharing mutual feelings this evening. Aimée spent most of the evening reflecting on the holidays of the past.

What a very foolish woman she had been to think that their traditional Christmas holiday could have remained the same! Oh, she was a very silly mother!

Tonight, Aimée faced the stark reality that their traditional Christmas holidays might not ever be the same. It was best that she prepare herself for change. Her youngest son would not be gracing their Christmas Day dinner table tomorrow. It was a bitter pill for Aimée to swallow.

By the time the evening was over and Mano and Aimée were climbing the stairs to go to their room, Mano knew without her saying a word that she was feeling, as he was, that the evening was lacking something. Perhaps it was because Mark was no longer living here now and he had been so somber this evening. Maybe it was the void that old Carlos's absence had created.

Mano was just as glad that the festivities had ended early for he was concerned about his father and ready to get upstairs so he could retire.

As soon as they were in their bedroom, Aimée inquired about the old man. "He's worse, isn't he? That's why Mark was late in arriving and why he left so early."

"Yes. Mark said he'd failed a lot this last week. I'm going to ride over there in the morning," he told her. She turned her back to him so he could unfasten her gown.

"Oh, Mano, I realized tonight that I've been so foolish to think that life would never change at Golden Splendor. Things never go on the same way forever. I dreamed a most foolish romantic dream," she sighed.

Mano turned her around to face him, and his dark eyes looked deep into hers. "No, *mi vida,* you dreamed no foolish dreams as long as you and I are here at Golden Splendor," he told her. "Our children may leave, but you and I will be here. We've made the magic happen, not our children, Aimée!"

She knew what he was trying to tell her. The two of them had discovered the magic of this place long before any of their children had come along, and it would still be there for them after the children were gone.

For more than twenty-five years, the two of them had lived and loved one another. On this Christmas Eve's night, they once again captured the glorious rapture of that passionate love they'd shared all these many years.

Early the next morning, Máno got up and dressed, letting Aimée sleep. He took the time to have only one cup of coffee before he rode for La Casa Grande.

Mano was still a fine figure of a man. He sat astride the fine black stallion that was the grandson of his prized stallion Demonio. It had been a sad day for Mano when he'd lost Demonio, but the horse had lived a long life. Now he prized this fiery young stallion that had Demonio's blood flowing in his veins.

When Mark had arrived back at the ranch last night, Estellita had a good report to give him. "He's had a very good evening, Señor Mark. He sat up in bed and read one of his books. I took him a warm glass of milk about an hour ago, and he's sleeping like a baby. I just checked him a few minutes ago," she told Mark. So he didn't bother to stop at his grandfather's room, but went directly to his own bedroom.

Estellita went to her bedroom relieved that Señor Mark had told her that she was to fix just a simple dinner tomorrow night. "There is no need for a big Christmas feast under the circumstances, Estellita. Grandfather can't be at the table, so make it easy on yourself."

Perhaps, it was talking to Deirdre tonight that made his thoughts roam back to Sacramento and Elena Fernandes. As soon as he got things squared away at La Casa Grande, he was going to go to Elena. This time, he would do what he should have done when he was last in the city. He should have asked her to marry him. Hell, he'd already made up his mind that she was the only woman for him!

Now there was no shadow of a doubt in his mind that she

was the only one for him. No woman had ever stirred him or haunted his sleep like Elena.

More than once when his thoughts had been consumed by her beautiful face and figure, he had felt like giving himself a swift kick in the rear, for he knew that if he'd asked her to marry him then that she would have returned here with him. He would not have been put through this torment.

He damned his fierce Mateo pride. The next time, he would not let that stand in the way.

Before he went downstairs to have his own breakfast, Mark stopped in his grandfather's bedroom and was delighted to see that one of the kitchen girls had brought up a breakfast tray. Old Carlos was propped up on the pillows, but he had an anxious look on his face as though he were anticipating eating the eggs, thick slices of ham, and biscuits.

"Well, look at you! You're looking great this morning, Grandfather. Now, you just get busy eating your breakfast and I'll go downstairs to have mine. Then I'll be back up to visit you," Mark told him.

"I slept wonderfully, *nieto,* and I'm as hungry as a wolf," he declared as he picked up the cup of coffee to take a sip.

That old man amazed Mark, and he was elated to see him looking that great this Christmas morning. Once again, he had rallied and appeared stronger.

Mark was having his own breakfast when Mano arrived. He told his father how hearty his grandfather seemed. "I haven't had a chance to tell him that you were coming over this morning. He was sleeping soundly when I got back last night, but I can tell you that he's doing fine this morning."

Mano laughed. "That old man is a fighter," he agreed. He poured himself some coffee while Mark finished his breakfast. Mark suggested that Mano go up to see his father while he attended to some chores in the barn. "I gave the foreman the day off to be with his family."

"You just go to do what you've got to do, son, and I'll see you later. I thought I'd come early and have my visit with him now, because Carlos and Deirdre will be over this afternoon," Mano told him as they rose from the table.

Mano went toward the stairway, and Mark went toward the barn. He was in much better spirits today than he had been last night.

Part Four

Splendor of Love

Thirty-six

Under the circumstances, it was a very pleasant Christmas Day at La Casa Grande. Old Carlos had a nice visit with his son. When Mano saw that he was getting weary he left so his father could take a nap. Old Carlos napped for almost an hour and then had a light lunch. Then he took another nap, which seemed to refresh him just in time to greet his oldest grandson and his pretty lady.

He was very talkative and alert when they arrived, and Carlos could tell that his grandfather approved of Deirdre. She found the old man utterly charming even though he was very ill.

He told young Carlos, "You're going to have to bring this beautiful lady back to see me again. She lifts my spirits!"

Deirdre laughed. "You're sweet, Señor Carlos, and I'll come to see you any time I can."

"I'm not sweet or kind, señorita, as Carlos can tell you, but I am honest."

But a visit of an hour was enough. Carlos saw that his grandfather was tiring when he closed his eyes and suddenly became very quiet. He whispered to Deirdre that it was time they left, and Deirdre agreed with a nod of her head.

Carlos took his grandfather's hand as he bade him good-bye. He had no doubt that it was the last time he would see him alive. He and Deirdre were leaving tomorrow at midday.

Deirdre also went to the bedside. Her gracious tenderness

was a pleasant surprise to both old Carlos and young Carlos. She took his hand in hers and bent down to kiss his wrinkled cheek. "It was a pleasure to meet you, Señor Mateo. Goodbye, señor."

His weak eyes gazed up at her, and he murmured, "Goodbye señorita. Nicest kiss I've had in a long, long time."

They left the room quietly and rejoined Mark downstairs. Carlos told his brother how the old man had suddenly faded into weakness with the need to sleep.

"That's the way it is with him, Carlos. He seemed to have a surge of strength all day today, but tonight he might be completely worn out. But it's been nice for him to have seen father and you and Deirdre this afternoon."

Carlos said, "I guess this is the last time I'll be seeing you on this trip, Mark. Deirdre and I have got to get started back to Sacramento by midday." He gave Mark a warm, brotherly embrace—which was out of character for him. Carlos had never been demonstrative like Mano and Mark. Mark decided that the beautiful Deirdre had performed many miracles where Carlos was concerned.

What was most important to Mark was what Carlos said to him after he'd embraced him. "Mark, I just want you to know that I'm glad you are taking over La Casa Grande. You are the right one to do it. I think it was meant to be this way. I honestly do."

"Thanks, Carlos," Mark told him. Their eyes met in understanding, giving birth to a camaraderie which would last a lifetime.

It was after three when Carlos guided his buggy back toward Golden Splendor, and Deirdre understood why he was quiet and thoughtful as they rolled down the dirt road. He had told his grandfather goodbye for the last time. There was no doubt about it in her mind: Old Carlos was dying.

But it really wasn't old Carlos he was thinking about. Carlos was thinking about Deirdre and what a beautiful lady she was not only of face and figure but of heart and soul. The more he was with her, the more he found to admire about her. It was obvious to him by now that she had charmed not only him but his family, including old Carlos.

Carlos had begun to realize new things about himself since meeting Deirdre Deverone. He could be as impulsive as his younger brother or his father. Carlos remembered after he and Mark had turned twenty some of the tales their mother had told them about their wild, reckless father when he was in his twenties.

For him to have invited Deirdre to accompany him here for the holidays had been impulsive for Carlos. But for him to have bought the gift which he had yet to present to her was *very* impulsive on his part. The gold bracelet was only one of the presents he'd bought at the jewelry shop in the city. He had also purchased a most magnificent emerald-and-diamond ring. He'd seen the ring on display and had been reminded of Deirdre's lovely green eyes.

It was only when he was walking out of the shop that it dawned on him how many hundreds of dollars he'd spent in less than a half-hour.

Going back to Golden Splendor, he knew why he'd bought that ring. He had definitely decided to ask Deirdre to marry him before they returned to Sacramento. But for Carlos, it had to be the perfect romantic setting, and Golden Splendor was hardly private. He decided that he'd wait until they were alone traveling back to Sacramento.

Before they reached the gates of the estate, Carlos brought the buggy to a halt and looked over at Deirdre. "I apologize for being so remote," he said. "I've had things on my mind, and I know this can't be very pleasant for you."

"Oh, Carlos, I understand. Your grandfather is dying, and we both know that," she told him compassionately.

He brought her hand to his lips. "Thank you, Deirdre. Thank you for understanding. You're a jewel. I never expected to find a lady like you."

He had yet to kiss her lips, but the kiss he gave to her hand was enough to tell Deirdre that he possessed the same hot blood as his younger brother Mark. She adored Carlos and understood his quiet, reserve. She, too, liked to have time alone, but she wanted desperately to be the woman to ignite the flaming passion she suspected was smoldering deep within him.

She'd never met a man like Carlos. He could be gentle and tender; she'd seen the gentleness when he'd stroked Amigo to show the cat his love for him. She'd seen a mist of tears in his eyes when he'd told his grandfather goodbye this afternoon in their final farewell. She'd never met a man that she could talk with endlessly as she could Carlos. Coming to Golden Splendor had convinced Deirdre that she was desperately in love with Carlos. But she also asked herself how she could feel this way when he'd never kissed her.

The atmosphere at Golden Splendor was more subdued that evening. Deirdre was pleased with the gowns she'd brought. Her emerald-green gown had been the perfect choice for Christmas Eve. But tonight when the family gathered for Christmas dinner, she wished to look more demure—especially with the shroud of sadness hovering over the Mateos. Her purple gown with its white collar and cuffs was ideal. She was satisfied with her image in the mirror as she put on her earrings and her amethyst broach.

Later, when Deirdre walked into the parlor, Aimée admired her impeccable good taste. She felt very proud to introduce this young lady to her parents. Deirdre found them just as warm and charming as the rest of the Mateo family. Paul Aragon was a jovial little Frenchman with a paunchy belly and apple cheeks. His tiny wife was a very elegant lady with snow white hair and delicate features like Aimée's.

Tonight, Aimée had had her cook prepare her family's traditional Christmas dinner of roast duck with rice. Last night they had followed the customs of the Mateos.

The Aragons left shortly after dinner, for they wished to return to Chateau L'Aragon before the night grew late. But they shared an after-dinner liqueur with their daughter and her family before they left.

Aimée told Deirdre, "We have tried to get them to stay overnight on Christmas and return home the next day; but no, my father is restless away from Chateau L'Aragon. He still feels that nothing would run without him there. My brothers, Emile and Armand, have been running the winery for the last few years."

Deirdre chuckled. "It has been so nice to meet them tonight—and Señor Mateo this afternoon. It's been a most wonderful holiday for me—thanks to the entire Mateo family."

"Well, Deirdre, you have been a most delightful guest. We're all enchanted by you, and Carlos must bring you here again or he will get a very harsh scolding from me." She smiled.

"And I will certainly come, señora."

Lamps and candles dimmed much earlier this evening. Mano felt the need to go back to La Casa Grande in the morning, so he said his farewells to Carlos and Deirdre that night. "I fear I'll not be back by the time you have brunch with your mother and Markita. I know you plan to leave right afterward, but I also know you understand."

"Of course, Father. I'll be leaving with a heavy heart," Carlos told him.

"He's lived a rich, full life. I guess that's all a man can expect. He had a dream when he came to California and he saw it come true. He shall die happy," Mano declared soberly.

Deirdre was not sleepy when she went upstairs, so she began to pack so that she would not have to do it in the morning.

She laid out her undergarments and the slippers she would wear with her blue gown and cape when they left tomorrow. In his room, Carlos was doing the same thing. The first thing he put in his valise was the leather-bound law book Deirdre had bought for him. He decided to leave behind the linen shirts from Markita. In the valise with the old law book, Carlos also placed the velvet pouch Mark had handed to him just before he and Deirdre had left La Casa Grande. Mark had told him, "Grandfather told me to give this to you, Carlos." Carlos had thanked him, but he'd not opened the pouch until he and Deirdre had returned and he was alone in his bedroom. It was the gold-etched pocket watch the old man had always carried. Carlos's eyes misted and he was glad that he'd waited to be alone to open the pouch. Old Carlos knew that he was dying and he'd not be putting that watch in his pocket again.

At La Casa Grande, Estellita had done as Mark had instructed her. She fixed a good meal, but not her usual Christmas Day fare.

Señor Mark told her to serve the holiday dinner in his grandfather's room. She liked his thoughtful gesture. He was a good grandson and so devoted to his grandfather. She admired this young man more and more all the time. She knew how hard he was working to run the ranch as his grandfather would have. Everyone, including the foreman, liked Señor Mark. He was masterful without being lordly.

Mark was pleased to see how old Carlos had seemed to enjoy his dinner, and he poured another glass of red wine for his grandfather.

Old Carlos remarked that it was fine a red wine. "Your father, my son, is a fine vintner, *nieto*. This is a superb wine!"

"It is, isn't it, Grandfather? And it went perfectly with the beefsteak Estellita fixed for us. That woman is one fine cook," Mark declared.

"She is that. Always take care of her, Mark. She has taken good care of me," he told his grandson with a serious look on his face.

Mark gave him a nod of assurance. "La Casa Grande is Estellita's home, Grandfather, even when she can no longer take charge in the kitchen. But she's not going to give up 'her' kitchen as long as she can hobble around." He grinned.

Old Carlos chuckled. "I think you are getting to know Estellita very well."

"We get along just fine."

Carlos finished his wine, and Mark summoned a servant to take the trays. Mark felt that the extra glass of wine should help him sleep well, so he gave his grandfather an affectionate hug and told him that he'd see him in the morning.

The old man grasped his hand with an amazing show of strength. He smiled up at Mark and said, *"Féliz Navidad, nieto!"*

"Felices Navidades to you, Grandfather," Mark told him. He was feeling encouraged as he went down the hallway to his own room. His grandfather seemed very alert this evening.

There was no hint of a sunrise when Mark rolled over in his bed to look out his windows. He assumed that it was still very early, but the hands of the clock told him it was time to get out of bed. So he crawled out of his bed to walk over to the windows to peer at the dark, grey sky. There was no promise of the sun shining today. A dense fog hovered over the grounds, and Mark could hardly make out the fountain and benches in the courtyard gardens.

He got dressed and went downstairs to have his breakfast. Since it was still dark outside, Mark decided to wait until after he'd eaten to check on his grandfather. He figured that he probably needed the time to sleep; yesterday had been filled with excitement for the old man.

An hour passed before Mark went back up the stairs to see if old Carlos was ready to have his breakfast. When he opened the door, the room was ghostly quiet and old Carlos's snores had ceased. He moved toward the bed with trepidation. Mark grew more apprehensive when he saw that the sleeping man's body was still. Mark pulled back the coverlet and rested his hand on his grandfather's chest. He felt no heartbeat, and he knew—as he'd sensed from the moment he'd walked through the door—that death was in the room.

"Oh, God! Oh, God!" he moaned as he sank onto the chair, Carlos's limp, lifeless hand in his. Tears flowed down his cheeks. He had not shed so many tears since he was a small lad who could cry freely from the hurt of a skinned knee or a cut.

When Mano entered his father's room and saw Mark was sitting there shaking with sobs, he knew that his father was dead. Mark didn't have to say a word. Mark felt his father's hand on his shoulder, and he looked up. "He's gone, Father. He's gone."

Mano gave him a nod of his head and bent down to embrace his son. At that moment, Mano sought to comfort his son. He had witnessed death before, but this was Mark's first time. "He died peacefully in his sleep, Mark. It is the kindest way a man could die. Father has a happy look on his face."

Mano took charge, for he knew his son was shaken by his grandfather's death. He pulled the coverlet over old Carlos's face and urged Mark to come downstairs with him. Then Mano went to the kitchen to inform Estellita about his father's death and have a carafe of coffee sent to Mark in the study.

"We've arrangements to make," he told his son. "I'll help you, but first I'll have to ride back to Golden Splendor to detain Carlos before he leaves for Sacramento."

He summoned Pedro to take the message to old Carlos's remaining friends in the valley. Mano knew his father's wishes and, since Carlos was at home, he made the decision that the funeral would be in the morning at ten. This was out of consideration for Carlos and Deirdre. They both had jobs to get back to; and as it was, they would be delayed an extra day.

Mark dried his tears and lit up a cheroot. Mano explained the funeral arrangements and took time only to gulp one hasty cup of coffee before leaving for Golden Splendor. "You, my son, ride for Father's priest. The funeral needs to be performed in the morning. Carlos and Deirdre can't delay their departure another two days. Besides, your grandfather told me many times that he wanted a simple funeral."

So when Mano left La Casa Grande, Mark went to the stable to get his horse saddled to ride to the rectory to get Father Gonzales.

Mano found his family in the dining room just finishing a pleasant lunch. Deirdre was dressed in the traveling ensemble she'd worn the day they'd arrived, and Carlos had had their luggage brought down to the hallway entrance.

His announcement shrouded the room in gloom. It came as no shock to Aimée and Carlos couldn't honestly say it surprised him; but he was in a quandary. He had to remain whether he wanted to or not.

It was Deirdre he was thinking about, for she would be forced to remain, too. She tried to disguise her feeling of concern, but Carlos sensed that she was worried about how this could affect her job at the hat shop.

She didn't fault Carlos, for he couldn't help it. But as the family made their plans during the afternoon, she sequestered herself in the guest room so the Mateos could talk and make arrangements which really didn't include her. But she had to face that this glorious holiday could cost her dearly. If Lisette were angry enough, she could lose her job and that meant that she'd be out on the street.

If that happened, then the splendor of this Christmas would not be worth the price she'd pay.

Thirty-seven

Carlos and Deirdre were rolling down the long drive of Golden Splendor twenty-four hours later than they'd planned. Deirdre was hoping Lisette would understand that she'd had no choice but to stay for the graveside services.

Deirdre was convinced that Mark was very much in love with her little friend Elena, for when he'd walked with them to Carlos's buggy he'd made a point of telling her to let Elena know that he'd be coming to Sacramento soon to see her.

"Tell her I would have been there sooner had all this not fallen on me to do," he'd said.

"I'll tell her, Mark," she'd promised him.

Mark watched Carlos's buggy roll down the drive before he went back to the house to join his parents and Markita. He was glad when the last mourners had departed and he was finally alone at La Casa Grande. He was in no mood for idle talk with old friends. The truth was, he envied his brother and Deirdre as they disappeared down the drive. He would have liked to have ridden away from all his responsibilities this afternoon. He was in no mood to deal with tears and lamentations.

His parents and Markita remained to share the evening meal with him; but he was glad to say good night to them, too. Mano sensed that it was a night that Mark wished to be alone, so he told Aimée, "It's been a long day and I think we need to get back home."

Mark said his good nights to his family and closed the front door of what was now his house. He walked down the hallway to the study which was now his study. It was overwhelming, for La Casa Grande was quite a dynasty.

He walked to the liquor chest to pour himself a glass of his grandfather's favorite cognac and sat in the leather chair at the desk. As Mark sipped the cognac, he thought about Christmas night and realized that that old man had put on a last show for him—a most gallant act!

Perhaps it was his weary state or the intoxicating effects of the cognac, but as Mark sat in the leather chair, he swore he heard the old man's voice telling him, "You see, *nieto,* you fit the chair perfectly. I knew what I was doing when I made you the patron of La Casa Grande."

When Mark left the study that night, he never had any doubts about himself or that he could be the master of this ranchero. It was enough for him that his grandfather had had that much faith in him. Damned if he'd ever fail him!

He was thinking of various things that would be needing his attention in the morning. He crawled into bed and laid his head on the pillow, and sleep came swiftly.

For the next two mornings, Mano came to the ranch to help Mark get the papers and documents in order, but at midday he rode back to Golden Splendor and Mark turned his attention to working the ranch.

Both days Mano went home pleased with the way his son was assuming his new role. The changeover was not going to require much of Mano's or Mark's time. Grandfather Mateo had taken care of the legal matters himself. His banker and old friend had been stunned when old Carlos made his last trip into the bank and had his name removed from his vast bank account. "I wish my grandson Mark's name to replace mine," he'd told Fred Garson. Garson just hoped the young man was worthy of such faith.

As old Carlos had advised, Mark had already started to establish his image in the house. Mano noticed this when he and Mark were in the study together about a week after Carlos's death. Carlos's personal mementos had been removed and packed away. All the articles now on the desk belonged to Mark.

Mark had even changed the furnishings to suit his taste and convenience. Mano had to admit he liked the changes. The long, black-leather couch that had been situated against the dark-panelled wall for as long as Mano could remember was now placed in front of the massive stone fireplace. The cozy leather chairs were now on either side of the hearth.

Mark was pleased to hear that his father approved of his changes. "Grandfather told me to make this house reflect my image and to remove his. Of course, I told him that he would forever be here in this house. But he told me that his memory would fade and that I must take over in all ways. The house must present my style and personality, so I decided to start with the study."

"As usual, the old fellow gave you some wise advice, Mark. You should make this place your home now. There will be a day when you'll bring a bride here; and as elegant as the parlor and dining room are, she'll want to change them. Her taste will not likely be like my mother's," his father pointed out.

As they prepared to leave the study, Mano glanced up above the mantel to see the portrait of his mother. He smiled. "One day, your bride's portrait should hang there."

"Whenever I get a chance to claim myself a bride, maybe it will." Mark laughed.

"You'll have a chance, Mark. Just don't let a lady you truly love slip away from you. Don't let anything stand in your way."

"Did mother ever give you any doubts about her love for

you?" Mark asked seriously. "Did you ever wonder if you were crazy in love with her but she didn't love you back?"

Mano grinned. "That lovely mother of yours taxed me to the limit. But I knew she cared, regardless of what she said, for her kisses told me differently."

Mark grinned. "I wish I'd had this conversation with you many weeks ago, Father. I could have been a lot wiser when I went to Sacramento."

"Then go back there, Mark, and do what you think you didn't do right the first time," Mano advised.

Father and son parted company that day feeling a great camaraderie with one another. As Mano rode back to his own home, he was sure that very soon he and his older son would share this same closeness, for he had seen many changes in Carlos on this last visit.

Deirdre Deverone was responsible for that, Mano was certain.

It was an ungodly long day for Carlos and Deirdre. They left La Casa Grande immediately after the funeral to get on the road to Stockton, but it was after six when they arrived and checked in at the same hotel they'd stayed in less than a week before.

He made arrangements for dinner to be served in his room, ordered warm baths for both of them, and saw her to her door. "I'll see you in an hour, and I thank you for being such an understanding lady, Deirdre." He bent down to kiss her cheek because she had such a weary look on her lovely face. He was afraid she'd never want to take another trip with him.

But once again, a warm bath did wonders to refresh her and tonight she wore the same comfortable dressing gown to walk the few steps across the hall from her room to Carlos's. As she gave her long, thick hair a firm brushing, she reflected that they would have been back in Sacramento by now had fate not intervened.

In the morning she should have been at the shop when Lisette arrived, but she wouldn't. She fully expected Lisette to be furious but prayed she'd understand when she told her of the sudden death of Carlos's grandfather.

She remembered how long the return journey was going to be and told herself that she'd better have dinner and get back to her room to get a good night's rest.

When she arrived at Carlos's door, he took her two small hands to lead her into the room. "You're amazing, Deirdre. After the trying day you've had, you look so beautiful and refreshed," he declared.

"I've not had as trying a day as you, Carlos. I have to admit the bath did wonders, but right now I'm famished." She smiled.

At that same moment there was a knock on the door and the waiter arrived with their dinner cart. Carlos laughed. "It would seem that you will now be able to eat, my lady."

Carlos, however, was equally hungry, and the two of them ate ravenously, like starving wolves. When they noticed each other's appetite, they broke into gales of laughter. That was what made Deirdre so perfect for him. He could thoroughly enjoy himself and have fun just being with her. She was a jewel, and he knew he'd never find another like her.

So he decided that he was going to delay no longer in asking her to marry him. They were finally alone as Carlos wanted them to be when he proposed, so he ordered another bottle of wine.

He told her, "We've both a need to indulge ourselves this evening, Deirdre. The hour is early yet."

Carlos poured each of them a glass of Mateo burgundy and offered a toast that they might share many more happy days together.

"I'll certainly drink to that, Carlos." She smiled warmly up at him as she took the first sip.

"Do you really mean that, Deirdre? Do you wish us to have many more days together?" His dark eyes searched her lovely face.

A soft, tender look came to her green eyes as she told him, "Oh, Carlos, of course I do. I've loved the times we've spent together. I thought you knew that."

"I hoped that I wasn't just imagining it." He was suddenly feeling very nervous about proposing to her. He'd never asked a woman to marry him.

"No, Carlos, you were not just imagining it. I care for you very much," Deirdre told him honestly.

That encouraged him. "Do you care enough for me to marry me? I want very much to marry you, Deirdre." He gave a nervous laugh, confessing, "I feel very awkward, for this is a first for me."

An impish smile came to her face as she told him, "I'm ever happier to hear that, Carlos." She'd already gotten out of her chair and come around the corner of the table. She sat on his lap and placed her hands on either side of his face, bending down to let her lips meet his. Carlos knew what her answer was from the ardent kiss she gave him.

His arms instantly circled her waist and his lips captured hers in a rapturous kiss. When he finally released her, he whispered huskily, "Oh, Deirdre, I never expected to love a woman as I love you!"

Deirdre discovered that her quiet, reserved Carlos could be a hot-blooded Latin when he made love to a woman. The two of them found themselves caught up in a whirlwind that had them soaring to the heights of the heavens.

After their passion's fury was calmed, Deirdre lay languidly enfolded in Carlos's arms. So, pleasantly exhausted, she fell asleep. The feel of her satiny, naked body snuggled against his felt so divine that he fell asleep, too.

Deirdre never returned to her room that night, but stayed with Carlos till morning.

He woke up first and dressed quietly, not wanting to rouse her because she slept so peacefully. But they had many miles to cover so, reluctantly, he went over to the bed to bend down and kiss her gently. "Wake up, sleepyhead. If we're going to make Sacramento this evening, we're going to have to get started."

Slowly, she opened her eyes and mumbled his name. Then she realized that she lay naked under the sheets. Sheepishly, she smiled at him. "It did happen, didn't it, Carlos? I—I didn't dream it."

He grinned. "It surely did happen, *querida,* and it was wonderful! Now you get yourself dressed while I go downstairs to see about having breakfast sent up."

He left, and she slipped into her dressing gown and dashed across the hall, still bedazzled.

By the time their breakfast trays arrived, she was ready to travel and her valise was packed.

When they left Stockton, it was still early. People were just beginning to stir. The sun was out, and the grey, dismal sky had disappeared.

Sitting in the buggy with the man she loved, she didn't care if she got a chilly greeting from Lisette. Carlos couldn't have been a happier man than he was this morning. His adoring eyes were constantly turning in her direction. He was thinking what a wonderful way to start the new year, for he intended that he and Deirdre would be married very soon. He wanted no long engagements.

Thirty-eight

It had been another long day of traveling for Carlos and Deirdre by the time Carlos stopped the buggy at the front entrance of the hat shop. Twilight was hovering over the city, so the shop was dark and Lisette had already left for her home. As tired and weary as Deirdre was right then, she was glad she didn't have to face an angry Lisette.

Now that they'd become lovers, Carlos was reluctant to say goodbye for the evening. "Let's have a simple wedding very soon," he implored. "I want you at the house with me and Amigo."

"And that is where I want to be. A simple wedding is fine with me."

"We can have a family celebration later. You just get busy picking out a date, and I'll take care of all the other details." He gave her a long, lingering kiss before he finally brought himself to release her.

Deirdre slipped inside and walked slowly through the dark shop to her quarters. She lit a couple of lamps and set her valise beside the bed. It might not get unpacked this evening. She felt no ambition other than to fill her empty stomach with a simple meal and seek the comfort of her bed.

In slow, lazy motions, she ambled into her kitchen in her stocking feet and fried three slices of the slabbed bacon and a couple of eggs. In the meantime, she relied on fresh-brewed coffee to refresh her.

She did get her valise unpacked and laid out a gown for morning. All evening the lamplight kept catching the sparkle of the diamond-and-emerald ring Carlos had slipped on her finger as they were preparing to leave Stockton. She had never seen a more beautiful ring. Not even the exquisite rings Aimée Mateo wore on her fingers were more stunning than this symbol of Carlos's love.

She put away the lovely gifts that the Mateo family had given to her. Since they had not known that she was going to be there as their guest, she realized that they had selected her gifts from their own possessions. She treasured the black lace shawl and reticule from Mano and Aimée, certain it had belonged to Aimée.

By now she was more than ready to get into her nightgown and get into her bed, for she wanted to get up early in the morning and have coffee made when Lisette arrived at the hat shop.

Sleep was upon her as soon as her pretty head rested on the pillow.

At Half Moon Bay, when Christmas Day was over, the fishermen and their boats were back out on the bay ready to resume their routine. But Sebastian could not resist asking his daughter as he bent to kiss her that morning, "I will be seeing you this evening, eh, little one?"

"I will be here, Papa." She'd giggled. This evening she would be, but she didn't know how many mornings she could continue to promise him that.

For the first two hours after her father and Vasco had left the cottage, Elena was busy putting things in order. Her father and brother were not the neatest housekeepers, and the last two days and nights had been filled with celebrating.

By midday she'd mopped floors, cleaned up the dirty

dishes, and dusted all the rooms. Elena had to admit that it had been a long time since she'd worked this long and hard, and her day was still not over. She needed to go to the marketplace.

It was obvious to her that her father did not shop two or three times a week for the fresh vegetables and fruits brought in from the valley by the farmers. His pantry and larder were almost completely empty, and they needed foodstuffs for their dinner this evening.

With the large wicker basket hung over her arm, she left the cottage to sashay up the dirt road. She had on her comfortable leather sandals and her floral gathered skirt with a tunic top. She concluded that she'd been eating too much of the rich food at the Towers Hotel, for her floral skirt was uncomfortably tight around the waist.

When she got to the marketplace she selected a variety of the fine fresh vegetables including two heads of cabbage, a dozen potatoes, a stalk of celery, and five large white onions. But when she had paid for all of the purchases, she realized that she could go on no more buying sprees like this while she was home, for she had very little left to get her back to Sacramento.

She saw several familiar faces in the marketplace. Some greeted her warmly, but there were others who barely mumbled hello. She wondered what gossip had spread about her after she'd left town. She knew how these people felt about anyone who dared to venture away from the village.

Out of the corner of her eye she spied two Portuguese women whispering and looking directly at her. Irritated, she vowed that she'd not settle for this place to live the rest of her life. Papa was just going to have to accept this.

With her pretty head held high and proud, she walked by them without even looking their way.

Elena had been right. The two women had been talking

about her. Rina Castelina was telling her good friend, "She's just like that snobbish mother of hers. You remember Miranda—she thought herself better than the rest of us even though her husband was a fisherman like ours."

Her friend spoke up. "I wonder what she's doing in Sacramento."

"It might surprise old Sebastian if he knew the truth about his darling daughter," Rina remarked sarcastically.

Elena was exhausted by the time she got to the cottage. As she had walked up the narrow dirt drive from the main road, she'd seen her father's nosy neighbor Maria staring out her window. She prayed that she didn't come snooping around. She'd always detested old Maria, who had constantly tried to boss her when she was growing up.

She'd not even had time to put her vegetables away before she heard the old woman coming through her back door. She called out to her, "Come on in, Maria. I've got vegetables to put away."

"Elena, you should keep your doors locked. You know what happened to your mother," she chided her.

"I know, Maria," Elena replied, considering that a lock would keep the likes of her from intruding as well.

Maria made herself comfortable in one of the kitchen chairs, quizzing her. "You came back home to your pa, eh, Elena? Did you get your fill of the big city?"

"Oh, no, Maria, I love Sacramento! I just came home for the holidays. I'll be going back to my job shortly," Elena told her.

"Going back, are you?" the old woman asked her with a surprised look on her face.

"Oh, yes."

"What kind of job have you got, Elena?"

"I work for an exclusive dress salon, Maria," Elena replied as she busily moved around the kitchen without bothering to offer her a cup of coffee. If she had, the old woman would have lingered another half-hour at least. Elena began to peel the peaches which she planned to use to bake her father and Vasco a fresh pie for their dinner tonight.

"Well, my, my, my! That would be enough to turn a young lady's head. Well, your ma always liked her fine gowns. She never dressed as plain as the rest of the women. Always liked to look real fancy she did," Maria remarked.

"Then I guess I'm like my mother, Maria, and I'm proud of it," Elena declared, wishing the old woman would leave. She'd still not offered her a cup of coffee or sat down at the table to chat. She bustled around the kitchen and set out her vegetables to peel.

Maria finally seemed to get the message that Elena was too busy to spend any time visiting. She got up and reluctantly announced that she better leave. "It doesn't seem like you've time to visit, Elena," Maria said in a huff.

"The truth is, I don't, Maria—not if I want to bake Pa and Vasco a peach pie for supper." A smile broke on Elena's face as the old woman marched out of the kitchen. Good riddance! she thought.

An hour later she had her pies in the oven and time to have a cup of coffee. She relaxed for awhile before she decided what she was going to do with the small amount of pork roast that could be combined with some of the vegetables to have what Sebastian called a "pot" dinner. She simply didn't have enough money to buy a good cut of meat.

During this idle moment, she considered that Delores Delgardo would certainly expect her back by tomorrow. Her romantic heart had hoped that the handsome Mateo would come to call. She murmured softly as if he could hear her, "Oh, Mateo, *caro mío,* come take me in your arms and tell me you love me, and I won't go back to Sacramento."

She had a conceit to match Mark's and she was convinced

that he cared for her. Why else would he have come to Sacramento in search of her?

But an inner voice tormented her, pointing out that he could have come back to the hotel to encourage her to leave with him. Instead, he'd delivered the ultimatum which she'd stubbornly refused to comply with. Oh, how she yearned to see him again, to have his arms hold her, and to feel the liquid fire that blazed in his kisses.

She tried to shake away thoughts of Mateo so she could get herself busy putting together a pot of something in which she could use the small amount of pork roast that was left. She cubed the roast and added it to the water simmering in the kettle along with some of the potatoes, quartered onions, and chunks of the green head of cabbage.

She figured with a big stack of cornbread cakes that this should make a very hearty meal for the three of them. It proved to be very tasty, and they ate ravenously that evening, finishing every bite of the pork stew and cornbread cakes.

But it seemed to escape Sebastian's attention that he had nothing in his pantry, and Elena was reluctant to mention this to him. But she had no more money to spend on food.

Vasco helped her clean up the kitchen and Sebastian went into the front room to read the paper he'd bought on the wharf after they'd docked.

As they were preparing to leave the kitchen, Vasco asked her, "Do you want to take a walk with me, Elena? I feel like I need to after all that supper I ate."

His invitation surprised Elena, but she quickly accepted and removed the apron she had around her waist. As the two of them went through the front room, Vasco told his father that they were going for a walk.

They had only taken a few steps when Elena asked him, "There's nothing wrong with Papa, is there, Vasco?"

"Oh, gosh no! Did you think that was why I asked you to take a walk with me?"

"I thought maybe that could be the reason. Thank goodness, it wasn't."

"Papa is fine. He is still as strong as a bull. I—I just wanted a little time to talk to you alone before you leave to go back to Sacramento. I know you will be going, Elena, and maybe I can understand it better now. I just wanted you to know that. You see, I had very hard feelings toward you, and I didn't like feeling that way at all," he confessed.

Her small hand gripped his firm-muscled arm. "I understand. I sensed your hostility that night I arrived back home for the holidays," she told him.

"It didn't take me long to mellow," he added quickly.

She laughed. "I noticed, and I was glad. Oh, Vasco, you and Papa are so dear to me and you'll always be, but I had to do what I did—whether it was right or wrong. Papa would never have agreed and there would have been a terrible scene. I wanted to prevent that."

"Maybe, Elena, this is part of the reason I wanted to talk with you alone tonight. You see, I feel quite differently than Pa does. Maybe I've seen the changes in you and Pa hasn't. I can understand why you'd not ever be content anymore to just clean and cook while we go out to fish every day. Since you've been gone, I have learned how much you did. Pa does the cooking, and I do the cleaning up. But there ain't much time in the evenings after I clean up the dishes to do much other cleaning," he admitted.

She laughed. "I found that out today, Vasco. I put the day in cleaning, and then when I turned my thoughts to tonight's dinner, I found that the larder and pantry were practically bare. I had to walk to the marketplace to get some vegetables or we wouldn't have had a decent meal."

"You shouldn't have had to do that. No wonder you look

ired tonight! And then I go asking you to take a walk! You
should have told me, honey."

"Oh, Vasco, I'm glad you asked me to walk with you. It
gave us time for a private talk. As you said, I will be leaving
before too long."

"Well don't you worry about walking to the marketplace
tomorrow. Pa and I will stop on our way home. You don't
need to be spending your money on our food. May I ask you
something, Elena?"

"Of course you may, Vasco."

"When will you be leaving?"

"I should have left today. I should really go tomorrow if
I want to have a job when I get back," she told him. "I can
only stay one more day and night."

Vasco told her that she was going to find what he was
about to say strange and perhaps surprising. "As I told you,
Pa's got it into his head that you'll not be going back. So
maybe the way you left the first time would be the way for
you to do it this time, Elena. It might be simpler on you and
Pa."

"You're probably right, Vasco. I want no harsh words between us. I'd been thinking about that, too," Elena admitted.
She gave his huge arm a gentle pat and told him that at least
this time he would understand and that that was a comfort
to her.

"No, there will be no hardness in my heart this time, little
Elena. You've the right to live your life as you please, just
as Pa and I do."

"It is good that we've had this talk tonight, Vasco. It's
meant more to me than you could possibly know." She saw
that he had turned her around to head back toward the
cottage.

Sebastian had finished reading his paper and took it to
put in the basket with the kindling to start a fire in his cook-

stove in the morning. He was feeling rather smug this evening. Everything was as it used to be. He and Vasco had come home to the nice fresh smell of beeswax, and the little cottage was spic and span. There had also been the aroma of the good supper simmering on the stove along with the smell of fresh-brewed coffee. Ah, how nice it was again!

Now, his son and daughter were enjoying an evening stroll together. He couldn't have been a happier man. What he'd not stopped to consider was that although this might delight him, Elena might not have found the daily routine that rewarding. She wanted more out of life.

Later, when Elena was in her own room and she'd told her father and Vasco good night, she sensed from her father's manner that he was assuming that she was perfectly content. She was hardly content. She was weary and tired from an exhausting day. Tomorrow would offer nothing different except that Vasco would go to the marketplace. She'd let them bring in the food and their dinner would be late going on the table.

Then she would take her brother's advice and leave a note on the kitchen table when she left the day after tomorrow.

Thirty-nine

Deirdre was up and dressed with a pot of fresh-brewed coffee on her stove when she heard Lisette coming through the front door of the shop. She tensed, dreading their encounter.

She questioned why she should feel such apprehension when Lisette had seemed to have such a warm, understanding nature. The only reason she could think of was the sudden change in Lisette when she'd announced her plans for the holidays. Something had told her that Lisette had resented her trip.

Lisette greeted Deirdre with sour sarcasm. "Well, you've finally returned from your *extended* holiday."

"I had no choice, Lisette. Carlos's grandfather died, and he had to remain to attend the funeral. It was out of my hands."

Lisette made no reply as she turned around to go back to the front of the shop. As the day went on, the atmosphere remained strained. It didn't help Lisette's mood that she had no customers the entire day, but that reminded Deirdre that she hadn't really needed her there. Business was still slow after the Christmas holiday. Right now, the ladies were concentrating on the annual New Year's Eve gala, which did not require a hat.

Lisette's frostiness did not melt over the next two days.

Deirdre tried to make up for her holiday by working in the evenings, but Lisette never acknowledged the extra hours.

Deirdre was disillusioned and perplexed. Lisette seemed completely different and reminded her of the selfish, cold Delores Delgardo.

The one bright spot for Deirdre was that she would be seeing Carlos on Sunday afternoon and that helped soothe her frayed nerves. She was glad to see the workday come to an end and breathed a sigh of relief when Lisette left the shop to go to her home.

She had been tempted to point out that had she been gone for the last few days, it would have put no hardship on Lisette because there was no business. It was ghostly quiet in the shop.

Deirdre no longer tried to get a conversation going between them. It was an act of futility. When Lisette did make a remark, it was laced with contempt. Her eyes had noted the magnificent ring on Deirdre's finger and she had no doubt that Carlos Mateo had given it to her.

But Lisette did not mention the ring until the last day of the week. It was as if she wished to prick Deirdre one last time before they parted company for the weekend. But Deirdre's French temper snapped after five grueling days of Lisette's overbearing attitude. All week she had tried her best to get back in Lisette's good graces, and each night she'd devoted two hours after dinner to working on hats so there would be an array of new designs ready to tempt customers when they started to come in after the first of the year.

"I see you got yourself an expensive trinket over the holidays." Lisette smirked, and Deirdre's green eyes sparked brighter than the emeralds in the ring.

"Isn't it a beauty?" she asked sweetly. "Carlos also asked me to marry him, and I accepted."

"I see," Lisette mumbled as she gathered up her reticule

to leave the shop. Deirdre did not know the frenzy she'd put Lisette in.

When Carlos arrived at the shop early Sunday afternoon to drive her to "their" park, he found a young lady who'd endured a harrowing few days.

Deirdre collapsed in his arms and gave way to tears when he questioned her about her week.

"She's been horrible, Carlos. She refused to understand that I couldn't get back. I've worked every night to try to make up for the extra time, but Lisette has ignored me. Oh, Carlos, I'm so hurt. I thought she'd get over being angry in a day or two when she saw how hard I was working."

His dark eyes looked down at her and he lifted her up from the park bench. "Come, Deirdre, we've got some things to do. You don't have to put up with that. You're coming home with me."

She quickly learned what a take-charge man Carlos could be. He propelled her into his buggy and returned immediately to the hat shop. He told her to pack all the personal belongings they could take in his buggy that afternoon and write a note to Lisette to inform her that her husband-to-be would be picking up the rest of her possessions tomorrow.

Deirdre did not question him but did as he'd instructed her to do. She had to admire the masterful way he'd ended her crisis. When she had packed the three valises, Carlos took them out to his buggy. That done, he asked her to point out the articles in the two rooms which belonged to her. There was nothing in the kitchen, but she showed him the wicker rocker and the footstool. She told him, "There really isn't much here that's mine, Carlos. But my valises are stuffed, and everything in the chest of drawers *is* mine."

Carlos saw the stressed, confused look on her lovely face, and he wished he'd known about her problems sooner. He'd have gotten her out right away. "Don't you worry your pretty head about anything, Deirdre. What's yours you will have, I assure you. I'll get it all tomorrow. Now write that woman a note so we can leave."

Like an obedient child, she sat at the little kitchen table and wrote to Lisette. To Carlos, she looked like a helpless child and he felt protective of her. It had pained him when she'd fallen, sobbing, into his arms. Carlos smiled warmly at her. "Shall we go home, Deirdre?" he asked.

"I'm ready, Carlos," she said. She got up from the chair, and he took her arm. But she suddenly dashed away from him to collect the chintz pillows from her bed. "Oh, Carlos, these little pillows are mine. I can't leave them. I'll hold them in my lap."

Carlos chuckled. "Amigo might try to lay claim to those."

Deirdre was laughing with him by the time he hoisted her and her pillows into his buggy. He went around to leap up beside her and put the buggy into motion. His dark eyes darted over to look at her and he told her, "I adore you, Deirdre Deverone!"

Amigo was at the door to greet them when they arrived. Carlos told him, "Well, Amigo, meet your new mistress." The Persian cat rubbed himself against the hemline of Deirdre's gown, meowing as if he approved. Deirdre reached down to give him an affectionate pat on the head. She hoped he approved.

Lisette had a rude awakening Monday morning. She raised the shades to let the morning light in and then moved to the back of the shop to find no Deirdre. The armoire was completely empty, but there were garments still in the chest. She found Deirdre's note on the table and was devastated. She read it a second time. She had to admit that she'd outsmarted herself and pushed Deirdre to the limit. Now she had to pay the price for her stupidity.

In very low spirits, she brewed up her own pot of coffee and tended to her shop, which was so quiet that two people weren't needed anyway. But Lisette did have time to see the number of hats Deirdre had trimmed and placed on display in her last days at the shop. Lisette hadn't noticed before. She'd been too busy punishing Deirdre for being naughty, for staying away two extra days. Well, she had been a foolish, silly woman, and no one knew that better than Lisette.

In the late afternoon a formidable man marched into her shop and announced his purpose. Lisette gave him an understanding nod and Carlos sought no further conversation with her as he amassed the rest of Deirdre's belongings. He emptied the drawers and had the wicker rocker and little footstool in his buggy in no time at all.

He did not say goodbye, but took his last load out of the shop, got into his buggy, and started for home. He didn't even take the time to put his coat back on or button up his linen shirt. When he came through the front door with his coat flung across his arm and his briefcase in his hand, Deirdre rushed to greet him with Amigo trailing behind her. It felt glorious to have both of them warmly welcoming him home.

He gathered Deirdre in his arms and planted a kiss on her lips. When he released her, he told her, "You're right where you belong. Now, tell Stella to hold dinner so I can get the buggy unloaded."

"Of course, Carlos," she said as she turned to go to the kitchen to pass his orders on to the cook. Deirdre had had the entire day at Carlos's house while he'd been at his office and she'd had two encounters with Stella. She could tell that Stella was very pleased that Carlos had installed her last night into one of the guest bedrooms. While Deirdre would not have objected to sharing Carlos's bed and bedroom last night, it had left a sweeter taste in the straitlaced Stella's mouth that he had followed a proper course.

But there had been a glint in his eyes when he told her last night that this arrangement was going to be brief. "We're going to be married much sooner than we planned."

Deirdre had to confess to herself that his gesture had endeared him to her more. The luckiest day of her life was the day she'd met him in that little park.

She was back in the parlor when he finally brought the last of her possessions through the front door. As he came in with the little footstool, he picked up his coat and briefcase and told her, "I'll join you in just a minute."

"And I shall have a glass of wine waiting for you, Carlos," she promised him.

"Ah, I'll be ready for it, *querida,*" he told her as he went toward the stairway.

He looked very sensuous to her with his white-linen shirt unbuttoned and his black hair slightly tousled. She had to admit that she wished she were to share his bed tonight.

Shortly, he came downstairs with his unruly hair brushed and the straying wisps no longer falling over his forehead. But he'd not taken the time to button his linen shirt.

He sank down on the settee with her and took a sip of the wine, reaching for her hand. "I think the lady was in a slight state of shock, Deirdre," he commented. "I went in and told her who I was and why I was there, and she just gave me a nod of her head. Come to think about it, I can't recall any words exchanged between us."

"I still find it hard to believe that she changed so drastically," she declared.

That ended their conversation about Lisette, for Stella announced that dinner was ready. Later, Deirdre insisted that he go to his room to look over the papers she knew he'd brought home while she went to her bedroom to get her things sorted out and put up.

Together they mounted the stairs but parted company in the upstairs hallway. He couldn't part from her without one sweet kiss. He could feel her firm breasts pressed against the front of his chest. *"Madre de Dios,* plan our simple wedding for the end of this week and get me out of this misery," he moaned with a grin on his face.

"I'll get busy on it tomorrow, Carlos," she promised him. With a soft laugh she urged, "Now go and get your mind on your work."

He turned away, noticing that Amigo hadn't followed him but had trailed along with Deirdre as she passed two doors to go into her room.

He called to Deirdre, "That Amigo is no fool! He'd rather be with a pretty girl than me."

"I'll leave my door ajar in case he decides to come to you." She smiled.

Out of curiosity, Carlos also left his door open when he entered his room. For the next hour the cat remained in the room with Deirdre. She placed the wicker rocker beside a window and put the footstool close at hand. Amigo, busy investigating the new objects in the room, decided that the footstool was just right for him to curl up on, so he did.

Once her clothes were neatly stored in the chest of drawers, she slipped out of her dress and into her nightgown. With her wrapper on and the sash tied around her waist, she settled in the rocker to make plans for her wedding. Since it was to be a simple ceremony at Carlos's home, she decided against a white gown in favor of robin's-egg-blue. She and Delores Delgardo were in agreement that this was one of the most flattering colors for her.

She was also thinking that this rocking chair might be

used in the months to come when she and Carlos had their first baby.

She wanted Carlos to turn one of these nice bedrooms into a study so he could have the solitude he needed in the evenings. Once she was occupying his bedroom with him there might be nights she'd wish to retire early while he was still engrossed in papers and documents.

Suddenly, she was aware that Amigo was no longer on the footstool and she searched the room for him. He was nowhere in sight, so she dimmed her two lamps and crawled into her bed.

Carlos wasn't sure just when he'd come to him; but when he dimmed the lamp on his desk ready to call it a night, he discovered Amigo curled up at the foot of his bed sleeping soundly.

When Sebastian and Vasco got to the docks in the late afternoon, Vasco told his father that they would have to purchase some food. "Elena had to go to the market yesterday, Pa, and I told her not to do that today. Let's admit it, Pa—we depended on Elena more than we realized. She was the one who kept the cottage running. We're not too good at it."

There was indignation in Sebastian's voice when he remarked to Vasco, "So, she mentioned this to you last night when the two of you were taking your stroll, eh?"

"She was just laughing about it, Pa. She said our pantry was bare and she'd had nothing to fix for our dinner. I felt sorry for her. She'd worked all morning mopping and cleaning. To be honest with you, Pa, I can see why Elena didn't find her life here too wonderful."

Sebastian bristled at his son's words. He did not wish to hear this at all. But he said nothing to Vasco. Vasco, not realizing how his comments were affecting Sebastian, went on. "Elena is young and pretty, Pa. She wants more than cleaning the cottage and cooking our meals every night. That has to be very boring for her, especially now that she's been in Sacramento working for Señora Delgardo."

Sebastian fell solemn. "I guess you could be right, Vasco," he muttered. That was all he said as they made their way to the store and walked on to the cottage that late afternoon.

The day for Elena had been endless. She'd had time hanging heavily on her hands. She'd packed her valise and pushed it under her bed. The other valise would not be taken back to Sacramento, for it had contained her gifts to her father and Vasco. And the tunics and floral skirts which she'd taken to Sacramento would remain here this time.

Sebastian sensed an intensity in his daughter tonight. He had to face something that he'd been fooling himself about. She wasn't going to remain with them.

But he was a man desperate to try to capture the magic of the past when his pretty little daughter had accompanied him on his fishing boat. So he suggested that she come out on the trawler with him in the morning.

"I'll think about it, Pa," she said with a warm smile on her face. How could she tell him that this time tomorrow she would be miles away? Her eyes met Vasco's in a glance of understanding.

Later that night as Sebastian lay in his bed, he had to admit to himself that going out on his fishing boat did not excite Elena as it had when she was thirteen or fourteen. As Aimée Mateo had discovered over the holidays, Sebastian realized that life did not remain the same as children grew up and sought to live their own lives.

Something else prodded him in the darkness—a memory of his beloved Miranda. He had never doubted her love for him, but there had been many times when he had sensed a discontentment churning within her. He'd chosen to blind himself to it. He had not dared to ask her about it, for he had feared what her answer might have been.

Days had passed into weeks and weeks into months. Sebastian had gone out on his fishing boat daily, and Miranda had stayed at the cottage tending Vasco and their little Elena. But like Elena, she often found time hanging heavily on her hands. She did not choose to associate with the other Portuguese wives, for she had little in common with most of them.

Maybe the other fishermen's wives had been right about her and she had been a bit of a snob, but she'd felt no qualm of conscience. Perhaps it was because she'd been brought up by a father who'd been a warehouse manager and owned property. Her Latin mother was gracious and well-bred. Miranda was pampered; but when her mother died, she had to face how cruel life could sometimes be. Although her father still protected her, she assumed the responsibility of running their home. For Miranda, that had been an undertaking. Yet, Alonso was always there to take charge if anything went wrong.

Everything in her life changed once again when her father died. She'd had no one to depend on but Sebastian. However, she didn't know what it was to be indulged after her father's death. She loved the Portuguese fisherman with all her heart, but his lifestyle was not the way of life she'd known.

Once the fires and passion of love began to calm, Miranda had been determined that her petite body would not be swollen with a baby every year. She made her wishes clear to Sebastian, and her arrogance had stunned him. A Portuguese wife did not give her husband such ultimatums; but then, Miranda was not Portuguese.

Tonight, Elena reminded him of her mother. He saw her determination in her eyes. It was as if he were looking into Miranda's soul.

When Elena went into her own bedroom, she made no effort to pull out the faded pants and shirt she always wore when she went fishing with her father. She was not going. She'd tell him in the morning that she'd decided to not go, and she'd tell the two of them goodbye.

When they got home tomorrow, Vasco would know that she had gone during the afternoon while they were out in the bay. She would leave a message for her father.

Elena lay in her bed considering that if she should lose her job with Delores Delgardo she might be as lucky as her friend Deirdre. Working in a shop would be more exciting than living in a fishing village.

Only one thing troubled her as she went to sleep: The Christmas holiday had completely depleted the money in her pouch. She would have precious little to survive on in Sacramento if Delores Delgardo said she no longer had a job with her.

Forty

The next morning she told her papa goodbye. Vasco lingered for a brief minute after Sebastian walked on toward the front door. He gave her a hug and told her, "Take care, little sister."

"You know, don't you?" she murmured softly.

He gave her a nod, and his huge hand took hers to place a leather pouch in hers. "Don't give me any fuss. Just take it," Vasco demanded as he swiftly turned on his heels to leave to catch up with his father.

She went back to the kitchen table and opened the pouch. It was stuffed with money. That dear Vasco! He wanted to take care of her as he always had all her life. She couldn't deny that she could be needing Vasco's money if the señora told her she no longer had a job. She placed the purse in her reticule.

She didn't know what to expect from Delores Delgardo anymore. Like a chameleon, her mood could change with a blink of an eyelash. It was a consoling thought to her that she had her good friend Deirdre and the dear Señora Gomez. Either of them would give her a haven should she find herself out on the street.

She wasn't going to allow herself to worry. She'd face whatever she must, for she was ready to leave Half Moon Bay. She put the cottage in order, neatly making the three beds and cleaning the kitchen.

She carried her valise to the front door, relieved that she'd only have one satchel to wrestle with going back to the city. Before dressing in her traveling ensemble, she went back into the kitchen to drink a cup of coffee and once again write her father a note.

This was a much easier letter to compose than the first one had been. She also took the time to eat a light snack of some of the cured ham with a slice of the bread she'd baked yesterday. Going back, she would be taking the *Morning Star* instead of the *Bay Queen*. It left the bay two hours earlier than the *Bay Queen*.

Shortly before two, she left the cottage. She wasn't surprised to see old Maria at the window. An hour later, the gossip would go around the fishing village that Elena Fernandes with her valise in her hand had departed again. Dear God, she was glad to be leaving this place and all these gossipy Portuguese women behind!

She didn't care what any of them thought about her. With a smug smile, she sashayed down the dirt road, thinking to herself that it would give them something to talk about the rest of the afternoon.

She thought about her mother this mid-afternoon as she walked farther and farther away from the cottage. She wished that she'd been able to have the vivid memories of her that Vasco did. Elena had come to the conclusion that the fishwives gossiped about Miranda because they were jealous. They resented that Sebastian had not married one of them but had chosen instead a pretty Latin bride.

The *Morning Star* left promptly at three to plow through the waters toward Suison Bay. She was glad that it was still not dark when she arrived at Rio Vista and caught a carriage from the bay boat into Sacramento. By seven that evening, she was at the front entrance of the Towers Hotel.

She went through the door, and Clarence gave her a friendly welcome as she breezed by the counter. She noticed a surprised expression on his face as he remarked, "I heard you weren't coming back, Miss Elena."

"Now who told you that, Clarence?" she asked with a pert smile on her face.

"I can't rightly recall, Miss Elena, if it was Miss Babette or Miss Camilla. It doesn't much matter, 'cause they were wrong," Clarence said. "I'm glad they were, too."

"Thank you, Clarence. Goodnight to you," she told him and moved on toward the stairway.

It was her hope that she'd be able to get to her room without an encounter with Delores, Babette, or Camilla. She would like to get a good night's sleep before her meeting with the señora.

But as she stepped up to the second landing she met Babette coming down the hall in all her finery. However, she wasn't on an assignment. She had a private date with a gentleman friend.

"Well, queenie, you finally decided to come back, eh?" Babette smirked. "It must be nice to have a whole week off."

"It was, Babette, and I doubt very seriously if my being gone put any extra work on your back, so what are you fretting about?" Elena asked as she moved past Babette. There were few people Elena detested, but Babette was one of them.

Babette trilled with laughter. "Well, maybe old Delores's disposition will improve now that her little pet is back." Elena ignored her remark and went into her room. She lit her lamp, but didn't wish it to burn so brightly that its light would gleam under the threshold.

The bed looked comfortable and she put her valise on one

of the chairs and sat at the dressing table to take off her bonnet.

But before she began to disrobe and get into her loose-fitting dressing gown, she realized she was famished. All she'd eaten all day was a slice of ham and some bread. She would have to go down to the dining room for dinner. Like it or not, she'd have to chance running into Delores if she wished to eat.

So she straightened her hair and gave her gown a couple of yanks and removed the little bobbed jacket she had on. She dimmed the lamp before she left her room.

To her great delight, the dining room had a small crowd this evening and she saw no sign of Delores. Elena heaved a relieved sigh and ordered a feast of lamb chops, new potatoes, and fresh garden peas. She even indulged herself with wine before her dinner was served and had another glass during the meal.

She was taking the last sip of her wine when she heard a deep voice behind her. "Well, you're back!"

She turned to look up at Miguel standing behind her chair. "Yes, I'm back, Miguel."

"Did you have a nice holiday with your family, Elena?"

"I did. How about you?" she asked him. She was hardly prepared for his boisterous laugh as he sat down at the table with her. His manner became very sober and he asked her, "Tell me, Elena—tell me what it is like to have a family Christmas?"

At first she thought he had over-indulged; but when she had studied his face, she realized he wasn't drunk. "You're serious, aren't you Miguel?"

"I am. Will you share a glass of wine with me and tell me about your Christmas with your father and brother?"

At her nod, he motioned to the waitress. Elena suddenly

found herself feeling compassion for Miguel, a man she'd always considered obnoxious.

"As you already know, Miguel, my father and brother are fishermen on the bay. You were there with your mother for a visit when I met her. We lived very simply in a modest cottage. There is nothing fancy about it, but at Christmas time that little cottage holds a magic I'd never want to miss. That is why I went home. I had to," she told him.

She told him that on Christmas Eve, after they had had a fine feast, they gathered in the front room around their Christmas tree to exchange their gifts.

"My father goes into a nearby woods to cut down the finest tree he can find to bring back home to place in our front room to decorate. I make wreaths of evergreens and pine cones. Ah, there are such wonderful aromas in the cottage at Christmas time, Miguel," she told him with a sparkle in her eyes.

Christmas Day, she went on, was a time when she and her father cooked together. "And, of course, we share a bottle or two of his treasured Portuguese wines." She laughed.

Miguel listened to her, intrigued. How he envied her!

A puzzled look came to her lovely face as she asked him, "Miguel, I fear I don't understand. Are you telling me that you and your mama do not celebrate the holiday?"

A weak smile on his face, he told her, "I wasn't as lucky as you, Elena. Delores Delgardo is too busy to concern herself with putting up a Christmas tree, cooking a dinner, or even buying a Christmas gift. My only home has been a hotel room."

She sighed, softness lighting her dark eyes. "Oh, Miguel. Miguel, I'm sorry to hear that. I—I wish it could have been different for you."

"So do I, Elena. So do I, for I might have turned out to be a nicer person. I'm glad you let me sit here tonight and talk with you. You see, I admire you, Elena. I like the way you stand up to my mother. Don't ever let anything change you," he told her.

She smiled at him. "Oh, Miguel, I'll forever be Elena Fernandes. Nothing could ever change that. I, too, am glad we had this talk tonight." True to her straightforward, honest nature, she smiled impulsively as she told him, "You see, Miguel, I didn't think I liked you and now I know I do."

Miguel laughed. It was refreshing to be around someone as open and frank as Elena. He assisted her out of her chair. "Good! Now we can be friends."

They parted company at the base of the stairs. Miguel strode back into the lobby, and Elena went up to her room. The young waitress in the dining room could not believe what a gallant gent Miguel Delgardo had been tonight with Elena Fernandes.

Clarence was just as surprised when he spied Miguel escorting Elena to the stairway. Delores's son was acting like a gentleman, and Elena seemed to be enjoying his company.

Before they'd parted, however, she'd patted his hand and told him, "One day, you will get to know the Christmas I told you about tonight."

A broad smile lit up his face. "You know, Elena, I think you're right!"

There was a definite reason Elena had not encountered Delores in the lobby or the dining room. The señora had sequestered herself in her suite and had her dinner served to her there. Tonight she'd not even sought the company of Colette, for she wanted to be alone to think.

She was vexed with Elena. The girl had been gone far longer than she'd promised, and Delores wondered if she'd even return. She realized that she'd never dominate and rule the free-spirited Elena Fernandes. Delores did not like that.

Had she been honest with herself, she would have had to confess that no requests had come in for Elena's presence at holiday balls and galas. But Delores had to have someone to blame for the seasonal decline in business, so she blamed Elena.

Her practical side told her that the little Portuguese girl had a loyal following of clients and she couldn't deal with her as she would Babette or Camilla. By the time she finally dimmed her lamps that night, she knew only that she had to hire a new girl to replace Deirdre. To be without Elena and Deirdre would devastate her. It was relatively easy to find a young lady like Deirdre, who had a touch of class, but to replace Elena would be impossible.

It was midnight when Delores finally went to bed, and she was completely unaware that it was New Year's Eve. She could not have cared less.

Babette returned two hours later, but she'd not had the evening she'd expected, although she and Julian had attended a grand party. In the past Julian had always been very generous, gifting her with exquisite pieces of jewelry. Babette had not cared for some of the gems, but she had no attachment to them and could always sell them. But tonight, there'd been no little gift. Even more insulting, Julian had spied a cute little miss who was the picture of sweet innocence and his attentions had gone to her.

Babette had had to restrain herself for the last two hours of the party when Julian rudely seemed to forget about her. Finally, as they were traveling home from the party, Babette tried a sob story on him which had worked in the past. Before, he'd handed over a handsome amount of bills to help her out. Tonight it had not worked. He'd politely dismissed her trials and said nothing. Babette had left his carriage *sans* jewelry or money.

It disturbed her so much that when she got to her room she carefully surveyed herself in the full-length mirror. After she'd disrobed, she carefully scrutinized her naked body. It looked the same to her. She suddenly realized it was not the body but her face that was etched. There was no sign of innocence there, and her eyes had seen too much to reflect any hint of sweetness.

Whether she liked it or not, Babette had to admit that her time of naive virtue had passed her by even before she started to work for Delores. It was beginning to frustrate her that lately her gentleman friends were not particularly generous to her. Working for Delores was providing her with only salary, a roof over her head, and her meals. There used to be many advantages in working for the señora, but there weren't anymore.

The next morning she was awakened by an annoying rap on her door. Delores walked into the room and announced that she wished her to come to the salon at two.

"This afternoon? It's New Year's Day. I thought the salon was going to be closed," Babette muttered.

"So it is, but Celeste and I are going to be working on two new gowns. The pearl-grey satin is a gorgeous creation, and it's just right for a tall, slinky girl. I want Celeste to fit it on you," Delores told her, starting for the door.

Babette couldn't resist commenting, "Well, I guess you know by now that little queenie is back."

Delores whirled back around sharply and inquired if she were referring to Elena.

"I gather that you didn't know. That surprises me, for she got back last night about the time I was going out to dinner with Julian."

Delores's lips went tight and she tensed as she turned to

leave Babette's room. It seemed she was going to be delayed a little longer before she went downstairs to Miguel waiting for her in the buggy.

Like Babette, Elena was awakened from a deep sleep and she stumbled to the door knowing that she was not going to be in the best state to come face to face with Delores.

Delores had cautioned herself to restrain her hot temper for right now she could not afford to do otherwise. She realized that it was going to take a lot of willpower not to give her a tonguelashing as she'd like to do.

However, her black eyes were glaring as she entered the room and inquired, "Are you ready to go to work again?"

"I am, señora," Elena mumbled, slightly surprised that the señora was so cold and remote.

"All right, be at the salon at two. Miguel will pick up both you and Babette." That was all she had to say to Elena before she left the room. The truth was she had no reason to have Elena come to the salon other than to just put her through the paces. She planned to do that constantly since Elena had taken off so much time.

Elena was looking forward to accompanying Babette to the salon, and it was only later after Delores had left that it dawned on her that this was New Year's Day. The salon was not supposed to be opened.

She'd ordered a breakfast tray and by one-thirty she had dressed and was ready to go downstairs to the lobby. She took a seat where she'd have a view out the front entrance when Miguel pulled up in the buggy.

Babette was not prepared to see her and, sulking, asked, "Are you going to the salon, too?"

"It wasn't my idea. Blame it on the señora, Babette," Elena snapped, for she was in no mood to put up with Babette's smart mouth.

More and more Babette was finding out that Elena Fernandes could be a spitfire when she wanted to be. She had no time to make a retort, for Miguel pulled up in the buggy and Elena hastily got up. Babette sauntered slowly behind her.

She couldn't believe her ears. Miguel greeted Elena and she returned his greeting with a warm smile. He actually helped them into the buggy.

Haughtiness gave birth to her acid tongue, and she remarked, "What's this, Miguel? Are you turning over a new leaf on New Year's Day?"

He just turned around and smirked. "Don't count on that, Babette. Next time you might not be as lucky."

Elena had to restrain her laughter for Babette puffed up like a toad. She knew why Miguel had been so cordial this morning.

When they arrived at the salon, Delores was at the door to meet them. Babette was taken to one dressing room and Elena was ushered to another. Delores told her, "Celeste will be with you as soon as she's through pinning Babette's gown." Elena disrobed and hung her dress on the peg. She knew how swiftly Celeste could get a gown pinned and ready to be stepped out of. By now she'd gone through the procedure dozens of times.

Delores was more than pleased about the pearl-grey gown and she raved, "Ah, Celeste, it is just what we envisioned, isn't it?"

"Oh, yes, señora! I, too, am pleased." Celeste placed her materials in her basket.

Delores told her that she'd be back in the sewing room once she'd talked to Babette. Celeste gave her a nod and scurried out of the dressing room. She was still puzzled. Why had the señora had Elena come to the salon this afternoon? She had not hesitated to tell Delores that the red gown was not for Elena. She'd told Delores, "Little Elena would be smothered in that red satin, señora."

But Delores had shrugged aside her comments by telling her, "Well, we'll see, Celeste." Now Celeste had worked too long for Delores to believe a woman with such a keen eye for fashion would ever select this red satin for the petite Elena. She went back to her sewing room perplexed.

Meanwhile, Babette had gotten dressed and Delores went to her office to get her reticule. She returned to the sewing room to tell Celeste that she was leaving. Celeste bade her goodbye, assuming that Delores had come to the conclusion that the red gown wasn't for Elena after all and that Delores and the two models were leaving together.

When she joined Babette, Babette didn't question why Elena was not leaving with them, and Delores told her she was due at her friend Charlotte's.

So Babette was taken back to the Towers Hotel, and Miguel drove his mother to Charlotte Gaudreau's home. As she was getting out of the buggy, Miguel asked Delores about Elena and if he were to go back to the salon to pick her up.

"No, Miguel, and you don't have to return here for me. I don't know how long I'll be staying, so Charlotte's driver will bring me back to the hotel. You are free for the rest of the evening. Now doesn't that please you, Miguel?" she asked in the syrupy-sweet voice which always made Miguel suspicious. She had a pleased, smug look on her face.

He, of all people, knew what a vindictive, spiteful woman his mother could be. He questioned how Elena would get back to the hotel unless she walked from the salon.

At one time he would have complied with Delores's orders, but this afternoon he had no intentions of obeying her. He knew exactly what her devious mind had plotted. She wanted to punish Elena, and she was leaving her at the salon so she'd have the long, long walk back to the hotel.

When he pulled out of the drive of the Gaudreau estate, he guided his buggy back in the direction of the salon instead of the Towers Hotel.

Elena was not going to be making that exhausting walk back to the hotel. He'd see to that.

Forty-one

Elena waited for an endless time in her undergarments. She did not know how long she'd sat there; but a fitting hardly took this long, so she began to dress.

When she emerged from the dressing room, the shop was quiet and there was no sound of voices as she moved toward the back of the shop to the sewing room.

She startled Celeste, who said, "Mercy, Miss Elena, you gave me a fright! I didn't know you were still here. I thought you left with the señora and Miss Babette."

Elena was seething with anger. "I've been waiting for an hour for you to fit a gown on me, Celeste."

"Oh, Miss Elena, I'm very confused. I—I was not told you were still here. I assumed the señora had changed her mind about the red gown. I told her before you arrived that this gown was not for you. I thought when she left that she took you with her. I feel so bad."

"You have no cause to feel bad, Celeste. It is neither you nor I who is confused. I fear it is Señora Delgardo who is befuddled. But if you could just let me out of the salon, I shall be leaving now."

Celeste accompanied her to the front door, remarking on the long walk she was going to have to get back to the Towers.

"I'll make it, Celeste." Elena smiled at the seamstress.

Celeste felt sorry for the pretty young girl and found it puzzling that Señora Delgardo would do such a thing to her most popular model. "A happy New Year to you, Miss Elena," she said.

"Happy New Year to you, too, Celeste," Elena told her as she went out to the street.

Celeste turned to go back to her sewing room, but she would have been pleased to know that Elena had had to walk only a few steps before Miguel pulled up in his buggy. A devious smile was on his face as he asked her, "Do you need a ride, lady?"

Elena threw her head back and gave a lighthearted laugh. "Ah, Miguel, you must have suspected that I might!"

He assisted her into the buggy. Setting the carriage in motion, he commented, "It wasn't hard to figure out what was on her evil mind when she and Babette left here without you. I knew she had some devilment in mind."

A sly smile came to Elena's face. "Your mother was having her sweet revenge on me for taking off too many days, but I thank you from the bottom of my heart for being so sweet and thoughtful."

He began to laugh. "You are amazing! Did you know that? Never has anyone ever called me sweet in my whole life!"

She laughed, too. "I say what I feel. That is my way."

"That is why I like and admire you so much. You see, I've never had people to admire in my whole life. I used to admire my mother; now I find her disgusting."

Elena suddenly realized that in a lot of ways Miguel reminded her of Vasco. They had the same black hair and black eyes.

He told her, "I think Delores Delgardo may have met her match. No other girl who has worked for her has ever challenged her like you have."

"Your mother does not intimidate me at all."

He smiled and dared to ask her if she would join him for dinner in the hotel's dining room.

Elena felt she knew sincerity when it was reflected on a person's face, and she saw Miguel's earnestness when he told her, "I wish I'd met you a long time ago, Elena. I could have been a different person if I'd had a good friend like you just to talk with. I sought friends in the wrong places."

"I'll be happy to share dinner with you, Miguel. We shall toast the New Year and hope that it will bring good fortune to both of us." She smiled at him.

They arrived at the hotel shortly after four, much earlier than Delores had projected. Actually, she was back only an hour later than Babette and took the other girl by utter surprise when they encountered one another in the hallway.

Babette was going downstairs to have a late lunch when she came face to face with Elena. "Are you back already?" she asked. "You must walk at a very fast pace!"

"I didn't have to," Elena replied sweetly. "A very gallant gentleman with a buggy was most obliging. I'm sure Señora Delgardo will be disappointed to hear this, just as I'm sure you will delight in telling her," she told her calmly, not pausing for a moment.

Babette was forced to believe that Elena Fernandes possessed a charisma that even Delores Delgardo—whom Babette had always thought the most clever woman she'd ever met—could not dent or compete with.

Elena had time to stretch out on her bed to rest for a while before she had to dress to join Miguel for dinner. She was pondering just how long she'd be able to tolerate these dirty tricks Delores would be playing on her. Pushed to a certain point, Elena knew her own volatile temper would erupt. Right now, she wasn't feeling kindly toward the señora. She knew now that Delores Delgardo was not the kindhearted, generous lady she'd first thought she was. She was cruel and totally selfish.

The more she was around Miguel, the more she liked him.

His mother had made his life miserable and that was why he appeared obnoxious. But now she knew he could be nice, for he'd proven that to her this afternoon.

She donned her berry-colored gown with the white lace collar and cuffs, and around her throat she wore the pearls her father had given her. Miguel was waiting for her when she descended the stairway. Once again, Clarence could not believe his eyes when he witnessed Miguel escorting Elena into the dining room of the hotel.

They took a seat at Elena's favorite table, and Miguel ordered wine, once again amazing the waitress with his gentlemanly demeanor. They laughed and talked as they waited for their dinner to be served. Elena insisted on the roast pork. "Oh, we must, Miguel, if we wish to have good luck this next year," she told him seriously.

Miguel agreed. Tomorrow night he'd have that thick beefsteak he'd planned to have tonight. He needed all the luck he could have coming his way. He smiled across the table at her. "Tell me, is that another tradition of the Fernandes family?"

"Oh yes, for as long as I can remember."

"You're enlightening me about things I've never heard about before." He laughed lightheartedly.

Both of them enjoyed their pork roast and lingered another half-hour before they finally left the dining room. At the base of the stairs, Miguel told her good night. Elena remarked that both of them should surely have good luck from all the roast they'd devoured.

As she began to move up the stairs, he called to her. "And I'm going to remember some things you told me about tonight, Elena. Thanks again."

She was sure Miguel had told her secrets he'd dared not mention to anyone else. It was apparent that he was ready to leave and go out on his own but he didn't know what kind of job to look for. He'd always worked for his mother.

Elena had told him about Vasco and that he was a big husky fellow about Miguel's age. "There are many fishing boats on the bays near here, and they're always hiring men. It's not a bad life, Miguel. You put in your day's work, and your evenings are yours to do what you wish. You always have Sundays off. At least you would be living your own life and be out from under your mother's thumb."

"That is an idea, Elena," he'd agreed.

"Vasco loves it. He says he loves the feel of the warm sun followed by the cooling bay breezes.

Later, in his room, he recalled their conversation. There was no reason why he couldn't be a fisherman. He was as strong as an ox. Maybe the wages wouldn't be much, but he could get by. It didn't matter to him if he had to live in one room at a rundown inn. One room was all he lived in now. It didn't have to be fancy.

At least, he'd be free! He should have sought his freedom five or six years ago.

The first week in January was tense for Elena and Delores Delgardo. Delores had quickly learned that her devious trick had not worked. Babette had rushed to let her know that Elena was back at the hotel, but she didn't know that Miguel was Elena's gallant rescuer.

But Delores learned from Clarence that her son and Elena had dined together that same evening. Furious, she demanded an explanation.

He casually replied, "I didn't know there was an order against that, Mother, since we didn't leave the hotel. As I'm sure Clarence told you, I walked her through the lobby and we said good night at the bottom of the stairs."

Delores swished around the room, back and forth, before she whirled on him. "Well, well, well," she remarked sarcastically, "I guess I just didn't know how friendly you and Elena were."

"I like Elena, Mother. She's a lady. We are friends, I'm happy to say," he told her, and he turned to walk away from her without waiting to be dismissed. Startled, Delores blamed Elena for his new attitude. She was beginning to wonder if this Portuguese girl had the ability to cast spells on people.

Señora Gomez, along with some of her other customers, thought Elena so special that they wished no one but her for their parties. Even her old friend Colette had nothing but the highest praise for her. Delores had heard rumors that Camilla and Babette were not getting along since Camilla had been going out with Elena on assignments. The gossip around the hotel was that Camilla didn't tolerate Babette's bossing her anymore.

Now her own son seemed to be under Elena's spell. The more she thought about Miguel's behavior, the angrier she got. How dare he turn his back on her and walk out of the room!

But during the first week of the new year, Delores received another jolt involving Elena and her influence on those around her. Delores had purposely scheduled Elena three nights in a row. This meant she had to go to the salon daily as well, and she was exhausted. Celeste sensed this and thought the señora was being unduly harsh. She couldn't understand why Camilla and Babette weren't having a share of the assignments.

Truth be told, Celeste had not been friendly with Delores since the incident on New Year's Day. Something wasn't right. Celeste couldn't put her finger on it, but all the same she knew.

On the third afternoon, Celeste told Elena, "There's no

sense in you going through the motions of another fitting. Mercy, I know all your measurements by heart. Get yourself back to the hotel to rest before you fall flat on your face. You look tuckered out, Miss Elena."

"Oh, thank you, Celeste, thank you so much." Elena sighed. Fifteen minutes later, Elena was in the buggy with Miguel to go back to the hotel. He'd lifted the canvas bag she had carried out of the salon with her slippers and accessories.

"Damn her," Miguel blurted as he helped her into the buggy. "Damn her to hell, Elena! You're worn out!"

"It's all right, Miguel. I'll do this one tonight, but I assure you I'll not go out tomorrow night. She can fire me and I don't care," she told him.

But after she arrived back at the hotel and talked with Camilla, she decided that she'd refuse to go out tonight. Camilla had innocently told her that the two of them had done nothing all week. Elena had assumed that they too had assignments.

"I guess the señora thinks you're the only one who can sell her gowns, Elena," Camilla commented.

"Oh, no, Camilla. It's not that at all. The señora is punishing me for those days I took off. She's pushing me to the limit. Well, I've reached that limit. I'm not going tonight."

Camilla saw that Elena was in a foul mood, so she left her room. Elena flung herself across her bed, giving way to exhaustion. She slept for the next three hours and made no effort to go to Colette's room at four as she normally would have done to have her style her hair.

Back at the salon, Delores expected to find Elena still in the fitting room, but Celeste was there alone. She looked up when Delores inquired about Elena to tell her, "Oh, she's probably already back at the hotel, señora, and I've the gown ready for you to take. It's hanging right over there."

Celeste noticed that the señora stiffened, but she couldn't

stop herself from saying, "Miss Elena could have saved herself a trip down here today. There was no need for her to try that dress on. I've her measurements. She looked mighty tired to me, ma'am."

Celeste's words and the look in her eyes made Delores wonder if Celeste were suspicious about what happened on New Year's Day. However she said nothing as she walked over to get the gown and marched out of the sewing room.

She arrived at the hotel at four-thirty instead of her usual five-thirty and went directly to Elena's room with the lovely pink gown flung over her arm. She knocked several times before Elena finally opened the door looking sleepy-eyed, her hair tousled.

"You look a mess, Elena!" she shrieked.

"And I don't care, señora! I'm exhausted so I've slept. Someone else will have to go out for you tonight. Camilla and Babette have done nothing for the last three nights while I've worked. I'd sell no gowns for you tonight, I can assure you," Elena told her, her black eyes blazing.

Delores was put into such a frenzy at that moment that all she managed to mutter was that they'd talk in the morning. Elena closed the door and went back to bed.

The next hour was hectic for Delores. She rushed to inform Camilla that she would be taking over for Elena, for the pink gown would be more flattering to her than to Babette. She ordered Camilla to get to Colette immediately to have her hair styled.

Miguel was taking his mother back to the salon so that Celeste could ease out the seams of the waistline to fit Camilla instead of Elena. Once again, Delores was rushing out of the sewing room with the pink gown flung over her arm and Celeste was preparing to leave for the day. It was one of those days when she was anxious to get to her peaceful apartment.

When she left the salon this evening, Celeste was seriously considering the offer she'd received a few weeks ago from a new dress salon in the city.

Elena, unaware of the flurry around her, slept peacefully, and her deep sleep lasted for the next twelve hours. However when she did wake up, she was famished. She'd eaten no dinner the night before and only a light lunch. She felt a great need for some strong hot coffee.

She slipped into one of her afternoon muslin gowns and took a brush to her tousled hair. She wasted no time leaving her room and going down to the kitchen. She knew the black cook Fanny very well by now. She asked Elena, "What you doin' down here this early, sweet child?"

"I'm starved, Fanny. I missed dinner last night," she told her.

"Well, Fanny will take care of you. You go over there and sit down," she ordered. Like everyone else in this kitchen, Elena obeyed her. Fanny was the boss.

While Elena took a few sips of hot coffee, Fanny filled a plate with a slice of ham, biscuits, eggs, and sausage. She added a mound of butter and jam.

Fanny chuckled. "If that don't fill your little belly, then we'll fill that plate again."

But that one heaping plate that Fanny had served her was enough to satisfy Elena's hunger. Having consumed three cups of coffee, Elena was feeling very alert and sharp.

She hardly knew what she could expect from Delores Delgardo this morning, but she was ready to face her. She was wide-eyed and awake and the long hours of sleep had done wonders for her.

Delores had also had time to calm down and do some thinking. She had found out again last night just how important Elena Fernandes was to her and her salon. She'd accompanied Camilla to the Montgomery home since Mrs. Montgomery was expecting Elena.

Gracious lady that she was, Mrs. Montgomery tried to mask her disappointment, but Delores sensed instantly that she wasn't pleased with Camilla.

So Delores Delgardo came to Elena's room with her fury spent. She was almost the syrupy-sweet woman Elena had first met.

"I know how hard I've been working you, Elena, but it's been difficult for me, too, after losing Deirdre. Some of my ladies just don't warm to Camilla and Babette. But I'm very interested to have your opinion about a girl I hired yesterday. She's coming to the salon at eleven. I'd like for you to be there. I'd like your opinion of her," Delores told her.

"I will be there at eleven, señora," Elena told her.

Promptly at eleven, Elena arrived at the salon looking very chic in a gold gown trimmed in black braid. She wore a short, bobbed, black-velvet jacket, a matching bonnet, and her own jet beads and earrings.

She was striking.

Forty-two

Meredith, like the rest of the women working in the salon, appraised Elena and concluded that she was the most fashionable young lady who'd ever worked for the señora. Meredith escorted her to Delores's office.

Cynthia, the new girl, had only to look up at Elena and admire her. Elena had been in a very similar situation when she'd first met the fair-haired Deirdre in her lovely fancy gown.

Delores made the introductions. What was interesting to Elena now that she'd lived this lifestyle for many months was the way Delores painted such an exciting picture of Cynthia's future with the Delgardo Salon. Elena recalled her conversations with Delores on the wharf at Half Moon Bay. Oh, Delores could be a charmer when she wished to be!

Elena could see the sparkle in Cynthia's eyes as she anticipated the glamourous life she was going to live working for Señora Delgardo.

And Elena remembered the naive, impressionable girl she had been only months before.

Delores didn't delay assigning Elena to take Cynthia with her the next evening. Cynthia looked stunning in her brilliant-blue gown, and she was a very attractive young girl with a shapely figure, so she and Elena made a lovely pair as they left the hotel at seven.

But it took Elena one evening with Cynthia to find out

that the wide-eyed twinkle she'd seen in Cynthia's eyes had nothing to do with sweet innocence. She was not shy.

Miguel took them to Jefferson Howard's impressive mansion. As they were traveling there, Cynthia told Elena, "Call me, Cindy, honey. I hate Cynthia. I introduced myself that way to Señora Delgardo because I thought it sounded classier."

As Miguel brought the buggy to a halt, Cynthia gasped. "Old Delgardo wasn't lying when she said this was a fancy party. I bet it will be!"

Elena sensed then just how bold and brazen this girl could be. She leaned over to whisper in her ear that Miguel, their driver, was the señora's son, but that didn't faze Cynthia. She just gave a shrug of her shoulders.

When they entered the opulent parlor, Elena expected Cynthia to stay close to her to see how she should conduct herself as Elena had done the first evening she'd gone out with Deirdre. But Cynthia had other ideas and roamed on her own.

Elena couldn't afford to fret about her, she decided, but she could tell the señora that this girl was never going to be able to fill the void that Deirdre had created.

Instead, she turned her attention to a guest who was admiring her gown.

It was an hour later before she finally spied Cynthia across the room speaking with a gentleman. While she had a free moment, she began to move in Cynthia's direction and didn't hesitate to walk up to them.

Very graciously, she nodded to the gentleman and said to Cynthia, "I must speak with you for a minute."

She could tell that this didn't please her at all, but she had to pass on Delores's rules before she could feel free of responsibility for the new girl's behavior. When they'd moved several feet away, Elena told her, "Cindy, we don't woo the gents. We woo the ladies. This is an ironclad rule of the señora's."

It seemed Cindy had a flippant answer for everything. "Well, honey, the women may pick out the gowns; but it's their wealthy gents who pay for them."

Elena began to get out of patience with her and made her own retort. "But the ladies must first pick them out, Cindy, so I'd advise you to try to get someone interested in your gown before the evening is over or the señora will not be pleased."

It was almost the end of the evening before Sarah Howard finally had a moment to speak with Elena. "Elena, my dear, I just wanted to tell you that you're as lovely and charming as Margarita Gomez told me. I particularly asked for you."

"How sweet of you, Mrs. Howard. Tell my dear friend, Señora Gomez, hello if you should see her before I do. Your dinner party has been a lovely affair and I met so many nice ladies," Elena told her.

"Well, you've certainly impressed my friends, I must tell you," Sarah remarked to her, but Elena noticed that her eyes were focused on Cindy, who was talking with a dashing young man. Sarah's disapproval reflected on her face.

It was not until she'd yanked Cindy away and told her it was time for them to leave that she discovered what had disturbed their hostess so much. She heard the good-looking young man address Sarah Howard as mother.

Once they were in the carriage, Elena told her, "I was supposed to instruct you tonight, Cindy, but you hardly gave me a chance to do that."

"Elena, honey, let's just say that I've done this work before. Oh, I didn't wear this fancy a gown and it wasn't as elegant a party; but high class or low class, it's all the same. I met two really good-looking fellows tonight." She smiled.

"We're not allowed to date gentlemen we meet at these

parties, nor are men allowed to come to our rooms at the Towers," Elena informed her.

"What's that?" Cindy asked, bolting up in the seat. Elena repeated what she'd told her.

Once again, it didn't seem to bother Cindy that Miguel, their driver, was the señora's son. Indignant, she declared, "Well, Delores Delgardo won't tell me what I do on my free time when I'm not working for her."

Elena smiled to herself in the darkness. Cindy was going to have a rude awakening.

Miguel had a sly smile on his face when he helped Elena out of the buggy, for he'd listened and observed the new girl this evening. Elena was just glad the evening was over. As she climbed the stairs, she pondered just what she was or wasn't going to tell Delores when she came to her room for a report.

She gave way to a devious impulse.

She had just had time to change out of her gown and get into her nightgown and robe when Delores knocked on her door.

Delores rushed into the room, her dark eyes sparkling with anticipation, and she asked Elena, "How did it go?"

"It was a lovely affair, and Sarah Howard is a charming hostess. Cynthia seemed perfectly at ease. She's a very aggressive girl. I couldn't exactly instruct her, for she moved around too much." Elena was telling her the truth and not lying, and Delores heard what she wanted to hear.

In response to Delores's next question, Elena told her she had no way of gauging Sarah Howard's impression, for their hostess had made no comment on Cynthia's demeanor.

Delores left the room happy and pleased. Elena went to bed to get some sleep.

To her delight, Delores didn't stop by her room the next morning and she assumed that she was finally to have a night off. She'd been back from Half Moon Bay two weeks now, and it had been a very busy, hectic time. She'd put those two weeks' wages in the pouch with the money Vasco had given to her when she'd left.

There was no question in Elena's mind that she was pregnant, and she knew the time was growing short for her to continue working at the salon. She was certain Celeste must suspect even though she'd not said a word during the last two weeks of fittings. Her tiny waistline had expanded at least three or four inches since she'd returned.

For the first time since she'd returned from Half Moon Bay she actually had time to give some thought to her dilemma. Should she go to Golden Splendor and announce to Mateo she was carrying his baby? Would he do the honorable thing and marry her and give her baby his name or would she be faced with having a bastard to raise on her own?

Fury churned within her. She felt a desperate need to seek out Deirdre or Señora Gomez, but she had only to look out her windows to see the miserable January weather to know it wasn't a day to venture out of the hotel. She had a leisurely breakfast, but after she'd eaten she made no effort to get dressed and remained in her silk dressing gown.

She sat by the window and wrote her father and Vasco a long-overdue letter, but it was the first moment she'd had.

At the same time, a dramatic scene was taking place at Delores's salon. Repercussions of that scene would be affecting Elena very shortly.

Meredith knew there was trouble brewing when she escorted a stern-faced Sarah Howard back to Delores's office. Apparently, something had gone wrong at her dinner party last night. She could not imagine that Elena Fernandes had done anything wrong, so the sharp Meredith concluded Mrs. Howard was here to complain about the new girl.

Sarah had never been a woman to restrain herself if something displeased her. When she stormed into Delores's office, she held her responsible for sending such a girl to her home. She refused to have a seat and towered over Delores, who sat at her desk.

"I've nothing but praise for Elena Fernandes, señora, but I was not only embarrassed but insulted by that strumpet you sent with her. She offended my guests, so you can be sure you'll not have any orders for her gown. She was too busy entertaining the men. Elena could not have known this, for she was occupied with the ladies. With my own eyes, I saw her outrageously flaunting herself in front of my son Jason. Well, I've had my say, so I shall leave," Sarah Howard declared, departing as quickly as she had arrived.

Delores was shaken by Sarah Howard's fiery blast and she knew that she'd lost a good customer. How could she have so misjudged Cynthia? Refusing to take the blame herself, Delores faulted Elena for allowing it to happen. Elena knew what she expected from her girls. Elena should have been more aware.

Ah, that was the flaw in the character of Delores Delgardo! Colette knew her better than anyone and over the years she'd wanted to shake her soundly many times. Delores could never admit responsibility for her own doing. Colette's heart had gone out to Miguel. Miguel had never known what it was to be loved or cared for. Delores was too self-absorbed.

So often, Colette had ached to tell her that one day she might need her son and then he would not have any time for her. But she hadn't.

* * *

Miguel had only to look at his mother's face to know that she was incensed when she boarded his buggy at noon, ordering him to take her to the hotel. This went against her usual routine.

"Stay right here, Miguel, for I'll be returning to the salon shortly," she told him and then sailed through the hotel door.

But he wasn't about to sit in the buggy in the chilly drizzle to wait for her to conduct her business, so he went to the dining room to have a cup of hot coffee.

The truth was Delores had not regained her calm and composure when she left her salon. She was a woman on the raw edge! By the time she marched up the stairs, she was trembling with the fury flaming within her which should have been directed at herself instead of Elena Fernandes.

Elena encountered an erratic woman when she opened her door and Delores came storming into the room. There was a high trill to her voice as she told Elena, "I want you out of here when I return this evening. You're fired, Elena. You no longer work for me."

Elena was in such a state of shock that it took her a moment to find her voice. "If this is what you wish. I'll try to be out."

"You're not to take any gowns I gave you. Do you understand me?"

"I'll take nothing but what I have rightfully earned, señora. I also expect you to pay me the wages I earned last night," Elena told her.

Elena's cool, calm manner unnerved Delores. She fumbled in her reticule and flung some bills to the floor. She spat at Elena, "I doubt that you were worth that."

Proudly, Elena declared to her, "Oh, yes, I was and probably more, señora! It wasn't my fault that the girl you hired acted like a slut! That was your fault and not mine. It's obvious that Sarah Howard has called on you this morning.

Well, now, she's your problem and not mine. I tried to handle her last night and I couldn't. The truth is I'm glad to be out of this hellhole!" Elena declared. She watched Delores exit the room, and the woman she saw hardly resembled the woman of charm and grace she'd met on the wharf at Half Moon Bay.

She didn't waste time shedding tears, but immediately packed her valise. She packed only what she had bought for herself, but those possessions were more than she'd realized. When that was done, she got dressed. She had to find Deirdre and see if she could stay with her for a few days, and she had only a few hours. She had no desire to be at the Towers when Delores returned at five-thirty.

So she flung the cape around her shoulders and picked up her reticule to walk through the chilling drizzle to the hat shop.

When she emerged from the hotel, a deep voice called to her. It was Miguel. He had figured she would be needing him, for his mother had ranted and raved all the way back to the salon like a crazy woman.

"Come on, Elena, I'll take you wherever you're going," he told her.

"Thank you, Miguel." She told him, directing him to the hat shop. When they arrived, he told her that he would wait for her, but she'd protested. He had already done her a favor in bringing her to Deirdre's.

"Elena, I've nothing better to do. Go speak with your friend, and then I will take you back to the hotel. You don't need to be walking in this kind of weather," he told her.

A few minutes later she was glad that he had waited for her. Deirdre, she learned, no longer worked there. She had married Carlos Mateo, it seemed, since Elena had last had contact with her.

As Miguel helped her back into the buggy, she recalled

Mateo's directions to Granada Street when he had wanted her to accompany him back to Half Moon Bay. Miguel easily located the two-story stone house. Once again he refused to leave until he knew she was with Deirdre.

Stella was busy in the kitchen, so it was Deirdre who opened the door. Miguel watched as the two of them embraced. He had a feeling that Elena was in need of Deirdre.

Deirdre was surprised to see Miguel in the buggy and wondered how Elena had ever managed to get him to bring her to her home.

"Miguel is really very nice when you get to know him," Elena assured her. Deirdre found that hard to believe, but she knew of no one more honest than Elena.

"Don't forget that I'm your friend," Miguel reminded Elena as they said goodbye. "I detest my mother for what she does."

"I know you're my friend, Miguel, and I am your friend, too." Elena wished him well, then whirled around to go back to the front porch to get out of the chilling drizzle.

Deirdre guided Elena into the parlor. Elena giggled. "Aren't you the sly one, Deirdre! I didn't even know that you and Carlos were acquainted and suddenly I find out you're married."

"I know." Deirdre shared her laughter. "I'd planned to tell you, but you never met me that Sunday to go to the park. Oh, Elena, I couldn't be happier." She told her how swiftly their courtship had progressed. "I think we both fell in love instantly," she confessed.

"You look happy—absolutely glowing, Deirdre!" Elena told her.

"Well, Carlos invited me to spend the holidays with him and his family at Golden Splendor so I got to see that glorious place you'd told me about and it was everything you said it was. I adored his parents and they couldn't have been nicer to me. I saw Mark, Elena and he gave me a message to give to you," Deirdre told her.

"Oh—and what was his message?"

"He's coming here just as soon as he can, Elena. He cares for you very much. I'm sure of that," Deirdre told her.

"He has not seemed to be in too much of a hurry," Elena replied with a sharpness to her soft voice that told Deirdre she was very impatient with him.

"There's been a reason, Elena. In fact, that was why we were two days later in arriving back here and why Lisette was so angry with me." She told Elena of Carlos's proposal and Lisette's meanness, which led to their getting married sooner than they'd planned.

"Old Carlos died, Elena, while we were there and Carlos was forced to remain for the funeral. Naturally I had to remain, too. I couldn't believe how quickly Lisette changed. She became another Delores Delgardo."

"I'm very sad to hear about Señor Carlos. I liked him," Elena told her.

"Elena, be patient with Mark. He's been carrying a very heavy burden that you cannot know anything about. There have been reasons why he's not come to you. He stayed with his grandfather when his health failed. He is now the owner of La Casa Grande. His grandfather left everything to him," Deirdre told her.

Elena stammered, "Mateo owns La Casa Grande?"

"That's right! I only plead with you to give him time to get things squared away, and he will come to you. I could swear he cares very deeply for you," Deirdre said.

Elena wanted to cry out to her that she could not afford to be patient and wait for Mateo to come to her. Instead, she gave Deirdre a weak smile. "I pray you're right, Deirdre."

Deirdre sensed that something was troubling her friend and that that was why she'd sought her out today. She asked if things had become unbearable with Delores, and Elena told her what had happened.

"Could I stay with you a few days until I can make arrangements?" Elena asked.

"Our home is your home as long as you need it to be. Delores Delgardo has cut her own throat. She will be left with Camilla and Babette. She's a real fool if she doesn't fire this Cindy immediately," Deirdre told her.

It sickened Deirdre to hear that Delores had worked her unmercifully after she'd returned late from Half Moon Bay.

Deirdre seethed. She could easily imagine why Delores had stormed into her room at midday to vent her fury on Elena. She knew Sarah Howard and had worked assignments for her. She was a sedate, dignified lady who expected proper conduct from the young ladies who came to her home as guests from the salon. A young woman like Cindy would have mortified Sarah Howard, who would not have hesitated to voice her displeasure. And Delores would never blame herself. She would put all the blame on Elena's shoulders.

"You're free of her now," Deirdre told Elena. "Let us go have a nice lunch."

After they'd eaten, she showed Elena to one of the guest bedrooms. "This is your room as long as you wish. Have yourself a rest or a bath. Ask Stella for anything you need. I've some errands to run before I pick up Carlos," Deirdre told her. As she prepared to leave the room, she remarked on the miserable day she'd picked to go out. "I think Carlos was nervous about my keeping his buggy today."

Elena told her, "You just be careful. The streets are wet and muddy. I'll be just fine. In fact, I think I might have a nice nap while you're gone. I do feel a little weary."

"Do that, Elena. I'll see you later," Deirdre told her as she left the room.

Forty-three

The chilling misting rains were falling over the city at mid-afternoon as they had since early morning. Deirdre guided the bay down the street toward the dress salon where she knew that she'd find Delores Delgardo this time of the day. If she could, then she'd get her two other errands attended to, but this was more imperative to her right now.

The clerks recognized her immediately. She had always been well-liked, and the señora's employees had always considered Deirdre a young woman with more class than Babette and Camilla.

As Deirdre was about to ask if she would find Delores in her office, Delores came out of the back of the shop and saw her.

"Well, Deirdre, it's been a long time since I've seen you," Delores said.

Deirdre didn't address her as Señora Delgardo as she had when she'd worked for her. "It has been awhile, Delores. I'm married now."

"I heard. You married Carlos Mateo. A fine lawyer, Señor Mateo," Delores said, trying to maintain a calm in the face of Deirdre's green eyes, which were flashing with fire.

"That's right. I'm sure that you're familiar with the name Mateo."

"Well, you must wish a new beautiful gown today."

"Hardly, Delores! I came here only to tell you my husband

will be coming to the Towers Hotel to pick up Elena's belongings and he'd better be given access to them. Do you understand me, Delores? Be warned that you'll play no dirty tricks on him as you did on Elena Fernandes." She whirled around, her black cape swinging out, and suddenly stopped to look back at Delores. "You're disgusting, Delores."

Not only had her clerks overheard all her harsh words, but two ladies shopping stood frozen, listening. Deirdre wanted everyone in the shop to hear her.

Humiliated, Delores stayed in seclusion for the next two hours. When she finally emerged, she told Meredith to lock up for her tonight.

On the ride back to the Towers she said not a word to Miguel, but he quickly noticed the strange look on her face. Helping her out of the buggy, he felt the trembling of her hand on his arm, but he could find no sympathy in his heart for her.

Let her hurt as she had made people hurt. His heart was cold as he led her through the door and turned away to take the buggy to the carriage house behind the hotel. His mother had no engagements this evening.

Deirdre left the salon with the sweet taste of revenge consuming her. She knew how devastatingly embarrassed Delores had been in her salon with her clerks and customers hearing every word she had spoken.

The weather might have been dismal, but she was in grand spirits as she urged the bay to move on. She still had time to get her other two errands done before she picked up Carlos at his office.

She pulled the buggy up as Carlos walked out the door with his briefcase. He got into the buggy and she turned the reins over to him. "I worried about you all day out in this weather," he confessed, planting a kiss on her lips. "To see you sitting in the buggy looking so gorgeous was like a load lifted off my chest."

"You see, Carlos, you had no reason to worry about me. I am fine, but my little friend Elena isn't," she told him.

Carlos, ever-practical, took charge. "All I need to know from Elena is what she wishes me to take out of that hotel room. Give me an hour, and then we can all sit down to a leisurely dinner," he told Deirdre.

They found Elena in the parlor with Amigo keeping her company. Elena instantly saw what a different man Carlos had become when he walked into the parlor with Deirdre, his arm around her waist. "With two beautiful ladies around the house, old Amigo is going to think he's died and gone to heaven," he quipped. Then he turned very serious, quizzing Elena on what he should take from the bedroom she'd occupied at the hotel.

"Only my valise, Carlos. It is packed, and I left it at the end of the bed," she told him.

"That's all I need to know," he said and excused himself.

Deirdre told Stella to delay dinner and returned to the parlor with a choice Mateo wine. Elena took a glass and sighed. "Poor Carlos, he's put in a long day. He didn't need this tonight."

"Elena, don't worry about Carlos. That man is a tower of strength. He will return within the hour, and the job will be accomplished. He amazes me. When I had to move in here so hastily, he wasted no time in moving me in and planning our wedding."

As Deirdre had foretold, it didn't take Carlos long to return to the comfort of his home, out of the chilling mist.

Elena found Carlos warm and outgoing throughout the evening. She appreciated his protective attitude when he inquired if Señora Delgardo owed her any wages. "I don't intend for you to be cheated out of anything due you," he told her as they sat at the dining table.

"No, Carlos. She owes me nothing, and I owe her nothing," Elena responded.

After dinner, Carlos excused himself to go upstairs, and Elena thought it was because of her.

Deirdre quickly enlightened her, outlining Carlos's nightly routine. "It's our way of life. I understand, and I never feel neglected. Carlos always makes up for those two or three hours he must work in the evening. Having met Mano and Mark, I think Mateo men are a special breed!"

This comment brought a smile to Elena's lovely face. No man but Mateo could hold her heart and have her all-consuming love.

"You've changed Carlos, Deirdre. He's so happy and outgoing—not reserved as he used to be," Elena declared.

Deirdre gave a girlish giggle. "Oh, Elena, there is nothing reserved about Carlos. He is a hot-blooded Latin, I can assure you. If I have changed him, then he has changed me, too."

"Oh, Deirdre, this has been a wonderful evening. I was so desperate this morning, and tonight I feel relaxed for the first time in the last two weeks."

"Well, honey, you take a few days to relax and rest before you make any decisions about what you want to do."

"Thank you, Deirdre. It's nice to have a good friend like you."

Deirdre had one more question before they went upstairs to their bedrooms. For the next half-hour, they sat in the parlor and Elena told her about the two dinners she'd shared with Miguel and what he'd told her about his life as Delores's son. Deirdre's heart softened toward him. Poor devil, she thought, he never had a chance to be anything but what he was. Delores had made him overbearing like herself.

A short time later, they said their good nights. Elena went

to the guest room, and Deirdre went to the room she shared with Carlos. Elena did not worry about her future tonight. She just changed into her nightgown, crawled into the comfortable bed, and went right to sleep.

Deirdre also got into her nightgown. Carlos had been very receptive to turning the third bedroom into his private study. Just this last week his desk had been moved into the vacant room and he'd bought bookcases and a comfortable leather chair. Their bedroom was now just a bedroom and not a combined study-bedroom. Deirdre liked it better this way.

Deirdre was still awake when Carlos came in from his study. As he unbuttoned his shirt, he told her what had happened at the hotel. "Señora Delgardo took me to the room and remained there as I gathered up Elena's belongings. Then she gave me this envelope with money in it. She said it was wages she owed Elena. Do you remember—I made a point of asking Elena before I left if the señora owed her any money?"

"I do and she said no. But you didn't mention this to Elena after you got back," Deirdre remarked.

"I know. I just wanted your opinion about it since you know the woman and I don't." Carlos had his own idea why the woman had given Elena more money.

"Knowing Delores, I can tell you exactly why she made her generous offer. She's had time to cool down and she realizes that firing Elena could be the worst mistake she's ever made. She's scared, Carlos," Deirdre told him.

"So you figure it is sort of a bribe."

"Definitely, but Elena may as well enjoy it." Deirdre laughed.

"There's no reason why she shouldn't." Carlos smiled as he handed the envelope to Deirdre. "Give it to her tomorrow, and the two of you can have a good laugh."

* * *

Three days at Deirdre's home did wonders for Elena. Her frayed nerves calmed, and her tired body finally felt rested. Now it was time to make some plans for herself, for she didn't intend to wear out her welcome.

It had been a delight to Deirdre to see Elena looking so much better, and it had been a joy to have her at the house, finally having time to talk as long as they wished. But on the fourth night Elena stayed with them, they had a dinner party to attend.

Deirdre told her, "This one I really need to attend with him. You remember Clarise Crauthers, I'm sure! Well, her husband has become Carlos's client recently. But I hate to leave you alone for the evening, Elena."

Elena laughed. "I won't be alone. Amigo will keep me company. Now you just go with your husband as you should and don't worry about me."

They sat remembering the Crauthers' garden party, exploding with laughter over Carter Junior and Tyler. It was only after Deirdre had left her that Elena let herself recall that late afternoon and a wave of sadness washed over her. It was the last time Mateo's arms had held her, and it seemed like years ago.

At six-thirty Deirdre and Carlos left for the dinner party and Stella announced to Elena that her dinner was ready. Later as Stella was taking her plate away and preparing to bring her dessert, she told Elena, "Miss Elena, Amigo seems to have taken a shine to you. He's all curled up there by your feet."

"I know. I felt his head resting on the toe of my slipper," she replied.

"That cat is a smart one! He knows a nice person right away, but he sure has his own dislikes." Stella chuckled.

Elena went directly up to her room after dinner, Amigo trailing her. She left her door slightly ajar so the big Persian cat could leave her room if he wished to. The room Elena was occupying was the one Deirdre had used until she and Carlos were married, and her wicker rocker and little footstool were still there.

Amigo made himself comfortable on the footstool and Elena slipped into her nightgown and robe, glancing at herself in the full-length mirror. She wondered if Deirdre suspected her condition. Her breasts were fuller, and her waistline certainly was, too. She realized that soon anyone would be able to tell she was pregnant. No gown could conceal it.

The Crauthers' dinner party tonight was typical. As Deirdre had told her weeks ago, Clarise didn't like long affairs. So the hour was early when Deirdre and Carlos returned. With her door ajar, Elena had heard their voices when they entered the front door. Amigo's keen ears had heard, too, and he jumped down from the stool and dashed out the door.

Elena was glad that she'd come up to her room after dinner, for they did not come upstairs for awhile. She was sure they were enjoying their privacy in the parlor tonight.

Elena heard Deirdre's infectious laughter. Since Amigo had departed, she closed her bedroom door.

Deirdre's laughter was because she was relating to Carlos parts of her private conversation with Clarise this evening. There were no ladies from the dress salon there tonight, but Clarise was curious to know about Elena and what had happened to her.

"Clarise told me that she couldn't get any information about Elena from the salon. She'd asked to speak with Delores, who said that Elena no longer worked for her. Clarise told her then that she didn't wish any of the others. She said Delores was indignant. Clarise left the salon offended by her manner. Delores lost another customer this week," Deirdre told her husband with a satisfied smirk on her face.

For almost three hours, Elena had done nothing but sit in Deirdre's wicker rocker and think. After viewing herself in the mirror, she'd known she had only one option left to her: She had to go home to Half Moon Bay. Once she got back there, she'd decide whether to confront Mateo.

The next morning, she told Deirdre of her plans. Deirdre was pleased. "Oh, Elena, that is where you'll find happiness—not here in Sacramento."

"I know, Deirdre. I was just a young girl, impulsive and too impatient. Things might have gone differently for me and Mateo if I'd not taken that notion to rush away with Delores Delgardo."

She told Deirdre that there were two favors she would like to ask of her. "Anything, honey. You know that," Deirdre said.

"Well, I'd like to see Señora Gomez before I leave here, for it may be a long time before I ever come back this way, and I'd like to buy my passage on the *Bay Queen*."

Deirdre smiled. "I think we can get that all done today for you. In fact, I'll leave you at Señora Gomez's home to visit with her, and I'll get your ticket for you and run my errands. When do you want to leave for Half Moon Bay?"

"Tomorrow, Deirdre."

Deirdre chuckled. "I'm convinced, Elena, that you are an impulsive lady. When you make up your mind you don't waste any time, do you?"

"Maybe that's my trouble, Deirdre."

"No, this time I think it's right," Deirdre told her.

An hour later, the two of them were in Carlos's buggy and Elena had a pleasant farewell visit with her dear friend Margarita.

Margarita Gomez gave her a warm embrace as they said

their goodbyes. "Yes, Elena, you go home and marry that fine young man of yours who cared so much about you he tried to track you down in this big city when he didn't know where to look. A man has to love a woman to do that, Elena."

But she assured her that they would be seeing one another again. She stood at her front entrance and waved to Elena and Deirdre as their buggy rolled down the drive.

A sadness engulfed Margarita. Her volatile temper was blazing, for Elena told her everything that had happened from the time she'd returned from Half Moon Bay.

She was glad Elena was away from Delores Delgardo. Margarita had decided that Delores would never sell her another gown.

Elena shared a gay dinner with her two dear friends Carlos and Deirdre. After dinner, Carlos excused himself quickly. Since this was to be Elena's last evening, he surmised the girls might like to spend it engaged in girl talk.

But he gave Elena a warm embrace before he went upstairs. "Have a safe journey home," he told her. "You know Deirdre and I care for you very much."

"I will, and thank you Carlos for everything. I love you both very much," Elena said, not knowing that Deirdre was thinking that one day Elena was going to be her husband's sister-in-law. She felt certain of this.

Before they dimmed the lamps in the parlor, Deirdre confided that she might be pregnant. "It's too early to know for sure. I hope so, Elena. Nothing could make me happier."

"Well, I might as well tell you that there's no doubt in my mind that I carry Mateo's child," Elena confessed.

"I know, Elena. I could tell. Carlos even noticed. I wondered about that the first time you came to the hat shop. That wasplike waist of yours had expanded even then. Elena, you must go to Mark. He has the right to know. You aren't being fair to him. Forget that Portuguese pride of yours."

"I will not beg, Deirdre."

"That is not begging, Elena. Give him a chance to refuse, although I know he will not do that. He loves you, Elena." Deirdre declared.

"I will go to him, Deirdre, and I will see if he is a man worthy of the price I paid when I gave him my love and my heart," Elena promised her.

"You'll see that he is, Elena. I firmly believe this."

"I want to believe you, Deirdre," she admitted and hugged her friend good night. In the morning, she would board the *Bay Queen*.

Miguel was finding his mother impossible to be around. She was more overbearing and foul-tempered than usual. Cindy had been dismissed, which left only Camilla and Babette. Business had to be down, for he'd taken neither of them on any assignments this last week.

With a lot of idle time on his hands, he'd spent several evenings at the Golden Nugget Tavern. He missed Elena and their talks.

Last night he'd chanced to meet a fisherman named Julio Carillo and they had shared a few drinks together. As it happened, Julio owned a fishing boat and was in dire need of two husky fellows. He offered Miguel a job and Miguel had accepted.

"I've got muscles and strength, but I don't know a damn thing about fishing," Miguel admitted to him.

Julio gave a roar of laughter. "Don't worry about that Julio will teach you. Learning to fish is easy. You mean your Papa never took you fishing, son?"

"I'm afraid not, Julio," Miguel told him.

"He should be ashamed of himself. All lads should go

fishing with their pas. You and I will go fishing, eh?" the ruddy-faced Julio told him.

When Miguel left the tavern, he not only had a job, he was feeling good about his future and this new venture with old Julio.

It was the first time he could ever remember being warmly embraced by a man or called son. He genuinely liked the old fisherman already.

Forty-four

The expression on Delores's face convinced Miguel to say nothing yet about his plans to leave her. When they arrived at the hotel, he asked her if his services were going to be needed that evening.

She glared at him and snapped, "For what, Miguel? There are no assignments for tonight or the next three nights. So you are free, but let me warn you not to spend your money so freely for the next week for I'll not have any to give you."

Her empire was crumbling and she was crumbling with it, Miguel realized as he watched her walk through the hotel door. She'd lived her whole life really caring about no one but herself and her selfish desires. Living around her all these years had made him the same way until just recently.

But Miguel was encouraged now that he could turn his life around. Elena had somehow softened his cold, hard heart and he would forever be grateful to her.

Liberated from the salon's usual, busy schedule, Miguel pursued his own pleasures. He ate dinner in the dining room and the same waitress who'd served him and Elena attended him. She found him as nice and as pleasant as he'd been the other evening with Elena Fernandes.

When he'd finished eating, he went directly to his room and began to pack two valises. He realized suddenly that he had no possessions except an expensive wardrobe. The venture he was striking out on didn't require fine-tailored suits so he packed four shirts and three pair of pants. One pair of good leather boots was all a man really needed for himself, but he had five. He folded a dark-blue coat.

He collapsed into the chair with a roar of laughter. He'd wasted twenty-five years of his life, and it was better to laugh than to cry. He was too old to cry.

He decided that it was best that he write a letter to his mother instead of telling her face to face. She was too erratic right now. He'd take her to the salon in the morning, and he'd be gone when she was ready to leave tomorrow afternoon. He'd give the letter to Clarence with instructions that Domino would have to pick her up.

The next day, he truly tried to be more gentle toward her as he helped her out of the buggy, for she looked weary and old.

"You look tired this morning, Mother," he remarked.

He could feel her stiffen, and she yanked her arm away from his hand. "Your eyes are blurred from drinking too much last night, Miguel. I am fine," she barked.

"No, Mother, you're wrong. I didn't put the evening in drinking. I stayed at the hotel all evening. Goodbye, Mother. Take care of yourself," he told her and turned to get back in the buggy.

She had already entered the salon and was walking to her office when she considered his parting remark. Something about it seemed strange, but she didn't dwell on it long.

Miguel stopped at the emporium before he returned to the hotel. He purchased some dark, cotton twill pants and a shirt similar to the garb the old boatman had been wearing last night at the tavern.

In his suite, he changed into his new clothes and looked at himself in the mirror. He looked like a different person, and Miguel liked this new image. A few minutes later, he was ready to leave this room behind him and seek a new life.

Clarence didn't recognize him at first. Miguel handed him the letter and told him, "Give this to Mother. I'm going to be out of town, so Domino will have to pick her up this afternoon at five."

Clarence took the letter, but he was too stunned to speak. All he could think of was how displeased the señora was going to be. The lady was in a foul mood already and this was surely going to put her in an even greater frenzy.

But Miguel had never felt so lighthearted and free-spirited as when he walked out of the Towers Hotel to head for Fisherman's Point to meet old Julio.

He felt liberated!

At two that January afternoon, the *Bay Belle* pulled away from Fisherman's Point into the river that branched out to the bay. There was a hint of a chill in the air and the light wind stung Miguel's face. He could never recall feeling so pleasantly excited. Being in the midst of the laughing, easygoing boatmen made Miguel wish he'd done something like this five or six years ago.

It had not been cowardice which had prompted him to write to his mother instead of facing her. He just didn't wish to endure her rage. Let her vent that anger to the emptiness of her bedroom after she'd read the letter. He was three hours away from Sacramento by the time Delores emerged from the salon to see Clarence sitting in the buggy. Domino was under the weather, so Clarence had appointed himself to the task.

She raised a skeptical brow and quizzed him. "You Clarence? Where is Miguel?"

"I am not sure, señora. He said he had to go out of town, and he left a letter for you. I've got it back at the hotel," Clarence told her. He, like many of the other employees at the hotel, had seen the drastic changes in the señora since Elena Fernandes had left. Rumors were running rampant.

Clarence felt nervous as they traveled from the salon to the hotel, and he was glad to resume his station behind the counter as soon as he handed her Miguel's letter.

She didn't tarry or go into her office. She went directly up to the second landing. Once inside her suite, she sank on the settee and opened the letter.

When she had finished reading, she flung the single page down on the thick carpet and went into a fury resembling an erupting volcano.

She shattered expensive pieces of porcelain, cursing Miguel's father and Elena Fernandes.

Completely spent, she collapsed on her settee. When she regained her strength, she reread the letter. This time she absorbed what her son was telling her. He was tired of being her lackey and had gone to seek his own life. He'd written that he'd taken little with him, for he had no further need of expensive clothes. A lavish wardrobe was never what he'd wanted anyway. He'd have much rather had her time and her love, he'd written.

The last sentence of his letter had a deep impact on Delores. He vowed that he'd never be a yoke around her neck again. He was determined to make it on his own. He wrote that he had never been proud of the weekly allowance he'd taken from her. He was sorry he'd done it so long.

She sat quite still for the longest time. Miguel was smarter than she'd realized. She had never taken the time to know her own son.

Like it or not, she had to confess this January night that she had no one to blame but herself that Miguel had become so shiftless. Now he wanted to change, but she could not take credit for that.

She'd had no time for him all these years, and she faced

the stark reality that from this day on he'd have no time for her.

Mark Mateo spent a reflective evening at La Casa Grande. He'd gone to what he now considered his study. The last few months paraded through his mind. Autumn had come and gone. When autumn had left the countryside, so had old Carlos.

Winter was upon them now. It was a slow time at the ranch, and he could set a slower pace for himself. Taking over La Casa Grande had been a tremendous undertaking, but he felt a certain amount of pride in himself for he truly felt like the patrón now.

He pulled out the desk drawer and spied the little velvet box which held the magnificent ring he'd had the greatest intentions of presenting to Elena. He realized that there was only one thing missing from his life which could make him the happiest man in the world. Some probably thought that he should feel that way now, having inherited the vast La Casa Grande. But he was damned lonely if the truth be known. He was lonely for the woman he loved with all his heart and soul.

He had never been able to accept that Elena didn't love him, even though she had refused to return with him to Half Moon Bay. No woman could so completely surrender herself to a man as she had that late October day unless she loved the man. It was that fierce Portuguese pride that had made her refuse to come to him at Carlos's house.

His own stupid pride had also stood in his way from marching back to the Towers Hotel and kissing away any protests she might have tried to give him. It was time for this foolish folly to be over. He was going to have her here with him at La Casa Grande, and he didn't care what he had to do to make that happen.

When he climbed the stairs, he didn't know that Elena was already closer to him than she had been last night. Over an hour ago, she'd arrived at Half Moon Bay. But the wharf was deserted, and little Chico wasn't around. She was glad she had only one valise. Just that proved taxing before she finally reached the cottage close to midnight.

No lamplight glowed from the windows, and she knew that her father and Vasco had long since retired.

A sleepy-eyed Sebastian responded to her knocks, but when he saw his pretty Elena standing in front of him, he became alive. "Oh, Elena! Elena, you are home again!"

"Yes, Papa, I am home!" she smiled weakly for she was so exhausted that she could have collapsed right there on the floor.

Instinctively, Sebastian knew that this time she was not going back to Sacramento. He carried her valise to her bedroom.

"Go back to bed, Papa. Tomorrow is a workday for you, and I'm ready for my bed. We will talk tomorrow night," she suggested.

"Yes, go to sleep and rest, daughter, and I will do the same," he told her. He left her then and returned to his own room to sink down on his bed and enjoy a most contented sleep for the next six hours.

Vasco slept through Elena's homecoming and was not aware of it until he woke up the next morning. A happy Sebastian told him that his sister had arrived home to stay.

Elena slept long after Sebastian and Vasco had left the cottage. But on the back of the cookstove was a hot pot of strong black coffee when she emerged from her bedroom to amble into the kitchen.

By the time Vasco and Sebastian returned to the cottage,

she had a tasty meal prepared for them, for this time she had found food there in the pantry. She had to admit that today she might not have made the effort to walk to the marketplace.

It was a night of jubilation at the Fernandes cottage as they dined and drank Sebastian's Portuguese wine. Sebastian announced to his daughter, "Our Vasco has himself a pretty little lady, Elena. Remember Maria Rico? Vasco is courting her."

Vasco gave a sheepish smile, and Elena could not resist teasing him. "Ah, Vasco, I remember Maria. You've got yourself a girl of pepper and spice." Elena figured that the feisty little Maria had been the bold one, for Vasco was so shy. Elena was pleased that her older brother had found himself a girl; it was time.

Elena indulged herself in their happy family reunion; but in the morning when her father and Vasco went out on the bay, she had very definite plans for herself. She had no intention of wasting one day now that she'd arrived back at Half Moon Bay.

Tomorrow morning she was going to head for La Casa Grande in her father's flat-bedded wagon. This time tomorrow night she'd know just how much man Mateo really was!

The next morning when she heard her father and brother leaving the cottage, she got up out of bed and went to the kitchen in her nightgown to get a cup of coffee. She had a second cup before she left the kitchen to get dressed.

She certainly didn't want to wear a muslin gown to travel in the old wagon, so she pulled down her yellow tunic and her black-twill, divided skirt, which would certainly be more comfortable. She slipped the tunic over her head and stepped into the black skirt. But she faced a problem when she tucked the tunic inside the waistband and tried to button the band.

She muttered and tugged, but it was impossible to make

the button meet the buttonhole. Even with her breath sucked in, the band needed another good inch. So she left the skirt unbuttoned and consoled herself that the black twill jacket would hide the gaping band. With the black, flat-crowned hat set at a cocky angle on her head and the strings tied under her chin, she was ready to leave the house.

A short time later she guided the old wagon down the drive to the main road. She made a fetching sight as she went through the village toward the outskirts and the open countryside. More than one head turned to admire her as the wagon rolled by.

She remembered how long it had taken her father to make the trip to Golden Splendor when they'd come to the festival and Deirdre had directed her to take the side road to the north about a mile before she would have arrived at Golden Splendor. Elena recalled the big archway on the north side of the road. She knew that she'd have no problem finding La Casa Grande, which was where she had to go if she wanted to find Mateo.

She knew that she could have her talk with Mateo and still get back to the cottage before her father and Vasco returned home in the late afternoon. A million questions paraded through her pretty head as she got farther and farther away from Half Moon Bay.

The long hour-and-a-half journey gave her plenty of time to think as she traveled through the quiet of the countryside. What would she do if Mateo refused to marry her and claim his child? She supposed that she would be faced with returning to the cottage to tell her father the truth. It wasn't a very pleasant thought that she would be bringing shame to herself and her family. What a flurry of gossip that would set off!

There at La Casa Grande, Mark had risen early for he had many things to attend to, so that he could leave today. He'd given one of his hands a large list of supplies to buy at the grain store and he'd placed his foreman in charge of the ranch for the next few days.

He'd told Estellita he was leaving this morning when she'd served breakfast to him. Young Alberto was preparing his buggy for him now that he had everything covered to make the ranch run in an orderly fashion during his absence.

Ready to leave, he was going from the barn to the house when his long, striding steps halted as he spied a billowing cloud of dust rising in the air and an old wagon came rolling up his drive. He wondered who it could be. He didn't want to have his departure delayed now.

But a few seconds later a slow smile came to his handsome face, for he saw the long, flowing black hair blowing back from the driver's face. Only one woman had such glorious hair as that.

He moaned with delight. "Dear God! Dear God, it's Elena!" His powerful legs carried him swiftly down the long drive. All the time he was making his mad dash toward the wagon he was thinking to himself that Lady Luck had finally shone on them. If she'd been just a little later, he would have been gone.

Seeing him running to meet her was enough to make her heart start pounding wildly. She could tell he was as happy to see her as she was right now viewing his firm, muscled body getting closer and closer.

By the time she had pulled up on the reins and was ready to leap to the ground, Mateo was there reaching up for her. Once she was in the circle of his arms, he vowed that she'd never leave them again.

He held her, managing only to say her name over and over again, and bent his head to kiss those sweet lips he'd ached for. It was a long, long embrace. He held her so tightly that she could hardly breathe, but she didn't care. When his lips finally released hers, his face was still pressed against hers as he whispered in her ear, "You came to me, *querida!* I shall never let you go again, my Elena. I never knew I could love as I love you, Elena Fernandes. Tell me you will never leave me."

His deep violet eyes probed deeply into hers. She gazed up at him. "Never, Mateo. I will never leave you. I love you, and I always have."

He smiled, for that was all he needed to hear. Swooping her up in his arms as though she were as light as a feather, he placed her on the seat of the wagon. He then leaped up beside her, taking charge of the reins, and guided the cart toward his barn.

He turned to ask her how she had known where to find him. She told him that Deirdre had told her. "I was sorry to hear about your Grandfather Mateo."

"That was what prevented me from coming to you, Elena," he told her as they pulled up to the barn.

"It doesn't matter now, Mateo, for we're together. That is all that matters." She smiled at him.

He dropped the reins and took her hands in his. His eyes danced over her face, for he wanted to absorb all that loveliness. "I want you here, right here with me at La Casa Grande, Elena. I want us to be married immediately—no more waiting."

He had spoken the magical words she'd yearned to hear him say. Deirdre had been right. He did love her, and it was she who had been wrong to have not had more faith in this man she loved.

"I'll marry you anytime you say, Mateo." She beamed at him, her eyes sparkling from the overwhelming joy she was feeling.

He grinned. "I'm going to hold you to that, Elena. Now

you just sit in the wagon a minute while I run into the barn to tell my foreman there's a change of plans."

He wasn't gone from her side long before he was back at the wagon and reaching up to take her down. As they were walking toward the house, he confessed to her that he had been about to leave La Casa Grande. "I was coming to Sacramento to get you, even if I had to hogtie you to bring you back here."

Elena threw her head back and laughed. "Oh, Mateo, Mateo, I adore you!"

If ever Estellita had seen a pair of young lovers, she knew she was seeing them walk up to the house when she glanced out the kitchen window. The tiny little miss walking by his side hardly came up to his broad shoulders. But what a little beauty she was! Señor Mark had such a happy smile on his face as he gazed down at her.

He didn't have to tell Estellita that he was not going anywhere now. She knew instinctively that he no longer had a reason to leave.

As he ushered her through the front door, he told Elena, "Welcome to your new home. You're all I need to make my life complete. We're going to have a wonderful life here at La Casa Grande, *muñequita mía.*"

"Oh, Mateo, it is such a grand house." She sighed as she gazed at the long hall and into the parlor.

She recalled the beauty of the family home at Golden Splendor, but this fine old mansion had its own distinctive structure and a Spanish influence which Elena found more intriguing. She was bedazzled as, looking around, she realized that marrying Mateo meant she would become the mistress of this grand home.

Wide-eyed, she looked up at him and sighed. "Oh, Mateo, this is overwhelming. I've never lived in a place this grand. I might not fit in here."

His hand tightened on hers, and he looked deep into her eyes. "You would fit in anywhere, Elena. This is my house now, and no woman but you could possibly be my wife or the mistress of La Casa Grande."

He explained to her as they roamed from the parlor to the dining room that his grandfather had done things in a grand style. They would make changes to fit their own tastes. He told her that he had already started putting his own imprint on the house. Elena had never seen such a long dining room table in her life as the one that was in that spacious dining room.

"Come, I've someone for you to meet, Elena," he said. He ushered her into the kitchen, where a middle-aged Mexican lady greeted her with a broad friendly smile.

With boyish enthusiasm, Mark announced, "Estellita, this is my Elena."

"Well, it's a pleasure to meet you, Señorita Elena. Welcome to La Casa Grande," she told her, taking a step closer to them. The young lady, she observed, was even more beautiful now that she was so near to her.

"Thank you, Estellita. It's nice to meet you, too." Elena smiled.

"This lady actually runs the house, Elena. She's the boss," Mark said grandly.

A gleam came to Estellita's eyes and she asked him, "Señor Mark, am I to forget your previous instructions to me?"

"I've no reason to leave La Casa Grande now." He smiled. "In fact, if I can reach Father Gonzales this afternoon, it is a wedding dinner you'll prepare tonight, Estellita."

His remark took both Estellita and Elena by surprise. Startled, Elena exclaimed, "Mateo, a wedding? I've brought nothing. How could I possibly be married tonight?"

His eyes darted from Elena to Estellita, who was in a quandary. How could she prepare a wedding feast on such short notice?

"You two just come over here to the table and let me ease both your minds. It will be a simple service for just you and me alone, Elena. Remember, you told me you'd marry me anytime I said. And I told you I was going to hold you to that promise. I meant it. I'll not let you leave again now that I've got you here," he said. Estellita, listening to him speak his heart to this pretty girl he obviously adored, began to smile.

Elena noticed her smile and she, too, broke into a broad grin of pleasure. "It will be as you wish, Mateo. But I'm not going to be a very beautiful bride in this old skirt."

"You look perfect to me, but you'll have a pretty gown to wear, *querida*. You just leave all that to me." He turned to Estellita. "You can fix dinner for just me, and my bride, and Father Gonzales. We'll have a family gathering later. That should make both of you feel better, eh?"

"Yes," she admitted, "but you two will have yourselves a wedding cake."

Elena and Mark sat at the little kitchen table and ate a light lunch. Estellita observed these two young people laughing and talking and was pleased that this old mansion would ring with laughter once again. Happiness was going to abide here.

As soon as they had finished their lunch, Mark knew he had places to go and people to see so he told Estellita, "I'm taking Elena to the south guest bedroom so she can relax and rest after her trip from Half Moon Bay. I'm going to be gone a couple of hours. Take good care of my lady for me, Estellita."

"I'll take very good care of her, señor. Now you just be on your way."

Mark showed her to the lovely guest room, which had a

marvelous view of the courtyard gardens below, and he gave her a long, lingering kiss before he forced himself out the door.

Elena sat on the bed surrounded by luxury. She felt giddy. Everything was happening so fast. Deirdre had been right when she said Mateo men were take-charge men!

Forty-five

Alone in the lovely lavender-and-white bedroom, Elena recalled that Deirdre had told her how Carlos had taken charge to put into motion their own hasty wedding. It seemed that Mateo men could be masterful in any situation.

When Mark had ushered her up the stairs and into the room, he had told her to sit at the desk to write a note to her father. "I don't wish Sebastian to worry about you. I'll send your message by one of my men, and he will deliver the wagon back to Half Moon Bay. He can tie his horse to the back of the wagon so he'll have a way back here."

So she'd done as he'd requested, and he'd tarried no longer except to steal one more kiss before he dashed out of the room.

She did not doubt that Mateo was impatient to make her his bride, and she could not have been happier.

Only one thing bothered her about these hasty plans. She'd not had a chance to tell him that she was expecting his child, and she wondered if he would be happy about it. If he weren't, then she would surely be shattered.

Mark had first ridden to seek out Father Gonzales, and the Mateo family priest could not have been more delighted to hear that Mark was taking himself a wife. La Casa Grande needed a woman. The padre told Mark he would be there at six-thirty.

Next he rode to Golden Splendor to announce his happy news to his family. He was sure that Markita would be delighted to furnish Elena with one of her gowns for the ceremony.

His news was greeted with great jubilation. Only Markita pouted when he told them that they would have no guests this evening.

Mark embraced and soothed her. "Soon we will have another ceremony for just you, little sister. Now go get a pretty gown for my lady."

Aimée announced that she had a gift for him to take to Elena and went upstairs. If the young lady had arrived totally unprepared and her impulsive son insisted on a wedding tonight, there were a few things the mother of the bridegroom could supply.

When she descended the stair, she brought a box containing a lovely coral nightgown and lace-trimmed wrapper which Mano had bought for her. She knew he would understand why she'd given his present to their new daughter-in-law. She'd also put a bottle of her sweet-smelling toilet water in the box with the lingerie.

Markita returned with her prettiest jonquil-yellow gown which she thought Elena would look beautiful in. Along with the gown, Markita had chosen some slippers and undergarments for Elena to wear.

"Tell Elena she is to keep this gown. It will always be treasured by her more than me. It's my gift to her, Mark. I've always known she was the girl for you, but I'd begun to wonder if you were going to figure that out," she teased her brother.

He gave his sister an affectionate hug as he took the lovely yellow gown and told her, "Elena will appreciate your generous gift, Markita, and you will be seeing her in a few days."

His perky little sister declared that her father and mother were not going to get off as easily when she married. "I want to have the biggest, grandest wedding that's ever been held in San Mateo County."

Aimée and Mano broke into gales of laughter, and Mark took his leave from the lighthearted gaiety in his family's parlor. He had accomplished everything that he'd set out to do, and he was now ready to go to his own home and Elena.

He was feeling very pleased with himself when he arrived back at the house. He informed Estellita that there would indeed be a wedding tonight. Father Gonzales would be arriving for the simple ceremony at six-thirty.

"After the ceremony, we will have dinner with champagne, of course," he told Estellita.

"I had no doubt at all you'd work everything out, señor." She smiled at him. "And your pretty bride will have a wedding cake to cut. It is in my oven already."

She saw the lovely gown flung across his arm, and she guessed that he'd ridden to Golden Splendor.

"You're an angel, Estellita," he declared, giving her a hasty hug as he dashed out of the kitchen to go upstairs.

He gave a light rap at the door and called out to Elena, "We're getting married, *chiquita*. The priest is coming at six-thirty, and you've a wedding gown, along with all the other little frilly things you ladies like."

"Oh, Mateo, the gown is beautiful."

"Markita told me to tell you that's her gift to you. This is from Mother. Now, I'm going to leave you even though it is sheer torment. Just a few more hours and you will be my wife, Elena Fernandes. That's all I ever wanted. One kiss to hold me, eh?" he asked, his eyes twinkling.

She went into his arms, and he held her close to him to

take the sweet nectar from her lips. When he released her, he told her, "You're going to be the most beautiful bride in the world, and I can't wait to see you in that yellow gown."

"As long as you think that, Mateo, then that is all that matters to me," she murmured as he reluctantly began to back away from her toward the door.

"The magical hour is six-thirty. Estellita will be coming up shortly to assist you in anything you need," he told her as he finally went out the door.

She laid the yellow gown on the bed and examined the contents of the box Markita had packed for her. She had forgotten nothing. There were lacy undergarments, slippers, and stockings. Next, she opened the box that Aimée Mateo had sent to her and found a diaphanous coral nightgown and a matching satin wrapper trimmed with ecru lace. Elena was touched by Aimée's thoughtfulness as she sniffed the bottle of toilet water. But what really brought tears to her eyes was the delicate headband of silk orange blossoms that lay underneath the wrapper. A note was attached to it which told Elena what a very sentimental woman Aimée was. She'd written that it was an old French tradition that brides should wear orange blossoms for happiness and good luck. She wanted Elena to wear the band she had worn and hoped that Markita would wear it on her wedding day as well.

Emotion washed over her, and Elena gave way to a moment of sentiment as tears flowed down her cheeks. But they didn't last long, for she was too happy this late afternoon.

The next hour went by swiftly. Estellita had two of the young housemaids bring in the bronze tub to prepare a bath for Elena. It was only when Elena was enjoying that leisurely perfume-scented soak that she gave way to a panic. Markita's gorgeous gown might not fit her now as it would have a few months ago. What would she do?

She lingered no longer in the tub but got out quickly to

dry off and slip into the satin wrapper Aimée had sent to her.

The lovely gown had silk-covered buttons running down the front a few inches below the waistline. There was also a wide sash. Nervously, she slipped into the gown and began to button up the front of the bodice. There was no question that the material was pressed tight across her full breast, but at least she could button it. She managed to make the next two buttons fit the loops, but not the last three. Those two inches of her expanded waistline made it impossible. A wild hope surged in her that the wide sash would cover the gap, and miraculously it worked. Elena heaved a deep sigh of relief as she began to unbutton the bodice so she could slip out of the gown. She was not ready to get dressed just yet.

In the lacy undergarments she sat at the dressing table to style her hair for the exquisite headband. She finally settled on leaving short little wisps of curls at her temples. She brushed the rest of her hair away from her face to cascade down her back so she could place the headband like a crown atop her head. The effect was attractive and most flattering. It showed off the radiant beauty of her face, and Elena decided to leave the headband on her head as she ambled around the room. It was still too early to put on the gown which she knew was going to be very uncomfortable.

Only one thing marred her happiness this early evening. She still had not told Mateo that she was carrying his baby, and she'd always been honest and frank with him. What if he thought she had tricked him into marrying her because she was pregnant? She knew how proud Mateo was.

What Elena didn't realize was that she herself was still naive even though she'd learned much about life during the time she'd been in Sacramento.

A man as experienced as Mark, who knew every curve of her sensuous body, had realized the minute he lifted her from the wagon that she was swollen with his baby. He believed that their child had broken her stubborn will and her fierce pride, making her finally come to him. Well, he couldn't be happier! Often, he'd thought about that glorious afternoon and wondered if he'd planted his seed within her.

His sharp mind knew exactly how far along she was in her pregnancy, and that they could expect a baby at La Casa Grande in July.

He knew what a headstrong, gutsy lady he was marrying tonight, but that was what made Elena exciting. A shrinking violet, docile doll would have bored him.

Since it was to be a simple ceremony in the parlor, Mark dressed in one of his fine-tailored black pants and a white ruffled shirt. He was thinking that Grandfather Mateo would have probably been mortified that he chose not to wear a coat, but Mark was doing things his way.

He left his bedroom and went downstairs to his study to get the magnificent ring that he'd yearned so long to put on Elena's dainty finger.

From the study, he'd gone to the parlor to see how lovely Estellita had it looking with flowers which were still blooming in the gardens even though it was January. Candlelight glowed throughout the room. The dining room looked equally nice. Candles illuminated a lovely centerpiece of white and yellow asters plucked from the south gardens.

He strolled into the kitchen to tell her what a magnificent job she'd done in making it look so festive. He asked her, "Estellita, would you go up to Elena and escort her downstairs when Father Gonzales arrives. She's here without any family."

Estellita could not have been more pleased. "I'll be glad to do that, señor. I have not been so happy in a long, long time. I like your beautiful lady. Señor Carlos is surely smiling down on us tonight."

Mark had to agree with her, for he, too, had felt old Carlos's presence this evening.

Just before the hour appointed for the wedding, Estellita knocked at Elena's door. Elena greeted her, and Estellita gasped, "Oh, señorita, you are so very beautiful! I've never seen a prettier bride!"

"Oh, Estellita, thank you. Now, if I can just walk down the stairs. My legs feel like jelly."

"I'm to escort you downstairs. Señor Mark asked me to do it. It is my pleasure to do so, and I will tell you that you're just feeling as any young bride feels. Shall we go? Father Gonzales is here, and your wedding is ready to take place in the parlor. Señor Mark is waiting for you." She gave a soft chuckle. "Don't ever tell him this; but he, too, is nervous I think."

Elena smiled. "Good. That makes me feel better."

As Estellita led Elena to the archway, Mark told the padre about his bride in most glowing terms. "Father, she is a splendor to behold," he boasted, "but you will see for yourself shortly."

Father Gonzales did, indeed. Turning, he saw a vision in yellow entering the parlor. He saw a lovely young lady moving slowly into the room. She resembled a fancy, dressed-up doll. But when Mark brought her to meet him, the priest realized that this was not a doll, but a young woman very much alive with spirit and great warmth.

Father Gonzales felt sure that Mark had picked himself the perfect wife to be at his side as his own mother had stood by Mano through the years. In fact, he was very much reminded of Aimée tonight and how her eyes had adored Mano the night he had united them. A wave of sadness swept over him this evening. He, like old Carlos, was no longer young. This could be the last wedding he would officiate for the Mateo family. But he was glad to see Mark married.

But the wise old priest suspected that he was going to still be around to bless their first child.

There might have been only the three of them at the long dining table, but it was a gala evening that gave Father Gonzales a chance to become more acquainted with Elena. He left there liking her even more. Like Estellita and Mark, he felt that Señor Carlos was smiling in heaven tonight!

Elena had insisted that he take a large serving of the delicious wedding cake Estellita had baked for her. So he saw a young lady with a kind, generous heart. Yes, he liked Mark's bride. She would be good for him and for La Casa Grande.

By the time Father Gonzales left, Mark knew that his little Elena had charmed him. It was already obvious to him that Estellita adored her, so he didn't anticipate that Elena was going to have any problem being the mistress of the manor. All she had to do was be her natural self.

She confirmed his belief when he started to guide her back to the parlor and she pulled away from him.

"I'll join you in just a minute, Mateo. I must tell Estellita how nice her dinner was and how much I loved the wedding cake," she told him as she dashed back into the kitchen. He watched her go, an amused smile on his face. She had no reason to concern herself about being the mistress here. She might not realize it, but she had already taken charge of La Casa Grande. Mark saw in Elena the same warm charm and grace that had always endeared his mother Aimée to her servants.

For as long as she lived, Estellita would never forget the moment when Elena had rushed into the kitchen to thank her.

The lovely bride sank down in the kitchen chair and moaned as she removed Markita's slippers. With a pathetic look on her face, she told Estellita, "I just can't stand these tight slippers another minute, Estellita. Markita's feet are much smaller than mine."

Estellita smiled. "When your feet hurt, you hurt all over, señora."

Elena heaved a sigh of relief and walked around the table in her stocking feet. "Ah, it feels wonderful. Well, I'll say good night to you, Estellita."

"Good night to you, Señora Elena," she smiled, watching her leave the kitchen in her stocking feet and carrying Markita's borrowed slippers.

It was a sight Estellita would never forget and one she'd recall often in the days to come. It told the Mexican cook that there was nothing put-on about this down-to-earth little lady. She was like a fresh summer breeze in the old house.

When she came into the parlor and Mark saw her carrying her slippers, he realized that Markita's slippers were cramping her feet. His little free-spirited wife could not tolerate that. To him, she looked adorable.

Sinking down on the settee beside him, she told him, "Oh, Mateo, it was a perfect wedding! We may have another ceremony for the family, but it will still not compare to this one in my memory."

"I feel the same way, *querida*." He poured them one last glass of wine before they went upstairs. She was not aware of the gap displayed in the front of her gown, but he sensed that she was as miserable in that tight gown as she'd been in the too-small slippers when he saw that three of the buttons were unfastened.

Elena was very aware that she'd not yet told him that she was pregnant and it was time she did. As she took the last sip of the wine, she said, "I've something to tell you, Mateo."

"Later, *mi vida*. You just get your pretty self upstairs and get comfortable. You've had a long day. I'll join you in just a few minutes after I see to all these lamps."

He wanted to give her a chance to undress in private so she would not have to feel embarrassed about the ill-fitting gown.

"I'll be waiting for you, Mateo," she told him as she left the parlor. It was as she was climbing the stairs that she was grateful to have a few minutes alone to get out of Markita's dress and into the full-flowing coral gown Señora Mateo had sent her.

Mark dimmed the lamps and sat down to light a cheroot. He took a few puffs, thinking that he, like Elena, would always feel that this was their true wedding date. His bride had been breathtakingly beautiful in Markita's yellow gown with his mother's headband atop her head. On her finger was the ring which had belonged to his Grandmother Mateo.

There in the quiet of the darkened parlor, Mark felt very much that the spirit of Grandfather Mateo was with him. He could have sworn that he heard his raspy voice say, *"Nieto, I am happy this night."*

Forty-six

When he entered the guest bedroom, he found his bride at the dressing table in her sheer nightgown, brushing her long black hair. She looked glorious.

She looked up at him and smiled. "Bless your dear mother, Mateo, for she furnished me with this lovely nightgown. I am overwhelmed that she allowed me to wear her headband tonight. She wrote me a note, Mateo. It said that in France brides always wear orange blossoms on their wedding for happiness and good luck."

He stood beside her as she sat on the little stool, and his hands rested on her dainty shoulders. "Mother is a very sentimental lady, as you'll find out as you get to know her better," he told her.

"Oh, I know that already, Mateo." But Elena was not going to completely relax until she had told her new husband the truth. She would be in torment until she did.

So she looked up at him, and her black eyes gazed directly into his. "I've something to say to you, Mateo."

"Tell me whatever it is you wish to say, *chiquita*," he urged her as he unbuttoned his white-linen shirt and removed it. He flung it over on the chair and faced her. He stood there with his broad bare chest exposed, and her eyes danced over him.

Her long lashes fluttered nervously. "Well, it—it isn't easy with you moving around, Mateo," she told him.

He came closer to her and she got up from the stool. He fought back an amused smile, anticipating her confession. "All right, Elena, I'll stand very still, I promise you. What do you want to tell me?"

She stood before him, her pretty head held high and proud. "I carry your baby, Mateo, and I have for three months." It was only a second, but to Elena the moment was endless before she saw a grin spread slowly across his face.

His arms claimed her as he told her, "I knew that the minute these arms of mine held you today. Oh, *querida,* why do you think I was so happy when you arrived? Why do you think I planned this hasty wedding tonight? I've gone almost crazy with you in Sacramento and me here. I think I knew I planted my seed in you that afternoon in the city."

By now Elena found herself pressed close to him. Any doubts she might have had about Mateo and how he would feel about her revelation were quickly swept away.

Amorously, he whispered in her ear, "Oh, *querida,* I left Sacramento in a torment, and I've been in one ever since until this morning."

"And I paid a high price for my stupid pride, Mateo," she confessed.

He looked down, and his violet eyes warmed her with the passion he was feeling. "That doesn't matter now. We're together and nothing is ever going to separate us again, my Elena," he promised as he bent to kiss her half-parted lips. That was all it took for a flaming spark of desire to blaze into a raging inferno of passion. All those long weeks of hunger had to be satisfied by caresses and touches before a calm finally settled over them.

Elena knew that no man but Mateo could have possibly taken her to such heights of ecstasy. Mark was certain that no woman but Elena could fire him as she did. Her supple body molded to his so perfectly that he swore she was meant to be his and his alone.

He held her close to him throughout the night. Tonight, he felt that the world was his, for he had the woman he loved with all his heart in the bed beside him. In that tiny body of hers was his baby. A most beautiful babe it would have to be with a mother as lovely as his Elena. He lay smiling, suddenly realizing that she never called him Mark. He was going to have to ask her about that one day. But he didn't mind at all, for no one could have made it sound as she did with her endearing Portuguese accent.

His bride slept peacefully the next morning, but he roused himself. Once he had his work clothes on, he slipped out of the room and went downstairs.

Estellita chided him good-naturedly when he merely gulped a fast cup of coffee. "Can't you take time to have some breakfast, Señor Mark?"

"I'll have breakfast later with my bride, Estellita. I want to get to the barn right now," he told her and rushed out the back door.

When he returned to the house, Elena was still sleeping, so Mark had Estellita serve him his breakfast. He was ravenously hungry by now.

"I can't wait any longer for that sleepy-headed bride of mine to wake up, Estellita." He laughed.

"Well, she had a very big day yesterday. She needs her rest after so much going on. I'll take her a breakfast tray later. Don't you worry about that, señor," she told him.

Mark smiled. "I think you like my new bride, eh Estellita?"

"I like her very much, Señor Mark. I think she is the nicest thing that could have ever happened to you. The little señora and I are going to get along fine," she declared firmly.

"That makes me very happy, Estellita," he told her.

As Elena always addressed Mark as Mateo, Estellita began to call Elena the *little señora* as the days went by.

Sebastian and Vasco had trudged up the path to the cottage after their day of fishing to find an old Mexican sleeping on their front porch. Sebastian saw his wagon by the side of the cottage instead of where it should have been, and many questions immediately cropped up in his mind.

Sebastian called out to him. "Hey, you—what's going on here? Why are you here, eh?"

Santos jerked alive. "Are you Señor Sebastian?"

"I am."

"Then I've a message for you from your daughter. That will explain why I'm here with your wagon," Santos stammered.

Sebastian raised a bushy skeptical brow as he took the message the old Mexican handed to him. A slow broad grin came to Sebastian's face as he read.

He turned to Vasco to tell him the good news. "Come, we go in the house and drink a toast to Elena and Mateo." He urged Santos to join them before he untied his horse from the back of the wagon to ride back to La Casa Grande.

Reluctantly, Santos accepted the Portuguese fisherman's offer, for he was a hard man to refuse. However, he politely refused the offer of a second glass. "No, Señor Sebastian, I must be riding for La Casa Grande now. I thank you for your very good wine, but I must go."

Sebastian walked with him to the door and watched as he mounted his horse. The old Mexican pulled the wide-brimmed sombrero atop his head and tightened the straps. Santos gave a wave of his hand and spurred the horse down the path to the main road.

Sebastian and Vasco spent a festive night in the cottage

celebrating Elena's marriage to Mateo. Sebastian told his son, "Now, it is time to think about getting yourself a wife, Vasco. A man is not complete without his woman. A man needs a wife."

"Oh, Pa, I don't know."

"Believe me, Vasco. You start thinking about it," Sebastian urged him. Vasco nodded skeptically.

The next afternoon when Vasco and Sebastian returned from their long day of fishing, another surprise awaited them. Elena and Mark sat in the buggy in front of the cottage. Necessity had demanded that she return for her clothing, since she had nothing to wear at La Casa Grande.

Mark told Sebastian, "I hope you'll forgive me, sir, but once I had her at La Casa Grande I wasn't going to let her get away from me again."

Sebastian and Vasco roared with laughter. Sebastian told him, "I like your way of thinking, Mateo. I would have felt the same way."

They shared dinner with Elena's father and brother, and Elena packed her belongings. It was long after dark when she and Mateo boarded his buggy to go back to La Casa Grande.

Elena had her light wool cape draped around her shoulders and she snuggled close to her husband to enjoy the moonlit ride back to La Casa Grande. But before they arrived she fell asleep. When Mark guided the buggy under the high archway, she awoke and exclaimed, "Oh, we're home, Mateo!"

He looked over and smiled. "Yes, *querida,* we're home." It pleased him how natural it had been for her to call the mansion home. He wanted Elena to feel that La Casa Grande was her home now.

He stopped the buggy at the front entrance and assisted her down. "Go on upstairs. I'll get the buggy over to Alberto and have him help me carry your things up to the house," he told her.

The first thing she did as soon as she got to the bedroom was to remove the black twill divided skirt. It was cutting into her waist after all the *paella* she'd eaten at her father's. It was a glorious feeling to have the sweet freedom of the loose gown. But she gave herself a stern warning that she must not eat so much in the next few months or she was going to be a horrible sight for Mateo to look upon.

A short time later, Mark carried in her gowns. He'd had Alberto set the two valises by the door, for he'd suspected that Elena might already be in her nightgown.

He had sensed that she was miserable in that binding skirt after they'd eaten at Sebastian's. She'd obviously wasted no time getting into the gown and satin wrapper. She gazed up at him with a very serious look on her face and declared, "Oh, Mateo, I think I ate too much *paella*."

"Are you not feeling well, Elena?" he asked, hanging the gowns in the armoire.

"Oh, no, I just feel stuffed and fat. I've got to watch my eating, or I'll grow too fat," she declared as she began to brush her hair.

He laughed. "You're going to grow a little fatter regardless of what you eat, *chiquita*."

She sat there with a pout on her face, mumbling, "Fat and ugly is what I'm going to be."

He walked over to where she was sitting and lifted her up from the stool. "You'll never look more beautiful to me, Elena Mateo. Don't you ever doubt that for one minute," he declared.

Sweeping her up in his strong arms, he carried her to their bed and removed the satin wrapper. She'd known the fierce passion of his lovemaking. Tonight she was to know his tenderness. She was a woman completely fulfilled.

There was no shadow of a doubt how deeply and devotedly her handsome husband loved her.

It took one more trip to Half Moon Bay for Mark to gather the rest of Elena's possessions from her bedroom. He'd told Sebastian of his mother's plans for a formal second wedding for them very soon. "You and Vasco must come. My brother Carlos and his new bride will also be there. Mother isn't going to be satisfied until she gets to see her two sons take their wedding vows. So Carlos and Deirdre will be going through the same ceremony as Elena and I."

"We will be there, I assure you, Mateo. You must tell Elena that the Fernandes men might be having a wedding, too, before the year is over. Vasco has finally become serious about little Maria," Sebastian said with a broad pleased smile on his face.

"I'll tell her and she'll be pleased to hear the news. It's time Vasco took himself a bride," Mark declared as he boarded his carriage and waved goodbye to Sebastian.

When he left Half Moon Bay, Mark didn't go directly to La Casa Grande. He drove to Golden Splendor, for he felt the need to speak with his mother. Poor Elena had let out seams of her gowns as far as they could go. She was in need of a comfortable wardrobe to take her through the next few months.

Elena was very distraught about what she could possibly wear for the formal affair Aimée was planning for a second reading of the marriage vows for both of their sons.

Mark was pleased that he found his mother alone in her sitting room, and he explained the situation. "Elena already carries my baby, Mother. She has for three months. I couldn't be happier about it. I've been through hell not being able to go to her, for I suspected it might be so."

"She's with you now, Mark, and that's all that really matters. You leave the rest to me. She and I will go to my seamstress, and she'll have herself some pretty and comfortable gowns." Aimée smiled at him.

"You're an angel, Mother," he told her as he planted a kiss on her cheek and made a mad dash out the door.

Memories flooded her as she watched her son go. She was no angel, nor had she ever been. She was already carrying Carlos when she and Mano got married. She had been a young woman like Elena who'd fallen helplessly in love with a Mateo man.

Forty-seven

On Friday afternoon, Aimée and Elena went to see Aimée's seamstress Melinda. For years, Melinda had stitched lovely gowns for Aimée and Markita.

Her soft wool cape had concealed her expanding figure, but Elena felt embarrassed. She knew that once she removed the cape at the seamstress' shop, her condition was going to be obvious.

Aimée sensed her tenseness the moment she boarded the carriage. They had been together only a few minutes before Elena looked over at her, her dark eyes pleading. "I carry Mateo's child already, señora. I can no longer hide it. My gowns have reached their limit."

Aimée's deep violet eyes, exactly like her son's, looked compassionately at her daughter-in-law and her hand went over to clasp Elena's. "Elena, I've a confession to make to you. I was pregnant with Carlos when Mano and I got married. So you see, you are not the first nor will you be the last. What matters is that you love my son and he loves you. It was the same with Mano and me. We loved one another so fiercely that nothing could have separated us even though our fathers were bitter enemies. Mano and I love you dearly, and the first time we saw you and Mark together we were reminded of ourselves."

"Oh, señora, how lucky I am!" Elena cried with mist coming to her eyes.

"No, no Elena. We are the ones who are lucky that our Mark found himself a beautiful girl like you. You see, Elena, you are beautiful of face and soul. We could not be happier to be becoming grandparents."

Elena spent a wonderful afternoon with Aimée and she felt as if a very heavy burden had been lifted from her shoulders.

They spent more than two hours at Melinda's shop. Aimée had insisted that Melinda make Elena six gowns in various shades and materials for her to wear during the next months. For the formal occasion, Melinda had come up with a marvelous idea. She had a lovely gold-satin gown which she proposed to layer with flounces of white lace which would conceal Elena's no longer petite figure.

But the most pleasing purchases of the afternoon were two gowns which gave her swollen figure the freedom to breathe. They took those two dresses with them when they finally left the shop.

It was late afternoon when the carriage brought the two ladies back to Golden Splendor. They were both in a jubilant mood when they greeted their husbands. The four of them shared dinner together before Mark and Elena departed for La Casa Grande.

Both Mark and his father saw that the ladies had formed a very close bond. They watched the two of them give one another a warm embrace. They exchanged smiles and both of them were feeling very happy this winter's night.

Later, when Mano and Aimée climbed the stairs to go to their bedroom, he told his lovely wife, "You look radiant tonight. I have to assume that you two had yourselves a nice time."

"Oh, a glorious time, Mano! I'm going to be a grandmother!" she exclaimed.

Mano ushered her into their bedroom, teasing her. *"Madre de Dios,"* he cried, "I shall be sleeping with a grandmother!"

"Yes, *grand-père,* I shall be sleeping with a grandfather." She smiled.

Everyone in the Mateo households seemed to be happy and content but Markita. She grew impatient waiting for her suitor to propose to her. Yet, he courted her devotedly.

As she helped her mother prepare for the wedding celebration, she complained to her mother, "I'm to be an old maid."

Aimée laughed. "Oh, hardly, *ma petite!* Francisco adores you."

"Well, Francisco sure has not asked me to marry him," she declared to her mother.

Aimée knew the reason why, for she and Theresa Renaldo were dearest friends. Francisco was fearful she'd refuse him. Theresa had told her, "Francisco would be crushed. He must gather more courage or Markita must convince him that she cares for him as much as he cares for her, Aimée."

So Aimée told her daughter, "Francisco will ask you when he feels that you will say yes to his proposal. Maybe, *ma petite,* just maybe you leave doubts in Francisco that you love him enough. Don't blame him so harshly. Maybe your flippant way unnerves him. Think about that, Markita. If you really care for Francisco, then let him know this in a most ladylike way."

Markita was to think about what her mother had told her that afternoon.

Carlos and Deirdre arrived in the late afternoon, and it was a most pleasant evening at Golden Splendor as the fam ily gathered in the spacious dining room for dinner. Aimée was as enchanted with Carlos's pretty wife as she was with Mark's. She'd seen changes in Carlos at Christmas, and she saw a different Carlos sitting at their dining table tonight. Deirdre had brought out the best in Carlos and it was obvious to her that her son adored his beautiful, fair-haired bride.

She had class and charm and looked most elegant in her exquisite gown. Aimée could imagine what pride Carlo must feel when he took her to the *soirées* in Sacramento. She was a lady any man could be proud of, and Carlos would not have settled for a woman who would not have measured up to his expectations. Deirdre Deverone seemed to have filled all his requirements in the lady he wanted in a wife. Apparently, he found them in Deirdre!

Aimée couldn't have been a happier woman. Her two sons had beautiful wives, and they both seemed so happy. One day she felt sure Deirdre would be carrying Carlos's baby.

Actually, Deirdre could have told her that she suspected she was pregnant right now. When she'd told Carlos that there was a very good possibility she was, he had been exuberant. He'd pranced around the house like a proud peacock and rushed to announce the news to Stella.

She found herself most anxious to see Elena now that they'd arrived at Golden Splendor, but she doubted that they'd have time alone for the estate was a beehive of activity.

About the same time that Deirdre and Carlos arrived at Golden Splendor, Sebastian and Vasco rolled up to the front entrance at La Casa Grande. They found it overwhelming that this was actually where Elena now lived.

Vasco stammered, "Our little Elena sure did herself proud, eh Pa? Our little princess got herself a real castle."

"She sure did, Vasco. I thought Golden Splendor was grand, but this surpasses that fine place."

Elena was still upstairs dressing, but Mark had gone down to the parlor so he'd been there to greet them the minute they arrived.

A servant ushered them into the tiled hallway, and Mark rushed out when he heard voices at the front entrance.

Elena was descending the stairs and she saw Mark coming into the hall. She called out to him, "Is it Papa, Mateo?"

"Yes, they're here," he told her, waiting for her. Together, they greeted her family. Elena got a big bear hug from both of them. It took only one fleeting glance to confirm what they had suspected: She was pregnant.

But that didn't matter to them. She was absolutely glowing with loveliness. They moved into the parlor, and Mark served wine after he'd instructed the servant to take their luggage to the guest rooms.

What really amazed Sebastian that first hour was the grace and charm with which his daughter moved around in these grand surroundings as if she'd been born there. Twice she left the parlor to attend to household matters, and Sebastian had seen her in the hallway speaking with the servants.

Mark showed them to their rooms so they could refresh themselves before dinner. They'd hardly expected to have separate rooms—and such spacious rooms at that! They were not accustomed to having their valises carried.

Vasco was particularly impressed. Since he'd not come to Golden Splendor with Elena and his father, he'd had no inkling of the grand style in which the Mateo family lived.

Twilight was gathering outside, and Vasco stood at the windows overlooking the courtyard. What pleasant times Elena must enjoy walking in her own lovely garden along the stone pathways bordered by shrubs and flowers! In the center of the courtyard was a bubbling fountain. Four iron benches were placed around the little fish pond. Roofed patios extended from two of the rooms below his bedroom. Exotic tropical plants grew profusely, and tall majestic palms towered to lofty heights.

Elena had her own little paradise just outside her own door!

Promptly at six-thirty, Sebastian heard a rap on his door. His daughter called out to him, "Papa, may I come in?"

"Of course you may, honey." A broad smile was on his face as she came into the room. "I'm such a happy man. You've got yourself a fine, fine husband who loves you, so I don't have to ask if you are happy. Your face tells me that. I wish your mama were here to share this happy time with us."

"I wish that too, Papa. But at least, I have you and Vasco. I know you can see that I already carry Mateo's child. I hope you're not upset about it," she stammered.

Sebastian had always been a man of deep emotions, and he was feeling the depth of them as he encircled his daughter in his arms, tears streaming down his face. With his deep voice cracking, he told her, "Upset—oh, no! I know this child is a child of deep love, and I couldn't be happier about being a grandpa. And Vasco will be the proudest uncle in the village."

They laughed and cried, and then Elena suggested that they go downstairs to join Mark in the parlor. Mark was already having a glass of wine when the three of them came in. A short time later, Vasco and Sebastian were eating huge thick beefsteaks which covered their plates. Estellita had fixed an enormous platter of small roasted potatoes and fresh green vegetables.

Sebastian finished every delicious bite of the steak and declared to Mark that it was the best steak he'd ever eaten. "You've got yourself one fine cook, Mateo."

"I shall tell Estellita you said that. She will be pleased. One day when you visit us, you will have to show Estellita how to cook your *paella.*"

Elena was amused. She wasn't sure that that was a good idea at all. Her father and Estellita in the same kitchen could prove disastrous.

They returned to the parlor after dinner, and Elena left the three men together when she retired. The next day and evening were going to be busy.

After Mark had seen Elena to their room, he suggested that Sebastian and Vasco come with him to his study. "We'll have ourselves a nightcap," he suggested.

Just to walk through the carved oak door was to know that this was a man's room. Sebastian and Vasco were astonished by the heavy, sturdy furnishings. The leather chairs that flanked the massive stone fireplace made a relaxed, cozy setting. Mark told them to make themselves comfortable while he got them a drink.

He pointed to his desk. "That's where I spend several hours during the week." After he'd handed them their drinks, he went over to the desk and picked up the teakwood box where he kept his cheroots. Offering them each a cigar, he took one for himself.

Lighting it up, he sank down on the leather sofa. He pointed out a large portrait above the mantel. "Next year, Elena's portrait will be hanging there. That is my Grandmother Mateo."

"A fine-looking lady," Sebastian told him. "You've got all that any man could possibly desire."

"Now I have everything I want, but without Elena my happiness could never have been complete. Yes, I have everything I ever wanted and I'm a most happy man. Now, I anticipate the joy of my firstborn, and I'll tell you that I'm as excited as the devil." He laughed.

An hour later, the three of them climbed the stairs and went to their separate bedrooms. Both Vasco and Sebastian admired and respected Mark Mateo very much.

Perhaps it was the excitement of her father's and brother's arrival that made her feel so weary. But Elena didn't know when Mark crawled in bed beside her, nor did she know when he got out of the bed the next morning. Mark intended that she should sleep and feel rested.

He dressed and took charge of entertaining Sebastian and Vasco. The three of them shared a hearty breakfast, and then he took them out to the corrals to see the fine Mateo bulls, boasting that they were the finest in the country. He told them of his grandfather's challenge to him to breed a finer bull. "I'm damn well going to try to," he told them.

"You'll do it, Mateo," Sebastian declared.

At Golden Splendor, Mano was taking charge of a gentleman guest at his home, while their two lovely ladies remained in their bedrooms sleeping soundly. Carlos accompanied them, for Deirdre, too, was still asleep.

"Remember they have to have their beauty rest. At least that's what Aimée always tells me." Mano laughed.

The dignified gentleman walked with Carlos and Mano as they toured the famous winery and later took a ride in Mano's buggy out to the vineyards. He also made a confession about his lovely wife. "She sleeps long after I've gone to my office."

It had been Aimée Mateo's idea to invite Ricardo and Margarita Gomez to this festive occasion, knowing how fondly Elena had spoken about Margarita and how kind she'd been to her. She knew how thrilled Elena would be to see her again. Aimée could not have been more pleased that they

had accepted her invitation for the weekend at Golden Splen
dor.

From the minute they'd arrived, Ricardo had been de
lighted that Margarita had insisted that they come here. The
country estate was an enchanting place, and the Mateo family
were the most gracious genteel people he'd ever met. Touring
the vineyards and the winery had intrigued him. Mano Mateo
had a right to be proud.

Margarita had been just as impressed as her husband after
the first evening they'd spent with Aimée and Mano Mateo.
She and Aimée had warmed to one another instantly, and it
was obvious to Margarita that Aimée adored her daughter
in-law. She knew that it was because of Elena that they'
been invited for the weekend.

Last night when they'd gone to their bedroom after a won
derful evening, Margarita had told her husband, "Aimée put
the ladies in Sacramento who think themselves such grand
hostesses to shame. That delicious veal with that sauce was
marvelous!"

Ricardo raved about the strawberry mousse, declaring that
he'd never eaten anything so delicious before. "You must get
her recipe for that. I heard her tell you that it's a traditional
Aragon family dessert."

Margarita could not resist taunting him, "Now aren't you
glad you came?" Sheepishly, Ricardo grinned and admitted
that he was glad to be at Golden Splendor.

When the men arrived back at the house, they went in
different directions. Carlos looked for Deirdre, and Mano
had many things to check on. Ricardo was ready to go to
his bedroom and rest his weary feet, for he'd walked more
than he was used to.

Carlos found Deirdre in a miserable state. She was awake
but still not dressed. She was having a queasy spell. She
moaned, "Oh, Carlos! I must get myself together before th

evening. You go have lunch with your family. I just can't make it. Perhaps, you could have a tray with some tea and a light broth sent up to the room."

"Don't worry about a thing, Deirdre. I'll have a tray sent up, and I'll go down and explain to Mother that you're not feeling well," he told her, bending to kiss her.

Carlos had only to mention to his mother that Deirdre was not feeling well for her to tell him, "She does not have to worry about not being able to come down to lunch. She is with family. I will take her a tray myself and assure her that she must never feel embarrassed with us."

Carlos had always admired his mother's cool, calm manner. She seemed to always be able to handle anything. She seated her family and guests at the table for the light lunch Celia had prepared. Then, she graciously asked them to excuse her for a few moments. Carlos knew what she was about, but Mano didn't. He watched her disappear through the kitchen door. Then, she rushed up the back stairs with a pot of tea and some chicken broth. She'd listened to Carlos describing Deirdre's discomforts. Did she dare to hope that Deirdre was pregnant, too?

It took only a few minutes for her to ease Deirdre's concerns and urge her to sip the tea and the broth. "You see, *ma petite,* you will be fine by this evening. You finish this and just rest this afternoon. Remember, Deirdre, we are family."

"Oh, señora, I think it is you who made me feel better," Deirdre told her.

"I appreciate that, Deirdre. Just know that I care for you and I'm so happy that my sons chose ladies like you and Elena to marry. I love both of you very much."

"Ah, Elena and I are blessed to have you, señora." Deirdre responded.

Aimée was an affectionate lady who gave her love without

any restraint. She bent down and kissed Deirdre on the cheek. "Carlos is our beloved son, so that makes you our beloved daughter, Deirdre."

She turned and rushed out of the room, and Deirdre sat on the bed thinking what an amazing woman Aimée Mateo was.

Aimée joined her family and guests at the table, and Celia served her. She gave a gay laugh. "Ah, at a time like this, things sometimes get hectic. I trust you will forgive my absence."

Mano did not know what had demanded Aimée's attention, but he smiled at her. "You are forgiven, *querida*. Now, enjoy your lunch."

Ricardo and Margarita remained at the dining table with Aimée, but then excused themselves to go to their room for a siesta. They surmised that their host and hostess needed the next hours to prepare for their affair this evening.

For the next two hours Aimée seemed to be going in a constant trot everywhere Mano spied her. She never ceased to amaze him, and she probably never would.

She finally went to her bedroom and collapsed across the bed to sleep for an hour-and-a-half.

Forty-eight

It was a gala occasion that evening at Golden Splendor. Aimée, dressed in her elegant purple gown, her amethyst-and-diamond earrings dangling from her ears, stood beside her husband to greet her parents when they arrived. Shortly afterwards, the Renaldo family arrived, followed by Alonso and his sister Lola.

Mark had escorted Elena up the back stairs so she could have her reunion with Deirdre before the ceremony. He escorted Sebastian and Vasco into the front of the house.

It was a very emotional reunion for Deirdre and Elena. It was obvious to Deirdre that Elena had been well into her pregnancy when she had finally left Sacramento. No wonder she had been so apprehensive. But Deirdre had been right: Mark had only to know to do the honorable thing and marry her. But then, she had never doubted that he loved Elena.

With great pleasure she told Elena her own good news that she and Carlos were to also be parents. But those were the only private moments they were to have for the next two hours. Markita knocked on the door to tell them that it was time to come downstairs and stand with their husbands to renew their vows in front of friends and family.

Father Gonzales's black eyes met Elena's as he performed the same ceremony that he'd just performed at La Casa Grande a few weeks before. There was an impish twinkle in the priest's eyes as he looked at her. He told her later that he couldn't have imagined that she could have looked prettier than she had on her wedding night, but tonight she certainly had. "I must tell you that my housekeeper and I enjoyed that cake," he told her.

The ceremony completed, Elena glanced at the assembled guests. She gasped and clutched tightly to Mark's arms as she exclaimed excitedly, "It's Señora Margarita, Mateo. She is here!"

Margarita walked to her. The two women embraced warmly, and Margarita told her, "Nothing could have kept me from coming to your wedding once I received the invitation from Señora Mateo. I am so very happy for you and your husband. The first time I met your young man I knew—oh, I knew he loved you and I was right," she declared.

Mark had joined his bride and heard Margarita. He told her, "Without your help, Señora Gomez, I don't know how long it would have taken me to find her. I shall be forever beholden to you."

But Elena was not able to speak with Margarita for as long as she would have liked; there were other guests who demanded her attention as well: Alonso and Lola, Mark's grandparents—the Aragons, and her own family. Elena lost sight of her father and Vasco in the crowd of people, but she didn't worry. Her father was a friendly fellow that everyone found likable.

This night, when all the wedding guests assembled around the long dining table in the spacious room, all the chairs were filled with the guests. Aimée had chosen flowers in shades of white, yellow, and lavender for her centerpiece.

Celia had baked two wedding cakes so each bride could cut her own cake. Deirdre and Elena agreed later that it was an evening out of a fairy tale, and they both knew who deserved all the praise: Their dear mother-in-law.

Elena finally managed some private time with Margarita.

Margarita told her of the demise of the Delgardo Dress Salon. "There have been rumors, but all I know is that the shop closed. I've heard she left Sacramento, but her worthless son left before she did. The Towers Hotel now has a new owner."

Elena felt no sadness at the news. Delores Delgardo had never been as nice as she'd thought her to be. She wondered about Miguel. Had he perhaps hired on one of the fishing boats? She remembered their talks.

Elena promised Margarita that she'd send her an invitation to her baby's christening. "I would love for you to be our guests that weekend at La Casa Grande, señora." Margarita gave her a warm embrace, assuring her that nothing would keep her from coming to that grand event.

Mark whisked her away to say goodbye to the Aragons. He sensed that Elena was weary, and he was a very protective husband. He wanted nothing to go wrong with his wife or his baby. He started saying his goodbyes and searched for Vasco and Sebastian. He had no intention of lingering another hour, for it could prove to be a long hour for Elena.

A short time later, Mark had corralled Elena, Sebastian, and Vasco. Mark noticed that Elena was asleep before they got halfway home. He laughed, remarking to Sebastian, "She is exhausted and she didn't even realize it."

When they arrived at La Casa Grande, Mark didn't wake her up. He gently gathered her up in his arms to take her into the house and up the stairs to their bedroom. He bade Sebastian and Vasco good night as he'd rushed on up the stairs ahead of them with his wife in his arms. Sebastian saw that Mateo was right about Elena, for she didn't even rouse from her sleep.

She was hardly aware of Mark disrobing her and slipping her nightgown over her head. He laid her back on the pillows and pulled the coverlet over her. Only then did he go back downstairs to take the buggy to Alberto.

* * *

The next morning Vasco and Sebastian started back to Half Moon Bay. Sebastian had never known his son to be so talkative, and he knew that Vasco would never forget this time he'd spent at La Casa Grande. He told his father, "Pa, Mateo worships Elena. I never saw a man so crazy about a woman."

"Ah, Vasco, I go home with my heart overflowing with joy," he told his son.

The same morning Carlos and Deirdre left to return to Sacramento. But Margarita and Ricardo stayed over an extra day at the urging of Aimée and Mano.

An early spring came to the California countryside. It was a busy time around Mano's vineyards with new cuttings being planted from his best grape vines of last autumn's harvest.

Mark was very busy at La Casa Grande and very excited. He had bred two of his prized bulls, and he was now anticipating that this union would produce an outstanding calf that would mark a superior breed.

Wildflowers were beginning to bloom profusely in the pasture where the bulls grazed. Elena, too, was in full bloom. She would only wear gowns that flowed loose and free from the shoulders. Her dear mother-in-law had had her seamstress stitch up five such gowns. She'd chosen bright, lively colors so Elena would not feel dowdy. Some had lace-trimmed necklines and others had ruffling or flounces on the bottom. Elena looked very pretty in these yellow, coral, and jade dresses.

She could only ride with Mark in the buggy, and she was looking forward to being able to mount a horse again to ride with him. She took her role as mistress of La Casa Grande very seriously, staying more and more at the house or in the courtyard.

Estellita admired her stamina. The little señora kept herself busy giving orders to the servants and checking to see if her requests were carried out properly. As she'd grown heavily into her pregnancy, Elena still forced herself to stay active and Estellita respected her more and more all the time.

Often she sat in the kitchen with the Mexican cook and they just talked. But she still never tried to boss Estellita in "her" kitchen.

Like Mark, Estellita became more and more protective of the little señora, especially as she watched her climb the stairs, a feat which seemed to take more effort as Elena grew larger. She feared Elena might feel faint and fall.

Many changes took place in the spacious old mansion during that early spring. Aimée eagerly helped her daughter-in-law make the changes in the bedroom to reflect her own taste.

Aimée suggested, "Shall we brighten it up, Elena? Would that not please you?"

Elena had been more than pleased with the changes, and Mark was pleased with the transition, for he didn't feel smothered by frills and fluffs. But most important to him, Elena was thrilled about the new look.

The next project was the nursery. A door was cut into the wall of their bedroom to give access to the adjoining room. By the time his mother and Elena had finished, that ordinary room had been transformed into a nursery with a canopied crib and ruffled curtains at the windows. Aimée had bought a rocker for Elena and every item the newborn baby could possibly need. Every drawer in the chest was filled with baby clothing.

Mark could not have been happier to watch his mother and wife as they spent time together, laughing like two school girls. They got along with one another so perfectly, his mother was so excited about the baby. "No baby will ever be as special to Aimée as this first one," Mano confided to him one afternoon. "It will forever hold a singular place in her heart, Mark."

Mark had laughed and pointed out to his father, "I don't know if you've noticed as I have that our wives are very much alike. I think that's why they get along together so well. I can tell you those two have worked like beavers for the last three weeks."

"I've heard she's bought out all the shops." Mano laughed.

"It looks like we've got our work cut out for us, Father. Can you imagine? The two of them are going to be going shopping together all the time," Mark jested.

Mano smiled. "We'll be able to handle them, Mark."

That evening as he and Elena were dining, Mark complimented her on the nursery. "Ah, *muñequita mía,* we may just end up filling all these bedrooms on the second landing."

Her black eyes sparkled and a coy smile came to her face, but her tone was serious and firm. "Ah, no, we will not. I do not wish to be pregnant every year, Mateo. I will not be like the Portuguese women in the village who are big with a baby every year."

His manner became just as sober as he assured her, "Elena, I'd never want you having a baby every year. We've too much living to do for you to be always heavy with a child."

"Oh, Mateo, I'm glad to hear you say that," she said with a lovely smile on her face.

"Elena—oh, my Elena, I love you so. I only wish I could help you carry that heavy load you carry now. But I can't. I'd never want you to have to be this uncomfortable all the time."

The days of June passed, and Elena grew even larger. It

seemed Mateo's eyes were always watching her as if he expected her to explode suddenly. She became indignant and snapped at him.

He gave a husky laugh. "I can't help it, honey. I've never been a father before. I'm anxious."

She cupped his handsome face with her hands. "I'd not wish you to be any other way, my Mateo," she said.

Everyone at La Casa Grande and Golden Splendor was becoming anxious about the upcoming birth. Aimée came over in the gig every week to check on Elena, impatient for the baby to arrive. Estellita swore that the baby had to come any day. No one was more impatient than Elena. She was ready for the little imp to make its appearance.

She had finally agreed with Estellita to have a breakfast tray sent up to her in the morning. Going up and down the stairs had become too much for her to handle two or three times a day.

A servant brought the tray, but Estellita still came up to her room to check on her during the mornings while Mark was occupied in the corrals. This morning she told Elena that she was glad she'd finally decided to save herself the trip downstairs. "There's nothing wrong with pampering yourself some, little señora," Estellita declared.

Elena gave a weak laugh. "Oh, Estellita, I don't know how you can possibly call me little. I look as big as those black bulls in the corral."

"Don't you compare yourself to those ugly things, little señora," she admonished her gently.

After Estellita left, Elena forced herself to get out of bed and strolled out on the balcony. In the distance, she saw her handsome husband standing by the corral fence talking with his foreman. How had she been so lucky to capture the heart of this man? she wondered, admiring him.

As miserable as she was feeling, she went back into the

room and tried to make herself as attractive as she could. She put on a thin silk dressing gown, for it was going to be a very warm July day.

She pulled her thick hair away from her face and secured it with a satin ribbon. She even took the time to dab some toilet water behind her ears and throat. She was setting the bottle back on her dressing table when she experienced a sharp pain. At the same moment, she felt a warm liquid creeping down her thighs and panicked.

She had to get to Estellita, for Mark could never have heard her call from the balcony. Fortunately, Estellita was making her rounds of the rooms and heard Elena's frightened shriek. Leaning over the railing, she cried, "Get Mateo quick, Estellita!"

"I will. You get back to your bed. I'll be right up to you." Estellita rushed to the back of the house. Luckily, she found Alberto sitting on the step. "Fetch the Señor pronto, Alberto. It's the señora. The baby may be coming."

She turned quickly. When she got to Elena, she found her sitting on the side of her bed, confused. "What is this, Estellita? It—it just came flowing from me after a sharp pain hit me." She motioned down to the damp front of her dressing gown.

Estellita had a quick answer for her. "Your water broke, little señora, so you're getting ready to have that wee one. Now, let me help you into a nightgown." It proved to be a struggle for the cook, because Elena had to bend over to give way to a new round of pains.

Mark rushed into the room. "Shall I go for the doctor, Estellita?" he asked her.

"No, señor, you stay right here with me. Send someone else for the doctor. This baby may make a fast arrival now that its decided to come into this world," she told him.

Meekly, Mark did as she'd ordered, then returned to sit with Elena.

"Now what do we do, Estellita?" he asked, watching his wife writhe in pain.

"We comfort her, señor. This is something a woman does herself. Just hold her hand and bathe the sweat from her face. I've got to go downstairs to gather up a few things," Estellita told him.

The next hour-and-a-half seemed endless to Mark; and he was getting vexed that Santos had yet to show up with the doctor, for Elena's pains seemed harder and more frequent.

"What's delaying Santos?" Mark snapped.

Estellita could tell the señor's nerves were frayed. "He might not be able to find him, señor, or the doctor could have been out on another call," she pointed out to him.

That possibility had not crossed Mark's mind.

A few minutes later, Mark heard the sound of galloping hooves on the drive, and he rushed to the windows to see Santos coming back alone. Before Santos could dismount from his horse, Mark was in the yard. "Where's Cerventes, Santos?" he demanded.

"He's delivering the Alfredo baby. He said for me to tell you that first babies take a long time. He'll come here directly from the Alfredo ranch," Santos said.

Mark dismissed Santos and went back into the house. He wasn't feeling kindly toward Dr. Cerventes. His wife was moaning with pain. She needed the doctor's services, and he wasn't here for her.

Most first babies might take a long time in arriving, but not this little Mateo heir. Estellita had already concluded that she would be the midwife, a service she'd not performed for a long, long time. She was nervous and prayed the baby would be tiny.

She sent Mark to the kitchen to have pans, kettles of hot

water, and towels brought to the room. "This little firebrand isn't going to wait around for Dr. Cerventes. It has a mind of its own. It's ready to get out of there," Estellita told him.

When Estellita told her to push hard, Elena did, gripping Mark's hands for strength. She was growing very weary.

"One more hard push, little señora, for I think I see its tiny head," Estellita told her. Elena screamed. The pain was excruciating, and she imagined she had felt the sting of death.

Estellita gave a chuckle of delight as she declared, "We've got ourselves a baby—a beautiful baby girl, as cute and sassy as she can be!"

A sublime peace of exhaustion settled over Elena. Mark kissed his wife's damp forehead before he moved around the bed to see his daughter. The next moments were ones of golden splendor that he'd never forget as long as he lived.

As soon as Estellita had the baby cleaned and wrapped in a blanket, Mark took her in his arms. As his violet eyes surveyed this tiny little being that his and Elena's love had created, he felt a pride he'd never known before.

"She's beautiful, Estellita!" he exclaimed. He planted a soft kiss on the baby's cheek and whispered to her, "Ah, *muñeca mía.* Now I have two little dolls!"

It was a glorious moment for Estellita and one she'd never forget. There was nothing awkward about Señor Mark as he cradled the tiny baby in his arms and his little daughter seemed to be perfectly content to have him hold her.

Mark lay the baby beside her mother. "Our daughter, *mi vida,* and she's as beautiful as her mother," he told her.

Estellita left the young couple to share this special moment in private.

Elena saw that her daughter was as beautiful as Mateo had said. She'd already decided weeks ago what she was going to name her baby if it were a girl: Miranda Aimée Mateo.

Mother and daughter fell into an exhausted sleep, and Mark left the room leaving the door ajar. He sent a servant to sit in the hall to keep a check on Elena.

For once he went into the kitchen and ordered Estellita to have Juanita take charge this evening. "I want you to go to your room and rest. You've had a hectic morning and afternoon. There will be no lamps lit in the dining room tonight. I'll have a tray up in the room with Elena."

Estellita gave him no fuss, for she couldn't imagine anything nicer than stretching out on her bed and sleeping for hours, which was exactly what she did.

The spacious old house was quiet, and Mark was ready to relax as well.

He sat in the parlor and poured himself a glass of wine. He knew he should send a rider to Golden Splendor with the news, but for Elena's sake—to allow her a period of rest—he delayed sending one of his men.

When Dr. Cerventes finally arrived at La Casa Grande, Mark was not cordial. He would not allow the doctor to go upstairs to disturb Elena or the baby when they were resting so well. He dismissed Cerventes curtly. "It was four hours ago that Elena needed you. She is fine now. Estellita delivered her baby. You're free to go to your next call."

When Mark escorted him to the front door, the doctor realized that he'd never deliver any more Mateo babies.

Mark and Estellita's tender loving care was all Elena had needed.

Forty-nine

· The long-awaited news finally came to Golden Splendor. A broad smile was on the hired hand's face when he announced to them that the señora had had her baby and it was a daughter.

Aimée was ecstatic, declaring to her husband, "Oh, Mano, I must see her, this little granddaughter of ours. I've waited so long."

Mano smiled, suggesting that perhaps they should wait for morning to make the trip to La Casa Grande. But Aimée would not be dissuaded.

"You couldn't be that heartless, Mano, to make me wait that long," she told him.

He laughed and kissed her cheek. "No, I could never be that cruel to you. But we must not stay long for Elena has had a difficult afternoon, I'm sure."

"I promise, Mano. Just a very brief visit." She smiled.

True to her promise to her husband, Aimée viewed the lovely little cherub swathed in a soft blanket and bent down to kiss Elena, telling her what a beautiful angel the baby was. "Now, you rest and we'll see you tomorrow." Motioning to Mano that she was ready to leave, Aimée slipped out of the room. Elena was so drowsy that she had hardly been aware of their presence.

Mark escorted them to the front door and told them that

t was Estellita who had delivered the baby. "I sent Santos or the doctor, but it was four hours later when he arrived."

"Don't fret, Mark. There's a nice young doctor in the valley now. Cerventes is getting too old," Aimée told her son.

After they left, Mark lit up a cheroot in the quiet of his study. He believed that old Carlos would be happy wherever he was. A new little Mateo had been born under this roof. That had to be a man's immortality. He had children; those children had children, and so it continued forever.

He felt a gentle breeze waft over him, and he saw that the doors leading out to the patio were ajar. He'd not opened them. He got up to close and secure the doors.

A swifter breeze rushed through the doors, and he swore that the old man's voice, carried along with the gusting breeze, said to him, "Nieto, now you are a father, a glorious experience. Cherish it, for time passes all too swiftly."

Just as suddenly as the breeze had invaded the study, the whispering voice was silent. Perhaps the brandy he'd drunk had gone to his head and he'd just imagined it.

In the morning he sent a rider to Half Moon Bay to take the news to Sebastian and Vasco and came downstairs to enjoy a hearty breakfast. Estellita was back in her kitchen. In his shirt pocket, he had a special gift for Estellita, for she certainly deserved it. He'd chosen a lovely sapphire-and-diamond broach from his mother's jewelry chest. Estellita would treasure the Mateo heirloom, and he didn't know what he would have done without her yesterday.

She was overcome with emotion when he presented the broach to her, and she pinned it on her dress immediately. She wore it constantly after that morning. There was no question about it: She was proud as a peacock that she'd been the one who'd delivered the little Mateo heir!

Once Sebastian received the message from Mateo that Elena had had her baby, he found himself impatient to see his first granddaughter. He told Vasco, "I'm going to see my granddaughter. Are you as anxious to see your niece?"

Vasco quickly replied that he was, so the next day the two Fernandes fishing boats remained idle at the docks and Sebastian and his son left Half Moon Bay to go to La Casa Grande.

When they arrived at La Casa Grande, Sebastian looked down in the cradle to see the babe with black ringlets covering her head. He touched the delicate face and swore he'd never seen a more beautiful baby except for his little Elena when she was born to Miranda.

Vasco's huge finger had gently caressed the baby's hand and when her finger clasped his, Vasco chuckled. "Elena she's a strong little imp!"

They spent only one night before they returned to Half Moon Bay. But during that afternoon Sebastian invaded Estellita's kitchen and instructed her in the preparation of *paella*. Elena did not know how it had happened, but obviously the two of them had gotten along fabulously.

Estellita liked the big bear of a man who'd raved about her skills as a cook and she liked the way he didn't hesitate to tie an apron around his middle to help her knead the dough for loaves of bread and peel the vegetables. They laughed and talked and cooked for most of the afternoon, while Vasco joined Mark in the corrals.

"This amazes me, Mateo! My papa and Estellita puttering around in her kitchen is hard to believe." She giggled when Mark described the scene.

"They spent a pleasant afternoon together. Sebastian might just take our cook away from us," he jested.

"I doubt that. Besides they leave in the morning." She smiled at him.

* * *

In late August, Margarita Gomez received her invitation to the christening of Miranda Aimée Mateo. Elena also invited them to spend the weekend that first week of September. Margarita began to make her plans and shop for a very special gift for the baby.

Elena understood why Deirdre and Carlos had to decline the invitation, for she was now too far advanced in her pregnancy.

No one but Mark knew what she was going to name her baby. She knew her mother-in-law was as curious as a cat, but Elena kept telling her that she hadn't quite made up her mind.

As Estellita had told her, she quickly lost all the excess weight she'd put on. She was delighted to be able to get into her pretty afternoon gowns. As her own mother, Miranda, had felt, she wanted to keep her trim figure for a long time now that she had it back. She was glad that Mateo understood how she felt.

This was a very special christening for Father Gonzales. Elena's and Mark's wedding had been the last he'd perform for the Mateo family unless Markita married soon. But he was almost sure that this would be his last Mateo christening. He, too, had been invited to be an overnight guest at La Casa Grande. He'd become very fond of Mark's pretty, little wife. She was just as sweet as she was pretty.

Ricardo and Margarita arrived late in the afternoon on Friday. Sebastian and Vasco arrived during the afternoon, too. It was a gala evening at La Casa Grande.

Both Ricardo and Margarita agreed that they were even more impressed with the grandeur here at La Casa Grande than they'd been with Golden Splendor. Margarita marveled about the gracious, charming little hostess Elena was at this fine, famous ranchero. It was as if she'd been born to play the role of mistress of this grand house.

She looked more beautiful than ever, and it was obvious that Mark Mateo adored his wife. Anytime he looked at her, his dark eyes warmed with love, Margarita observed.

The christening was the next afternoon, and it was a very sentimental occasion when Father Gonzales blessed the baby, Miranda Aimée Mateo. Aimée Mateo and Sebastian both cried, and a slight mist came to Mano's eyes, too. He was thinking how much joy Elena Fernandes had brought to his family.

Sebastian was telling himself that he was damned well going to hang around this old world for a long time yet. He had to watch little Miranda grow up. One day, he was going to take her aboard his fishing boat just as he'd taken her mama when she was a little girl.

When Ricardo left La Casa Grande he was as intrigued by the prized Mateo bulls as he'd been by Mano's winery and vineyards. Mark had taken him on a tour of his corrals. Margarita enjoyed every moment of the time she got to spend with Elena on Sunday, which was a quieter, more relaxed day. Sebastian and Vasco had left on Sunday morning, and so had Father Gonzales.

Monday morning, the Gomezes left to return to Sacramento, but they were to return to La Casa Grande for many visits during the future years.

Six months after Miranda Aimée's christening Father Gonzales did perform a wedding for Markita and Francisco Renaldo. Even though her sons and daughter were in their own homes, Aimée did not set herself a more leisurely, lazy pace. Once a week, she went to La Casa Grande, and she and Elena often went on shopping sprees. Twice a year, she and Mano traveled to Sacramento to visit Deirdre and Carlos. Their firstborn had been a son, and Carlos could not have been a prouder father or Deirdre a more doting mother.

Francisco's father had deeded his son several acres of his

vast ranch and built a fine house for the two of them. Mano couldn't have been more pleased that Francisco had an intense interest in becoming a vintner like him, so Mano began to teach him the business. By the time he and Markita had been married a year, they had become the parents of twin sons. By the time they were two, Markita found she had two rambunctious boys on her hands.

Since he had a huge gathering during the holidays at Golden Splendor, Mano had decided that the Festival of the Grapes could not continue, but he compensated his workers in other ways.

Family gatherings were a big undertaking. After one of these reunions, Mano and Aimée sought the delightful quiet of their courtyard gardens. Looking up at the moonlit sky as they sat on the bench, Aimée declared, "Ah, it's so nice to be surrounded by all this serene quiet, Mano."

He gave a husky, deep laugh. "See what the two of us started with our wild, torrid love affair."

She gave a lilting laugh. "I've no regrets about that."

"Nor I, *mi vida*," he declared as he bent to plant a kiss on her cheek.

Elena and Mark had arrived back at La Casa Grande after their evening at Golden Splendor. Mark suggested that she turn Miranda and their infant son over to their nanny. By the time Miranda was almost four years old, Elena had decided she did want one more child. She wanted to present Mateo with a son, and she had gotten her wish. Mark could not have been more thrilled. The baby was named Sebastian Manuel.

To Mark, Elena had become more and more beautiful in the last five years. His little Miranda Aimée was the image of her mother with her feisty little walk. She even placed her hands at her waist when she was indignant.

Tonight she struck this pose as she shook her black curly head to protest going to bed. But Elena firmly told her, "Sleepy or not, Miranda Aimée, you will go upstairs and get in your bed."

"I won't go to sleep," she told her mother as the nanny took her hand.

"But you'll get into your nightgown and into your bed," Elena ordered.

She whirled around and marched up the steps, her long hair bobbing back and forth around her small shoulders. Mark watched, amused.

Elena turned then to take Mark's arm so they could take a stroll in the courtyard. He had exciting news to tell her tonight.

She sighed. "Oh, she is so stubborn and headstrong! But so adorable."

He grinned down at her. "I can't imagine where she got that, can you?"

Sheepishly, she smiled up at him. "I know, Mateo! I know she gets it from me."

Mark reached down to kiss her cheek. "Ah, Elena *mía,* I've got all a man could ever want."

Elena knew what having a son meant to Mateo, and she was so happy she'd had this second baby. "Now I've got everything to make my life complete, Mateo. I've a darling daughter and a new son. I have you, Mateo, and I just keep falling more and more in love with you."

They sat on the bench by the fountain and he teased her. "Such talk, *chiquita,* could get you in trouble."

She smiled. "Oh, no, it won't, for I wish not to grow huge again so soon."

In every sense of the word, Elena had truly become the

patroness of La Casa Grande. She did not walk in the shadow of Mark's grandmother anymore than he walked in old Carlos's shadow. He was the patrón.

This serene courtyard garden was one thing they had not changed. As far as they were concerned they both wanted everything here to remain the same. But inside the sprawling mansion, many things had been altered over the years. Elena had established her own style and taste.

The second landing now had four occupied bedrooms. The first year of their marriage all the bedrooms except for hers and Mark's had been guest rooms. But then Miranda Aimée had come along to occupy the nursery adjacent to their room and a nanny was ensconced in the next room.

A fourth bedroom was changed to lovely shades of pink with frills and fluff for little Miranda when she was ready to leave the nursery. Like her Tía Markita, pink was her favorite color.

Elena reasoned that the remaining bedrooms were needed for guests. They had all the family she desired.

Mark could not restrain himself any longer telling her his news. *"Querida,* I think I've done it! I've met Grandfather Mateo's challenge. I've bred a finer bull. The calf was born this morning just before we left for Golden Splendor. He's sheer perfection!"

She flung her arms around his neck and excitedly exclaimed, "Oh, Mateo, I never doubted that you would. Why didn't you tell me sooner?"

"We've not had a private moment until now." He laughed.

"Oh, Mateo, I'm so proud of you; and Grandfather Mateo is, too, I bet!" she declared, reaching up to kiss his lips.

Mark knew he had to be the luckiest man in the world and the luckiest day of his life had to be the day he went fishing with old Alonso and chanced to spy a feisty little

Portuguese girl walking down the wharf at Half Moon Bay. Meeting her had changed his life.

His arms went around her tiny waist and he bent down to kiss her honeyed lips. He told her, "You've made every dream I ever had come true, *muñeca mía*. Without you, I would have had nothing. With you, I have everything."

Elena knew that she had her own golden splendor right here at La Casa Grande!